Kay Stephens was born and brought up in Yorkshire. She spent the first seven years of her working life as a librarian, and since then has written several short stories and a number of novels, including THE SOARING FELLS and STONES OF CALDER DALE, both set in her native Yorkshire.

Also by Kay Stephens

West Riding
North Riding
Pennine Vintage
The Soaring Fells
Stones of Calder Dale

Acknowledgement

For assistance with my research into traditional methods of carpet manufacturing I am grateful to the Wilton Royal Carpet Factory Limited. I am particularly indebted to Gill Coveney, the Curator at Wilton Royal, for all the information provided at the time of my visit to them.

Chapter 1

The clacking from rows of massive looms was swamping everything, including Laura's confidence. Penetrating the office windows, the racket was as relentless as the weavers' stares which had examined her every step of the way from the outer door of the shed. The men, faces honed by the slump, challenged her as openly as Roy Lindley's words.

'What are you doing here, Miss Crabtree? You don't know the first thing about carpet making.'

I hope I'll prove that I do, maybe even before 1937's out, thought Laura. But, stung by his brusque manner, she glanced down. Jewel-bright greens, reds and blues shimmered; delicate pastels merged. All her meticulous designs blurred as she widened her azure eyes, willing them to reveal no emotion. She mustn't let on that she felt like bolting.

She faced him with a determined smile. 'I believe I do understand getting my ideas down on to paper.'

'Mmm.' Whatever Mr Lindley meant by that, his grey eyes scoured the dozen or so patterns that Laura had brought with her. *Was* he interested? 'Some of these are more like stained glass than . . .'

'Aye,' she interrupted. 'That's the way they're supposed to look. The one in your hand's inspired by that lovely west window in York Minster.'

Briefly, her smile ceased to be forced. Nobody at the other mills had recognised this source of many of her designs, the thing that made them truly original.

'Learn this from your dad, did you?' Roy Lindley inquired casually.

1

Laura smoothed down a strand of freshly permed fair hair. She had had it styled recently, copying the way the new queen wore hers two months ago for the coronation. Somehow, though, despite her navy blue costume, Laura looked younger than ever, about as mature as Princess Margaret Rose!

'Actually, no. My father's in fishing – owns a fleet of trawlers.'

So she wasn't from round Halfield. Roy Lindley might have known. He'd have come across an attractive lass like her otherwise. About twenty, he guessed. He'd become a connoisseur in the past ten years, to compensate himself for joining the family business straight from college the year after the General Strike.

'My mother's family were the creative side,' Laura informed him, her self-assurance resurfacing. 'They fashioned jewellery from Whitby jet.'

Whitby seemed like another planet, and sitting alone in that urgently chugging train like a different lifetime. Already, she hungered for the sea air. She drew in a deep breath, and coughed, trying not to choke on the cloying odour of moist wool.

Roy Lindley noticed and grinned. 'The dyehouse is just round the corner. Come and have a look.'

The smell of hot, wet wool was overwhelming, the steam dense, screening the big oblong vats, enveloping the men who were submerging the hanks of yarn. Laura had never been anywhere more horrible.

He led her back to the office and resumed their earlier conversation. 'I didn't know there was much call for jet any longer.'

Her blue eyes glinted ruefully. 'Happen not, but it can still be made to look very beautiful.'

'You'd rather have stayed at home perhaps, if there were a job . . .?'

'Not really,' Laura responded, very quickly. He was putting words into her mouth. And although leaving home had been a wrench, she was too certain about her ambition to have

2

stayed where she was. Couldn't he see that, from the way she'd put hours of work into these designs? Didn't he know succeeding *mattered*?

'Have you relations in Halfield then, Miss Crabtree?'

'No, I can manage on my own. I am of age.' And I'm the one who's had to look after other folk, she thought.

Mr Lindley was smiling now. It needed considerable effort to stop herself from staring. No ordinary man had any right to look that handsome, with hair all rippling and golden like ripe corn on her uncle's farm. And eyelashes that would have been gorgeous on a girl. But his smile appeared . . . patronising, as if he thought he knew all about her, when she herself barely did. This was her first chance to discover her own potential.

'I have got friends here, actually. One of them found me digs on t'other side of Halfield, with Miss Priestley.'

'Not the Miss Priestley connected with St Martin's – Secretary at the Liberal Club?'

'That's the one. You know her, do you?'

Roy Lindley smiled again. 'Know of her. Who doesn't? If that's where you're staying, we can let you know, one way or the other.'

Tell me now, thought Laura, it's written all over your face. You'll no more buy my patterns than fly. Only she wouldn't say that, would she? She could button up her lip when need be. She'd had plenty of practice. She'd not put a spoke in things while there was the slenderest chance. And he was studying her designs again, very carefully.

She wouldn't give up. Wasn't it years since she'd begun to love carpets, when Grandma Crabtree had taken her to Nostell Priory? The carpets there had enchanted her with their glorious colours and such beautiful patterns.

It was through Clem Hargreaves, though, that she'd become seriously interested in the way carpets were made. He had worked manufacturing them all his life until the mill he owned burned down. Although upset by hearing how he'd only been able to stand and watch while the blaze consumed all his work,

3

and his dreams as well, Laura had found her own dreams taking direction.

She had been in her teens when Clem Hargreaves arrived in Whitby after the fire. His sister Millie had offered him a home there while he recovered and sorted himself out. He'd not only lost the factory, his house near Halfield had adjoined the mill yard and was virtually gutted.

The Crabtree family had all got to know Clem. Millie was the widow of one of the best trawlermen who'd ever worked for Laura's father, and Yorkshire folk don't forget. Welcoming Clem at their table had been as instinctive as keeping a friendly eye on his sister. And he'd brought with him exquisite carpet samples which he had rescued from the fire.

Laura had grown more fascinated with every piece that the elderly man showed her. Glad to take his mind off the destruction of his mill, he'd studied them repeatedly with her, had encouraged her to run her fingers deep into their pile.

Some designs were oriental in style, more luxurious than Laura would aspire to; others were the sort she could picture in ordinary homes. And they all were in beautiful shades, and none of today's geometrical patterns either. Clem had explained how carpets were made, and had nodded sympathetically while she enthused about how much brighter and cosier they were than the cold linoleum in every room of her own home and countless others locally.

Long before Clem and his sister had moved from Whitby to their present house in Halfield, Laura was certain how she wanted to use her flair for art. She'd be so excited if she could design carpets for folk like herself who'd really appreciate something lovely which had been beyond their parents' means.

Laura had missed both Clem Hargreaves and his sister after he'd found he couldn't settle away from the West Riding. Busy with helping in the home, she had feared that she would have to forget the enthusiasm that he had roused in her. But then in the public library she had found books that reminded her of everything he'd taught her about the manufacture of carpets. Studying them time and again, thinking of those beautiful

4

samples, she had yearned and waited, until she could shelve her ambitions no longer. All those years she had searched for something that would make her work different. And then one day she had seen a blaze of sun slanting down through stained glass, carpeting the stone of a church floor with vibrant colours.

Now at last she was here in Halfield, a town famous for carpet weaving. She'd make her own opportunities. Nobody was given talents unless they were meant to use them. Waste not, want not, was her favourite motto.

She wasn't going back to live in Whitby. Now sixteen, her sisters were always needing something new. Even when the fishing was good, the family budget was greatly reduced by their requirements. There were other reasons as well for keeping away, but she didn't mean to dwell on them.

Coming back to today, Laura noticed Roy Lindley was looking at her again.

'Here's the address.' She smiled as she took a neatly written card from her handbag. 'I'll look forward to hearing something before too long.' She couldn't afford to hang on if this was going to come to nothing.

Before too long? Roy's lips tightened as he restrained an approving smile. She certainly wasn't going to procrastinate. He personally was responsible for the design team, though, and always kept Lindley's ahead of other manufacturers, creating fashions and fresh trends. He could tell her now that they'd no need of anybody new here, but that didn't suit his purpose. He'd like to keep her . . . dangling, to keep open the lines between them.

She smelled of Evening in Paris scent, reminding him of his young sister, but Laura had a more exciting air, despite the sensible navy costume.

He rose when she did, strolled with her to the outer door. 'As I say, Miss Crabtree, we shall be in touch.'

Passing between the looms, she flinched. He saw how overwhelmed she was by their height, to say nothing of their din. But then she squared her shoulders, raised her chin, and he noticed the assertive tilt to that pert little nose. Not a biddable young lady, he decided, but a challenge he wouldn't wish to ignore.

I don't hold out much hope, Laura silently admitted on the tram rattling down towards the town centre. And even though she couldn't think of any other local carpet factory that she hadn't tried, she wasn't altogether sorry that Roy Lindley hadn't snapped up her patterns. She wasn't keen to do business with him. There was something too knowing about him, and he was smooth. Oily, her mother would have said.

The tram lurched down the incline, and the clattering intensified as the rounded front of its twin approached on the adjacent track. Even when the other tram had passed, Laura still felt the racket and vibration continuing inside her head. She was so keyed-up, torn between her determination to succeed and her dread that she might not possess enough talent.

Wryly, she smiled, glimpsing her set face reflected in the dusty window beside her. She suited Halfield, proper grim on a working day! It was a good thing she hadn't seen it like this that first time she'd come to hear Michael playing the organ in his new church, or despite being the heart of the carpet industry it wouldn't have tempted her to live here. She'd missed Michael when he was no longer the organist at their church in Whitby, but they were only friends. She would not have left home just to follow him here.

Smoke as dense as any fog hung about church spires and mill chimneys – the only parts of buildings that weren't obliterated by that dismal grey cloud. Any trees there were in the town were submerged, along with shops, factories and densely packed rows of back-to-back houses. It might as well be November down there, not July. It was only out here on the surrounding hills that you knew the sun was shining.

That first Sunday it had all looked so different: dignified, splendid almost, with workplaces stilled, the few drifts of smoke wafting up from domestic fires. The sun had bestowed

6

what haze there was on that day, she recalled, softening the contours of the distant moors, lending a mystical quality to the crags.

And if she wanted an explanation of why she'd jumped at the idea of living here she needn't be so fanciful. She knew she had more of a chance of selling her designs here than anywhere. Halfield was nicely placed as well – not too near Whitby, and not too far away either – if she went home, she wouldn't have to stay the night. Ever since Dad had encouraged her to go after the only work she wanted, her mother had been furious. She hadn't really appreciated that Laura had waited until their Sybil, Netta and Greta were old enough to be a bit of use at home.

She herself still felt guilty; her mother had relied on her so much for keeping an eye on her sisters when they threatened to get out of hand. Triplets had been such a shock, especially since they arrived years after Laura herself was born. It was no wonder their mother's spirit never recovered and, after the hysterectomy the doctor had advised, her health wouldn't permit shouldering all that responsibility. The girls couldn't help being undisciplined, Dad's long absences at sea had meant there was no one to exert parental control, and had prevented their growing as fond of him as Laura herself had always been.

In the end it was their father who had seen that Laura might very easily sacrifice any hope of a career. Away with the trawlers so frequently, he had returned home each time to fresh reminders that his eldest daughter was letting her love of her sisters run away with her. She'd been good with them while they were tiny, and still followed them around when they were in their teens. 'Time you stopped,' he'd told her. 'It's not doing anything to make them stand on their own feet, and you're going to end up getting nowhere with your carpet designing. Just think on – your Aunt Constance never got as far as she deserved with her ballroom dancing, did she?' He hadn't mentioned on that occasion an earlier admission that he'd been obliged to follow his father as a trawlerman, regardless of his own ambitions. Nor his reminder to Laura that *she* should be free to choose her direction.

She sighed now, thinking of her aunt, and how caring for Grandma Crabtree had left her single, as well as frustrated in her longing to be a professional dancer. For Aunt Constance, there hadn't been as much time as she had supposed. Maybe Laura owed it to her, as well as to Dad, to ensure that the encouragement she'd been given resulted in a worthwhile future. And it might reconcile her mum and dad if she showed them he hadn't been all that wrong to persuade her to come away like this and concentrate on designing. She just wished she could tell somehow that she really had it in her . . .

Since arriving in Halfield she'd been dismayed by how readily she felt daunted, living in a strange town while she struggled with work that she'd mainly studied in books. She needed assuring that she wasn't wasting her time.

Clem Hargreaves might tell her. She'd been pleased to see he was a senior member of Michael's church choir, but he'd been laid up for weeks with a broken leg. This tram passed the end of Park Road where he lived. Before they reached the stop Laura was ready for getting off. She strode past four imposing detached houses and up to the next.

'I hope I haven't come at an awkward time,' she began breathlessly when his sister Millie opened the door of their Victorian stone home.

'Eh, Laura – you're allus welcome here.'

'How are you keeping? And Mr Hargreaves, is he in?'

'Aye, he is that. He'll be glad to see you. He's tired out, though, so happen you wouldn't mind not staying too long.'

One leg extended awkwardly towards the empty firegrate, the elderly man was sitting on a Windsor chair. The sun glinted off all the brass in the room, the heavy fender, fire irons, and gas mantle brackets, and brightened the otherwise sombre effect of dark oak furniture.

'Good afternoon, Mr Hargreaves. Now don't get up. How's your leg?'

'I've just had the plaster off today. They say as it's mending

8

nicely. It isn't half giving me gyp, though.'

'They've put him through it and no mistake,' his sister added. 'Still, the worst should be over. You'll have a cup of tea, won't you, now you're here?' she finished, heading towards the kitchen.

'On your own then? Your young man's busy practising, I suppose.' Her last visit had been with Michael. Seeing the change in Laura's expression, Clem Hargreaves appeared amused. 'Speaking out of turn, am I? Nowt between you, is that what you still reckon? Aye, well – it'll come soon enough.'

Why did people want to see her married? wondered Laura, not for the first time. But she'd more important matters to resolve.

'If I ask you something, Mr Hargreaves, will I get a straight answer?'

Renewed amusement lit the brown eyes, added an animated glow to his rather heavy features. 'You will that – so long as you'll bear no ill will. What's to do then, lass?'

'Is there anything wrong with my designs? Some way in which they don't work? When you said they were good, were you just being kind?'

'How long have you known me? I thought we were pals in Whitby. You shouldn't be asking that! I flatter nobody, Laura, never have. You're having a job getting somebody to buy 'em – that it?'

'I've trailed from one carpet mill to the next ever since I got here. I've just been told today that I know nothing about the way they're made.'

'And do you?'

'There's what you taught me years ago, and I've studied since, read all the books I could find, but mostly they covered them that are made by hand.'

'Aye, well – they're still the best, but this is 1937, think on. There aren't many folk can pay those sort of prices. You remember me saying ours were hand woven, do you?'

'I hope I haven't forgotten anything you told me.'

'The principle's still the same, of course. Has been since the

9

Turks first made carpets. It's all done by knotting of one sort or another . . .'

Smiling, Laura nodded. 'Yes, you showed me.'

'That'll do for a start.' Mr Hargreaves glanced over his shoulder. 'See yon' sideboard – fetch us t' stuff you'll find in the left-hand cupboard.'

He smiled approvingly when Laura returned with a heap of papers.

'I managed to save this lot when the mill burned down. Bring up a chair and we'll have a look together.'

His expression wistful, he sifted through until he found what he was seeking: a design on large-scale graph paper.

'Point paper, this is called. Have you seen owt of the sort before?'

Laura examined the sheet of squared paper. 'No, I'm afraid I haven't. As you know, nobody round Whitby made carpets.'

'So until now you've not had a proper chance to study the practical side? Well, as you see, this is what we use for designing. It has to be accurate, every square representing one knot. As you can tell, every shade is hand-painted on here, just as it is on t'original draft.'

'So, not using point paper, and not realising that each knot has to be shown in detail could be the reason my work hasn't been taken?'

'Aye, it could that. You could offer to study all this – next time you approach somebody with your patterns. Or . . .' Mr Hargreaves hesitated, weighing her possible reaction. 'Or you could come round here, regular like, and I'd give you a bit of coaching.'

'I'd look forward to that,' Laura said quickly, 'it'd be very useful, thank you ever so much. Could mean the difference between not getting anywhere and producing the work I believe I'm capable of.'

'You can take a couple of these designs with you, if you like. If I go through this stuff while we're having our tea, I'll maybe find the drafts they were copied from. Now that would give you a good start . . .'

When Laura left Clem Hargreaves she couldn't thank him enough. She would scrutinise these designs time after time, until there was nothing about them that she didn't understand.

As she ran to catch the tram she felt excited, her ambition to earn her living designing could become a reality, confirming her wish to settle in Halfield. What she would need, eventually, would be a place of her own. She wasn't keen on living under somebody else's roof. She needed to be able to concentrate.

She wasn't after anywhere grand, somewhere small would be enough. And owning a house would show everyone that she'd become independent.

The tram was lurching towards the town centre, passing the ends of narrow grey streets. Inwardly, Laura sighed. Men were grouped on the corners; collarless, unshaven, trying to make the best of a three-day working week, or losing the struggle to retain their self-respect with no work at all.

The houses were in the main neatly kept, their steps and window-bottoms whitened or yellow-stoned, lace curtains at sash-framed windows. But she'd never feel thrilled about living somewhere like this, even if she was ashamed of the reluctance which she would keep to herself. Halfield might be growing on her, but she couldn't eradicate her past. She was used to space, Goathland Moor, Roxby High Moor, Fylingdales . . . and that cold, wind-tossed infinity called the North Sea.

Even if the money she'd been left only bought a blackened stone terraced house, though, she would make it *hers*, furnished as she wanted. She could be content, she need only put her mind to it.

Deep inside her Laura ached for something more than contentment. But that was expecting too much too soon. She picked up a copy of the local *Courier* which someone had discarded on the wooden slats of the next seat. She read a tribute to George Gershwin who'd died the other day, then looked for something to cheer her up instead. The advertisement seemed to jump right off the page at her, she couldn't have missed it.

FOR SALE – Leasehold, the Coach House adjoining
Arncliffe Hall.

The house was only small, comprised of two bedrooms and a bathroom, together with a living-room and kitchen.

And I know nothing at all about it, Laura reminded herself sharply. Had she gone quite potty? She hadn't sold one of her designs, why in the world was she even considering buying a house yet? And leasehold – whatever difference would that make?

'I wonder, though . . .' she murmured aloud, and grinned at herself when a middle-aged man in greasy blue overalls and a flat cap glanced round to see who had spoken.

Arncliffe Hall was described as occupying a hilltop site, two miles outside Halfield on one of the routes to Bradford. There was a telephone number in the advert. If there hadn't been, Laura might have waited.

As soon as the tram shuddered to a halt, she jumped off and hurried across the setts at the corner of the road, risking ricking her ankle she was so busy looking for a telephone kiosk, instead of where she was going.

A Miss Pilkington, secretary to Mr Patrick Horsfall, the owner, answered, and suggested Laura make an appointment for that same day. 'Mr Horsfall is taking a short holiday at present, and wishes to conclude this matter.'

Laura was told it was an orange and green bus, not a tram, that would take her to within a quarter of a mile of Arncliffe Hall.

Hurrying towards the bus, she smiled. Mr Horsfall's secretary had been surprised that she would be using public transport instead of hiring a taxi. As if she'd more money than sense! The brass she'd been left would be put to good use, not frittered away.

A young maid, in a dark dress and a scrap of frilly white

12

pinny, opened the door and showed Laura into a room that made her stare it was so splendid. She couldn't take it all in at once, it was so lovely – good solid furniture, heavy curtains, and silverware all over the place.

She'd never been inside a private house as impressive as this. Her own home had been terribly cramped, although she'd been thankful it was no bigger while she was helping to keep it clean as well as washing, ironing, and getting the triplets off to school. But seeing the house made her feel daunted by the prospect of meeting Patrick Horsfall. Halfield folk seemed to have a habit of making her ready to retreat.

'But I'll not do that,' she promised herself under her breath, admiring the Axminster carpet and wondering if it was hand made. Curbing the urge to run her fingers over each piece of highly polished furniture, she crossed to one of the enormous windows. She wouldn't let anybody panic her. The Arncliffe Coach House wasn't the only possible home for her. She didn't even know yet if it was suitable. And she'd only today started looking. This was a lovely spot, though, and no mistake. From this side of the mansion, Halfield's mill chimneys were obscured by a fold of the hill. All she could see for miles was the green of the valley, interrupted only by the blackened sandstone of isolated farms, and matching dry-stone walls, veining the landscape as far as the rugged moors.

She'd picked a good day to come here, she reflected, enjoying the expanse of countryside which contrasted so vividly with the town's clustering streets. In winter time Arncliffe might be a shade remote.

How would she get back and forth to work, though? If she got work. But then, she'd be designing from home. She closed her eyes, imagining herself sitting before a window like this, inspired by her surroundings . . . Oh, definitely *inspired* – Arncliffe was a very inspirational place ! She'd got to make a go of it all.

His lips unsmiling and his expression carefully non-committal,

13

Patrick had heard out his old acquaintance, Carter Ainley. Now, with a promise that he would be in touch, he dismissed him. Ainley's displeasure was ill-disguised, and had no effect upon him. As Miss Pilkington ushered the man out through the door Patrick was beginning to feel his initial interest in Ainley's proposal waning.

Briefly, he'd been tempted by the scheme to adapt the Coach House as a production unit for the latest kind of wireless sets. Partly for the income it would yield, he was too much the businessman to ignore that, but more for the prospect of avoiding filling the Coach House with inquisitive neighbours. People who would come and go at all hours of the day and night and over the weekends, growing increasingly curious about his family. With a workplace there instead, he might enforce certain regulations . . . Unfortunately, though, the entire atmosphere of his estate would be altered. Maybe the young woman his secretary was about to show in would have an acceptable use for the place?

Laura had started when the door was opened by Miss Pilkington, an austere lady whose greying hair in an outmoded Eton crop did nothing for her pallid appearance. Trying now to hurry across what felt like half a mile of that lovely carpet, Laura was smoothing down her own hair. She cleared her throat, managed a watery smile for the secretary who appeared to be thawing slightly and, only just in time, remembered to ram her spectacles into place on her nose.

He was waiting the other side of the door. Nervously hastening in, Laura nearly collided with him. A tall man, dark-haired, though with grey streaks above his ears, he towered over her by several inches.

'How do you do, Miss Crabtree?'

His hand was cool but very firm on hers, his voice quiet but deep.

'How do you do, Mr Horsfall? Thank you for seeing me at short notice.'

'This suits me very well, I'll be glad to make a decision. Let me show you round straight away. If it isn't what you have in mind, you must please say so and save us both valuable time.'

'Of course.' And if my offer isn't what you expect, I'm sure you'll not waste time either, thought Laura.

Patrick Horsfall hastened through the room in which he had waited and along a corridor. The small windows, set at intervals, gave glimpses of Halfield. They crossed a cold, stone-faced entrance hall with an inglenook fireplace, also of stone with intricate carving. Even in July, the place would have benefited from flames soaring from the black iron grate.

'This is the shortest route from inside the main house,' he told her, opening double doors of some very dark wood.

He stood back and Laura walked through, mesmerised already by the magnificence of a huge reception room.

'Gracious, this is impressive,' she exclaimed, and whipped off her glasses to have a proper look. She'd never been in a lovelier house, seeing it clearly seemed more important than trying to appear businesslike.

'Princes have dined here – and more than one foreign monarch.'

I can believe that, Laura thought. She swallowed, over-awed by its size. Slowly, trying to contain her delight, she gazed around the panelled walls and over towards the line of tall windows hung with gold brocade. Surreptitiously, she slid one foot along the floorboards, testing. At one end of the room stairs with a carved balustrade led up to a balcony.

'The minstrels' gallery,' Mr Horsfall explained.

Laura inhaled. She imagined a dance band playing. All about her she pictured couples moving to the rhythm which she could almost hear.

Steady on, Laura, she thought, you're only passing through. He's not inviting you to a grand ball!

All at once she felt deflated. This reception hall was so large, the entire house so splendid, that her living anywhere near seemed highly unlikely. And she couldn't bear the prospect now of settling for a tiny house, hemmed in by hundreds like it down in the town. She hadn't even seen the Coach House yet, but she could imagine the price. And she only had the

15

thousand pounds Aunt Constance had left her.

'Eh – I am sorry,' she exclaimed. 'I was forgetting that we're on our way through here, it was just . . .'

Patrick smiled. 'We'll move on then, shall we?'

The Coach House was visible as soon as they went through a door at the far end of the room. Two-storeyed, it stood only fifty feet from the main building, and was constructed of a similar sandstone. Its windows were arched and divided into small panes. The only door she could see was painted cherry red and matched the remaining woodwork.

'Until quite recently my sister lived here, but her husband farms, and took over from his father who died last year. They're expecting a family in the near future, anyway, and this would soon have proved too small.'

'How much are you asking?' Laura enquired, not risking falling for the place then learning it was beyond her means.

'That would depend upon what was included. It is carpeted, and my sister has left the curtains. She would expect something for them.'

Aye, thought Laura grimly, that'll send it up quite an amount. And she had a nasty suspicion that he would want far more than she possessed.

'Apart from the items mentioned, the house itself should fetch seven hundred pounds.'

'I see.'

The figure was less than she had feared, but she wouldn't go committing herself until she'd seen inside. And even then, she thought, I'd better not do anything. Her first priority would be her work.

But what if somebody else snapped this up in the meantime?

'I have to tell you I've had several offers,' Mr Horsfall revealed, feeling in a pocket for the keys. 'Well – here we are then.'

Even the narrow hall was carpeted – right to the edges. It was a lovely, plain moss green, and toned with the patterned carpet showing through the open door of the living-room. She'd need a new Ewbank sweeper for that, she wasn't sure

16

she trusted vacuum cleaners yet.

'In here, first, shall we?'

He preceded her and went to stand by the fireplace which was mahogany-framed surrounding opalescent tiles.

The room was large for a two-bedroomed house, and the high ceiling increased the feeling of space. Laura went to look out of the window. The view was virtually the one that she'd admired from Arncliffe Hall itself.

This is what I want, she decided. But she must be practical; there'd be rates to pay, gas bills, she'd need furniture, and food. How could she expect him to hang on until she proved she could earn enough?

'I'd like to look at the kitchen, please.'

'Certainly. You'll need to be fully aware of what you're contemplating.'

The kitchen occupied the entire rear of the building and, if narrow, compensated by being long. It had more cupboards than she'd ever seen in any kitchen anywhere.

Laura sensed Mr Horsfall looking at her, glanced at him, and grinned.

'You know what the trouble is, don't you? It's all too nice – I can picture myself here. I shan't want to see myself living anywhere else.'

'But you can't meet the figure, is that it?'

'Oh, I can – providing too much isn't asked for carpets and so on. The trouble is, I've only just come to live round here. I don't know for sure that I can keep myself.'

He didn't say one word. Laura's hopes foundered. Had he decided in favour of some other potential buyer? Maybe he thought she was a bit of a scatterbrain, even looking at houses before getting a job.

The stairs and landing had pale apricot wallpaper which complemented the green of the carpet. Their feet made no sound as they went upstairs.

'This is the master bedroom.'

Without furniture it appeared large, and with windows in three of the four walls was extremely light. One side faced the

17

moors where a single dead tree was outlined against the summer sky.

'I'll bet this catches it in winter time.'

He smiled. 'You could say that. Although the prevailing wind comes from the east, so you'd be sheltered by the main house.'

The other bedroom was hardly any smaller, the bathroom had a modern suite. And Laura decided it was time that she left. Any longer in this house, and she'd certainly never consider any other.

'Are there any questions?' Mr Horsfall enquired, as he showed her down the stairs and out to inspect the compact garden set to one side.

'There's probably lots I ought to be asking, but I've never bought a house before. There is one thing I'm uneasy about, though. I've never really understood leasehold. It is all right to sell a leasehold place?'

She must have said something funny. He was standing staring down at her, his rather severe features lightened by a smile.

'Do you know who I am?'

'I'm afraid I don't. I told you, I'm new to Halfield.'

'I run the largest building society there. I think you may take it that I know what's permissible.'

'Aye, I reckon that'll be so.'

Laura was grinning up at him, amused by her own naivety. And unable to resent *his* amusement because it wasn't at her expense.

Back in his study, he invited her to sit the other side of the massive desk. He unlocked a drawer and withdrew a sheaf of documents. Before speaking he glanced across at Laura, wondering. Not usually so patient, he was waiting for some clue as to how she could manage the asking price. Although saying little she had conveyed a delightful eagerness, a refreshing change from his business acquaintances and the over-sophisticated women who considered themselves their equals.

And she had pluck, even contemplating the responsibility of

taking on a house of her own. Her neat costume was neither fashionable nor well-tailored. He'd like to see her in a Chanel suit, less severe and far smarter. He felt so certain she wasn't accustomed to having money behind her, maybe he should caution her against buying?

'My sister and her husband spent a lot on carpeting the Coach House,' he began, reluctant to spoil the gleam in those glorious blue eyes.

'How much?' she prompted. 'I'm not as soft as I look.'

Patrick smiled, recalling the glasses she'd worn. He had guessed they were normally used for reading, and adopted today to appear more efficient. 'Does roughly a hundred sound astronomical for carpeting?'

Laura laughed. 'Not if you say it quick. And you do mean for the curtains, an' all?'

'Yes, indeed.'

'So, eight hundred all told? It's a lot of brass.'

'It is that!'

'Not more than I could manage, though. I've had some money left me. That's what made me believe coming to live over here was possible.'

'But perhaps you wish to consult someone on the advisability of such a purchase? Was the legacy from within your family?'

'Yes, but there's nobody I want to ask about it, thank you.' She wasn't sure even her father would understand well enough to advise her to go ahead. 'It's nowt to do with any of them really. Aunt Constance left me the money specifically so that I could become independent. She was a lovely woman, taught me ballroom dancing. She had pernicious anaemia.'

Patrick saw the clouding of her eyes.

Laura swallowed. 'Do I have to make up my mind in a hurry?'

'On the contrary. You must give this careful consideration, Miss Crabtree. Please leave your address with Miss Pilkington as you depart.'

'Depart' sounded final, Laura decided, after he had pressed a button on the mahogany desk and his sombre secretary had

19

returned to show her out. His goodbye was formal as well, with no hint that they might ever meet again.

'I won't even think about it, I won't,' she muttered, walking slowly towards the bus stop. It would be tempting Providence even to dream of living here in country as open as any around her Whitby home.

She noticed from the time-table attached to the gas-lamp that the buses were infrequent. She'd have to make sure she brought her bicycle if she came to live here. *If . . .*

Chapter 2

'So how did it go?' Michael asked, his ready smile belied by the guarded expression in his hazel eyes.

He was waiting for her in Miss Priestley's living-room, drinking tea from one of the Royal Doulton cups reserved for visitors. Paying guests were given everyday earthenware. Laura hoped Michael had been given better tea as well. Miss Priestley seemed over-generous with water and milk.

'I doubt if Lindley's Carpets will be taking my designs,' she said, her smile rueful. 'But they did hang on to them, for the present, so happen there's still hope.' She told him about visiting Clem Hargreaves and how helpful he was.

For some reason that she couldn't have explained, Laura didn't intend giving even a hint to Michael about that lovely house. Being secretive troubled her, though, especially with him.

Michael had been a good friend who had seen her through the death of her Aunt Constance. And earlier, visiting Mrs Crabtree following her operation, he'd always encouraged Laura to reserve time for herself. He was a stimulating person and seemed determined that she should do more than help her mother. With him, she had taken Mondays off, to go wandering through tiny villages reached by cycling over the rolling Cleveland Hills. They had talked a lot. Michael was the first man to treat her like an adult who could think for herself. When he'd moved to the West Riding she'd been devastated, until she realised Halfield was an excellent place for selling her designs.

'Where else have you been?' he asked, running both hands

through his brown hair, and frowning.

Laura gave him a look as she sat in the other brown leatherette armchair. How could he have known she'd been to view the Coach House?

'Carpet mills, Laura,' he reminded her, smiling again. 'Your mind doesn't seem to be on what we're discussing.'

'Oh – most of them by now.'

'You could try further afield.'

'I'd been thinking that.' She was only selling them her designs, it wouldn't matter very much where the mills were situated. It wasn't like having to go there every day.

'I'll make enquiries,' Michael promised. 'One of our churchwardens runs a dyeworks, he should know all the local carpet manufacturers.'

'Thank you,' she said, trying hard not to resent being organised.

'Your designs are good, my dear, very original.'

'Thanks.'

She smiled at him, trying to make amends for not being properly grateful. Wasn't he the first person who'd made her feel that she mattered, and not only as another pair of hands for coping with the triplets?

'I do wonder though, Laura, if you shouldn't perhaps have some other work to fall back on. With your experience of caring for your sisters, especially when they were younger, you could be very useful to some mother with a large family.'

If he had hit her she couldn't have been more astonished, nor more upset. Not *you*, Michael and all, she thought, horrified. She'd believed he, of all people, understood.

'Some people are born to serve others, you know,' he continued. And she realised he had no idea how he had distressed her. But *his* life hadn't been all menial tasks. He hadn't spent hours following three sisters around, tidying their toys when they were little, sorting out comics, then magazines, helping mend their clothes. Seeing they were turned out so nice that, even when their mother was too tired to bother, the triplets still had people stopping to admire them in the street.

22

No, Michael was different, he'd been to a college of music in London. He had become so well known for his playing that people were surprised he was still only in his late twenties. When he conducted choir practice, eyes alight and his brown hair gleaming, everybody looked up to him – and not only because he was over six feet tall.

He glanced at his watch as he set down his cup and saucer. 'Sorry, my dear, but I'll have to be making tracks. I've promised to talk to the Mothers' Union. They've got their annual service coming up, and we're going to make it rather special. I didn't want to leave before seeing you, but – well, you were rather later than I'd anticipated.'

About to apologise, Laura checked herself. She was certain she hadn't arranged to see Michael today. They had met yesterday but nothing had been said about this afternoon. If he'd merely calculated how long he thought she ought to be out, that wasn't her fault. Even for Michael, she wasn't going to forget that she'd come here determined to make up for always having to put everybody else before her own ambitions.

But I mustn't be niggly about summat and nowt, she reminded herself silently, and followed as Michael walked towards the brown grained door.

He had a hand outstretched for the knob when the door opened and Miss Priestley bustled in, as though she'd heard him set down his cup and must escort him to the front door.

'It's been so nice seeing you again,' she beamed, fluttering short, spiky eyelashes as if she were twenty years younger than her middle-aged frame suggested. Her solid pink hand sought Michael's, gave his fingers an energetic pumping, and held on.

'Do feel able to come here at any time. Even if Miss – er, Crabtree happens to be out, you will find a warm welcome. You know that, don't you?'

'Thank you, Miss Priestley.'

Michael retrieved his hand, resisted the urge to shake his fingers to restore the flexibility essential for playing. He looked beyond her to Laura, prevented by her landlady's bulk from leaving the living-room doorway. 'See you later, Laura.'

Miss Priestley had the front door open now and was reiterating that it had been so nice to see him.

Her eyes seemed misty as she closed the door and trapped Laura between herself and the ornate umbrella stand before she could hurry from the lobby and up to her room.

'Such a lovely man! And so brilliant with the choir. I've always loved singing, you know. And so handsome – so very like . . .' She paused, sighing, her puffy eyelids lowered. 'So like my fiancé. I lost him, you know, in the Great War.'

'I'm sorry,' said Laura, wishing she hadn't been told already about Miss Priestley's young man, who hadn't been killed as she implied, but had found some lass in Blackpool more attractive. Perhaps that meant Miss Priestley warranted *more* sympathy, though? And she clearly was lonely – why else would she be so fascinated by her lodger's life?

Pale eyes wide open now, she was scrutinising the third finger of Laura's left hand. No, there's no engagement ring, Laura felt like telling her, and wondered why she sensed Miss Priestley would be reassured by that.

Michael's suggestion about the kind of work she might do sickened Laura. Her legs leaden and her spirit weary, she began climbing the steep, narrow stairs. Did he really not understand that she'd come to Halfield determined to make her name designing carpets?

She opened the door and went into her serviceable room, wondering why she was so disturbed by his thoughts regarding her future. If Lindley's didn't take her patterns, she'd find somewhere else. She'd visit every carpet manufacturer in the North of England. That way, although she wouldn't enjoy asserting herself with Michael, she would demonstrate that she'd never go back to devoting her life to her sisters or to other folks' youngsters.

She would have to look sharp, though, and get her career started because now she had this other ambition. She had set her mind on having that house she'd seen today. At least I'm not frightened of hard work, she reminded herself, and I don't believe in giving up.

* * *

Laura awakened next morning bursting to get on. She would telephone Michael, even if having anyone's help went against the grain. She would find out from him what other carpet mills there were, and then she'd get out there and make them consider her designs.

She was half out of bed when she remembered that she'd left those designs at Lindley's factory. She couldn't ask to have her work returned if there was a chance Roy Lindley was going to make her an offer. She would have to bide her time. But she cared too much about establishing her independence for waiting to be easy.

Laura felt low-spirited from her inability to get something done. She wasn't used to hanging about. Killing time was a luxury no one in the Crabtree household had experienced since the day Greta, Sybil and Netta had yelled their introductions there.

She washed and dressed, then sat in front of the pockmarked swivel mirror, savagely attacking her hair with the brush. She reminded herself of a Reynolds' cherub today but, with her frizz of hair instead of angelic waves, an unruly cherub. If she could only get it away from her forehead she might look more than about eight, might resemble a businesswoman of twenty-five.

'Are you there, Miss Crabtree? There's a letter for you.'

Miss Priestley's shout made her smile to herself. Why ever was she worrying about how she looked? To read through a letter from her mother by the sound of it. She'd not have been forgiven yet for deserting home. If she didn't feel like tearing out her hair before she'd read to the end, she'd be surprised.

Miss Priestley came bustling out of her sitting-room to the rear of the house as soon as Laura's foot reached the bottom step, making her wish she didn't mind this feeling that her landlady spent every minute listening.

'I wondered when you were getting up,' Miss Priestley said, her silvery eyes boring into Laura's, then flicking just as interestedly towards the envelope she was holding. 'Delivered

25

by hand, this was, not more than a minute since. By somebody in a big posh car.'

Thanking her and taking the envelope, Laura ran back upstairs. 'I'll be down again in a minute or two,' she called over her shoulder, without waiting for a reply.

The bed springs twanged as she sat down and slit the envelope. The notepaper inside had the Lindley Carpet Factory crest and address. But where were her designs? They'd have to let her have them back.

Roy Lindley was not returning them. He was making a proposition, suggesting that Laura worked with his design team. This would necessitate her going through every process in the mill, learning how their carpets were manufactured. And then, he felt sure, she would readily interpret her designs in such a way that they could go into production.

'Oh, heck!' she muttered, appalled. He'd got completely the wrong end of the stick. She only wanted to sell him her patterns, not spend every day in that deafening place.

She would go there and explain; that way she'd get her designs back straightaway. She asked to use the telephone and arranged a meeting, then tackled breakfast. She had more than a suspicion that she was going to need all the sustenance coming her way. And Miss Priestley provided lovely breakfasts: eggs and bacon, lots of home-baked bread, and best butter from the Maypole Dairy in the next street.

When she went rushing out of the house to stride along between the rows of blackened stone houses, Laura felt ready for anybody. She was right, wasn't she? She had come all this way to work as a designer, nothing else. She would have to tell Mr Lindley. Unless . . . maybe she might as well hear about any possible advantages of doing as he suggested.

The tram today seemed to echo her need for action: busily whirring over its tracks, the metal arm whooshing along the overhead wires, even the shuddering as it lumbered onwards was a part of her going somewhere. And surely the somewhere that Laura Crabtree had intended going was to have been more congenial than working in that mill?

Her appointment was with Roy Lindley, but when she was shown into his cramped office she found his father there as well. I could have done without this, thought Laura, anxiety tightening her throat. She could hardly speak. But she needn't be feeling nervous at all. She only had to explain that she meant to work from home.

She was introduced to Robert Lindley who was nearly as striking in appearance as his son. He might have lost most of that glorious hair, but he had all the other handsome features and a lot more besides – seeming altogether nicer, not fancying himself nearly so much.

Laura wished she'd seen him first. He'd not have made her feel so defensive, would have understood exactly what she intended.

'Do have a seat, Miss Crabtree,' Roy Lindley said, beaming. 'So – you're eager to take up my suggestion. That's good, I need your enthusiasm. Father, here, was a little sceptical about a woman coming in on the design side.'

'I like your work, though, Miss Crabtree,' the older man assured her. 'Even if it does need modifying before it is going to be of any practical use.' His smile was more constrained than his son's but for some reason Laura felt that it meant more.

Not that she could allow herself to be influenced by anybody's smile. She sat across the desk from the pair of them, flummoxed, wondering how she was going to convey her reservations about the way they saw the job. So far, she hadn't managed to slip in more than an odd word.

Mr Lindley senior was telling her about the carpet factory, and how it had been started by his father and had grown into one of the principal suppliers of carpets in the whole of Britain. 'I hope you realise that it's exceptional for us to take on somebody who hasn't either worked their way up in the trade or had specific training? There are classes teaching design for our industry, you know. You are fortunate that we aren't insisting that you go away and come back only when you have studied.'

27

'Er – yes. I do appreciate that such an appointment would be out of the ordinary,' said Laura.

Again, though, Robert Lindley continued swiftly: 'At my son's request. He'll be answerable for your usefulness to us – and he's no more easy to please than I am.'

Laura swallowed uneasily, wondering what precisely was expected of her, and why.

Before she could speak the door opened after a perfunctory rap on its glass panelling. A smart young woman put her pretty dark head into the room and murmured to Robert Lindley that he had an important telephone call in his own office.

As he left Laura tried to conceal her relief. His son noticed and grinned conspiratorially.

'You don't need to worry about the old man, though you'd best not let on that I've told you so. I have a pretty free hand these days, especially over designing.'

'It's not that.' She mustn't let him think that she was readily intimidated. 'Your offer was something of a surprise. I wasn't really contemplating a job where I'd be working here all the time.'

Roy Lindley looked taken aback. He'd come up with the idea to ensure their close acquaintance. Now she was as near as dammit rejecting it. 'You could have said so in the first place! You've put me in rather an invidious position. I've fought to have you accepted by my father. I hope you're not telling me I shouldn't have bothered?'

'Not at all. I do want to design for your company, but I would like to know more about why you'd want me here every day.'

'Is there something preventing that? I thought your family were over on the east coast, that you had no obligations. You haven't got a bairn tucked away somewhere, have you?' If she had a child or, worse, a man in tow, he would dispose of her now.

'No, I have not.' Shocked, Laura rose. Nobody had ever spoken of anything of the kind to her. 'If you're going to talk to me like that, I'm afraid I've come to the wrong place . . .'

'Here – steady on.' He was recovering now, restoring his customary suave manner which surely couldn't have been shaken by this ingenuous slip of a girl?

Laura's hand was outstretched to gather together her designs. Her wrist was grasped firmly. When she looked at Roy Lindley he was smiling at her, his rather heavy eyelids lowered.

'Sit down again, won't you, Miss Crabtree. I'm not an unreasonable man, there could be some compromise we might reach – providing you remained aware that concessions are a rarity here. Now, suppose you explain why you won't consider working on the premises?'

Alarm bells were jangling somewhere in her mind. She didn't want to be beholden to anybody, much less Roy Lindley. And yet she didn't want to waste all these lovely patterns either.

'Do you really want to waste all these?' he asked.

How did you know that was what I was thinking? Laura wondered, even more distrustful. But that ready smile worried her most. Was that how he got his own way?

'Together we can make them work,' he continued. 'Don't you long to see carpets coming off the loom and know that you've created their designs?'

Laura had wanted nothing more for almost as long as she could recall, but she still hadn't contemplated designing anywhere but at home. And nor was Roy Lindley someone with whom she wished to work constantly. 'I didn't know it would be like this . . .' She swallowed. Was she repeating herself? Eh, they'd got her worked up! 'I thought I could just sell you the patterns.'

'And have somebody else do the donkey work? You expect some fellow to bore the pants off his backside, do you, converting your pretty pictures into designs that we can use?'

'Not at all,' she said earnestly. She was losing hope of selling her work here, anyway, and that loosened her tongue. 'I don't want anyone touching them. I expect to convert these patterns myself. I only need you to give me half a chance.'

'Well – if you're to succeed, you'll certainly have to acquire some practical knowledge of how carpets are manufactured. That will only come through experience of every process.'

That sounded reasonable enough to Laura and she nodded. 'All right then, I can give this a try.'

'You'll need to put your back into it, Miss Crabtree, and to stop conveying the idea that working in our mill is rather beneath you.'

'Eh, is that the impression I give? I'm sorry. I'm not like that at all, you know.'

'I must admit you've disappointed me today by appearing that way. And by seeming as if you aren't quite serious.'

'But I am, Mr Lindley, very serious.'

'You're sure? It seems that now I've grown enthusiastic about your designs, you appear to be losing interest. Is that a tendency of yours as soon as the newness wears off one of your schemes?'

'No, I never do that.' Laura gave him a direct look. He was goading her, but she certainly couldn't tell why he should. 'My dad's worked hard all his life, and he's never given me the idea that my path would be any different. He encouraged me to go in for this. I want to learn and I'm not scared of hard graft. I'd love to show you how serious I am – providing you're offering a sensible wage.'

Roy contained a satisfied smile. He had been afraid that he would have to let her go, and that would have deprived him of an interesting situation. As it was, she would be stretching herself to the limit, proving her worth. She'd hardly notice what he was about.

Some time during the conversation and without intending to, Laura had sat down again. Her designs remained on the desk.

'Leave those with me,' he suggested. 'I'll use at least some of them to illustrate the difference between what we require and what you have produced so far.'

They discussed her pay and the hours she would work. She would be getting up at dawn and working till five-thirty, but nothing now would induce her even to hint that she might expect one single concession.

They were walking between the rows of heavy looms towards the outer door when they met Robert Lindley. He paused with them, turning Laura so that she might examine a partly woven carpet.

'What do you think of this, Miss Crabtree?'

'Oh, that's beautiful.' The carpet was in muted shades, predominantly greens, blues and browns with just an occasional touch of red. It reminded her of an old tapestry and she said so.

Mr Lindley senior beamed. 'You certainly have a good eye. That, my dear, is precisely what we intend. You like tapestries, do you?'

'Very much.'

'Locally there are some fine originals – Patrick Horsfall is a connoisseur. I suggest you visit him at Arncliffe Hall.'

Laura was about to explain that she was hoping with all her heart to live on the doorstep when she sensed Roy Lindley's awkwardness. Surprised that he appeared uncharacteristically perturbed, she stared at his handsome face which was turning from deep red to deathly ashen. Unable to credit that he could so quickly lose all his poise, her gaze flicked towards his eyes. He was looking at his father as though he could have clamped a hand across his mouth.

After briefly registering a surprise that equalled her own, Robert Lindley smiled easily towards his son. 'I will see Miss Crabtree to the door.'

He motioned her to pause beside the nearest loom then pointed upwards to a lot of oblong cards, all full of holes and joined together. Once away from the machinery, standing near the lime-washed wall where he could be heard, he explained, 'We call that the Jacquard system. It's similar to what's used in a pianola. One day there'll be wider applications of cards like that. Here, it's what sets up the pattern going through the loom.'

'How does it do that? What do the holes represent?'

'I'm glad you've asked that, the system's very interesting, but we'll explain more fully once you start here. There's time enough.'

I've gone and done it now, thought Laura, walking dazedly along the flagged pavement, scarcely aware of the drizzle falling from drab skies. She was so disturbed about agreeing to work in Lindley's factory that she walked all the way back to Hanson Road, and still felt no better. Even when she'd completed whatever training they deemed necessary, designing for them wouldn't be anything like she'd pictured.

When Miss Priestley's home, 'Bien-être', came into sight among the row of terraced houses Laura's footsteps slowed. She was in no mood for talking, and certainly not for enlightening her landlady about the result of her outing. Could she dash indoors and up to her room without having to gather her wits and face an interrogation?

Suddenly, though, trying to avoid Miss Priestley made her feel guilty. The woman meant no harm, was only interested. And if her own career was beginning now she herself would be happier, could be generous with her free time for as long as she lived here.

The lack of privacy was still just as apparent. As Miss Priestley emerged from her own quarters Laura returned the welcoming smile. While she promised to be only a moment before she would be ready for dinner – which she felt much too agitated to eat – Laura realised that her landlady reminded her slightly of an older Aunt Constance.

I might be glad of this one day, she reflected, struggling rather with Miss Priestley's excellent steak and kidney pie. When I've been hard at it in that mill the last thing I'll want will be to think about cooking. Nothing, though, would detract from her independence. She wouldn't be sorry to be on her own, to be free to shape her life the way she intended.

Laura was deep in thought about how different that life was becoming when Miss Priestley came in to clear away and paused by the sash window, her eyebrows soaring. 'That's him again,' she exclaimed, half to herself, then remembered Laura and pointed. 'Getting into that big black car.'

Glancing out, Laura saw a large man who looked singularly unappealing to her.

'Carter Ainley – he's allus stirring summat up,' Miss Priestley continued. 'Very friendly, he is, with that lass in the end house. And him a married man. She was telling me t'other day that it's only that he wants her to work for him, that he'll take her on to do the books for a new business of his, making wireless sets. Not round here, mind. He reckons he's buying a coach house or summat over at Arncliffe Hall.'

Not my Coach House! thought Laura, horrified. She'd only just begun realising that no matter how uneasy she might feel about working at Lindley's it did mean she would be justified in making a firm offer for that lovely house. She'd even been thinking she'd have to fetch her bike over from Whitby. There could be no late arriving at Lindley's Carpets. She didn't intend putting one foot wrong there. Roy Lindley would be made to understand that Laura Crabtree always flung her heart into anything she tackled.

The drizzle that she had scarcely noticed on her way to Miss Priestley's had intensified during her meal, It was bucketing down, slanting like steel rods towards the lace-curtained windows. She couldn't let that keep her in now. She must get to Patrick Horsfall as soon as she could and prevent him from selling that house to Carter Ainley or anybody else.

So long as a deal with Ainley wasn't agreed she might still stand a chance – he had seemed dubious about her buying, but now she had a job. A proper job.

'You want to get a proper job.' She heard the words in her mother's voice. That had been when she'd spent so much time producing carpet patterns. 'You'll never make a living at it.' Mum would have preferred it if she'd been like Cousin Emily and gone to work in the baker's, or Bessie from next door who served in the fish and chip shop. Her father hadn't been forgiven for supporting Laura's ideas. There was something to be said for that noisy mill, she thought now, more resolved than ever to make Dad proud of her.

Asking permission to use Miss Priestley's telephone, she rang Arncliffe Hall. A woman answered, and Laura wondered why she'd been counting on speaking to Mr Horsfall himself.

'Is that Miss Pilkington?' she enquired.

'I'm afraid it isn't, you should find her at the office.'

'And is Mr Horsfall there as well?'

'I should think so, unless he has a meeting somewhere.'

The woman didn't sound pleased to have been troubled. Laura wondered if it was Mrs Horsfall. Perhaps she was on the point of going out; someone in her position would like as not sit on various committees. Or maybe she was entertaining.

'I'm sorry I've interrupted whatever you were doing,' she apologised swiftly, though meaning to find out as much as she could. 'I was ringing about the Coach House – do you happen to know if Mr Horsfall's decided who he's going to sell it to?'

'I believe he has decided, but I'm afraid he hasn't told me yet.'

'I see. Thank you.' Her heart sinking, Laura sat down with a thud on the bamboo chair. She couldn't believe it. It seemed only a few hours since Patrick Horsfall had been showing her round the place. He hadn't said a word then about knowing who the fortunate buyer was. Now she'd heard this rumour about Mr Ainley it made her wonder why she hadn't been warned that the Coach House was spoken for.

If she had been a girl who went in for weeping, she'd have been crying her eyes out with frustration. Conditioned by long years of not showing what she felt, emotion tended to be contained, a hard little ball jammed just below her throat.

Gazing out from her bedroom, the street veiled by the downpour, Laura felt imprisoned, trapped. Agitation churned inside her, as sour as if she'd eaten green apples. She felt like telling Mr Horsfall what she thought of folk who let you believe in something, then let you down.

She certainly would have to find out who was buying the place. Was it Carter Ainley with his plans for a workshop? Why did he have to choose somewhere which would make such a beautiful home?

34

Half an hour later Laura was calming down, thinking more rationally. Nobody had told her who the new owner was to be or even for certain if the deal was settled. But *knowing* did matter – it mattered a very great deal. Until she found out she couldn't read a book or write a letter home or put a record on her battered old gramophone.

She caught herself pacing the room, every floorboard creaking beneath the worn, mustard-coloured linoleum. Miss Priestley would be calling up the stairs wanting to know what was wrong.

Laura couldn't stay in a minute longer; she thrust on her macintosh, ran downstairs and out of the front door.

Putting up her umbrella, she splattered along wet pavements towards the tram stop. There was nobody else waiting; she almost decided to turn back. Happen it would be fine tonight. She could go and see him then, at Arncliffe Hall.

I've got to find out straight away and tell him how I feel, she asserted silently, with rain drumming on her umbrella, the over-sickly smell from the nearby toffee works soaking into her.

The silvery rails began shuddering and the vehicle trundled into sight. She'd be in Halfield in a few more minutes. She'd go up to him in that building society of his, and . . . Well, she'd think of something.

Sitting in the tram Laura began to realise that she hadn't handled her decision to buy the house as efficiently as she might. Michael would reprove her for not being practical and would want to take her in hand. Well, she couldn't let that happen, not any longer. From now on she would do things herself. She'd learn how. She would make fewer mistakes, and they couldn't all be as upsetting as making a mess of this.

She was thankful when the tram rattled to a halt in the town centre. Thinking wasn't agreeing with her today. All she need concentrate on now was finding that building society.

Opening her umbrella, Laura glanced along Commercial Street, wondering which one was Mr Horsfall's. There were three building societies here, in the one street. However many more were there elsewhere in the town? What was she going to look like, traipsing into first one and then another, asking if it was Patrick Horsfall's? She couldn't do it.

Somebody would be able to tell her. But who – or who that she knew in Halfield? She wouldn't go telephoning anybody from the church – they were curious enough about her as it was, thinking she had followed their organist to the town. Michael would soon be told what she was up to. And she would do her own talking about her plans, when she was ready.

On impulse, Laura hurried up the steps into the Gothic-style Post Office. Five minutes later she emerged with the information that Patrick Horsfall's building society was the Yorkshire West.

It was only five minutes more before she was shaking rain off her umbrella as she stood nervously in its doorway. She knew it was because that house mattered so much to her, but she cursed her own anxiety for making her legs feel weak.

Laura made up her mind she'd not be daunted by the building society offices even though they were imposing, all highly polished counters and panelling on the walls. And packed out with customers. There was only one young man who didn't have a cluster of waiting people.

'Is it possible to see Mr Patrick Horsfall, please? I haven't an appointment, I'm afraid, but this is very important.'

'And your business, Miss – er . . .?'

'Oh – Miss Crabtree. The business is a private matter. He does know who I am.'

Startled, the young man scanned Laura from her damp fair hair, over her serviceable fawn raincoat, to her saturated shoes. Should he take it on himself to turn her away? What personal business might she have with the big boss? On the other hand, he was well-schooled in displaying good manners and would not risk being reported as otherwise.

'One moment, if you please,' he said grandly. 'I will enquire if Mr Horsfall is available.'

The shock came when Patrick Horsfall arrived to usher her

36

personally through the heavy door that led on to quiet corridors and his office.

'I hope you're not going to tell me off for asking to see you here,' Laura began as they approached his desk. She was determined to get in first with her explanation. 'I had to come into town to find out which building society was yours. I tried to speak to you at your house – daft of me really.' She gave a tiny shrug.

He had lovely eyes, very dark brown, a pity they were so grave. Not that they wouldn't be graver than ever when she'd had her say.

She swallowed. 'You could have told me that you'd already got somebody for the house. Is it that Mr Ainley? Because if it is I'm surprised at you.'

His dark eyebrows had jerked upwards already. Laura ought to have been warned not to continue, but she was beyond caution.

'Letting somebody like him take over that beautiful little place, for making wireless sets! Sheer waste, that is, throwing away that gorgeous view and everything. Haven't you thought what a lovely home that Coach House is? Have you no idea?'

One dark eyebrow remained raised, his lips compressed. There was a glint in those brown eyes which could have been anger. On the other hand, Laura began to suspect, it might be a very different emotion.

'Who told you this?' Patrick asked her.

'I telephoned your house. Somebody there said you'd decided. It'd be your wife, I suppose.'

'No, it wouldn't.'

He *was* cross now, his eyes hardened. Laura didn't like annoying him, but she needed to get at the truth.

'I've always been one for knowing the worst rather than living on false hopes. And if you have sold that house to somebody else, I do have to start looking round. I've got work in Halfield.'

'I did advise you to give the purchase careful consideration, Miss Crabtree.'

'I have done, Mr Horsfall, I know what I want.'

Patrick gazed at her, marvelling at the fire in those exquisite blue eyes, tantalised by the half-smile that hovered on and off her piquant face. Logical thought was impossible.

He had surprised himself by sending away Ainley only that morning, just as he had dismissed everyone else interested in the Coach House. He couldn't recall when last he'd reached a financial decision without relying on his innate commercial instinct.

'I wondered if you were trying to put me off before, but you've only got to say "no" and I'll go away. I won't make a fuss.' Laura grinned, and the amusement returning to her voice compelled Patrick to look at her again. 'Well – happen not much of a fuss. I suppose I might try to change your mind. If it is made up . . .'

His answering smile was rueful, but Laura was glad to see it just the same. He'd said hardly a word and his expression hadn't altered at all, how could she work out what he was thinking?

'You're not afraid of taking on responsibility then, Miss Crabtree?'

'Well – maybe a bit. Not enough to be anything but sure about what I'm doing.'

'On your head be it.' He leaned back in the big leather chair, a hand on each arm, studying her expression, anticipating her response. 'I certainly don't believe you'll wish to change my mind for me. You see, I have decided in your favour.' And don't, for God's sake, ask me for the reason behind an impulse that is totally inexplicable to myself.

'You won't regret it, I promise – you won't, you won't!'

Her delight pleased him more than he'd have admitted. Perhaps he hadn't been too misguided in indulging her as he might have indulged his own daughter.

'What do I have to do to make this happen quickly?' she demanded. 'You could have the money tomorrow . . .'

And that, thought Patrick, might prove useful. With a property the size of Arncliffe Hall, dependent parents, and the

38

building society to run, money was not so readily available as people supposed. Eight hundred pounds did not appear so large a sum to him as it must to this young lady, but he could use it to good purpose: for the cause that wearied each day and gnawed into every night.

'What you should do is leave me in peace for all of forty-eight hours, by which time I should have seen my solicitor about the legalities. You may call on me again, therefore, the day after tomorrow, but at Arncliffe Hall. Shall we say eight o'clock in the evening?'

I could hug you, thought Laura, then checked herself, saddened despite her own elation. Why had she not seen earlier this remoteness about him, this air of harbouring a secret?

His smile was genuine enough, though, as he escorted her through the offices and to the main door.

'In two days' time then,' he said, still smiling, and watched as she walked away from him.

Her umbrella furled despite the downpour, Laura Crabtree seemed to be springing along the wet pavements, her head high, the froth of blonde hair darkening as it grew wetter. Time you learned a bit more sense, he warned her silently, and hoped she wouldn't alter.

Chapter 3

Michael was coming down the steps from Miss Priestley's. For a minute Laura resented what seemed like his repeated checking up on her. But then his face lit up as he saw her, and she knew she couldn't do anything but share her good news.

'I've got so much to tell you,' she began, smiling into his hazel eyes. She hesitated then, aware that she hadn't confided earlier.

He glanced at his watch. 'I didn't think you'd be out on an afternoon like this. And now I've got choir practice in ten minutes, can't hang around any longer.'

'But I've got to tell you, I can't wait! Is the practice in the church? I'll walk you there while I explain.'

Wryly, Michael smiled. 'You're drenched already. I don't suppose staying out a few more minutes will make much difference. But shouldn't you calm down slightly? You're as excited as a little girl.'

And that's precisely the way I feel, thought Laura, like a child at Christmas, only better than any of my Christmases. All the waiting had culminated in obtaining the thing she most desired – the home where she could give her mind to shaping her own future.

'I'm going to be staying on in Halfield,' she told him, trying to choose her words, though they seemed to be tumbling around in her head. 'The folk seem nice and . . .'

'You've sold some of your carpet designs?' Michael exclaimed, astonishment ill-disguised in his voice.

'Not straight away. But Lindley's are setting me on. When they're satisfied I know enough about making carpets, then

41

they'll use my patterns. Well – after we've got them right for their looms.'

'So you'll be settling round here? That's good news, love.'

'Er – well.' Laura paused again. 'Not so near to St Martin's. That's the other news I've got. I've found a lovely little house. Aunt Constance would be that glad I'm putting her brass to good use.'

'But –' Michael swallowed, hard. Dismay engulfed him. He had never for one moment supposed that Laura would contemplate using the legacy without first consulting him. He had believed it represented security for them both, for their future together. She must know, surely, that the pittance he earned wouldn't enable him to support a wife? He had understood when she followed him to Halfield that . . . that . . . And now she was spending the money on a house for herself.

'It's only a small place, but just what I want. I never thought I'd live anywhere so lovely. It's the Coach House at Arncliffe Hall – Mr Horsfall's. I shan't have to go back to Whitby now. Can't you say something, Michael? Wish me luck, *something*?'

'I would first need to know more about this house. I can see all manner of snags.'

Laura read in his eyes the intention which he'd never mentioned, and immediately felt guilty.

'Eh, love – there's plenty of time. You've only just settled in at St Martin's. I thought we were all right as we were.'

'Until you proposed moving further away. Dash it all, you haven't been here more than a few weeks.'

'I'd no intention of upsetting you, Michael.' She wouldn't hurt him for worlds. How could she have failed to see how seriously he was taking everything?

No, thought Michael glumly, because you have not considered me at all. The fact of what she had done alone spoke far more cruelly than the baldest words. He could have shaken her. And somehow he must still behave in a manner appropriate to a man involved so heavily with the church. He swallowed a sigh.

'I would like to know more about your plans,' he said quite briskly, 'but I'm late already. I take it that you're not joining us to practise tonight?'

'Sorry, love, I've not had my tea, have I?' And he knew that she hadn't really decided yet to become a permanent member of the choir. She needed to think about that now, to work out whether she'd be better avoiding anything that involved her more deeply with Michael.

'I will call round afterwards. Perhaps then we can talk?'

Trying hard not to resent the reproof in his voice, Laura turned away and hurried back to her lodgings.

Miss Priestley waylaid her in the lobby. 'So there you are then. We were wondering what had become of you. You shouldn't ought to go worrying a fine man like Mr Dawson.'

Laura succeeded in checking her sigh. Miss Priestley couldn't help wanting to know what was going on. Michael couldn't help smothering her with caring.

'I hadn't arranged to see him, you know.'

'No? He seemed to think that you had. And you could have said summat to me about being late for your tea. I'd done you a nice pair of kippers, they'll be cooked to a frazzle.'

Eating the dehydrated kippers, Laura tried not to dwell on Michael's visit later that evening. She was sorry, but she couldn't believe it would serve any purpose. Whatever he might say, she was buying that house. She'd been that upset when she thought somebody else had got it, she didn't need further proof that she was doing the right thing.

Discovering how seriously Michael viewed their friendship was a shock; she still felt quite sick with alarm, appalled that she hadn't noticed sooner that his hopes didn't match her own. Admittedly, she got on better with him than any man except her father, but she'd never understood what Michael was feeling. He might have kissed her once or twice, but it had seemed to be merely affectionate. Where was the excitement of being in love, the attraction that was supposed to be like electricity between couples, so strong they couldn't leave one another alone?

43

It's not my fault that I'm not swept off my feet, she reminded herself, wishing that she felt less inadequate. Unfortunately, she couldn't believe this wretched confusion was Michael's fault either. Looking back, she wondered guiltily what she had done or said that he might have misinterpreted. It seemed now as though she'd only just escaped her mother's expectations to be engulfed by Michael's.

At nine-thirty that evening, he came striding into the living-room of 'Bien-être'.

'You'd better hear what I think, it's for your own good,' he began.

'All right, Michael, I'm listening.'

He did not sit but crossed to stand over her, scowling, looking like somebody's angry parent. A father more domineering than her own ever was. I'm not a child, she wordlessly protested, and prayed Michael would stop treating her as though she were.

He was fighting the urge to haul her to her feet and crush her against him. Wanting her was goading him, as it had for months. The ferocity of his desire alarmed him. If they weren't to marry, what could he do but shield her from what it might do?

'Since you have come to Halfield, away from your family, I have considered your well-being my responsibility. You must forgive me, Laura, for seeming to condemn your ideas. But I am seriously disturbed – by what I have learned from you, and since then.'

'Disturbed? What about?'

'About Patrick Horsfall.'

'I'm only buying a house from him, what's wrong with that?'

'From what I hear, any contact with that man should be regarded with suspicion.'

'Have you met him?'

'No. But in my concern for you I mentioned this scheme of yours to one of our churchwardens. You know I'm the last person to heed gossip, Laura, but I cannot disregard his warning. Horsfall, it seems, was almost voted off the board of

44

his own building society a few years ago. There was some scandal – he was interviewed by the police. Afterwards, the shareholders called an extraordinary general meeting to decide whether or not they continued to support him. Fortunately for Horsfall, he had the backing of the then mayor of the borough. By a narrow majority, he retained control.'

'And what was it all about?'

'I was told no details. They must have been suppressed. Horsfall's an influential man, knows how to hush things up.'

And you wish you could pin something on him, Laura realised, shaken. This wasn't the Michael she knew. Grubbing about with gossip? She could see him the way he'd been in Whitby – looking rather severe against their flowery wallpaper. But listening so warmly to her mother's accounts of her ailments, aired regularly over cups of tea. He was like a teasing elder brother to Netta, Greta and Sybil, even when they inevitably went too far, acting like the chumps they were, and Laura herself itched to knock their pretty dark heads together.

'Alderman Fawcett doesn't exaggerate. And he is a magistrate.'

Uneasy, Laura stood up, crossed to the sideboard, and stared hard at a photograph of a much younger Miss Priestley, framed in silver.

'Was Patrick Horsfall brought before him?'

'I think not. It sounded as though the police lacked evidence.'

'Ah.' Relieved and smiling, Laura faced him. 'It sounds also as if they have never seen fit to follow it up, doesn't it? You say you don't heed gossip, love. You'll understand then that I don't either.'

'Laura . . .' Quietly now, regard for her shining in his eyes, he was walking towards her. His hands took her gently by the upper arms.

'I can't let you do business with someone like that, can I, dear?' She gazed sideways, beyond his arm, looking steadily at the blackleaded firegrate so he wouldn't read the rebellion in her eyes.

45

'Not without forewarning me, which you have done. I'm grateful.'

His face was hardening, the skin tautening over high cheekbones, lips narrowing into a thin line. His hazel eyes glinted dangerously.

Don't take on so, Michael love, she thought. You're a good man. Too good to quarrel with when you only want to look after me. Just let me do what I have to, about my work, about a place to live. One day, I shall want to settle down. It could even be with you.

'You'll go your own way, I suppose?' he said, speaking softly now, drained. Eternity to him had always meant the infinite time of the God he trusted; now it became months of separation, an abyss. She might as well be living back in Whitby as out the other side of Halfield, with him tied up with services and practices with the choir evenings and weekends, and her working long days in the mill. 'You'll need advice on the legalities, no doubt. Let me know how I may help.'

Laura didn't answer. She'd asserted herself enough for the one night, hadn't the heart to explain that she needed to do things for herself. After Michael had left she realised that it was hardly surprising she hadn't grasped the extent of his emotions, nor was it a wonder that she had still to struggle to appear adult. Living at home for so long had been no preparation for dealing with this situation.

The morning felt refreshingly cool as Laura travelled to her job at Lindley's Carpets. The inside of the mill, though, was stuffy and warm. Yesterday's sun had penetrated even the walls, to say nothing of the windows at the top whose coating of whitewash failed to keep out all but a fraction of the heat.

'Wicked in here, isn't it?' said Roy Lindley cheerfully, greeting her from the doorway of his office, 'You look cool enough, though – a sight for sore eyes!'

Laura grinned. 'Are you always full of compliments, Mr Lindley?'

'Only for the pretty ones, naturally.'

'I'll have to steel myself against it, won't I?'

'I was hoping not.'

Laura gave him a look. She hadn't been wrong about him, had she, and she'd decided there was only one way of managing fellers like him. It mightn't seem over polite towards somebody who was her boss, but if it didn't suit he could always start behaving like a boss ought to.

'Where do we start then?' she asked, smiling. The place didn't seem quite so unbearable today. Happen she would be able to stick working here. And then the looms started up. The racket made her cringe; she felt herself shrinking down inside the neat little collar of her blue and white print frock.

Roy Lindley laughed. 'You hadn't forgotten what it was like?'

'I was hoping I'd remembered it wrong and it wasn't too awful really.'

He ushered Laura into his office and closed the door. 'For now, we'll work in here. Afterwards, I'll take you to the studio and introduce you to the rest of the design team, and give you the grand tour of the mill.'

He indicated the smaller of two chairs placed too closely together behind his desk. 'Make yourself at home.'

Deliberately, but without making a fuss, Laura drew the chair a little away from his and then sat down.

He was overpowering beside her; even from a foot away she felt uncomfortable, acutely aware of his male assertiveness. When he glanced sideways at her, his eyes were frankly appraising. I am going to keep calm, Laura resolved, and I am going to learn my job. I'm going to confound this clever beggar, if it's the last thing I do – and that's going to happen, somehow, by keeping him in his place.

'These are some of the designs we work from. I'll go over them with you, explaining in detail how they relate to the finished carpet. Then when we go round the weaving shed you'll see what I meant about your patterns not being practicable.'

The first of the designs was placed in front of her on the

desk, but some way to her right, whereas Roy Lindley was sitting to her left. His arm progressed along the back of her chair. Laura pushed the drawing nearer to him. Without looking, she knew that he raised an eyebrow.

He was smiling, though, when he spoke again. She might have foiled Roy Lindley, but he didn't bear grudges. There were one or two things about him that she might grow to like.

'This is really the second stage in the process,' he began, 'on point paper – a sort of graph . . .'

'I do know what point paper is,' Laura interrupted swiftly. Feeling in her large handbag, she found a folded design. From Clem Hargreaves she had learned where to purchase a supply, and how to reproduce one of her best designs. She'd sat up far into several nights, determined to get it right.

'But why didn't you use this originally?' He didn't take to being given a surprise like this.

'I couldn't get any in Whitby. There's not a lot of call for it round there.'

Roy didn't smile. When he shrugged Laura contained her satisfaction and continued.

'I wasn't sure of your standard widths so I've taken this as being twenty-seven inch.'

'That'll do.' He could see she had used each square to represent one knot made on the loom, and was too taken aback to disguise his admiration of the pattern itself. 'You've a good eye for colour, Miss Crabtree.'

'Thank you.' She'd been told that before. Hearing it from him gave her another boost.

'And yet you took no account of showing each individual knot in your initial designs.'

'I'll soon put that right. I'll transfer every one of them on to point paper.'

'We'll see. First, though, you need a thorough understanding of the system. From here, the design is next transferred on to Jacquard cards . . .' Before she could tell him what his father had said, Roy Lindley explained: 'A series of punched cards was first used by silk weavers as early as the eighteenth century.

48

The system is more or less the same today, but you'll see for yourself very shortly.'

'Your father showed me them cards the other day. They're rather like the innards of a pianola, aren't they?'

'Very similar. And each square on here becomes a circular hole on the corresponding card.'

'How many cards are needed for one carpet?'

'That depends upon the complexity of the pattern. It's not unusual for us to require over four thousand.'

And Clem Hargreaves isn't likely to explain that to me, thought Laura, certain that hand weaving would be different. In one of the books which she had studied she had seen illustrations of women sitting at a great wide carpet loom, with the pattern they were following fastened just above eye level.

They eventually left the office and began touring the factory. Concentrating, initially, on the basics which would govern her designs, Roy led her immediately between the high looms.

'These are the spools of yarn. On this type of loom the yarn is inserted with a needle stitch, rather than by using a shuttle. You know what a shuttle is, I take it?'

Laura smiled. 'Yes, I was watching them when I came through the shed the other day.'

Roy promised her a detailed demonstration of shuttles in operation, when they moved on to the Wilton style of carpet. So long as she didn't astonish him too often with knowing more than he'd supposed, he would still enjoy his role as tutor.

'How on earth does anybody put up with all this clattering?' she asked, scarcely able to hear one word that he was saying.

The man in charge of the loom where they had paused grinned sympathetically and said something to her, but using his lips alone without any sound emerging.

'She can't lip-read yet, Dennis,' Roy Lindley explained, then led Laura away between ranks of similar looms, all making a terrible racket.

Through double swing doors at the far end, they reached yet another big, stark shed, filled with clacking machinery.

'These are mainly Wiltons. I'll show you a shuttle as I promised, and give you a quick run-through of what happens here. I shan't go into much detail though as yet, or you'll only remember half of it.'

Laura was thankful that she would be allowed some time in which to absorb the differences between methods of production. Later that day she met the rest of the design artists – all male, and all, she sensed with alarm, reluctant to accept her.

'I hope they're not worried for their jobs,' she said in concern to Mr Lindley as they left the studio.

'Anybody new is a threat when there's limited employment.'

Laura nodded. She was looking forward to working in the studio, though. It mightn't, after all, be so different from the way she imagined designing.

'Oh, by the way,' Roy Lindley said, before she went home, 'You'd better fix yourself up with an overall for tomorrow. You'll be starting in scouring.'

'Scouring?'

'The wool is spun already when it comes here, but it isn't dyed or anything. Scouring removes the excess spinning oil, dirt, and any anthrax that might remain in the yarn.'

'Do you mind if I ask you something?' Laura began.

'Not if you don't mind my answers.'

'You've soon explained to me the main stages in transferring a pattern on to the loom. Does that mean I shan't be all that long after all before I get down to some actual designing?'

His smile looked triumphant again. 'As I said, you need to understand every process here. You want the job, don't you?'

Having a job did indeed seem to reinforce Laura's decision to buy her own home. And only just in time. That evening, when she got back to Hanson Road, a letter from her mother awaited her.

As she might have guessed, Maggie Crabtree was bemoaning her eldest daughter's absence, refusing to believe that it would prove permanent. The triplets were brimming over with first one enthusiasm and then another. And when were they not? thought Laura. And when did any of their enthusiasms last, or turn out to be more than a disturbance to the entire household?

This evening, thank goodness, she was going to see Patrick Horsfall again, getting further ahead with the process that would secure her that lovely Coach House.

He had an important-looking document waiting for her. Handing it across the desk, he smiled. 'You didn't tell me the name of your solicitor, Miss Crabtree. It may be quicker if you pass this on to him yourself.'

Her solicitor? that was a laugh! Still, she must have one, it seemed, so she'd find somebody to act for her right away.

'Of course,' she said smoothly. She wasn't as daft as a brush. She glanced down the succession of clauses, but they were in complex legal language; one look revealed hardly anything of their meaning.

'If you need an explanation of any points now, perhaps I may assist . . .' Concealing a smile, Patrick was watching her expressive features as she scanned the first page.

Laura's blue eyes moved upwards to study his face. 'Is that because you're not accustomed to doing business with a woman?'

He allowed his smile to show. 'No – because I understood you hadn't bought a house previously.'

Laura smiled back. He was very kind, friendly as well. Only she wasn't sure he was the one who would best advise her. Surely she should ask her solicitor, when she got one, if there was anything she did not fully understand? She said what she was thinking, and Patrick Horsfall nodded.

'That would be the correct course, yes. But if there are any ways in which I might be of assistance, you need only ask.'

'I don't mean to be a nuisance to you, but I'm grateful for what you've said. It's just . . . actually, I've been wrapped up in family for far too long. I'm dying to tackle something on my own.'

'Are you from a large family then?'

51

She grinned. 'You might say that. I've three sisters younger than me – triplets.'

So, that's it, he thought. You haven't enjoyed their demanding all the attention. Most likely you were roped in to help with chores. And who could be expected to take very kindly to that?

'Well, just in case you wish to consult me at all – my card. You may telephone me here, or in my office.'

'Thank you very much.'

'You must instruct your solicitor to contact mine in the event of any queries, but I think we've covered everything.'

I'll bet you have, thought Laura. Still, he was being very agreeable, and she liked his smile. She could tell a lot from smiles, and she suspected she'd done Patrick Horsfall an injustice. He wasn't patronising. He's simply not used to being very free with folk, she realised, and wondered why he need be wary.

'Would you like to see the Coach House again today?' He was surprised that he did not wish her to leave. Whenever she came into a room it seemed to brighten. No doubt because she was fresh, not so predictable as some of his acquaintances.

'I was afraid you weren't going to ask!' Laura exclaimed, springing to her feet, dropping her handbag in her eagerness. Her face was flushed when she'd retrieved the bag. 'Butterfingers, aren't I? I'm that excited – there'll never be another time like this. Ever since my aunt left me that nice bit of brass I've been daring to hope that I might one day have a place of my own. She was my ballroom dancing teacher as well, did I tell you?'

And you loved her a great deal, Patrick observed. He longed to say or do something that would take the sadness out of her eyes. She looked so young too, younger by far than she probably was.

'Didn't you say you're from Whitby?'

'Aye – my mother's folk were well known there. They created jewellery from the jet. Of course, that went out of fashion after Victoria. Some say there was too much of it worn for mourning.'

'I see.'

'Just listen to me going on. Holding you up. I hope your wife gave you your tea before I got here, or you'll be fair clemmed! Were you busy?'

'Nothing that won't keep.'

He rose and came round the desk to her side. They left his study and began walking towards the large reception room which she remembered as leading outside in the direction of the Coach House.

'What work are you doing then, Miss Crabtree?' he enquired, as they went.

'I'm learning to design carpets. I've always loved drawing the patterns but I've got to learn more about how carpets are made before they'll be much use.'

Warming to her straightforwardness, Patrick smiled again. 'You might say I have an allied interest – I have quite a collection of tapestries here.'

'Oh, yes, Mr Lindley told me. You're very lucky.'

'You may see them any time you wish.'

'Do you mean that? Like – after I've seen the house again?'

'Certainly. I'll unlock the house for you, then meet you back in the large reception hall in – what, half an hour?'

'That'd be lovely, thank you ever so much.'

Seeing her prospective home was such a thrill Laura had to contain a gasp of pure excitement. Watching her, Patrick experienced a rare surge of delight. He'd never known anyone more naturally appreciative and enthusiastic.

Beside him in the gathering dusk, she gleamed in a simple frock only a fraction deeper than the palest gold of her hair. When he unlocked the Coach House door, she hesitated.

'Well, go on in then.'

He touched her shoulder only briefly but Laura remained aware of his fingers long after they had been withdrawn. As she listened to his footsteps retreating towards the main house, she felt the warmth resulting from that momentary contact. And warmth was something that she needed over here, while everything felt so new and strange, and her job seemed rather daunting. She couldn't help looking forward, after re-examining this little house, to returning to Patrick Horsfall.

Each room was just as lovely as she recalled. She nearly ran from one to the next, renewing acquaintance with them. In a way, she almost regretted carpets and curtains having been left in place. She would have enjoyed choosing everything herself. Especially the carpets. But then the practical side of her nature reasserted itself. She didn't possess one item of furniture; saving for it and selecting to her own taste ought to satisfy any need to express her individuality.

Following her initial dash around the place, Laura slowed down and travelled back through every room, measuring the available space and taking notes of existing colour schemes.

She noticed in the kitchen that the light was fading fast. She had been too enthralled to observe the storm clouds moving in across the moor, intensifying the darkness of approaching night. She glanced overhead, saw electric lights fitted rather than gas mantles, and crossed to the switch by the door. As she'd supposed, the electricity was turned off at the mains. She would have to work swiftly and get back across that area of paving before the evening grew much blacker. And Patrick Horsfall could even be waiting for her already. She wondered what he must be thinking of her for taking up his time.

Patrick had paused by an open window in the long upper gallery. Beyond the hills, the darkening sky seemed plush-textured, the shade of his favourite indigo delphiniums which were still visible against the flush of pink roses. He inhaled the night scents wafting in from the garden, feeling as tranquil, for once, as the breeze here. He had loved Arncliffe Hall, through his boyhood – and afterwards; until the cares descended, pressures that prevented him from really noticing his surroundings as well as from looking ahead.

Recently, he had begun seeing all this again, through her eyes – with some of her eagerness. Smiling, he half-turned, gazed towards the expanse of barely discernible tapestries. He shouldn't have been surprised that she shared this interest. So much, he felt sure, would capture her lively imagination, her appreciation of craftsmanship.

His smile continued, was directed at himself. He shook his head slightly over his preoccupation. But who could this harm? The emotions she evoked were his, would remain private; more private even than that twin burden marring his existence here. And, for the present, he might look forward to whatever he would permit himself.

There would be meetings, not only as the sale was finalised but in the future when she moved into the Coach House. On innumerable occasions Laura would be only a few feet away, her fragrance alerting all his senses.

And in a few minutes he must collect his thoughts, turn on all the gallery lights, then make his way through the rest of the house to meet her, or he would keep her waiting.

Laura wasn't sorry to have a moment alone in the enormous ballroom. A couple of wall-lights, red-shaded, warmed the brown, burnished panelling, gleaming a pathway across the polished wooden floor.

After a hasty glance all around, she experimented with first one foot then the other, gliding backwards in the foxtrot she had ceased to dance since the dreadful day Aunt Constance went into hospital.

The room which earlier had conjured dancers in her imagination as well as an orchestra, again reproduced music, and her movements gained rhythm. Heedless now of anything but her love of dancing, Laura whirled over the boards.

She was halfway along the room when she thought she heard some sound above the music in her head. As she turned, reaching a corner, she saw something moving beyond the balustrade of the minstrels' gallery. It wasn't him. The figure was small, slight, looked like a girl.

'Hallo, love,' Laura called. 'Come on – why don't you?'

Still dancing, she reached the foot of the stair. Did the child shake her head of long flaxen hair? It was too dark up there to be certain. Sensing the girl's interest, though, she continued dancing. When, from the far end of the room, Laura faced her, the child was part way down the wooden stair, seated, a slate and slate pencil discarded beside her.

Approaching once more, Laura spoke again encouragingly. 'Can you dance? Have they learned you at school? Don't you want to have a try?'

The child seemed to withdraw, regarding her with solemn eyes shadowed with dread. Thin arms were wrapped across her chest, as if locking herself in. But by the time Laura had completed another circuit of the ballroom the girl was standing at the foot of the staircase. She didn't respond, though, when Laura again called, 'Come on.'

Please yourself then, she thought, but didn't stop dancing. She felt an urgent tug at the back of the skirt floating out behind her.

'Eh, well! That's right, give us your hand. This dance is easy, almost like walking. And we do it like this. Quick, quick, slow . . . quick, quick, slow . . .'

The girl seemed insubstantial as Laura held her, guiding her around the room. A strange, ethereal creature, she might have been as unreal as the manner in which she had suddenly appeared.

'What's your name, love?' Laura asked.

The girl did not reply.

'How old are you, five – six?'

Again, there was no answer. The child could have been totally deaf, but no deaf person could have responded to her counting of the beat.

'Do you live here, love?'

'What's that to you?'

Patrick Horsfall was striding towards them, his shoes clattering across the boards. As he came nearer, Laura saw the enraged glitter of eyes as black as the fire-back.

The girl shrank against Laura then was taken from her, led away, Mr Horsfall's hand firm at the back of her slender neck.

They were leaving the way that the child had appeared, through the minstrels' gallery. The man seemed as disturbed as the girl, distressing Laura so much that she had to glance away. Hearing them reach the top of the stairs, she felt compelled to look up again.

He was staring down at her. She'd never seen so much anger in anyone's eyes.

Sickened, all grace knocked out of her, she staggered towards the nearest chair. I wish I knew what I'd done, she thought. He's mad at me, absolutely livid. Somehow by trying to befriend that little lass, I've completely put his back up.

Laura closed her eyes, fearfully upset, certain now that he wouldn't let the sale of that lovely little house go through. He wasn't going to want her anywhere round here. And wasn't the saddest part of all that there would be no chance now of helping that uncannily silent child to relax? Or was that the saddest? she wondered, moments later. Wasn't it sadder still to be denied the opportunity to help ease the pain which, she suddenly understood, was not quite masked by Patrick Horsfall's rage.

The banging of a distant door seemed to echo right through her head. Her body numbed with shock and disappointment, Laura struggled to her feet. I've only felt like this once before, she thought, recognising the reaction experienced on that terrible day her aunt told her she had pernicious anaemia.

She would have to go away. She hadn't an earthly chance of living anywhere near. If she had any sense at all, she'd be out through these doors, and out of his life as well before she unwittingly caused any more trouble.

Laura reached the double doors and turned the brass handle, ice-cold to the touch.

She couldn't walk through the doorway. There was no way that she could compel her feet to obey commonsense and take her out. Her back to the ballroom, she stood there, still grasping the cold metal of that handle.

Minutes were passing, three, four, five, it could even be ten. And those minutes felt like hours, but would never be enough because they would be her last here – where the people and the place were tugging at her heart.

I can't walk out without seeing him, she realised, slowly released her grasp of the door handle, and turned back to the room.

He was waiting as quietly as the child had, in that same position in the gallery. The pain in his expression hadn't altered, nor had the near-concealing anger.

Then why is it, thought Laura desperately, that I can't just go away? Where are the words that will see me through that door? She couldn't seriously still wish to live so closely to Patrick Horsfall.

Before she could begin to analyse what might be holding her there, Laura experienced, across that massive room, an irresistible compulsion. She had been conscious earlier of the warmth she had drawn from him, and now was strangely sure that he needed some response from her.

Half-smiling, she shook her head; maybe hoping to clear it, certainly deriding her sudden fancies. She swallowed, struggling without much success to rein her fierce intuition. Not running across the floor and up those stairs to him required considered effort.

What a powerful man he was. How *aware* he made her – aware of his commanding features, his seriousness, and of her own irrational wish to get to know him.

You're not to let him affect you like this, she silently told herself. You'd better get over it sharpish, my lass, you'll not be seeing him again now that you've made him so angry.

He was sure to tell her it was no use – he would take back that legal form, like as not tear it up, so that there'd be no chance of her buying that house from him.

And she had thought that she cared about designing carpets, about having her own little home, about having this home, here. She had no idea, no idea at all! She wouldn't have believed there was anybody outside her own family who could make her feel so shaken. Wouldn't have credited that being concerned for them could be so fierce.

Oh, do get on with it, she silently urged him. Tell me to clear out, that you're no longer going to sell that Coach House to me. And that'll be best for everyone. It's not right to feel this way, not about a stranger. There's neither sense nor reason in all this surging interest that I cannot control.

When Patrick eventually spoke, though, he only increased her need to remain. 'Beth is not deaf,' he announced stonily, into the echoing stillness. 'Nor is she dumb. She isn't stupid either.'

'I know,' whispered Laura huskily.

Was it the gathering storm that had drained the room of air, so that she seemed unable to breathe in the painful stillness? Or was it the tension constricting her chest while she waited, interminably . . .

His dark hair might have been a black cap as he stood there, about to judge. And Laura knew, in that moment, that whatever his decision now there was no escaping his power over her.

Chapter 4

'The tapestries are this way.' His voice as dull and weighty as lead, Patrick sounded as though he were under some obligation to show them to her.

Laura almost told him not to bother. They were in no mood for appreciating either art or craftsmanship. But suddenly she recognised that this was his acknowledgement that nothing that had occurred during the past half hour would alter their arrangements.

Swiftly, she obeyed her earlier urge to cross the floor, run up the stairs and join him.

'Mr Lindley – Robert Lindley, that is – tells me you're quite a connoisseur,' she began, trying to keep up as he strode ahead of her towards the long gallery.

'Is he your new employer?'

'That's right. Only his son Roy is the one who's responsible for the design side. Do you know Roy at all?'

'No, we've never met.' At the entrance to the gallery he smiled towards her while his dark eyes remained weary. 'Not the best of days for seeing my collection,' he observed, and she sensed that he didn't mean on account of the gloomy weather. 'Here they all are though.'

Laura gasped, astounded. Did he really own all these tapestries?

Patrick grinned when she glanced up at him. 'Yes, I do have quite a few.'

'And how exquisite they are,' she exclaimed, hurrying from one to the next, all along the hundred feet and more of wall. 'They're in superb condition. How old are they?'

'You tell me – they're historical scenes, many of them battles.'

'Aye – and studying them properly would take me about a year!'

'That might be arranged, once you're living in the Coach House. If you're as interested as you claim, I'll expect you to be able to date them. Do you know anything about where they were made?'

'Not so much. I just know I always like looking at tapestries when I come across them.' She gazed the length of the gallery where, their muted colours merging, they looked like one enormous closely woven picture.

'Are they all about the same period?' she enquired.

He shook his head. 'Not at all. I'll tell you about them some time, if you wish.'

'But just now we've both had a long day.'

'And, providing you've seen all you want of the Coach House and have no queries, you ought to think of getting home before the downpour that's threatening.'

Laura agreed, thanked him, and left Arncliffe, well aware that he needed to be rid of the reminder of those uncomfortable minutes in the large reception room. And things could be so much worse. He was speaking already of the time when she would be living just that small paved courtyard away from him.

Sitting in the bus, though, she discovered that she wasn't much less perturbed than Patrick Horsfall had been. She had come very close to losing any chance of owning the Coach House. But he had wanted her there – before she happened to meet his daughter. Somehow she'd win back his approval or they'd be uncomfortable neighbours. Both the means she would use and the length of time that she would require seemed incalculable.

Miss Priestley's house appeared a welcome haven, and the middle-aged lady herself seemed by now like an old friend. As usual, she opened the door of her sitting-room as soon as Laura closed the front door.

'Eh, lass – you do look tired, proper done-up! How would you like a nice cup of tea?'

'That's just what I need, thank you very much.'

'You can come through to the back here, if you want. It's cosier than the parlour when there's only me and you.'

Following her through, Laura hoped she was managing to disguise her surprise. Miss Priestley had a nice modern fireplace, rather than an old blackleaded range, and the walls were distempered a soft creamy colour and had an attractive frieze of leaves in autumnal shades. The sofa and armchairs were in rust brown uncut moquette.

'Happen you're wondering why I've kept the parlour so old-fashioned while I've modernised my own room?' she said, startling Laura who felt her neck and face flushing.

Miss Priestley grinned. 'I see I was right. I do mean to do it all up, someday. I began on this room after my mother died. I'd been given to understand she'd left me a fair bit of brass. Unfortunately, what she had thought of as a small fortune turned out to be very little for the mid-thirties. I'd given up me job to look after her, and what with the depression and all that, I somehow haven't been able to get back to work again since.'

'What was your job?' asked Laura, taking the armchair she was offered while her landlady disappeared into the adjacent scullery to put on the kettle.

Miss Priestley's head appeared around the door frame. 'I were a weaver, for donkey's years. In Dawson's cotton mill. There isn't much cotton woven round here, you know. Most of it is done over in Lancashire. I could have got a job a while back, but that were in worsted, and I hesitated because it were summat I weren't used to. I should have snatched it up; while I were thinking about it, some little whipper snapper of a lass got taken on instead.'

'Oh, dear.'

'Aye – well, like most things, it isn't all bad. I do a lot of knitting, so I get plenty of time for it these days. There's lots of folk can't manage to do stuff for theirselves. They're not all Rhona Hebdens!'

'Rhona . . .?'

Miss Priestley chuckled. 'Don't tell me there's someone in Halfield as hasn't heard of her! Making quite a name for herself, she is. Not undeservedly, mind you – it's just that she's doing so a mite quickly. Began as a school teacher, she did, but only in a modest way, teaching 'em to sew and knit.' She interrupted herself to go and attend to the kettle which was whistling away now on the gas stove.

'Her father left her a lot of brass,' Miss Priestley continued, returning with the teapot and taking cups out of her smart oak sideboard. 'He also left her shares in Bridge House Mill – spinning. She took the bit between her teeth, all right. Made sure she worked her way through all the processes, then got them to produce the knitting wools she wanted, while she went over to making up patterns.'

'Sounds like she's ambitious.'

'Aren't all you young 'uns, these days? You can't tell me you've come here just because of our new organist. I've noticed that you're not exactly rushing him up to the altar at St Martin's!'

Accepting the tea that her landlady had poured, Laura smiled at her over the cup and saucer. 'I don't want to appear secretive,' she began, and went on to explain about the job at the carpet mill, and how designing was the career she'd always wanted.

'Well, I never!' Miss Priestley exclaimed. 'If you'd been taking any ordinary situation in a strange town I'd have said you were doing all right, but something so unusual . . .'

'You'd better reserve judgement, I haven't got started yet.'

'Well, I certainly hope you do all right. I sometimes wish I'd been born with more ambition. But some of us have it too engrained that we have to look after our own.'

Laura smiled. 'I know.' She had felt before that she didn't understand enough about Miss Priestley. Now she was reminded of Aunt Constance, and she could also see her old home, with a room very like this one. There was a similar light-coloured tiled fireplace, with a design of darker tiles and a raised hearth. On the rug patterned in red and brown rectangles sprawled Netta and Greta, arguing over which picture they should see at the new Odeon. Sybil was stretched out on the settee, protesting that the other two were keeping the fire off everybody else. Between the three of them they were making such a din that Laura couldn't even think her own thoughts. She wasn't wrong insisting on a life of her own.

'You're quiet tonight, love,' Miss Priestley remarked, 'you must be tired out.'

'Aye, I think I must. I'm afraid I'm not much company.'

'Never mind. Do you want your tea freshening up?'

'No, thanks, this is fine.'

At least her landlady understood when Laura stood up and said she was off upstairs. Sleep, however, was the last thing that seemed possible as soon as Laura had undressed and got into the narrow bed. She wasn't surprised that Patrick Horsfall's face appeared before her closed eyes, nor that the frail, silent child was there as well. It's not my problem, she told herself over and over again. That little girl has a mother and father with plenty of money to see she gets attention, if that's what she needs. Somehow, though, she could dismiss neither father nor child for long enough to settle down and rest.

Laura's unease carried forward into the following day. I look proper washed out, she thought, as soon as she glanced in the bathroom mirror. She had allowed herself an extra hour in bed, she'd have to wait until the shops opened in order to purchase an overall as instructed, but looked as though she could have done with a day's sleep. Before she arrived at the mill she would have to brighten herself up.

Instead of taking the tram, she walked the mile or so down into the centre of Halfield. Once clear of the sickly sweet smell of the toffee works, she inhaled the warm, summer air. On the same level as all the factories and mills, like this, the smokiness wasn't nearly so bad as it appeared when viewed from the neighbouring hills. And she liked the folk who were so friendly; the woman in the draper's shop wanted to know all about her job while she advised on the most suitable overall.

Roy Lindley glanced from her to the clock as soon as Laura walked into his office.

'I had to wait for the shop to open up,' she said very quickly.

'And then you got here as swiftly as you could,' he finished for her, smiling. 'Well, put that thing on then, and come with me.'

The scouring department was beyond the dyehouse, a long area almost filled by enormous tanks. Moisture saturated the air.

Thank goodness my hair's permed, thought Laura, or with a few minutes of this it'd be as straight as a yard of pump water.

'Did you tell me why the yarn has to be scoured?' she asked. 'If you did, I'm afraid I can't remember.'

'Although already spun when we receive it, the wool still contains a certain amount of winding oil which must be removed.'

'Or the dye wouldn't take?'

Roy smiled again. 'Right. We also must remove any dust, not to mention anthrax.'

'Aye, that can be bad. I've an uncle farms, I do know a bit about some of the diseases man can pick up from animals. What do you use for scouring?'

'Glauber's salt – hydrated sodium sulphate.'

'Will I need to know how much is added to the water, and all about temperatures and so on?'

Briefly, Roy considered. 'I don't think that'll be necessary. The main thing is that you should acquire some knowledge of all our processes, as I told you earlier.' He was no fonder of the scouring department than anyone in their right senses would be. And wasn't he determined that he would supervise her instruction personally?

'I'll introduce you to Amos Kitchen who's in charge here, then leave him to explain the details of what goes on.'

Laura liked Amos at once. He was about forty-five and walked with a limp. He also possessed the gentlest brown eyes she had seen.

'I'm not used to having a young lady like you working wi''

me,' he said immediately. 'You'll have to pardon my blunt ways. I'll admit it'll be a treat, though, to have a bit of feminine company.'

'You sound as if you don't get much of that, Mr Kitchen. Aren't you married?'

'Me?' He tapped his leg. 'With this? I've been like it since 1917 – shrapnel.'

'I'm sorry.'

'Aye, well. Now you've got that off your chest, let's forget it, shall we? There's not so much I don't manage, and as quick as any of t'others,' he said, leading her towards the start of the process.

'Have you always worked here?'

'No. I started off apprenticed to Clem Hargreaves afore joining up.'

'I know Mr Hargreaves, have done ever since his mill burned down.'

'That were a bad do! He didn't deserve that. Even after I copped this in the Great War he took me on again. 'T weren't his fault I couldn't stand in one spot long enough to continue weaving. And he found me plenty of work, first in one department then another. Finishing was what I was doing at t'time yon place caught fire.'

'How did that happen? He was so upset I never liked to ask.'

'So far as I know, nobody ever did get to the bottom of it. There was some talk of arson, but nowt were proved. It was such a shame, though. Old Clem had established a good community round that mill.'

'You must find working here in scouring very different?'

'Aye. But you can't turn down work these days. And they've promised they'll consider me if a vacancy comes up in finishing. Any road, we'd best get on. This is where the wool starts going through. I'll show you all the stages, until it's rinsed over yonder.'

Laura was determined that she would absorb enough information to surprise Roy Lindley. She'd never been slow to learn, and Amos Kitchen made it easy for her. Throughout that day and the next he kept her by his side, explaining what he was doing and why, his pleasant manner the only good thing about the department.

'He shouldn't ought to have kept you in here for more than a few minutes,' Amos remarked, after Roy had looked in on one of many occasions. 'That would have been sufficient for you to grasp what goes on.'

Laura smiled. She was beginning to agree with his assessment of the situation. The frequency of Roy's visits had made her suspect he might even be contriving her discomfort for some scheme of his own.

'I'll put up with it. It can't be forever, and I am getting paid. So long as I end up designing carpets, I can endure quite a lot.' But she would have to say something if Roy Lindley was taking her for a ride. By Thursday that week Laura was feeling ready to doubt her own tenacity. She had never loathed anything as much as she loathed the damp atmosphere, and the perpetual smell of wet wool. If it hadn't been for Amos Kitchen, she'd have been at her wits' end. He was a lovely man, with a dry sense of humour which helped her to forget the misery of their surroundings. And he offered her the loan of a bicycle.

Laura had been telling him about the house she was buying and how she would have to make time to go home to Whitby to collect her bike when he made the suggestion.

'You can have it for as long as you want. It's been sat in my garden shed since last backend. It were my mother's, you understand, and she rode it right up till the last. When she passed on I hadn't the heart to get rid.'

When she had been persuaded into borrowing the cycle, Laura was only too eager to collect it from him. Miss Priestley had a lean-to where it could be kept and Laura would save tram fares getting to and from the mill.

'Why don't you come home with me straight after work tonight,' Amos suggested. 'I'm not doing owt particular.'

They settled on the following evening instead, so that Laura could warn her landlady not to expect her in at the usual time. Amos asserted that Laura must have a bite to eat with him. 'I'm a dab hand at ham and eggs, and I won't take no for an answer.'

Well aware that Amos Kitchen led a lonely existence, Laura thanked him and agreed. She wasn't particularly pleased with her own life which seemed to be at a standstill, with nothing concrete on her purchase of the house and no word from Michael since their disagreement. Discovering that Amos lived on the way to Arncliffe, she decided to telephone Patrick Horsfall to ask if it was convenient for her to have another look at the Coach House.

'I don't see why not,' he responded quickly, sounding amused. 'I suppose you're itching to get busy on the place. I'm sorry there's no further news yet but . . .'

'You must think I'm proper daft,' Laura exclaimed.

'On the contrary. I've always admired enthusiasm – and what better cause than your own home?'

Long before evening, Laura was aching for something to take her mind off Roy Lindley and the mill. The day was exceptionally hot which made the scouring department even more unbearable. For some time now Amos had been repeating that he couldn't teach her any more about the process. Encouraged by him, she tackled Roy about moving out of there when, yet again, he appeared at her side while she was enveloped in moisture, reducing her hair to damp strands and condensing down her back.

His grin revealed that he was still enjoying her discomfort. 'Had enough in here, have you?'

'Since you ask, yes. And I could have learned sufficient inside an hour to give me all the understanding I need of everything involved in what is, after all, no more nor washing!'

'All right then, we'll let you do something that's much more relevant to designing . . .'

'Thank you,' said Laura, relief flooding through her as she pictured herself in that lovely airy studio.

'Report to the dyehouse on Monday, first thing.'

'The dyehouse?' But that was as bad as this wretched scouring place – couldn't he have given her a break somewhere decent first? It wasn't as if dyeing was the next stage in production. After passing through the massive mangle, the yarn went to the winding room. 'You've got it in for me, haven't you?'

'Anything but,' Roy Lindley assured her, his eyes gleaming. 'But I believe my office is the place for this discussion.'

Feeling ridiculously conspicuous as everyone paused to stare, she hurried through the factory at his side. When they reached his office, Roy held the door for her, then closed it after them.

'I've been admiring your tenacity, Miss Crabtree, don't spoil that,' he said, leaning easily against the edge of his desk while he gazed deep into her eyes. 'I had the feeling you wished to be thorough in learning, and also that you wanted to prove something.'

'Go on,' she prompted when he paused.

'There are, you know, certain means of getting round that – for instance, I wouldn't necessarily demean a personal friend by expecting them to explore quite so exhaustively all the ins and outs of every manufacturing process.'

Laura stared incredulously into the eyes confirming that he was trying it on with her. Did he think she was born yesterday?

'Well, Laura? What else need I say?'

'Nothing. Not one more word. I'm afraid you don't understand me, Mr Lindley. Your suggestion seems totally demeaning. I think perhaps I shall enjoy the dyehouse.'

And that's telling me! he thought, excited by her spirit which was proving almost as strong as his own. He took one step towards her, smiling, this time in delight.

'Excellent, Laura – you're my own sort, even if that's the last thing you'd care to admit.' Standing so close that she could feel his breath on her forehead, he grew serious. 'You have it in you to do anything you set your mind to. I only hope that in so doing you don't disappoint the people who can give the help you will need.'

'Is that a warning?' she asked. 'Because if it is, I'd better say straight out that you do look like being disappointed, Mr Lindley.'

'Warning?' He pondered. 'No – no, I don't believe so, not at this stage.' The battle was only just commencing, after all. He would not toss it away without some show of strength. And since she had chosen the dyehouse she could not complain about the instruction she might receive there.

Disturbed, Laura walked away from his office without noticing the looms clacking away around her. He might say his words were not meant as a warning, she knew differently. From the first she had recognised Roy Lindley as unscrupulous. She knew already that it would be only a matter of time before he again attempted to blackmail her into responding to his interest in her.

Even when they finished for the day and she ran for the bus beside Amos Kitchen's uneven sprint, she was conscious of alarm. Roy Lindley held too many good cards in this gamble of theirs in which the stake was her career, and he did not play by any known rules.

'Did it do you any good, that chat with Mr Roy?' Amos enquired after the conductor had collected their fares.

'What do you think?' Laura's expression was rueful. 'He's got the whip hand, hasn't he? And he knows it. There's just one thing, though, Mr Kitchen – he's only the boss over what goes on at work.'

'I hoped you might manage to call me Amos once we were clear of that place,' her companion remarked, then smiled. 'I know I'm old enough to be your father, you needn't make me feel it all the time. But as for Mr Roy – you seem to have him weighed up already. You'll not need me to tell you he's a ladies' man.'

'Hardly! I've never met anybody so lacking in subtlety. It's time somebody told him that's not at all attractive.'

'Happen you'll be the one. He likes you, you know, might take a bit of advice from you.'

'Like heck he might! I'd not risk saying owt anyway, not before they've started buying all them designs of mine.'

Amos Kitchen had a neat flat above a branch of the Maypole.

'Comes in handy,' he confided as he led the way up the narrow staircase. 'I haven't quite got the hang of shopping for myself even yet. I'm always running out of groceries.'

Whatever he might say about his domestic failings, Amos was well prepared for her visit. Winding up the gramophone, and leaving her to select a record from his collection of dance band music, he disappeared into the tiny kitchen. Laura was only just beginning to wonder if he'd enjoyed dancing before being wounded when he came back into the living-room.

'Nearly ready now,' he told her, starting to set the table.

'Can't I do that?'

'Indeed not – I don't often have visitors, let me enjoy doing it proper.'

Amos refused help with the washing up as well after they'd eaten their ham and eggs. 'I can do that when you've gone. You'd better come and have a look at that there bike. See if it'll do.'

'That'll do very well, thank you ever so much,' Laura exclaimed, noticing how well cared for the old-fashioned cycle was. 'I'll see you have it back when I've had time to go and fetch my own.'

He said that there was no rush, and seemed so delighted to be able to offer her something that Laura felt happy about borrowing it.

The only thing she wasn't happy about was the situation at the mill. After she had thanked Amos Kitchen again for the bike and for her tea, and was riding off, it came back to her how much Roy Lindley had annoyed her. In company she'd been able to rationalise, had been cheered by Amos Kitchen's assessment that Roy fancied himself with the ladies. Now she realised again how insulted she'd been by his assumption that she'd be glad to make up to him in order to avoid some of the more unpleasant aspects of working in his mill.

If there were anywhere else that had shown interest in her patterns she'd not stop, not another week. The only trouble was they were paying her to learn her job, enticing her to stay with their promises of using those designs of hers.

72

Roy Lindley had spoilt everything. Even the prospect of seeing the Coach House again was diminished by her sense of fury at being trapped. Laura pedalled faster and faster, determined to get him out of her system.

By the time Arncliffe Hall came in sight, she was so breathless that she knew she ought to get off the bicycle and push. The last mile or so had been uphill; only because she was driven by the rage building within her had she been able to continue.

Once inside the grounds she allowed herself to dismount, but found that pushing the bike was almost as hard. Much heavier than her own, with the handlebars at a different height, it seemed most ungainly.

Then she saw Patrick Horsfall over by a bed of crimson roses. He turned and noticed her, and she waved.

'You haven't cycled all the way?' he asked, concern in his dark eyes as he hurried towards her.

Too breathless to speak, Laura shook her head. He took the bicycle from her, and she managed to murmur her thanks.

'*Have* you ridden all the way from Halfield?'

'No – only the last mile or so. I've been to collect this, it's on loan till I get mine from Whitby,' she gasped. 'When I'm living here I'll have to have a bike – can't go spending all that on bus fares every day.'

'But . . .'

He appeared so perplexed Laura was compelled to smile. 'We're not all made of money,' she exclaimed, then paused. 'Sorry, that wasn't giving you a dig.'

'I know.' Smiling, Patrick continued in the direction of the Coach House, where he leaned the cycle against the wall and waited.

Still out of breath, Laura was several minutes reaching his side.

'Are you all right?' he asked, unlocking the door. He placed an arm about her shoulders as they went indoors.

His touch made her realise how vulnerable she had felt at the mill. She sensed his anxiety for her, and it was an enormous

73

relief to feel that this was one man she could trust not to try anything on. Not relaxing against him required a massive effort. He seemed so approachable; wearing an open-necked shirt and grey flannels, he'd shed the businesslike manner with his normal dark suit.

Laura grinned. 'I'll be as right as rain in a minute or two. It's all my own fault. I got mad over summat somebody said at work. Because I want to keep my job I couldn't tell him what I thought of him. That was the reason I was pedalling demented, not thinking about it being uphill.' She swallowed, appalled. Tears were stinging the back of her throat, threatening to well into her eyes. And all because Patrick Horsfall was being sympathetic.

Was it because of there being nowhere to sit in the empty house that he continued keeping his arm about her shoulders? He was making her feel much better; she was reminded of the way her father always cheered her when things at home were getting her down.

'Better now?' Patrick enquired.

His voice was quite solemn. Laura glanced up at him. He smiled. 'Don't just bottle up your resentment about the job, it isn't good for you. I'm here now, ready to listen.'

'Why should you have to?' she asked, and read in his eyes how glad he would be simply to have her here.

He had admired her from the start for beginning afresh away from her home, and especially when the current situation was anything but propitious. Here in the West Riding there was still widespread unemployment – if not quite on the scale that, less than a year ago, had prompted Jarrow men to march on London. Abroad, the Spanish war continued; in Baghdad, Iraq's dictator had been assassinated. The other day our Ambassador to China had been wounded by Japanese planes, and Hitler's Nazis were steadily gaining power. What a time for anyone to begin a new career.

Laura could feel tiredness and irritation draining from her. Talking with Amos Kitchen had been good, being invited to share her difficulties with Patrick was even better.

Although he had lowered his arm now, they remained standing close to each other. The genuine concern seemed to continue in the way he scrutinised her expression. But then she remembered, collected the last few shreds of her self-assurance, and shook her head as she looked up at him.

'Whatever would your wife think, finding us alone like this?' she joked nervously.

Patrick remained serious. 'She's not here.' There was a silence. 'I don't know where she is.'

'Oh.' So that was it. Laura tried to steel herself against him. 'You mean she's gone out without telling you?'

'Magda hasn't just "gone out".'

Laura couldn't quite understand, it sounded so peculiar. 'You mean she's – you don't mean she's dead?'

He shook his head.

She swallowed and cleared her throat, wishing the action could do the same for her mind. 'Look, I'm sorry,' she began, then words shrivelled on her tongue. How could she sort her own emotions now, much less express them? This seemed to explain so much; the way she had sensed that he could be just as alone here as she sometimes felt, for instance. And the reason perhaps that she'd wanted to mother his little girl.

Patrick appeared to understand the tangle of her thoughts. She didn't know he was experiencing grave difficulty with his own. Never in what frequently seemed a very long experience had affinity developed so rapidly between Patrick and any young woman. Was it her unpolished speech that had warmed him to her, lowering defences raised against a world that might learn too much? Summoning his honesty?

'You're not the only one who's had a hard day,' he said quietly. 'Meeting you here was the first bit of brightness in mine.'

There was no way now that she would ignore her impulse to get to know him better, no way either that she could harden herself to regret becoming involved. She had immediately felt for Patrick this strong sympathy. And here she was today, worn out, no less in need than he, and maybe more susceptible.

Her gaze searched his face, locking its lean contours into her memory while she silently willed away the pain visible behind his eyes. She sensed him focusing on her lips, already felt the kiss which she knew would be withheld.

'I must go and see Beth,' Patrick announced abruptly.

'Can I come with you?'

'No, no.' He was at the Coach House door when he remembered. 'Just drop the latch, will you, when you're ready to leave?'

He didn't say goodnight or goodbye but hurried away from her, his footsteps echoing across the paving slabs. He might have been leaving the most casual of acquaintances.

Laura realised then how hurt she would be if that was all they were to be to each other. It was irrational and far too soon, but she wanted reassurance that Patrick would come to depend on her as much as she already seemed to rely upon him.

Slowly, pensively, Laura began to look around her future home. In every room she paused, savouring the fact that it would be hers. In those where windows overlooked Arncliffe Hall, she paused even longer, wondering how it would feel to live so close to this man who appeared to have become a part of her life even before she was ready for moving in here.

Laura was tired, though, and too disturbed to linger. For tonight, she needed to shelve contemplation of all these challenges to the calm solitude she'd anticipated finding in a place of her own. Checking that the door locked behind her, she headed towards her cycle then pedalled rapidly down the drive. Thank goodness it *was* downhill, she was shattered.

Out on the open road, the wind in her hair and the rich green of the valley easing tension, she felt better and very thankful that she wasn't obliged to sit in a bus. Could she have sat still? And wouldn't the other passengers have known that she was different – was discovering that, however inexperienced she had seemed, she was a mature woman now with the need to care. How draining this was. Her legs were weak, every thrust of the pedal an effort.

She was potty to feel this way about the owner of Arncliffe, though, to have it matter so greatly that he should show not only interest in her plans but concern for her as well.

And this is coming down to earth with a wallop! she thought, approaching Halfield. The bicycle rattling over the setts as she rode between the ranks of grey back-to-back terraces seemed to be drumming into her that this was where she really belonged. With a job in a mill and digs in a drab little house.

Today, she had needed a reminder of the beauty of her future home – her hope. Because of Patrick, she hadn't really concentrated on it. And now she must start having more sense – Patrick had a wife, wherever she was. Suddenly, though, Laura could understand why he had got through to her. Hadn't his concern, if only for a moment, reminded her of her father? From leaving Whitby until tonight, no one else had shown her the degree of interest for which Dad had always made time.

She was no longer a child yet she could still yearn for her father, even without needing his practical support. They had always been such pals. Laura pictured the old days clearly. Before the triplets came on the scene Dad had taken her out and about so often, telling her of Whitby's history or recounting tales of the sea.

Rare days when harsh weather prevented the boats putting out had been spent poring over old books together or listening while he fired her imagination with local legends.

After her sisters were born time alone with him had been scarce, all the more precious. But still their special affinity had continued. He it was who unfailingly encouraged her to create her own life. For his sake as much as her own, she needed to devote all her attention to designing. She had waited for years to be free to begin, and shouldn't be forgetting already that she mustn't let anything distract her from the only career she wanted.

As soon as she had something to show for all the work, Laura decided, she would invite her family over here, most of all so that Dad might see what she was doing.

Chapter 5

'I thought you'd be back before now. He's been here looking for you.'

Astounded, Laura stared at Miss Priestley who had met her in the lobby. How could he have? Had he passed her on the road? Having a car, Patrick Horsfall could have got here more quickly from Arncliffe – but why on earth would he come after her?

'He was that determined to see you, he wants you to go round there. You know where it is, don't you, in Honley Place? That nice flat the Vicar's wife found for him.'

Oh, Michael. 'Did he say what he wanted?'

'Well . . .' Miss Priestley seemed embarrassed but her smile was sympathetic. 'He did mention that you'd had a bit of a disagreement. He said I wasn't to hang on to you that he'd said owt, mind. Evidently, though, it's bothered him ever since.'

Laura wasn't up to facing Michael tonight. He would read in her eyes, in her entire being, how she had been drawn to Patrick Horsfall. She'd often felt that Michael could see right through her skull, lay bare her emotions. And they were private, especially for the present while she couldn't separate her affection for that little house from her feelings towards its owner.

'Would you mind if I rang him up, please?'

'So long as you pay for any calls, you can telephone whoever you like. I don't use it much, except on Liberal Club business. You'll have Mr Dawson's number, will you?'

'Somewhere, yes. Thanks.' She would need time first, though, to gather her wits.

Laura sat for a long while beside the umbrella stand in the lobby, staring at the telephone on its bamboo table. How could she even begin without her voice or her manner revealing how different she felt?

'Michael,' she said breathlessly, as soon as he answered.

His interruption relieved her of the need to say any more immediately. 'You're not coming round then?'

'Eh, love – I'm worn out. I've been working in that wretched scouring department all this week . . .'

'Not till this hour?'

'No, but I've got the use of somebody's bike, I went to fetch it.'

'Miss Priestley thought you'd have been back sooner.'

Laura stifled her groan. Between them, Michael and her landlady weren't allowing her much freedom. She wished she felt glad they were both concerned for her. And Michael was her friend, she couldn't snub him. Telling him where she had gone after picking up the bicycle would only make matters worse, though. Even without giving anything away about the encounter with Patrick Horsfall.

'I'm sorry,' she said. 'What was it you wanted, love?'

'We didn't part on the best of terms, did we? Whilst I'm not sorry for what I was compelled to say, I would be sorry if we fell out over it.'

'I'm not really the falling out sort. You'll see that next time we're together. We could go off on our bikes tomorrow, the mill's shut,' she promised rashly. 'And I shall see you at church, shan't I? I'll come and cook your dinner afterwards if you like.'

Being with Michael would do her good, help restore a sense of proportion. She was daft thinking so much about Patrick Horsfall, and before she knew more about him. She glanced around the walls which badly needed redecorating, then made her way heavily across to the worn stair carpet. This was real life – not that strange affinity that seemed to be developing over yonder. When she was living in that lovely Coach House that must be enough. She had a career she'd hardly begun, she was making friends through her work, and she had managed to remain on good terms with Michael. That surely must satisfy her.

Cycling out to Ilkley next day made Laura believe she could be contented without hankering for anything else. The sun was warm but a breeze made the activity bearable. And Michael was his old self.

She loved the scenery. Although she sometimes longed for the sea, the West Riding's moors and valleys thrilled her. Away from the smoke of industrial towns, everything was so green. That would be because of all the rain, she thought, doubly thankful today was dry. Ilkley's clean streets rising up from the river delighted her.

They wandered around, pushing their bikes, then left them against a dry-stone wall while they explored the square towered church whose rough stone interior smelled of old hymn books.

Afterwards they cycled as far as the Cow and Calf rocks where, surrounded by moors, Laura unpacked sandwiches from her saddle bag.

'Miss Priestley's specials,' she announced, grinning. 'She insisted, when I told her what we were doing. Potted meat, with plenty of mustard. You do like mustard, don't you?' How could she have forgotten? She'd once thought she knew most things about him.

'She's a good woman,' Michael began, then stopped abruptly. He'd been going to say he didn't know why on earth Laura was so eager to get away from 'Bien-être'. Then he remembered his resolution. He was going to let her go her own way, and without any remarks from him. He had thought about Laura's intentions until he felt sure he understood. She had to have her head. Hadn't she spent most of her life fitting in around the triplets, being compelled to help out, especially while her mother was ill? This was a predictable reaction. She needed freedom to develop, and if having a home of her own seemed to her the only way, he wouldn't restrain her.

He didn't believe she would enjoy living alone. When the

novelty wore off, he would be there.

'Aye, she is that,' Laura agreed, winning a curious look from him. 'We had a talk the other night. Did you know she'd had to give up her job while she was looking after her mother? By the time she passed on, Miss Priestley couldn't get more work.' Laura could have developed a conscience about her own plans which would deny her landlady her rent but you couldn't spend your whole life putting others first.

'I do love the moors, don't you?' She glanced around at the rugged slopes of coarse grass, heather and rocks. 'There's some not so far away from Arncliffe. You will visit me when I'm living there, won't you, Michael? It'll do you good, as well, getting out of Halfield.'

Not that there was much wrong with him today. He looked smashing, in a white cricket shirt and matching flannels, not nearly so old as he seemed in the dark clothes he wore in church.

'I'm in reasonable form now. I do a lot of walking and some of the hills here seem as steep as Whitby's – that's tightening up the flab.'

'Go on. You never had any.'

'How do you know?'

She laughed, testing his ribs with a prod, surprised that he didn't possess any surplus flesh.

Even her one finger pressing into his side aroused him. He was so aware of her, had been all the way to Ilkley. Much of the time they had cycled side by side, but when traffic approached from behind he had sent her ahead. He had wondered then if he'd never really seen her before, why he hadn't noticed how firm her body was with her thin print frock drawn tight by the saddle.

Still leaning towards him now, she was no less inviting: her hair curled towards her laughing blue eyes, her lips moist and parted. The vee of her neckline revealed skin touched by the sun.

'Won't those sandwiches be getting dried out?' He must find something for his mouth to do or he'd be devouring her.

82

If he didn't engineer her sitting away from him, he would pull her hard against him, thrust her beneath him. Alone with her out here, with skylarks overhead and so much air and space, he might believe he should be unfettered, as free to love her as in the dreams that plagued him nightly.

Laura was smiling. 'I'm glad we've come here – I don't mean just to Ilkley, but to the West Riding. There's nowhere else I'd even have started on my career. As long as I'd stayed in Whitby, Mum would have gone on producing reasons why she couldn't do without me.'

'But she's managing all right with you away?' he asked, picturing Mrs Crabtree who through her very ineffectuality managed to dominate.

'According to her letters, no. But I'll have to harden myself. It isn't as if them three were little lasses any more. They haven't chosen to start growing up, that's all. They'll do that better without me there.'

Michael nodded, said no more. Laura might appreciate the life here; for him, it didn't even approach what he had pictured of her coming to Halfield. She should have been as involved as he was at St Martin's, singing in his choir, meeting him at every service.

'I saw Clem Hargreaves the other day, did I tell you? He's given me some proper patterns to study, and will teach me if I need him to.'

She was so absorbed in this work of hers now, scarcely conscious of what they had discussed, her mind so overflowing with her own plans that nothing else really registered with her. He set aside his sandwiches, aching to compel her into total awareness of him.

'If he's not in church tomorrow we could go and see him,' Laura suggested. 'He's a lovely old man, and he must hate being kept in with that bad leg.'

'Yes,' said Michael, wishing she wasn't only interested in people concerned with carpets. Staring beyond grey rocks towards the expanse of hills and the town set among them, he began telling her it was a garrison in Roman times. 'And I've heard that it was a choir from our church who composed "On Ilkla Moor Baht 'at" during an outing here. Have you heard anything about it?'

Laura shook her head. 'I daresay Clem Hargreaves could tell you. He seems to enjoy explaining things. He's especially good . . .'

About carpets! thought Michael. Ah, well, if she made a go of her ambitions maybe she'd realise there was more to life. He only hoped she'd be quick about it. He could understand how living at home had kept her from becoming experienced, but she seemed to have no idea of how she affected him. And he'd been brought up to behave immaculately, barely trusted himself with more than a few kisses.

Sunday was almost as bad, although Michael found it less exacting. In church, as always, his entire being was concentrated on perfecting his playing of the organ, and leading the singing. The years following his acceptance as a full-time organist had made him recognise his own gift for bringing people out, making them better singers. There was always a kind of elation to Sundays.

In his flat, though, with Laura cooking dinner on the tiny gas stove, pretending that she was the domesticated girl that he had supposed came too readily to him. By the time they were sitting either side of his table he was immersed again in longing.

'Have you got a sore throat, love?' she enquired, noticing that he swallowed hard before beginning to tackle the roast lamb.

Michael shook his head, containing a wry smile. Inwardly he toyed with the prospect of revealing where the hurt lay, and its substance. He would be done with all the circumspection, with the supposition that getting involved in church matters removed all earthly passion.

Laura did most of the talking when they called on Clem Hargreaves and his sister. Michael listened, conscious of the new alertness in her eyes, of the enthusiasm which even a week in the scouring department hadn't quite suppressed.

She told Clem about working with Amos Kitchen, was pleased when he was so interested.

'Well, I never! A good chap, Amos, always has been. I was as sorry for him as I was for myself when I had to close down after t'fire. But he's not in scouring, surely?'

'I'm afraid so. I gather that was all they could offer.'

'Eh, dear. And he had a long spell on the dole first, if I remember rightly. But he's wasted there is yon . . .'

'So I gathered. He's a trained carpet weaver, isn't he? And a finisher.'

'It was for folk like him that I tried to set up again, but nobody would invest in rebuilding. Yon chap at t'Yorkshire West had the audacity to suggest I were past it. Me – that had supplied several of the big new banks in London, prestigious hotels, ocean liners!'

'That's what I'm going to do,' Laura told Michael as he walked her back to Hanson Road. 'Every time I see Clem Hargreaves he spurs me on. My carpets will be admired by famous folk all over the world.'

'I hope so, love,' he said, and avoided mentioning that tomorrow she would begin in the dyehouse.

Roy Lindley was late in that Monday. He had been away for the weekend and wouldn't arrive back until during the morning.

'I'm rather glad he isn't here,' his father told Laura, smiling as she walked towards him down the long shed. 'I've been noticing how you were getting on – don't think I haven't just because I've not said much. I leave our Roy to handle a lot of things, these days, and I'm a great believer in folk being allowed space to work. You're to start in the dyeing now, I gather?'

'This morning, yes.' Laura tried not to grimace.

Robert Lindley grinned. 'I think you're being put through it, lass. You were kept for a good while in scouring. No, I'm not about to interfere – just to tell you to keep on as you are. You've suited me already with the way you've tackled everything, and I've decided it's time you had a bit of acknowledgement. Help in finding your feet in Halfield. My wife's having a few friends in next Friday night, and we're both agreed we'd like you to come.'

'But . . .' Laura was staggered.

Mr Lindley chuckled. 'You'll appreciate we can't ask all the workers home, there wouldn't be room! But you're rather special, being a potential designer. And . . . well, I hope you'll endeavour to be there.'

'Thank you, I – yes, I'll be pleased to. Thanks.' But what about Roy? she thought anxiously. Will he take that as permission for his heavy-handed flirting?

His father might have seen right inside her mind. 'You don't need to worry about our Roy. He does take no for an answer. And I've never had any funny business yet in our house.'

Her eyes sparkling, Laura met his gaze.

'Not everybody knows Roy, not properly,' he continued. 'He hasn't had an easy time, not with girls. Something happened a year or two back, he didn't confide and I didn't ask. But we knew he was hurt, and he's not been any better to get on with since.'

Robert Lindley then sent for the dyehouse foreman, Steven Rushworth, introduced him to Laura and explained that she would be working under him until she had acquired a thorough knowledge of dyeing.

He was a large man, and appeared inscrutable until he heard this. Immediately his impassive features darkened, his grey eyes narrowing. He said nothing of his misgivings to his boss, however – only a frown directed towards Laura revealed his reaction.

'This is news to me, tha knows,' he grumbled, after being told by Mr Lindley that that was all, and they might go to the dyehouse.

Laura was on the point of saying she was sorry when she realised that none of this was her fault. Even if she'd had the slightest desire to spend more than the necessary few hours in learning what went on there, she would have had no hand in the arrangements. As it was, she was simply being frustrated in her longing to get to work in the design studio. And she wasn't frightened of saying so.

'This wasn't my idea, Mr Rushworth. I can only do as I'm told.'

'Happen,' he muttered, glancing sideways at her as they walked swiftly between the rows of clattering looms. 'Well, you'll have to learn by watching what we do, or not at all. There's none of us in there can be bothered explaining every little detail.'

'I'll try not to be a nuisance . . .'

She was interrupted. 'Can't help but be, can you? We all have our jobs, can't be doing with somebody just hanging around. And mind there's no messing about with young Geoff, the apprentice. He has work to do like the rest on us.'

With an apprentice? thought Laura. How old did he imagine she was? On account of her young face, she supposed, and had a good mind to remonstrate. But maybe leaving him to find out his mistake would be more dignified.

She hadn't forgotten one aspect of the dyehouse from her brief visit on the first occasion that she'd come to Lindley's. Remaining here was worse, of course, allowing the heat and the steam to grow really oppressive. And she was terrified of the vats. The first time she saw the hanks of wool on their poles being withdrawn from the boiling dye, she felt desperate to run out of the way.

It was as she glanced instinctively towards the entrance that she saw she was being observed. Grinning, Roy Lindley strolled towards her.

'No need to be scared, Laura.'

'Who says I am?'

'Those lovely blue eyes don't keep secrets. You don't have to worry though, I'll look after you.'

'But surely it was you who decided I needed a spell in here?'

'It doesn't all have to be unpleasant.'

She gave him a look. Did he never learn, or did making up to every girl compensate for the one he'd lost? Roy's expression was altering, though. He might have been regretting his old attitude.

'Have they shown you where the dye is measured out?' he asked.

'Not yet, no.'

'This way then.'

Getting out of the dyehouse was a relief. When Roy began telling her about his visit to London over the weekend, Laura discovered she could enjoy listening to him. He had attended the Summer Exhibition at the Royal Academy, something that made her envious, and had been to inspect one of their carpets newly installed in a Park Lane hotel.

'Do you know London, Laura?'

'Not so far.'

'You say that as though you mean to rectify the omission.'

'That's right. When I'm earning enough brass, and have got my home as I want it. I mean to see more than Yorkshire, you know, nice though it is.'

Roy smiled, delighted by her eagerness. He hadn't been wrong to believe her a cut above the rest. Worth spending time on.

'This is where Joe Bradley works, our head dyer.'

He stood back while she entered the small room that had windows on three sides, two of which were outer walls of the building.

After Laura had been introduced to the small elderly man with greying hair, Roy left him to tell her about his work.

'It's up to me to provide the right quantities of dye to produce a given shade,' Mr Bradley said, and went on to explain in more detail. The capacity of the vats varied from 10 to 1100 pounds, and he must take into consideration the number of hanks suspended in any particular dye lot.

'Yes, but *how* do you know how much dye to use?' Laura persisted.

A wide smile spread over his lined face. 'Experience,' he said firmly, and looked across at Roy Lindley.

'I'm not supposed to be aware of this, Laura,' Roy

confided, 'but Joe goes by guesswork.'

The statement was not disputed. Laura smiled, and won a chuckle from Joe Bradley.

'Who am I to argue with a Lindley!' he exclaimed. 'All I know is there's not many complaints.'

'None, surely, Joe?' Roy corrected.

'Maybe I'll remind you of that when we come round to new pay deals. Any road, Miss Crabtree, for your purpose we'll reckon I weighs out the dye, eh? Officially, that is how we do it.'

'And how do you maintain a shade?'

'That's called colour-matching. You'll see how that's done, no doubt – all by eye. And it's basically by studying the end of the yarn.'

'I'll demonstrate presently,' Roy assured her as they left the head dyer.

'He doesn't really go by guesswork, does he?' Laura asked, amused as well as astonished.

'You don't think that's something he'd admit if there weren't more than a grain of truth in it, do you?'

'And you don't mind?'

He laughed. 'We'd never find as good a head dyer.'

She was beginning to like him again by the time they reached the dyehouse. When he offered to explain more of the process as the men were going off to the canteen for lunch, she felt quite pleased. Whatever else, Roy Lindley was personally ensuring that her grounding in everything relating to dyeing was thorough. And understanding the techniques would help her to make her designs practicable.

She watched as Roy told Steven Rushworth that he and his men could leave everything to him, assuring them that they needed their break, even chivvying the young apprentice, Geoff, who seemed reluctant to relinquish his watch on one of the smaller vats.

'You can stand by the door there where it's cooler, just for a second, Laura. I'll call you across when there's anything to see.'

She wasn't sorry to remain where it was relatively cool, and far, far drier. She hated the moisture as much as the heat, if not as fearfully as the vats themselves with their bubbling contents.

Roy was examining one vat after another, obviously aware of what stage in immersion each one had reached. Again, she was impressed: he could have claimed such an appalling place was hardly the province of one of the bosses.

Evidently satisfied, he strode towards her again. 'Am I forgiven, for putting you in here? Going to give me the opportunity to prove it can be interesting and worthwhile?'

She smiled. 'Why not?' She couldn't afford to harp on about his inflicting discomfort on her. And today he wasn't nearly so annoying.

'I do care about carpets,' Roy told her, 'it's bred in me. And I am impressed by you, you know. Now, just come over here . . . I'm going to show you there's nothing to fear in this dyehouse.'

He had raised the poles together with their hanks of wool just clear of the dye in the vat beside him.

'Have a look now – everything's under control, isn't it? It's only like something simmering up on your stove at home.'

'But it's so vast! I think it's all that steam gushing out worries me most.'

'Nay, you mustn't let it. You've plenty of pluck, Laura, tackling designing. I might have my own way of ensuring you pick this up, but it's not calculated to make you alarmed.'

When he had re-immersed the wool, checked that all was in order and turned away from the vat, Laura met his glance.

'It's not really because *you've* had me working first in scouring and now in dyeing that I'm perturbed, you know.'

'Isn't it – in part, at least?' Taking her arm, he led her with him further into the dyehouse. 'You've an admirable ambition to carve your own way through life, you're not to be reproached for resenting someone else's intervention. I understand more than you know, Laura. If I had my way, I'd be running my own works.'

'But still manufacturing carpets?'

'Now, yes. But that wouldn't always have been so. When I left college I was no more eager than you were to follow family tradition.'

'I could hardly take up trawling like my dad,' Laura began dryly.

He laughed. 'It wouldn't surprise me if you said you'd had it in your head to do just that! But are you beginning to understand now that we might not be so totally different? There could be some common ground between us.'

'Happen so.' Laura smiled, recalling the invitation issued by his father. She felt she ought to accept and would need to be more than civil to Roy. Today there seemed less cause for being otherwise.

'I know I've been crass,' he admitted, 'you should take no notice. That's just my way with an attractive woman.'

Still smiling, Laura said nothing.

'What're you thinking?' Roy enquired.

She didn't answer. Where was the sense in stating that she found his new approach equally as resistible as the old? No matter how straightforward he appeared, she'd never grow fond of Roy Lindley.

Despite his evident assurance, though, he was sensitive to her disapproval. He read the absence of interest in her manner, and was unable to accept its permanence. She was a lovely woman, with eyes as clear as a summer sky, that pale froth of hair making her seem deceptively fragile. Even in a drab overall, she made it difficult to accept his own decision to stop playing the philanderer.

This past weekend he had thought about Laura a great deal. He had satisfied his physical needs while he was away, but that had been all. He'd already wasted enough of his life going after women who attracted him, regardless of their inability to maintain a stable relationship. Even apart from that time which he was managing to thrust to the back of his mind, there'd been plenty of other situations which had proved he needed more than sex.

'How are you liking Halfield?' he asked sincerely. 'Are you making friends here?'

'Yes, thank you. As many as I've time for. I'm going to be quite busy away from here as well, you know. I'm buying a house, there'll be that to furnish.'

'I say – that is something! There aren't many young ladies even think of owning their own home.'

'To be honest, it's not simply my own doing – I've been left a bit of money.'

He saw the tears fill her eyes, and had a guess at their cause. 'Someone you were very fond of, and that you miss?'

'Yes, I do, as a matter of fact. Only Aunt Constance wouldn't have wished me to be all morbid about her.'

'I'm sure. Maybe we should make allowance for your loss, give you time and a bit of space . . . You shouldn't forget, though, that while you're at work you're not without someone to turn to.'

Laura shook her head. 'I'm over the worst, thanks. Quite all right.'

Roy frowned. But surely this was a way in which their relationship might develop? Hadn't he found the key to cracking her steel-hard resolve? He'd always liked cheering people. She was the one who'd shaken him into recognising that his old tactics must cease. Even if it didn't work out, he had to try for a relationship founded on more than desire.

The hiss of steam, erupting like a thousand bursting kettles, made him swing round. Laura screamed. Jets of scalding dye soared ten feet to the rafters then dropped like a boiling Niagara only yards from their feet.

'Christ! This way . . . *out!*'

Too horrified now for screaming, Laura was riveted motionless, staring as the seemingly endless stream of crimson dye surged towards them.

'I said out, Laura!' He gave her a shake, saw her eyes transfixed in terror, lifted her bodily.

Turning from the boiling vat, he carried her around the one where they had been standing, then ran with her, bumping arms and shoulders against hot metal as he staggered towards the door. Out in the yarn store he leaned her against the nearest stack of bales. Her eyes wild, she was sobbing hysterically. He crushed her to him. Thank God he'd got her out. This was his fault, *his*, his own fault entirely. And he'd known better than to presume he might dismiss the vats even for one moment.

'Laura, don't – you're safe, love, all right now.'

From inside the dyehouse a lad's screams rang out. They intruded on her sobbing, soared higher, more desperately, penetrating her fright. Renewed dread widening her eyes, she met Roy's sickened gaze.

'No – no,' she gasped, 'no, please – there can't be.'

'Stay where you are.'

He hurtled towards the dyehouse entrance, tore through the scalding steam, his feet splattering in hot dye. Taking the shortest route meant enduring the worst of that scorching torrent, any other would be too late. Trousers and shoes drenched, heavy with the stuff, each step grew harder. Yet still he ran, stumbling, slithering, shaking his head to clear his eyes of the moisture.

The screeching bundle of reddened clothing was Geoff Appleyard, the quiet apprentice whose unassuming nature had contributed to his remaining undiscovered. Mercifully, the lad was puny and Roy could lift him. As he gained the yarn store he was shouting Laura to call the ambulance.

She was telephoning already. Shaken out of her own fear, she had gathered enough strength to urge her shaking legs as far the head dyer's room. The place was deserted, thumping on the door had brought no one, but she had kicked out the glass panelling and reached the lock that way.

'The ambulance is coming.'

She couldn't look at whoever had been in the dyehouse with them. Covered in gory dye, Roy looked bad enough, ghoulish, his face the colour of lard gleaming with sweat above the nightmarish mess.

He set the lad down, leaning him gently against one of the

bales. Geoff was having difficulty breathing and seemed better like this than he might lying down.

'Quick, Laura – fetch Steven Rushworth out of the canteen. The other dyehouse chaps as well. You'll have to tell Rushworth what's happened, but try not to create widespread panic.'

She hared off across the yard, and rushed into the canteen. All she could see was a lot of men and a dozen or so women sitting at the cheap wooden tables. None of them looked familiar. She ran the length of the canteen to the serving hatch.

'Can anybody tell me if Steven Rushworth's in here?' she asked the woman dishing up tripe and onions.

'Aye – I've just served him, love, he's over there, getting a knife and fork.'

Laura darted towards him. 'Mr Lindley's sent me to fetch you, Mr Rushworth. I'm afraid there's been an accident.'

'Accident? What sort of accident?'

'With one of the vats.'

'Bloody hell!'

Leaving everything, calling 'Come on then' to his men, the foreman ran through the canteen, overturning a vacant chair that was in the way. In the hush following their exit the clatter of a ladle dropping to the stone floor made Laura swing round. The woman who had been serving meals came tearing out of the kitchen.

'What did you say?' she demanded, seizing Laura by the arm.

'I'm afraid there's been an accident.'

'In the dyehouse?'

Laura nodded grimly.

'My Geoff's in there . . .'

Laura couldn't keep up with her as she scuttled out of the canteen and across the mill yard. She was just in time to see the woman keel over. Her son was being lifted into the ambulance.

About to rush across to see what she could do to help bring her round, Laura was stopped by a touch on her shoulder.

'It's all right, love, it'll only be a faint. I'm one of her mates, we'll look after her. Is the lad . . .?'

94

'He's alive, that's all I know.'

'We'll tell her that, soon as she comes round. She'll be best here for a while, they'll have things to do at the hospital.'

Laura nodded, glanced towards the ambulance again. Geoff, on one stretcher, was being tended by an ambulance man. Roy was sitting with his head in both hands. Even from where she was standing, she could see he was shaking.

She turned back to the woman who had spoken. 'Get a message to Mr Robert Lindley, will you – make sure he knows? Looks like I'd better go with them.'

'If young Geoff doesn't pull through, it's me that's killed him,' said Roy through his hands as she clambered into the ambulance.

Chapter 6

They didn't take long treating Roy Lindley. His hands were scalded, as were his feet, but evidently not too severely. Once they were dressed and he'd been given a sedative to subdue the shock, he was demanding to see Geoff Appleyard.

This could not be allowed. Geoff's injuries were far more serious; it would be some time before the doctors were even prepared to express an opinion.

'They must know something, Laura. You can't tell me that they haven't any idea whether he's going to survive?'

He had joined her sitting on a bench in the cheerless waiting room.

'Happen it won't be too long before they come and tell us.'

Nothing she might say seemed to be any use. 'I rang the mill,' she told him. 'Had a word with Joe Bradley. Your father was in the dyehouse, wouldn't come to the telephone.'

'I'll try and get hold of him in a minute.'

'Mrs Appleyard came round straight away, they said.'

'Came round?' Roy interrupted.

'Oh, you were in the ambulance by then. She passed out.'

'Not surprised, he's all she's got. And it's Miss Appleyard.'

'I see.' That made it all much worse.

'If he doesn't pull through . . .' Roy began again.

'We'll both be dreadfully upset, the whole factory will be. But there isn't a thing we can do now. Except wait – pray, happen. And look after his mother when she gets here.'

'She's not coming here!'

'On her way now. Your father got her a taxi. I think one of the creelers is coming with her. Has she a cousin works there?'

97

'I think so.'

A nurse brought in Miss Appleyard while they were speaking. When the nurse left she looked sharply from Roy Lindley to Laura.

'What were you saying? He's gone, hasn't he?'

'No, he hasn't, Emma.' Rising, Roy went to take both her hands in his bandaged ones. 'We're simply waiting to hear what the doctors say.'

'Are you sure? You soon shut up when I walked in.'

'Don't, Em.' Her cousin, Sally Broadbent, came into the room from the doorway where she had hesitated, timid as the mouse she resembled.

'I suppose when we saw the nurse we wondered if she had something to tell us,' said Laura swiftly.

Emma Appleyard looked down at Roy's bandages. 'You were in it and all then?' Her thin features didn't soften.

'Mr Lindley got him out, Miss Appleyard.'

She glanced towards Laura. 'I don't really know you, do I?'

'No. I've not been at Lindley's very long.'

'Were you there when it happened?'

'Yes. Mr Lindley got me out, then we heard Geoff's – heard Geoff. We didn't even know he was in there. Being dinnertime, we thought . . .'

'I'd told them all to get off to the canteen,' Roy added.

The lad's mother released her hands from Roy's, walked thoughtfully over to sit beside Laura. She glared at Roy.

'He was barred from the canteen, wasn't he? And you know the reason.' Aggression made her nondescript little body quiver.

'Em . . .' her cousin protested warningly.

'It's all right, Sally. It's all going to come out now, isn't it? They'll have found them canteen plates where my Geoff were. You see, you didn't stop me, Mr Lindley. Not when you threatened to sack us both 'cos I were slipping Geoff dinners on the quiet. But it were only leftovers I give him since, I swear. And that were t'only place where he could eat what I saved, without anybody being any the wiser.'

'There's a telephone call I've got to make,' Roy announced, and left them.

'He wants to try and feed a growing lad on what bit we earn, and keep a roof over our heads!'

'Have you gone barmy, Emma?' her cousin demanded. 'Can't you keep your trap shut? We all know you're out of your mind with worry, but you'll both be out of jobs and all, even if he does survive. You can't go talking like this and nobody do nowt afterwards.'

As Sally Broadbent sat at the other side of her cousin, Laura turned to them. 'I don't suppose Mr Lindley will do anything about what you've just admitted, Miss Appleyard. We shall all be just very thankful that Geoff gets better.'

'Do you think he will? You saw him, didn't you? How bad did he look?'

'I didn't see him close to, not till we were in the ambulance, then one of the men was attending to him.'

Roy returned, bringing a doctor with him.

'The news isn't too bad, Emma,' he began, and the doctor continued.

'Miss Appleyard? Well, as Mr Lindley says, the situation could be far worse. Your son is quite badly scalded, but not so severely as to diminish his chances of recovery. He will have to stay here in hospital for some time while we do what we can to ensure that he heals without too much scarring . . .'

'How long?' Miss Appleyard interrupted. 'There's only me and him.'

'You mustn't worry about that aspect, Emma,' Roy told her quickly. 'Naturally, Lindley's will pay for any treatment Geoff might need, in hospital and when he's discharged.'

'Oh. And how badly will he be scarred? Is – is it his face?'

'No. Fortunately, that is scarcely touched. It was his back caught the worst of it, and to some degree his shoulders and thighs.'

'Thank goodness for that. Oh, thank goodness. Will I be able to see him now?'

'Certainly. Come this way.'

Emma Appleyard glanced towards her cousin. 'Oh, Sal . . .'

'Now come on, you'll be seeing him in a minute or two, you'll feel a lot better then.'

I hope so, thought Laura wearily, wondering how on earth Geoff's mother would react to his injuries.

'We'd better wait and see if they'll let us go in after his mother has left,' said Laura, watching the two women hurrying through the door in the wake of the white-coated doctor.

'Well, I certainly must wait,' Roy asserted, 'but there's no reason why you should have to.'

'I was there, as well, wasn't I?' Ever since the accident she had realised how involved she'd become, how concerned for everyone at Lindley's. In some ways the mill seemed like one big family. She had been moved by the way so many folk had been shattered, including Roy. Her reasons for remaining went deeper, though: there was no mistaking his genuine remorse. Leaving him alone with it would be brutal.

'You might as well sit down,' she observed, and met his eyes as he sat beside her again. 'You got me out of there unharmed, anyway. I can't thank you enough.'

'We should never have been there, not at lunchtime.'

'No,' she agreed solemnly. 'But we were, you can't alter that now.'

'You must consider me totally incompetent, unfit to take charge of anything.' He paused, staring down at his bandaged hands. Where was the justice when this had happened while he'd just been acknowledging to himself that he was done with his old techniques?

'Whatever went wrong back there,' said Laura, 'I'm sure you'll not forget this day. But you're doing all you can for that poor lad and his mother. Nobody can do more. Did you get through to your father?'

'Yes.'

'How much did you tell him?'

Roy snorted. 'He needed no telling. And he didn't mince his words. Luckily for me, he sets great store by family, and the business as well. He's agreed we'll help young Appleyard. And

I shall pay – if only by the way Father treats me. But he won't let the details of my neglect of the vats come to light.'

'Will he be able to keep it quiet? Won't there be an inquiry?'

'We're hoping to avoid it, by looking after the lad and his mother.'

Laura's fair eyebrows shot up. She hoped that wasn't the sole motive for helping the Appleyards. And she felt uneasy about hushing up the accident.

'You don't like that, do you?' said Roy. 'Believe me, I'm anything but proud myself. And, as you will realise, you're the one who can ruin us.'

'Aye. Do you think I would?'

'I don't know, Laura. I wish I did.'

'If I'd been carrying on with you, I might have felt obliged to admit we were up to something. As it is . . .' She paused, considering, reflecting how she'd begun thinking of the mill as a family. They stuck together. 'Nay, it's not up to me. You understand these things.'

Roy nodded. He'd been brought up sharp before, and this time the person who had suffered was totally innocent. Laura was well aware that he'd originally contrived to get her on her own in the dyehouse. He felt idiotic, but what could he say to put things right?

'You may count on my behaving impeccably in the future.'

'We ought to get on rather better then.'

'I shan't compel you to go back into the dyehouse, either, nor anywhere else not absolutely necessary to your work.'

'That should save us some time,' she said, smiling at last. 'But I don't mean to keep right away from the dyehouse. If I don't go back in there as soon as I can, keeping out's going to become an obsession.'

They both looked towards the door as Emma Appleyard appeared there. 'My poor lad! Poor little devil!' she exclaimed. 'I hope you never forget how bad he looks today, because I shan't be able to, not ever. They might say he's going to be able to work again, that he'll be more or less all right, but you can't wipe out what's happened. Have you any idea what a scare like that has done to him, and to me? Well – have you?'

'Mr Lindley had a fright as well, you know, Miss Appleyard,' Laura observed, 'and he did carry Geoff out of there, regardless of his own safety.'

'Aye, I know.' She looked at Roy. 'One day I might thank you – right now all I know is that you're going to pay for this.'

Her face, which had been the shade of the beige-painted wall, flushed and her blue eyes narrowed.

'We'd better be going, Em,' her cousin prompted from just outside the door. She was afraid for herself as well. If Emma persisted and lost her job, the rest of the family might be given the sack.

'Order a taxi to take you home, the firm will pay,' Roy said quickly before the two women walked away from him.

Emma turned. 'I'm going to, don't you fret. I'll have every penny I can out of you before I've done.'

'Will she sue, do you suppose?' Laura asked him as they hurried down the long corridor towards the wards.

'I doubt if she'd know where to begin. But I don't consider that any real cause for satisfaction.'

Geoff Appleyard was lying flat on his stomach, so full of the medication they had given him to ease the pain that he hardly knew that they were there.

'He'll sleep all right now,' one of the nurses told them. 'And the doctors say he isn't in any danger.'

'Thank goodness,' said Roy huskily. He'd never really noticed Geoff Appleyard in the past. No doubt the apprentice had felt he hadn't much to boast about. Given a chance, though, he could make something of himself. And he owed it to the lad to ensure that this appalling incident didn't wreck his chances. From now on Roy personally would ensure that Geoff made headway in the company.

Laura glanced from the prone figure on the bed to the subdued man at her side. All at once she suspected that Roy was the one who would be most affected by the accident. A massive wave of sympathy swept right through her, nearly making her weep. She stared around her at the green curtains of the ward, the brown and green paint. Swallowing, she glanced back to Roy again. 'I don't think we're doing much good here, do you? We can come back tomorrow.'

By the following evening the apprentice was improving. Fortunately, youth ensured him a healthy body which was resistant to infection and would, in time, help promote total recovery. Any scarring would be out of sight except when he went swimming, and the optimism of the doctors had been absorbed by Geoff himself who saw no reason to feel gloomy about the future.

Even the peculiar antiseptic hospital smell didn't seem as bad to Laura and Roy when they were walking towards the exit.

'Thank you for coming with me,' he said, as he held the heavy outer door for her. 'I'll give you a lift home, of course. You'll have to remind me where that is.'

'In Hanson Road. But you don't have to bother, I can get the tram.'

He wouldn't consider that. 'Don't be daft, Laura. You know I'm glad I didn't have to face him on my own.'

It was quite an admission from Roy Lindley. She couldn't be sorry that he was being so straight with her. And she was utterly exhausted. She had insisted on spending the day in the dyehouse, and the experience had been far from easy.

The first few minutes had been bad enough. Although the floor and the vat that had boiled over had been cleaned, the crimson dye had stained everywhere, reminding her how much like blood it had looked when wet. All the time that she was watching the men immersing the woollen hanks she was cringing, terrified of each gush of steam and the proximity of that potentially lethal liquid.

'Them there vats don't boil over unless they're neglected,' Steven Rushworth told her, 'and there'll be no accidents while I'm in charge. It's all controlled when it's done proper, and that's the way it's been done in here since the day I were made foreman.'

It would take more than Steven Rushworth's pride in his work to reassure Laura, though, and she wouldn't be sorry to agree to Roy Lindley's suggestion that she should learn as much as she could that day and then move on to other processes.

In any other circumstances, she would have had another go at him for making her endure the conditions in the scouring department and dyehouse. As it was, she reckoned he had enough on his plate, and said no more.

His attitude towards her had improved as well. Once away from the gaunt grey hospital, he began talking about her landlady.

'Has Miss Priestley got you going to the Liberal Party meetings yet?'

'She's only ever mentioned it in passing. And I'm not really interested in politics.' She was surprised, though, that he seemed to know quite a bit about the Liberals, and said so.

Roy smiled as he concentrated on the road ahead. 'Lindleys always were supporters of Lloyd George. Father holds that if he'd remained in power this country would be in far better shape than it is. But I'm no great enthusiast and if you're not interested in such matters, I won't bore you. Tell me, instead, what you do with your spare time. Or is it all spent designing?'

'I've always gone to church, and I'm beginning to get involved in Halfield – it was a friend of mine who came as organist to St Martin's who gave me the idea of coming to the West Riding, you know. And, of course, I'm busy planning my own home.'

'Are you getting married shortly?'

Laura laughed. 'They'll all think that. Didn't I say? I'd some brass left me, and decided the time had come to strike out on my own.'

'Of course, I was forgetting.'

His expression again revealed that he was impressed. Laura hoped he understood now why she hadn't thought much of his empty flattery.

'And what else do you do, Laura? Go to the pictures, dancing . . .'

'I used to dance a lot. And I love a good Gracie Fields picture – she's that *ordinary*, yet look how she's got on.'

'I look forward to learning more about your interests,' he told her as they approached her lodgings. 'And I gather you're included among the visitors to Lindley Lodge this Friday evening?'

Laura was rather surprised that the occasion was going ahead despite the accident at the mill, but wouldn't embarrass him by commenting on that.

Roy appeared to have read her thoughts. 'No, we're not cancelling,' he said. 'We are hoping to avoid publicity about what happened yesterday. The surest way of having people believe everything is normal is to behave as though it were.'

She sighed. 'And I don't suppose stopping folk coming to your house would help Geoff or his mother. Have you seen her today, by the way?'

'No. She wasn't in. Father gave her a day off to recover.'

'I should think so as well. She looked that poorly.'

'I had someone go round there – to their home. Evidently she was getting over the shock.'

'And how are you feeling?' She hadn't seen him at all during the day at the mill, and had tried to talk about other things on the way to the hospital.

Roy indicated the bandaged hands. 'As you see, I can handle the wheel, just about. I won't pretend they aren't sore, but I can do most things. My feet feel pretty raw, but so long as I don't spend much time on them they're bearable. According to the hospital people yesterday, the dye must have cooled slightly before it got to me. Could have been far worse.'

'And the shock?' she enquired. As soon as they'd met he had asked if she was any worse for that.

Roy grinned. 'Like you, I'd have been better without the incident, but I'm a natural survivor – again, like you.'

'Steady,' she teased, 'that might be interpreted as a compliment.'

'So I'll never be allowed them now?' he asked, turning to face her as he parked the car outside 'Bien-être'.

'That's right. Blotted your copy book, haven't you! Thanks for bringing me home, any road. See you tomorrow.'

Michael was sitting in the front parlour with Miss Priestley. All Laura had told her landlady was that she was going to visit somebody in hospital. She was thankful now that she hadn't said more. If the Lindleys were trying to hush up the accident she wasn't going to talk about it all over Halfield.

'How was the patient?' Michael enquired as soon as Laura came in.

'Improving, thanks,' she said, trying to smile.

'Not one of our parishioners, is it?'

'If he is, nobody's told me. No – it's one of the apprentices from Lindley's.'

'And you got a lift home?'

'From my boss. He'd been there as well.'

'Very considerate of him.'

'Aye.' Laura was uneasy, but could say nothing. It was growing increasingly plain to her that if Roy hadn't insisted on getting her out of the dyehouse, Geoff might have been less severely injured. If she'd been in a position to discuss her feeling of guilt with Michael he might have rationalised it with her. As it was, she must bear it on her own, and behave as though nothing was wrong.

'I called round to see if you're doing anything Friday night, Laura? We're thinking of running a few dances in the church hall next winter. Some of the youngsters are frightened of coming because they can't do the proper steps. I told them I knew somebody who'd soon put that right. You will, won't you? I said Friday so's you won't have to be up early the following day.'

'We do work some Saturday mornings, you know, Michael.'

'Do you? I thought maybe, doing designing . . .'

'But I'm not really, not yet. So far I've been in scouring and

106

the dyehouse. While I'm learning, I work same hours as everyone in the mill. And I'm afraid this Friday's no good. I'm going out.'

'You hadn't said.'

'I didn't know, Michael, not when I saw you last. The Lindleys are having a do and they've invited me. I can't think why.'

'Never mind – I'll tell them classes will start next Friday.'

Laura gnawed her lip. 'I'm sorry, love, I don't dance any more.'

'Don't . . .? But that's ridiculous, Laura. You've got all your medals, are qualified to teach.'

'Even so, I haven't danced since Auntie died.'

Miss Priestley who had been sitting there, interested, got up and glanced from one to the other. 'Do you fancy a bit of supper?'

'Please, I'm famished,' said Laura, smiling.

As soon as they were alone Michael crossed the room to take her by the shoulders. 'You shouldn't grieve for ever.'

'I'm not, but this is too soon. I don't want to dance.'

'It would only be very informal . . .'

'Please don't go on at me, I'm tired out.' And she was beginning to realise how reluctant she was to become more deeply involved at St Martin's. Michael had been misinterpreting their relationship for long enough. She always felt torn now, between the need to convince him that they were no more than friends, and dread of being unkind.

Laura remembered suddenly that, unwittingly, she had told Michael less than the truth. She had danced, only quite recently, in what she privately thought of as the ballroom of Arncliffe Hall. When she pictured herself dancing again it was there, and her partner wasn't Beth Horsfall.

Always scrupulously honest, this increased her feeling of guilt. She waited, wondering how she ought to respond if Michael suggested that they should go out together on Saturday.

When he said nothing of the kind Laura was relieved. She

had enough on her mind, and seeing Michael seemed to generate tension.

'Is the house purchase going ahead all right?' he asked, moving away from her.

'So far as I know. I haven't heard owt for the past few days.' And that house is bothering you, she thought. I do wish you could accept that owning my own home is something I've got to do.

Michael choked back a sigh, acutely conscious that Laura was growing increasingly distanced from him. And each time that she placed some new interest between them his longing for her grew.

'Come round to the flat . . .' he began impulsively, checked, and added: 'Some time soon.' Was he going out of his mind? How could he overlook the danger of their being alone there, when each time that she was near every part of him yearned for her.

Frequently now he questioned the standards he'd always set himself. This searing passion seemed totally incompatible with his way of life. Looking at her now, her face nearly as pale as her froth of hair, the exquisite blue eyes heavy with tiredness, he felt his heart surge with love. He ached to remove her from working in the mill, from the planning and purchasing that would go into fitting out that damned house, and place her in the home that he would provide.

And there, he recognised grimly, this idealised love would become displaced by the urgency of his desire.

He glanced at his watch, 'Tell Miss Priestley I'm sorry but I can't stay, will you?' he said stiffly, 'Enjoy yourself on Friday.'

Cycling over to Lindley Lodge, Laura remembered Michael's words and grinned to herself. If he only knew! She was alarmed by the prospect of meeting all the Lindley family and their friends, but nothing would have made her cry off. Before that dreadful accident in the dyehouse she had felt that she ought to accept as an adjunct to her career: since then she had been determined to demonstrate where her allegiance lay.

Anyone less than blind and deaf was bound to have noticed the way many of the workforce had picked on the accident to illustrate their dissatisfaction with 'the bosses'. For the past day or two Laura had worked with the winders preparing yarn for the looms, but it wasn't only in the winding department that unrest was stirring. Passing through the weaving shed, eating as she now did in the canteen, all she heard was grumbling.

The only good thing was Geoff Appleyard's continuing progress. And if his mother perpetually bemoaned the cause of his hospitalisation, she wouldn't have been justified in claiming the Lindleys neglected either of them. Both Roy and his father visited Geoff daily and found ways as well of showing their concern for his mother.

Roy's parents were at the open door of their substantial Pennine stone home. Mr Lindley swiftly introduced Laura to his wife Inez, an elegant grey-haired lady wearing Wedgwood blue, but immediately she was drawn aside by the maid who was handing around drinks.

'Another domestic crisis,' he exclaimed. 'She'll have more time after dinner. And here is our other son.' Laura spotted a leaner version of Roy approaching from a room to the left.

'Laura, my dear, I'd like you to meet Alan who is studying medicine. Alan – Miss Laura Crabtree, our new designer.'

'How do you do?' Laura began, warmed already by the easy smile on Alan Lindley's face and by the eyes so like his brother's. His hair was a shade or two darker than Roy's, the thinner face made him seem even more handsome.

'Where are you studying?' she asked, after he had responded to her greeting.

'Oh, in London. The best place, although no Welshman or Scot would agree.'

She smiled. 'And how many years have you still to do?'

'God willing exam-wise, only one more. Then there'll be my hospital stint, of course, before I start seeking work in practice.'

'You're not going to specialise then, or become a surgeon?'

'Well, not for some long while. It was the regular contact with my own patients which first appealed. I will at least give that a chance to pall.'

'You sound as if you're prepared for anything.'

He grinned down at her. 'One wouldn't presume to tackle medicine if one weren't.'

Laura smiled back. 'All very philosophical. You'll have to give me a few tips. I'm afraid I've become a bit obsessive about the line I want to take. And about other things I plan. I'm not certain it's a very comfortable attitude to have.'

'But one way of ensuring success,' said a voice behind her.

Glancing over her shoulder, Laura met Roy's eyes and was glad to see that they had lost some of the haunted quality that had shadowed them for days.

'Have you been here for ages?' he asked her, concerned. 'I must confess to dozing off in my bath.'

'Bit risky, old chap,' Alan observed.

'Don't tell me *you're* concerned that I survive!' He turned back to Laura. 'You've seen Father, I hope? He soon handed you on, didn't he?'

'Only after ensuring that I was in good hands, and supplied with a drink.'

'Oh, all right.'

He was still smarting from his father's rebuke earlier in the week, and was more sensitive than he would have admitted to the constraint between them.

'Anyway, Laura, now you're here there's someone I'd like you to meet. Excuse us,' he said to his brother and, taking her elbow, steered her between two groups of people, towards the staircase.

'Cynthia – my kid sister – is considered too young for Mother's parties. Being excluded is the bane of her existence. I thought we might alleviate that for her till it's time for dinner.'

'So long as your parents won't mind . . .'

'If they notice, having Alan there will more than compensate. Just to fill you in – being the younger son, he was allowed freedom to choose the life he wanted. His choosing medicine

110

gave them cause to boast about him, his absenting himself made them appreciate his visits home.'

'If you hadn't told me you loved the business, I'd feel quite sorry for you.'

Roy laughed. 'And so you should.' They had reached a door to the right of the head of the staircase. 'You there, Cynthia?' he called.

At first the girl who turned to face the door as they entered appeared more than old enough to have joined the party downstairs. The Lindley looks and glorious hair enhanced a stylish dress with butterfly sleeves. It was only as she beamed then rushed to fling her arms around her brother that Laura saw she was no more than fifteen.

Roy confirmed this age as he introduced them. Cynthia groaned as she thrust herself away from him. 'Brothers, why do I have to have them!' she exclaimed, then smiled at Laura. 'Hallo – glad old Roy's sneaked you away from the parents' do. Like your frock . . .'

'Thank you.' Laura smiled. She'd had difficulty deciding what would look right, and had settled for a pale green linen which she'd made a few years ago from a pattern in *Film Fashionland*. Despite its pleated bodice, it didn't really feel dressy enough, but she'd never had much need for posh frocks. 'I was rather limited by having to come on my bike.'

'You didn't!' Roy exclaimed, staring at her, amazed.

'I don't like going home late on the tram.'

She read in his eyes his intention of driving her back afterwards, wondered if anticipating that had confirmed her intention of being independent.

'Have you any brothers?' Cynthia asked her, linking her arm in Laura's and taking her over to the window seat which was upholstered to match ruby brocade curtains.

'No, sisters.'

'More than one? Gosh, aren't you lucky.'

'They're triplets – and lucky isn't the way I'd describe it.'

'But you must miss them, now you're away from home.'

Somebody's been talking, Laura thought, and glanced

towards Roy who had joined them near the window.

'Oh, I do,' she agreed emphatically.

'Like when you lose a sore throat?'

Laura laughed. 'You're catching the general idea. But I suppose I do miss feminine company. Most of the people I've met so far in Halfield are men.'

'How gorgeous. I think I'll have a job like yours.'

'Are you still at school? What do you want to do?'

'Oh, I'm going to do medicine like Alan.'

'You must have a lot of tenacity, it's a mighty long training.'

'She'll never stick it out, you can save your admiration,' Roy observed quite sharply.

'You'll see,' Cynthia retorted, and was interrupted by Alan's arrival at the door.

'Thought I might find you in here. We're about to go in to dinner and, Roy, the parents are beginning to make noises about your dragging Miss Crabtree away.'

'Oh, Laura, please,' she corrected him.

'Well, it'll be mud, the same as Roy's name, if you don't both come at once.'

'Make Roy bring you again, won't you?' Cynthia pleaded as they left her.

'Nice girl,' Laura remarked, once they were out of earshot of his sister.

'Very. Pity she's so set on medicine, though.'

'She seems determined.'

'Unfortunately, that isn't enough. Cynthia had rheumatic fever when she was nine. It left her with a weak heart. They'd never pass her as fit.'

'Oh, no. But she must know, surely?'

'What kid of fifteen will accept all they are told?'

'What will she do then?'

'Father hopes she'll join Lindley's, of course. Don't know in what capacity. But that's way into the future, anyway. She'll go to university first.'

Laura would almost have preferred to remain talking with Roy and his young sister rather than sit with a crowd of people she did not know around the long walnut table. Although she had been introduced to everyone present as they filed into the dining-room, she felt overawed by its opulence and out of her depth in conversation with the other guests. They all knew each other, and all appeared to have lived for ever in or around Halfield.

As soon as the meal was over, she decided to make some excuse and leave. Both Robert Lindley and his wife objected immediately. 'Eh, love,' Mrs Lindley protested, all her sophistication evaporating, 'we haven't made you feel at home, have we? I said to Roy's dad that this wasn't the best sort of occasion to ask you here the first time. He swore he was right inviting you though, convinced me that it'd be a good thing for you to meet lots of new folk.'

'And it has been, don't worry, Mrs Lindley.'

'Nay, don't try to kid me, love. But if you haven't felt too comfortable tonight, we'll have you here again, soon. You'll see us with our hair down then, that'll happen be more to your liking.'

'Yes, of course,' her husband agreed. He was less sure than his wife how to put this right, whether or not simply to let Laura go home.

They were all deliberating in the light and airy entrance hall when someone clattered the knocker on the outer door. It was rattled again when no one opened immediately.

Robert Lindley went to answer the door, and Laura choked down an instinctive groan when she saw the man Miss Priestley had pointed out as Carter Ainley storming across the parquet floor.

She hadn't liked what she'd heard about his carrying on with other women, to say nothing of his attempt to turn the Coach House into a workshop. Now that he appeared furious she sensed that he could be extremely unpleasant.

He looked from Robert Lindley to Roy. 'Glad you're both in, that'll make it simpler to put my case.' He glanced beyond the group in the hall towards the open door from which conversation drifted. 'Didn't know you had owt to celebrate

113

this week. You'd better make the most of it, all on you – I'm going to put you out of business.'

'What the hell . ...? What right have you to come blustering your way in here?' Robert Lindley's usually pleasant features sharpened with indignation.

'You'll know soon enough,' Carter Ainley snapped.

'You'd better begin by introducing yourself or I'll have you out of that door before you know what's hit you.'

'It's Mr Ainley, isn't it?' said Laura, so astounded that she spoke up to the hefty intruder before realising that she was interfering in something which didn't concern her.

'I don't know you, do I?' he said, his broad face scowling.

'*Carter* Ainley?' Roy's father enquired.

'So, you have heard of me? That's a start. I'm here to see right done by my own. And I'd advise you to listen before I take this to court. Which is what I have every intention of doing.'

'Court?' Roy echoed, coming to stand beside his father. 'Why the blazes should you think you're justified in taking legal action against us?'

'You must have very short memories if you've already overlooked that catastrophe in your mill.'

'Oh.' Robert Lindley turned to his wife. 'Inez, would you excuse us for a minute, and take Miss Crabtree back to join our other guests?'

Roy looked pointedly towards the study door as the ladies left them, but his father had no intention of encouraging Ainley to hang around. Without inviting him to sit, he prompted him to continue.

'Go on with what you were saying – about your having some connection with the accident in our dyehouse.'

'That lad who were injured, who's fighting for his life, is my son. That's what the connection is, Lindley, and that's why I'm going to make you smart.'

Roy stepped forward slightly to stand almost between his father and Carter Ainley.

'I was present at the time, my father wasn't, I suggest you address any remarks to me.'

'Remarks!' Ainley thundered. 'Nay, it'll be far more than that.'

'Well, before you begin, I'm going to correct one statement you made – young Geoff is not fighting for his life. If he ever was that serious, the condition was overcome during his initial treatment in hospital. Since then he has continued to make good progress, his doctors are satisfied . . .'

'They might be, he's not their lad. Now let me tell you something – *I'm* not satisfied, and I won't be till we get proper compensation.'

'We are paying all hospital costs, Mr Ainley, and will pay Geoff's wages for as long as he is off work,' Robert Lindley asserted.

'You'll do a damned sight more when I sue for negligence!' He faced Roy. 'I understand it was you as were in charge when it happened.'

'Correct.'

Although trying to contribute to the conversation going on on the other side of the door where Mrs Lindley and these people she hardly knew were sitting, Laura could not avoid hearing virtually every word being said out in the hall. Ever since she had come back in here she'd been struggling to contain the anger aroused by the injustice of Carter Ainley appearing to support his son only when years of evident neglect had caused the boy and his mother hardship.

She heard him shouting again, and could sit still and silent no longer.

'And it's only your word against his, isn't it?' he was saying to Roy when Laura opened the door.

'That's not so, Mr Ainley. I was there as well. In fact, it was in order to demonstrate the dyeing process to me that Mr Lindley was there at all.'

'*You!* No wonder summat drastic went wrong. Having a look round, were you? Is taking an interest in dyeing one of your fancy notions?'

'No – a part of my job.'

115

'Miss Crabtree is joining our design team,' Robert Lindley informed him evenly.

Carter Ainley was not impressed. 'Well, that's it then, isn't it? The dyehouse is no place for a woman. It's easy to see who's really to blame now for mistakes being made, for carelessness.' He looked straight at Roy's father. 'I take it you are covered for negligence by your employees? Because if not, by God, you're going to wish you were.'

Astonishing them again, he swung round and opened the front door. He was through it and running down the steps to the drive before either of the Lindleys had decided to restrain him.

'You're not letting him get away with that?' Laura couldn't believe it.

Roy and his father exchanged glances, both so shaken by Ainley's sudden arrival that they could not think straight.

Laura was horrified. Carter Ainley would have them all up in court. In no time at all he'd have gathered some sort of evidence that would raise doubts about her suitability for her job. And she wasn't going to let that happen, not without a battle.

Ainley was getting into his car when she caught up with him. Placing one foot firmly on the running board after he closed the door, she rapped on the window until he wound it down.

'Aye? What now?'

Laura was thinking rapidly, but not rapidly enough. She'd have to get time on her side, nothing else could help her.

'I was only wondering why you hadn't hung on back there – if only long enough to learn how the Lindleys intended compensating young Geoff?'

'They've offered nowt no more than medical care and the wages they'd have been paying him anyway.'

'While they'll be paying somebody else to do Geoff's work as long as he's off.'

'That's their hard lines, isn't it ? Happen they'll soon be saving your wages, any road.'

Happen they will, thought Laura, especially now she was

interfering again. But she couldn't keep quiet. There was something that had bothered her about not knowing earlier who Geoff's father was. She remembered now what it was.

'Have you seen your son?' she asked him, wondering how much of the man's bluster was due to not having done all he could even now.

'I'm going tomorrow evening. I only heard tonight what had happened.'

'He doesn't live with you then?' she asked innocently, as if she didn't know full well what the reply would be.

'No, of course he doesn't . . .' He checked himself. 'He lives with his mother.'

'Aye – Emma Appleyard. Does your wife know of her existence, Mr Ainley? Does she know Geoff?'

He started the car engine. 'I don't have to stop here listening to your threats of blackmail.'

Laura flinched. She didn't like that word, but maybe it was justified. And she mustn't be deflected by her dislike of being made to feel she was trying something nasty.

'That's right,' she agreed. 'I only thought you might like to consider the repercussions there could be to the publicity of fighting this in court.'

'Eh?'

'Your wife learning about Geoff and his mother. And then there was the reason your lad was in there after he'd been told by Mr Lindley to get along to the canteen. He was sitting having his dinner in the dyehouse, did you know that? Well, he called it his dinner. To most folk it would've seemed like scraps. Scraps that his mother sneaked to him from her job in the canteen. Because neither of them ever gets enough to eat.'

He made to drive away then, and she let him go. He didn't appear to have changed his mind at all, but at least she had had her say.

Chapter 7

Laura ought to have felt better for speaking up; unfortunately, it had taken so much out of her she could only just stagger back the few steps to the Lindleys' front door.

'Laura!' Letting her in, Roy looked astounded. 'We thought you'd stormed off, upset by that chap. Where on earth have you been?'

He drew her inside and pulled forward the nearest chair.

Laura ignored the chair, she didn't feel up to staying. 'Talking to him – Carter Ainley. It's not right, the way he's suddenly found out that he cares about his son when he never gave a hang before.'

Roy's father spoke from the doorway of the room where their guests were gathered. 'Laura? We – we were afraid you'd simply gone home because you'd had enough of the trouble.'

'I have. But I didn't like my first glimpse of Carter Ainley. He hasn't improved with keeping. I'm sorry if I've been butting in, but it does concern me as well, if I get the blame for that accident . . .'

'My dear.' His hand firm on her shoulder, Robert Lindley was looking down at her, as concerned as if she'd been his own daughter. 'Even if the worst comes to the worst and we do end up in court, no one will be permitted to lay any of the blame on you. We have no intention of letting him destroy either the business or our good reputation as employers. If there is a fight, so be it. I shall be instructing my solicitor tomorrow, first thing. And so long as we are in existence, Laura, you will have a job.'

Both Roy and his father volunteered to drive Laura home,

but Inez Lindley insisted she would do so. 'Neither of you is in any state to handle a vehicle,' she said. 'You can just see the rest of our guests out to their cars. They're none of them in any mood for staying long.'

'Has it upset everybody?' Laura asked, concerned, after Roy had placed her bicycle in the boot of the Lindley car. Inez grinned as she got in behind the steering wheel.

'Some of our friends were staggered by a row going on at Lindley Lodge. Those that're proper friends won't let it make any difference, though. And I suppose the rest'll think it's made their evening. I'm only sorry it's been such a washout for you. I was hoping we'd be able to introduce you to folk who might help you settle in Halfield.'

'I think I'm doing that, but thanks for the thought. I'm afraid it's partly my fault I haven't started getting to know more people.'

'Our Roy has a soft spot for young Cynthia.'

'You knew where we were then?'

Roy's mother laughed. 'I haven't brought up them three without becoming good at guessing. Have you any brothers or sisters, love?'

Inwardly, Laura sighed, remembering how she had felt compelled to leave her mother to cope with them. 'Three sisters, just a bit older than Cynthia.'

'What – all of them?'

'I'm afraid so, yes. Triplets.'

'Your mother must be a very capable woman.'

Laura sighed again, watching Mrs Lindley's steady hands grasping the wheel, noting the ease with which she changed gear and judged the big car's distance from other road users. If only somebody like this were looking after the girls, she wouldn't feel half so guilty.

'I don't think you really appreciate your own mother.'

Her companion laughed again. 'I can see you and I are going to get on, Laura. I shall remind Roy and his father that we must ask you to join us again.'

'Thank you, I'd like that.'

Laura felt exhausted though, and wasn't sorry when Mrs Lindley drew up at the kerb outside 'Bien-être'.

'Remember me to Mavis Priestley, will you? It's a year or two since we met, but I don't think she will have forgotten me. You're lucky having lodgings with her, she'll put on a good table.'

'Yes, she does,' said Laura, too tired to go into details about her projected move to her own home. 'Well, thank you ever so much for a lovely meal, and for driving me home. If you'll open the boot, I'll just get my bike out.'

She waved as Mrs Lindley drove off, and went indoors still feeling regretful. She'd been reminded tonight that she'd once loved looking after her sisters, until they were old enough to do more for themselves. She wished she could be reassured that no one in her family was suffering from this decision of hers to move to Halfield.

The following morning at the mill the atmosphere was so gloomy that Laura was thankful she only had to work the half day. Overnight, it seemed, Roy and his father had re-examined the likelihood of Carter Ainley's prosecuting them for negligence, and had concluded he was capable of doing so. Naturally, this had resurrected Robert Lindley's original annoyance with his son, and evidently had led to further sharp exchanges.

'What exactly did Ainley say last night, Laura, when you went out to talk to him?' Roy asked, walking with her the length of the winding department in order to be out of earshot of his operatives.

'Much the same as he'd said in your house – that he was going to sue. But I gathered from something he said that his wife knows nowt about him having carried on with Emma Appleyard.'

'And nothing either, presumably, about young Geoff?'

'Nothing at all.'

'Well, we can only hope he sees the sense in keeping it that way, by not suing us.'

Laura agreed. She didn't feel she ought to raise false hopes by telling him that she had emphasised this to Mr Ainley. And, anyway, by this morning her memory of the previous night was so disturbed that she had difficulty recalling anyone's precise words.

'If it does come to court, you can count on me,' she assured him, nevertheless. 'You did get me out of there very quickly, and so there wasn't a mark on me. You didn't hesitate either to run straight back in for Geoff.'

Although Roy thanked her, he wasn't any more optimistic, and Laura spent a gloomy morning trying to concentrate on the Hattersley machine where wool was wound ready for the looms. She preferred that to picturing herself giving evidence before a judge.

Cycling back to Hanson Road, she wondered what she could do that afternoon to cheer herself. Despite feeling it was wiser to spend less time with Michael, she did miss his company. She hadn't made any real friends since arriving in Halfield and, having relied on him for years, was left with a gap in her life.

But I shan't let that depress me, she thought fiercely, opening Miss Priestley's front door. She had plenty to get on with, adapting carpet designs. She hadn't come here looking for social life.

An official-looking envelope addressed in handwriting that she didn't recognise was waiting for her on the bamboo table.

'That came for you first post,' her landlady announced from her living-room doorway.

'Thank you, Miss Priestley, I'll just go up and wash my hands, then I'll be down if the dinner's ready.'

'It is that – I've done you a nice chicken salad today since it's that hot.'

'That'll be lovely.'

Hurrying upstairs, Laura realised that she hadn't noticed the heat even in the mill. She had been too perturbed about Carter Ainley's threat to her future there. Still preoccupied, she tore open the envelope.

Her eyes lit up with excitement, all anxiety banished. Patrick Horsfall was informing her that the legalities of purchasing the Coach House were almost completed. This seemed to be happening very swiftly. She wondered if his position as head of the building society accelerated such a deal. He was suggesting that she go over to Arncliffe some time during that weekend. She couldn't have asked for a better tonic.

Getting off the bus Laura felt her excitement increasing. Telephoning to ask when it would be convenient to call, she'd been invited to join the family for a meal.

'My sister and her husband are here. It would give you an opportunity to find out more about your future home,' Patrick had told her.

Although she suspected that wasn't really necessary – hadn't she thoroughly examined the property? – something in his voice had revealed the invitation wasn't so casual as it sounded.

Laura was thankful she'd had time to wash and iron her other linen dress which was sky blue. Nothing else she possessed seemed suitable. This time she had left her bike at 'Bien-être'. She couldn't think they would wish her to stay long after they had eaten, and she didn't want to be even more hot and bothered than necessary when she arrived.

On previous occasions Laura had been too preoccupied to notice more than that Arncliffe Hall was large and stone-built. Today, walking up the long curve of drive with the breeze wafting through her hair, she studied its pleasing construction.

The main part of the mansion was two-storeyed, with seven large windows beneath a grey slate roof. Below the central window was the stone arched doorway, flanked by further windows to either side. Set forward of this main section were the two smaller wings, each of which was connected by a curving, single storey to the principle building.

Beyond the left-hand of these, Laura caught a glimpse of the house which soon would be hers. And all at once, despite having been so sure that she wished to live here, she felt alarmed. She'd felt rather out of place at the Lindleys', hadn't she? Their home couldn't have been half as big as this. What was she letting herself in for? The other evening she'd hardly got to know anyone present.

That, surely, was due to circumstances, though – she had gone with Roy to see his sister which had prevented her mingling with the other guests and afterwards . . . Nobody could pretend Carter Ainley's disturbing arrival had been conducive to relaxing in strange company.

Is it me, though? Laura still wondered. Is it because I'm not used to meeting wealthy folk?

She felt worse rather than better when the door was opened by a solemn middle-aged woman whose substantial figure was as ramrod straight as the long-cased clock beside her.

'I believe Mr Horsfall is expecting me. My name's Laura Crabtree.'

'Aye, that's right. It'll be you as is taking the Coach House. Well, come in do, and I'll tell him you're here.'

Before the housekeeper disappeared a smiling young woman in a silky maternity smock came swiftly down the stairs.

'Yes, tell Patrick, please, Mrs Harrison,' she responded to the glance that sought approval. 'Meanwhile, I'll introduce myself.'

Her hand outstretched, she came towards Laura. 'I'm Jenny Rawnsley, Patrick's sister.' Her grasp was warm and her smile even warmer. 'Do we call you Laura, or haven't we got to that stage yet?'

'Oh – Laura, please.'

'I can see straight away that you're just right for the Coach House. It's a load off my mind, I can tell you. Ted and I were so happy there, because it was our first home, I suppose. Are you wanting to have another look now? There's time, I think, before we're due to eat.'

'All right then, only . . . won't Mr Hor— your brother wonder where we are?'

'There is that, of course. If he's not in the middle of

124

something when Mrs Harrison locates him. Better wait till after the meal. Come along through then, and we'll find you a drink. Ted should have come off the phone by now – we'd no sooner arrived here than he had to ring our stockman.'

'Farming's a very demanding business, isn't it?'

'I'll say! You know a bit about it then?'

'Used to. My favourite holidays when I was small were on my uncle's farm.'

'But your parents aren't farmers?'

Laura shook her head. Jenny opened the door of a room that Laura had not seen before, and they walked together across to one of a pair of pale matching sofas set at right angles to the white marble fireplace.

'Do take a seat,' Jenny invited her. 'I'll see to the drinks. It looks as though Ted's still caught up.'

'I'll take care of that, Jenny.'

Hearing a familiar voice, Laura glanced over her shoulder as Patrick hurried towards his sister. He smiled at Laura as he picked up glasses.

'Hallo again, glad you could make it. I take it that Jenny's introduced herself? You'll discover we're very informal here – all first names, don't forget. I believe we shall be eating in twenty minutes or so. What'll you have? This is quite a good sherry.'

As soon as Patrick approached with her drink, Laura felt herself relaxing. His smile had seemed very genuine, and made her glad there would be opportunity to get to know him better. Maybe she would come to consider him a friend, although she must remember she was in Halfield to establish her career and her independence. She couldn't permit anyone to take her mind off her ambitions.

'You didn't go straight to your new home then?' he exclaimed, smiling, dark eyes challenging her own.

'Nearly,' Jenny answered for her, and Laura smiled.

'Since Mrs Harrison was on her way to let you know I was here, I thought I'd better not disappear.'

'We're going across after dinner,' his sister said. 'All right?'

'Why not? I'll be looking in on Mother and Father.'

Laura was wondering why on earth their parents didn't eat with the family when Ted Rawnsley strolled in. Patrick introduced him to Laura before returning to the drinks tray.

She liked Ted Rawnsley at once. His smile was as ready as his wife's and his blue eyes glinted with humour.

'When are you moving in?' he enquired, sitting facing her and feeling in a pocket for his pipe.

'Not quite yet – I've only heard today that it's definitely going through.'

'I'm sure if you twist Patrick's arm he'll not compel you to wait until all the legalities are formalised.'

'That's as may be, but I haven't one stick of furniture yet.'

'Will you enjoy choosing everything?' Jenny asked, as she shook her dark head at the offer of a drink.

'Can't really believe this is me. I'll have the time of my life.'

'I hope the colour scheme we left you won't clash too horribly with your ideas,' Ted remarked, glancing across over the pipe in which he was tamping down tobacco.

'Not in the least. Couldn't have been more to my liking if I'd picked the shades myself. And I love those carpets.'

'Jen's choice, and the curtains. I leave all that to her.'

'And a lot more besides,' his wife commented ruefully. 'Never marry a farmer, Laura, if you want to grab their attention for more than seven consecutive seconds.'

It was Patrick who laughed. 'You'd better add that the situation suits you to a T. Haven't you always known precisely what you want? Anyway, you don't understand the extent of the compliment Laura has paid you. Carpets are her business.'

'Really?' Sitting beside Laura, Jenny looked astonished. 'You sell them, do you?'

'*Designs* them,' he corrected his sister, coming to stand with his back to the hearth.

'I'm learning design, yes,' she told them. 'The hard way!'

'How come?' Drawing on his pipe now, Ted was intrigued.

'They're putting me through the mill, literally – and it feels like being under a grindstone some days, as well.'

126

'I didn't realise you had to go through all that,' Jenny remarked.

Laura laughed. 'Nor did I!'

'But it'll be worth it,' Patrick said. 'I'll certainly know where to come when we're recarpeting our Head Office in London.'

Laura grinned at him. 'What sort of thing do you have in mind?'

'Something light to counteract dark panelling. Incorporating our insignia, of course. Perhaps the white rose of York.'

'Against a gold background.' Although it was all in fun, Laura privately named the design Yorkshire Gold as they entered the next room. She soon saw how popular the shade seemed to be in here.

The long table was mahogany, agleam with silverware and crystal glasses. The matching chairs had gold velvet seats toning with floor-length brocade curtains.

'Here, beside me,' Patrick insisted, drawing out the chair to the right of the head of the table.

His sister came to sit at her other side, with Ted seated opposite. Again, Laura wondered about the absence of Patrick's parents.

Only when they had finished the delicious meal and she and Jenny were walking through the ballroom in the direction of the Coach House did she begin to learn the reason.

'My parents have their own suite of rooms, these days. Sadly, Mother has a stomach tumour and can only cope with specially prepared food. Father's the only one she'll tolerate around her at mealtimes. They're a devoted couple, always have been. He invariably has his meals served up there as well.'

'Oh, what a shame.'

'Their lives aren't quite so dismal as that sounds. They both have a love of classical music, and a massive record collection. They read a lot as well, and listen to the wireless. I still feel guilty for moving away, but I couldn't expect Ted to remain around here when Buckstones Farm was crying out for us to take over. At least we're not all that far away. Can get here in a crisis.'

Meanwhile Patrick bears the responsibility of a sick mother as well as a daughter who plainly is not as she should be, thought Laura, her concern for him growing.

'When are you going to move in?' Jenny asked, as she unlocked the door of Laura's prospective home.

'Eh, I don't know. I'd like it to be as soon as possible, I've completely fallen for the place. But I literally don't have anything I shall need. And I don't mind admitting I haven't as much behind me as I'd like, now I'm planning my first home. I'm prepared to take my time, mind, wait for some things. So long as I furnish one bedroom and get a table and a few chairs, and the things I'll need for cooking, of course.'

'I take it your family aren't going to help out?'

'I wouldn't let 'em,' said Laura quickly. 'In any case, there's enough of them at home still. Everything they have is in constant use.'

As they entered the living-room, she gazed around her, beaming. 'I do like it here, though. It's not going to worry me if it takes me a while to get it as I want it. I shall enjoy it all.'

They went through to the kitchen next, and Laura opened the cupboards and drawers one after the other, just for the sheer delight of reminding herself that they would be hers.

'I wish now I'd left you the cooker,' Jenny said. 'There's an Aga at the farm, I hardly use the gas oven.'

'Nay, don't talk like that. I don't care, honest – I have my eye on a nice little electric stove, anyway, a Baby Belling.'

As she was speaking she experienced a strange feeling that she and Jenny were no longer alone. She felt the hair at the back of her neck rise, and glanced anxiously around. She saw the face then, behind her, staring in, only a little above the level of the sill.

'Oh, heavens!' Jenny exclaimed, following her glance. 'Beth. I forgot her room overlooks this way, she's supposed to be in bed. Wonder if I can coax her back there, before she's missed. Sorry if she gave you a scare, she . . .'

'It's all right, it was only that I was startled. I've met Beth.'

'Have you now! Patrick doesn't normally . . .'

'We met accidentally. And I don't need that explaining – he wasn't over pleased. What – what's wrong with the girl?'

'If I could only say, my brother would be more than grateful. Sadly, we know very little, only that something traumatic occurred. Since that day she's never said one word.'

'Eh, dear.' Laura met the dark eyes, so like Patrick's. 'Do you have to rush her back to bed? She must want to come in here or she wouldn't be standing there that longingly.'

Together, they went out of the front door and round to where Beth was balancing on tiptoe, her pale hair stirring in the breeze and her nightgown fluttering about bare feet.

'You can come inside, Beth, but only for a minute or two,' her aunt told her.

The child did not even turn her head to look at her.

'She's not deaf,' Jenny confided.

'I know.' Laura touched Beth lightly on the shoulder. 'Do you remember me, love? We had a bit of a dance, didn't we, the other week?'

'Dance?' Jenny murmured, astonished.

'Only for a little while, then her father reappeared.'

'He doesn't mean to be harsh with her. I think – well, men sometimes are at a loss with children, aren't they? When there's something wrong it makes everything more difficult. And he seems to have it firmly fixed in his mind that Beth mustn't be permitted to become a nuisance to other people.'

'Doesn't she have any company then?'

'Mostly Mrs Harrison, who's always been very good with her. But she's in charge of running the place as well, of course.'

Beth appeared totally unaware of the conversation taking place only a few feet away from her, yet when they turned from her Laura was conscious that the child had noticed. Her fair head swivelled to watch.

'This is going to be my house soon,' she told her. 'Don't you want to have a look inside?'

Beth did not move and when Jenny tried to take her niece's hand she resisted.

'Leave her just for a second,' Laura whispered. 'See what

129

she does when we go back inside.'

Before they had reached the door she felt a tug at the belt of her linen dress.

'I wondered if she might.'

Jenny was astounded. 'She *has* taken to you. She's usually so careful to avoid contact. You'll have to watch it when you're living here, or you'll not be able to call your life your own.'

'I shan't be here that much, shall I? By the time I get home after work and make myself something to eat, she'll be in bed.'

Jenny laughed. 'As she should have been tonight!'

'Aye. I'll have to be careful of that, shan't I? I shall make myself unpopular if she keeps getting up again to visit me.'

'And we'd better hurry her back there now before she's missed.'

'Can't we just let her go round all the rooms here with us? I wasn't going to take long over it.'

Silent though she was, Beth appeared interested in the house devoid of furniture, staring all about her from the centre of each room in turn, her blue eyes urgently raking its bare walls.

'Did she visit you while you lived here?' Laura asked Jenny.

'Very occasionally, and only ever for about ten minutes. She would go to the door then, indicating that she'd had enough. Her behaviour used to disturb Ted, because it's so unchildlike.'

Returning to the main house, Beth refused to walk with them and wandered instead two or three paces behind. As they went indoors, though, through the large reception hall, she began tugging at Laura's skirt. As she glanced down Beth held out her thin hands and executed a strange little bare-footed dance.

'Well, only as far as the stairs, this time,' said Laura, taking hold of her. 'Do you remember? Quick, quick, slow; quick, quick, slow.'

The child had not forgotten, she moved easily to the beat Laura was counting, disconcerting as well as surprising her.

'I'll teach you some more when I come again,' she promised, and was even more surprised when Beth meekly went upstairs.

As the three of them approached her room, Patrick was coming towards them. Jenny answered the question his raised eyebrows were asking before he spoke one word.

'Your daughter's been exploring. But here we are now, no harm done.'

Laura smiled up at him. 'She wanted to see inside my new home, but didn't quite know what to make of its not having any furniture. I'll have to take her to have another look when I've settled in.'

'Want me to put her back to bed?' Jenny offered.

Patrick was still unsmiling. 'If she'll co-operate.'

'I'll get Mrs Harrison if she won't. You'll be looking in later, as usual?'

'Of course.'

As the bedroom door closed on Beth and her aunt, Patrick turned to Laura. 'Has my sister also told you about my parents?'

'Yes.' Was he going to be angry that she was learning so much about his family, about his grief?

'Good. They would like to meet you. They see so few new people, these days, and naturally are interested that you are coming to live so near.'

'Lead on then.'

His smile was genuine enough now. 'Not quite yet.'

Without explanation, he led the way to the tapestry gallery. When Laura began inspecting them, however, he smiled even more brilliantly and shook his head at her.

'This way.'

As Patrick opened a door the evening air rushed towards them. She followed him out on to the balcony which overlooked his garden with the grounds of the Arncliffe estate stretching beyond, almost as far as she could see in the twilight.

'This is all so lovely,' Laura exclaimed.

'I have an excellent head gardener, Mrs Harrison's husband, Tom. He keeps everything well maintained. Given the time, I'd do more myself.'

'But the days are never long enough anyway.'

'Precisely.' He turned from the view to gaze into her eyes. 'You might be good for Beth, Laura.'

'I hope so.'

'But,' he persisted, 'I have to caution you. Once you're living in the Coach House you mustn't let her encroach on your time too much.'

'I'll remember you've said that.' But she would still use her own judgement.

She's not the only one who will be happier to have you near, he was thinking, but did not feel justified in telling her so. Why should he burden her with the complexities of his life?

Seeing the gravity in his eyes, and knowing a little of his domestic situation, Laura shivered.

'You're not cold?' Anxiously, he touched her bare arm.

Sudden attraction became a pulse deep inside her. His hand remained on her arm, and his glance seemed riveted through her eyes as though it would reach right to the heart of her. Laura swallowed down a gasp.

Patrick had spent too long alone to be able to withhold the surge of mingled affection and desire. Wordlessly, he brought her towards him. One hand was still grasping her arm, the other tilted her head until their lips met.

His kiss was fierce with longing, and with the pain of bearing for too long so many private sorrows. He'd never needed anyone more.

His mouth on hers should have alarmed her, thought Laura amid confused emotions. But how could she move away, when she sensed that the waiting of years might be ending? When the life he awakened in her sang along every vein?

'Patrick,' she murmured, her voice as unsteady as her inner tumult.

They were standing very close, his chest firm against her breasts, his breathing urgent as her own. On the evening air the fragrance of the garden came as a caress, enhancing awareness of all her senses.

'One day,' Patrick said gruffly, as the sky around them darkened. 'One day, perhaps . . .

'Shall we go and see my parents?' he suggested at last.

'Well, yes – but what's the time?' Being kissed by Patrick had hardly encouraged frequent checking of her watch!

'Ten-thirty, but Mother sleeps so badly they never retire early. And naturally I shall drive you home.'

Naturally? Laura hadn't assumed anything of the kind. 'Right then,' she said, hoping it wasn't after all as apparent as she suspected that they had been holding each other close.

'You look lovely,' he assured her, smiling as she attempted to smooth down her hair while they hurried side by side through the corridors connecting them with the East Wing.

I only hope I can manage some coherent conversation, thought Laura, and noticed that Patrick's brown eyes glittered and even the tan induced by the winds of moorland Yorkshire failed to disguise the flush on his cheeks.

'You'll be busy, I know,' he said. 'But I hope this evening's proved that I'm looking forward to having you live nearby.'

Laura gave him a sideways glance. 'Aye, I did get that impression,' she said dryly.

Patrick smiled again but said nothing, which didn't surprise her, even though she suspected he was the last person to make a habit of kissing on impulse.

Rather too swiftly for Laura, they had reached the door of a sitting-room which proved to be beautifully furnished, and Patrick's father was hurrying to greet them. 'How nice of you to come and see us, Miss Crabtree.' He took her hand in both of his own.

'Please call me Laura,' she insisted, smiling.

'This way then, Laura. My wife is eager to get to know you.'

He led the way to a high-backed armchair. Mrs Horsfall possessed the same alert brown eyes as her son, but they appeared startling in her thin sallow face. The hand she extended was so fragile that Laura felt as if the pressure of her own might fracture the bones.

'Thank you for coming to introduce yourself,' Mrs Horsfall

said quickly, her voice quite strong. 'I'm only sorry that I couldn't play hostess this evening, but Jenny would deputise ably.'

'And compensate for any shortcomings apparent when I'm in charge,' Patrick added as he joined them and offered Laura a seat.

'Er – yes,' his mother agreed, affectionate reproof in the glance angled towards her son. She turned back to Laura. 'Once you're in the Coach House, I'm hoping Patrick will be less solitary. Perhaps something might be arranged about your eating together occasionally? Mrs Harrison tells me all too often of the meals he hardly touches.'

Laura didn't know how to reply. Although she had been drawn to him almost from the start, she had never seriously considered being involved to this degree in Patrick's life. Despite that kiss and what he had said, she had supposed that it would be some time before they saw much of each other. As if to confirm this, she sensed his embarrassment now, and read in his eyes annoyance which only his mother's illness prevented him expressing.

Mr Horsfall went to stand beside his wife, a gentle hand going to her shoulder. 'Mothers are the same the world over, aren't they, Laura? Never quite capable of crediting that their sons and daughters would survive without their intervention.'

Laura smiled again. Although rather the opposite of her own mother's attitude towards her, she knew there was a lot of truth in his generalisation. And, being aware of some of the anxieties confronting Patrick, she felt some concern was justified.

'I'm just very glad that it looks like we're all going to get on. I only knew I wanted to live in that lovely house. Learning that I'm going to have friends here is a real bonus.'

'And don't you make friends wherever you go, my dear?' Mrs Horsfall enquired. 'You remind me greatly of our youngest, Elaine. She's in Canada now, but always filled the place with young people before she emigrated.'

'Actually, I haven't had all that much time in the past for building up a social life.'

'Laura has triplet sisters, several years younger than herself,' Patrick announced.

'Don't blame you for escaping,' his father exclaimed.

Laura laughed, but Mrs Horsfall gave her husband a look. 'I'm certain Laura would not leave home for so slender a cause.'

Still laughing, Laura leaned towards her. 'There were times!' she exclaimed. 'But I'd probably still live over there in Whitby were there a place where I could do the work I've set my heart on. Although it'll be good for me as well to stand on my own feet.'

'And I understand you're a designer?' Patrick's mother continued. 'You must be very artistic. None of us has any latent talent, but that doesn't mean we're total philistines. We used to haunt all the galleries, abroad as well as in England. Florence is one of our favourite cities.'

Mr Horsfall indicated a pile of large volumes on a nearby table. 'We still keep our interest alive.'

Talking about books somehow led to discussing radio also. Suddenly Laura noticed that the black marble clock showed eleven-thirty.

'I'm afraid it's high time I was making tracks. It's true that the time flies when you're enjoying yourself. It's a good job it's not a working day tomorrow or I'd be late at the mill.'

As they were leaving, she noticed the photograph on a side table. It showed Patrick beside a glamorous bride with sleek hair of roughly Laura's own shade. The jolt it gave her threatened to spoil the entire evening. She reminded herself that theirs had been only one kiss, after all, and started by him. She had no cause to feel guilty.

In the car she thanked Patrick for inviting her. 'I've had a lovely evening, the meal was very nice, and I enjoyed meeting your family.'

'Good.'

She had sensed his unease ever since they were alone

together again, and she wasn't at all surprised. She herself was shocked that she could have forgotten earlier that he had a wife.

When they reached Hanson Road Laura wasn't taking any chances. She thanked him crisply again, and was out of his car before he could even echo her goodnight.

Chapter 8

Looking so serious that he alarmed her, Robert Lindley waylaid Laura as she went into the mill on the following Monday morning.

Whatever's wrong now? she wondered. Ever since the other evening, she had felt totally unnerved, scarcely able to cope. Going to Arncliffe for a meal had been exacting enough in the first place; and although the family couldn't have been nicer, a part of her had felt she was entering a completely new world. Being kissed by Patrick Horsfall had unleashed so many conflicting emotions that she'd returned home scarcely able to recognise herself. And now it seemed there were further problems here as well.

When her boss spoke, however, he was simply trying to learn more about the same difficulty that had troubled Lindley's for some time.

'Roy tells me that you had quite a few words with Carter Ainley the other evening. Can you remember what you said?'

Relief made Laura smile slightly. 'Not very much really – I just pointed out that if he sued the company he'd not get away without having folk learn he was young Geoff's dad.'

'I thought that was it. Well, Laura, you've done us all incalculable good. I made them an offer of compensation, you see. Last night Ainley telephoned saying it was acceptable.'

'Oh, I am pleased. And what's the latest about Geoff?'

'He's not doing so badly at all. The doctors are right suited with his progress, and his mother's getting over the shock. She actually came to me this morning to thank us for doing what we could since the accident happened.'

'So, providing Geoff doesn't have any setbacks, we can begin to put that behind us?'

'Let's hope so. We don't want the factory inspectors in.' He paused and smiled. 'Well, Laura, we've decided it's time you were learning something different. You'll be working as a creeler for a while. That means you'll be helping one of the weavers.'

'That should be more interesting.'

'That's what we intend. There's things about the yarn which you haven't come across yet, like colour matching for instance, but you can always catch up later on. We're putting you with Dennis Jagger for a start.'

Laura couldn't have been more thankful. Studying something new was just what she needed to take her mind off other matters. Much as she disliked the noise among the looms, she would relish being surrounded by carpets actually in the process of being woven. It should make her feel nearer to the day when she would really get down to serious designing.

She would need to give her whole mind to concentrating on what was being explained. There would be no opportunity now for thinking back to events at Arncliffe Hall. I'll only allow myself to recall one fact about Patrick – that he might one day give me the chance of designing a carpet for his building society, she resolved.

Trying to keep up with Robert Lindley, she allowed herself an inward smile. This factory was one place where she could make a niche for herself, she realised, as they entered the shed where the Wilton type of carpeting was produced. When Robert Lindley stopped beside the loom where she would be working, she recognised the weaver.

'I think you've met Dennis, haven't you? He's one of our most experienced young men, and has worked in the other shed as well as in here.'

Laura nodded as the weaver glanced towards her. 'I thought so – you weren't in here when I came round that first time were you?'

Dennis Jagger smiled. 'You've got a good memory. Have

you practised your lip-reading yet?'

'I'm afraid not.'

'You'll need it, Laura,' Robert Lindley said with a grin before giving Dennis a few words of instruction and departing.

They must have arranged that this particular loom wouldn't be started up until the way it functioned had been fully explained to her. She was glad of the reduction in noise; there was quite enough of that from the other looms in rows on all sides of them.

'Basically, a creeler's job is to make sure that all the bobbins of yarn are in order,' the weaver told her. 'In your case, since you'll not be going on to become a weaver like most creelers, it's just as important that you keep an eye on the process as a whole. I'm used to learning creelers what to do and I'll soon let you know if you're neglecting the bobbins, but I'm going to make sure you understand how these 'ere carpets are made.'

'That's what I want.'

'Happen you'd like to watch my lips now, while the machine is stopped and I'm explaining. Once this one's running you'll have difficulty hearing a thing.'

Laura grimaced. So much was new to her, she didn't want to worry about learning to lip-read as well.

'Don't look so anxious.' Dennis grinned. 'I shall demonstrate an' all, you ought to be able to follow. If you can't, you must say so.'

And will you hear me? wondered Laura. But Dennis was speaking again, repeating some of the detail that Roy had explained earlier.

'As you can see, the bobbins of yarn are arranged in these 'ere frames. After a bit, I shall expect you to know what order they've to be in. You can see, as well, how the yarn is fed into the machine.'

'What I can't remember is how the pile is formed.'

'Hang on a minute, can't show you everything at once. Go on, though – since you've asked, this is what does that . . .' He indicated a long piece of metal inserted under the yarn. 'This is called a wire – there's a sharp blade fixed into it and that's

139

what cuts the pile. That's after it's been formed into loops as the loom's weaving.'

'And is this what holds it all together?' she said, fingering a strong, hard thread.

'Aye, you're catching on fast. That's the weft – jute. Ours comes from Dundee. Now, just stand to one side a bit, we're setting her going. You'll have to remember not to touch owt while you're working in here – not unless I tell you to, that is.'

Laura was thankful not to be too close when the loom was clattering away, adding to the din filling the entire shed. She watched, fascinated, as the shuttle went back and forth.

'Is it the shuttle that weaves the weft in?' she asked, exaggerating with her lips as she'd seen the weavers and other creelers.

Dennis grinned, unable to tell what she was saying. But when she tried again he understood and nodded.

Laura loved that day, watching the pattern emerging as he wove, staring intrigued at the shifting Jacquard cards. She longed to know how exactly they translated the series of holes into the design emerging in the carpet, but there was so much to absorb at once, and more things that she needed to know. It would be some while yet before she'd feel justified in digressing to fathom the ins and outs of the Jacquard system.

The whole week was exhilarating, far more satisfying than any so far at the mill. By Saturday morning Laura felt elated. She was confident that she had grasped the main principles of carpet weaving. And Dennis Jagger had promised he'd let her have a go herself, under his keen supervision.

After dinner she caught the tram into the town centre. Patrick had confirmed that she should go ahead with ordering the furniture she would need to start her off in the Coach House. Any day now it would be hers, and she intended being ready for moving in as soon as she could. Explaining to her landlady had been awkward. She could see now the disappointment that had overshadowed Mavis Priestley's face.

'I'll be sorry to see you go, Laura lass. But I do understand about you wanting a place of your own. Happen I'll have somebody else here afore so long,' she'd added, regret clouding her silvery eyes.

'You'll have to come and visit me when I've got everything straight,' Laura had said. She would be sorry if she saw nothing more of her landlady. Beginning to like Miss Priestley had been an important factor in adapting to life in Halfield.

I still can't really believe I'll be living out at Arncliffe, she thought, looking out of the tram window and feeling thankful that she wouldn't have to settle amid the smoky streets of the town. In fact, everything about Arncliffe seemed insubstantial. Not least the other evening when Patrick had kissed her.

And I know well enough why that seems unreal, she thought ruefully. Why I've decided not to think about it. I'm quite well aware that I oughtn't to have let it happen. It was one thing to acknowledge privately that you were drawn towards a person; letting them do something about it while they still had a wife somewhere was terrible.

The tram had stopped in Commercial Street. Laura was glad to get off, and leave at the back of her mind these regrets that she'd never had an opportunity to learn how to cope with such a situation. At least, looking after her mother and sisters had taught her to get on with something practical and dismiss whatever was bothering her.

Laura didn't mean to be extravagant. She needed an overwhelming number of items for her home, she couldn't lash out on any one of them quite so freely as she wished. She went to the Co-op Furnishing first of all and found a nice bed with good solid oak for the headboard and at the foot. There was a little wardrobe to go with it and, although she'd have preferred the double one on show, she hadn't all that many clothes, had she?

A table and four chairs were next. Again she chose oak, and steeled herself not to look at the sideboard that matched. One day, she promised herself, she'd have saved enough for a sideboard. She had a good kitchen with all those cupboards,

141

and drawers in the table Jenny had left there. They would more than accommodate the crockery and utensils needed to cook for one.

Laura was busy selecting knives and forks, pans, mixing bowls and basins when she sensed somebody watching her from across the shop. Looking up she saw Geoff's mother, Emma Appleyard, and beside her Amos Kitchen.

'Hallo,' she said, surprised to see them together, and hurried around the counter to join them.

'Amos has just been with me to the hospital,' Emma told her.

'And how's Geoff today?' Laura enquired.

'Mending nicely, thank you. And now we're getting all that compensation I'm thinking of brightening things up a bit at home. We've made do for that long with stuff that were my mother's. I'm buying a new frying pan today.'

'And Emma's not the only one,' Amos exclaimed. 'I've gone and burnt mine, so I'm choosing a new 'un while I've got somebody with me who knows summat about 'em.'

'Good idea. Well, I'm glad your son's going on all right now, Emma. And that you've had company for today's visit.'

''T were Amos's idea. He's been asking after Geoff every day, you know. Him and me were in the Infants' together, so you might say we're old pals.'

After she had left them Laura began to wonder if something might come of their friendship. She would be delighted for them both: even with the compensation at the back of her, Emma would benefit from having a man around. And Amos deserved looking after following all the years of looking after himself.

The shops were shutting by the time Laura had bought all the utensils she would require for setting up house. She felt exhausted with trailing around after a morning spent in the mill, but she'd never been happier. Maybe living at Arncliffe was becoming more real, after all. She certainly hoped it was. Carpet designing and her new home were the only things that seemed satisfactory in her life.

Her unease about her friendship with Michael rather spoiled the following day when she went to church. During the service she was as thrilled as ever by the music, and was pleased to notice again what a splendid contralto soloist Miss Priestley was, but when she saw Michael in the porch afterwards his attitude made her uncomfortable.

'I thought you might have wanted to go out somewhere yesterday,' he said, frowning.

'Yes, well – actually, I was out buying the things I've got to have for my new home.'

Michael stifled a sigh. He might as well resign himself to accepting the way things were. Even while she was still living in the parish, Laura was so taken up with her plans to move away it almost seemed that a part of her had already left.

'We could go out today if you like, after dinner?' Laura suggested. 'I'd have come and cooked for you if I'd thought to warn Miss Priestley that I wouldn't be home.'

'It's all right, doesn't matter. We've a big Christening service, anyway, this afternoon.'

'What about tonight then, after Evensong?' She had planned to work on some designs but salvaging their friendship was important as well. Once more, though, Michael would be too busy.

'Oh, well – we'll have to get together as soon as we can. Will you ring me at Miss Priestley's if you can manage one evening during the week?' asked Laura.

Michael didn't promise. Recalling their early friendship and how good to her he'd been, Laura again felt guilty. But nothing she had done since arriving in Halfield had been intended to distress him, and he had known all along that she would put everything she'd got into her work. As she'd already been thinking, she wished she'd had more experience while she was growing up. She didn't know how to stop men developing expectations which she didn't share. She was beginning to feel she was particularly inept at interpreting their behaviour.

That week Laura threw herself even more wholeheartedly into life at Lindley's. Having had the rest of Sunday free, she had spent a couple of hours receiving tuition from Clem Hargreaves, then had worked on transferring more of her designs on to point paper.

First thing on Monday morning, she asked Dennis if he could spare her for a few minutes and went to find Roy Lindley. He was in scouring, but came out to see what she wanted as soon as she appeared in the entrance.

'Have you nearly finished in there?' Laura asked him. 'Because if you have time, I'd like you to look at these.'

Roy led the way through the factory to his office. 'More designs?' he enquired, smiling as he offered her a seat.

'Here you are. I have to know, you see, whether or not they're up to standard.' Clem Hargreaves had said these were very good, but she needed reassurance from either Roy or his father, the only people who could convince her she was mastering her job.

He was spreading out the point paper on his desk, scrutinising her colouring of the intricate design, counting the shades used, checking the number of knots represented. Slowly, he stood up, still gazing at the pattern, his eyes half closed as he visualised the finished effect.

'Excellent. Laura, this really is extremely good.' He glanced at her. 'How long have you been in the weaving shed?'

'Since last Monday.'

'Mmm. Not long enough, not by any means. But – well, we could try you out for a while in the design studio. So long as it was understood that you've still a lot to learn on the practical side . . .'

She would be designing properly, like all the others, working in the studio.

'. . . you would spend time again, later, in the shed.'

'Of course. That'd be all right. I wouldn't kick up a fuss.'

Roy grinned. 'No, I don't believe you would. And, just for the record, I couldn't be more pleased with the way you've buckled to, and with the patterns you're turning out now.'

It was arranged that she would spend that day creeling for

Dennis Jagger, but the following morning she would occupy a place in the studio.

Laura was so excited that she hardly slept that night. But she was too elated to notice any tiredness as she cycled to the mill next morning.

Roy took her along to the design studio, and re-introduced her to her future colleagues. The man in charge, Wayland Rogers, was a flamboyant character, with dark wavy hair, eyes that matched, and an eccentric style that emphasised his artistic leanings. His shirt was more yellow than cream and he sported a brown velvet bow shades darker than his rather loud suit.

Very Noël Coward, thought Laura, and had to suppress her amusement. It wouldn't do to put his back up, not when he was in charge here.

'You've met the others, I believe,' he said, languidly, and did not offer to remind her of anyone's name. 'You're over there.' He pointed a long finger in the direction of the darkest corner.

Laura had been thinking how nice and bright the studio was. It would need to be and all or she'd not see the point paper, let alone the colours she was applying to it. Still, she was beginning at last on the work at which she'd been determined to succeed – she'd not let niggling little difficulties spoil her day.

'Good morning,' she said, settling into her corner and glancing sideways at her neighbour. 'I'm Laura, in case you've forgotten, Laura Crabtree.'

'Yes,' said the rather attractive young man with red hair cut very short and a smart navy blue suit. His manners appeared less attractive and did not run to reminding her of his name. He didn't look up either. If he was aiming to convince himself that she did not exist he was making a good shot at it.

Roy had left as soon as he'd seen her heading for her seat. She wished already that he'd hung on a bit. She would have asked him to refresh her memory about all their names. She'd only been in here the once before and couldn't be expected to recall them all, especially when she'd met so many other folk since then.

'Is that yours?'

Startled, Laura glanced up from the crimson water colour she was already painting in on the design in front of her. Wayland Rogers was standing staring at her brush. He was tapping one foot.

'That's right.'

Even when Laura spoke and looked up at him, he didn't meet her eyes.

'Oh no, lovey – you can't do that, not for ages yet. This is what you should be doing. Put that away, there's a good girl.'

Humiliated, but not wishing to protest that Mr Lindley had approved what she was tackling, Laura pushed aside her own design.

'You're to work on these.' Wayland Rogers presented her with a batch of original drafts and a supply of point paper. 'You know what to do, I take it?'

'Copy them.'

'There's a clever girl.'

Laura held her breath or she'd have sighed out loud. She flicked through the designs he had given her, chiefly to see how interesting they were. They were not. They looked old, neglected.

'If there's any you can't manage to copy, Angus will explain how.'

Angus, it seemed, was the man sitting in front of her. Even from behind, everything about his brown bullet-shaped head was dour. She could only be thankful that the work, so lacking in complexity that it would bore her, would require no explaining.

Although the rest of the team talked and laughed quietly as they worked, no one spoke to her during the rest of the morning. When the hands of her watch eventually registered twelve o'clock, Laura turned towards the red-haired fellow.

'What time do we go to the canteen?' she enquired.

'Lunch is twelve-thirty, but *we* don't patronise the canteen.'

'Thanks.' She ignored the dig. There's one here who does, she thought, desperate for a breather.

Laura was glad to see Amos sitting at a table near the window, and headed towards him when she had chosen her meal.

'How are you getting on?' he asked.

'Oh, all right, thanks.' She hadn't the heart to admit how much her first taste of the studio had disillusioned her. 'Did you get your frying pan on Saturday?'

'Aye – a right champion one. Just the size for me on my own. I haven't tried it out yet, mind. Emma would have me go back for a bite to eat with her.'

'That was nice.'

'It was that! She's a real good cook, not that you'd suppose otherwise with her working in here.'

'So you didn't mind for once not doing your own cooking?'

'Mind? Don't talk daft. I'm glad I can fend for myself when I have to, but it's a treat to be looked after like that.'

'And I'll bet Emma's glad not to be left on her own as much, with the anxiety she has at present.'

'I daresay. Although now the lad's improving she can relax a bit. 'Specially now she's got rather more security.'

'Yes, I'm pleased about the compensation.'

'Eh, I don't mean only that,' Amos corrected her. 'I advised her to tell the boy's dad that it were time he contributed to their needs on a regular basis. And he's coughing up, an' all – and so he should, he's worth a mint o' money.'

Laura could tell that Amos was enjoying looking after the Appleyards' interests. Had he always, perhaps, liked Emma? He confirmed this while he tackled treacle pudding and custard.

'Me and her used to reckon we were sweethearts in the Infants', you know. It were a bit of nonsense, I suppose, at that age, but I kept an eye on her for a long time afterwards. She was a gradely lass in them days. Trouble was other lads saw that, as well. She were never short of somebody to walk out with. And then she met him. For a long time, I reckoned I'd have no more to do with her. Well, she should have had more sense, if not more about her. She knew he'd a wife and family, that there was no future in it.'

Laura pushed away her plate, all appetite vanished. This was how decent folk thought about women who became too friendly with men who were married. She didn't want Amos, or anybody else, thinking of her in this way. She would have to be careful about Patrick Horsfall.

'Any road,' Amos continued pensively, 'I've always said as them that make no mistakes don't make anything.'

Determined not to be late back from the canteen, Laura was the first to return to the studio that dinnertime. Interested to discover what kind of designs the others were turning out and if her own could compete, she paused beside one of the desks to look. The pattern was in the modern geometrical style that didn't appeal to her, but she could recognise how skilfully it was interpreted.

'Do you mind, that is mine!'

Laura had been too fascinated to hear anybody approaching. Now the man whom she seemed to remember as Henry something was at her side, seizing the point paper and turning it face down.

'What did you want to do that for? I was only admiring it.'

He shrugged lean shoulders.

'I am here to learn,' Laura reminded him. 'How am I going to do that if nobody lets me see what's expected of us?'

'You'll learn nowt from me, think on. And you're in my way. Can't get to my chair.'

The rest of the group were no more kindly disposed towards her, and Wayland Rogers himself took scarcely any more notice of her presence. Laura was thoroughly dejected by the time she got ready for home that evening. Halfway across the mill yard she bumped into Roy Lindley.

'Laura – what's wrong? I thought you'd be full of yourself today.'

'So did I. I'm afraid I'm not very welcome in the design studio. Do you remember that first week I said I wondered if they were frightened of losing their jobs?'

'Making things unpleasant, are they? I'm sorry to hear that, Laura, but I'm sure this will only be temporary. Give them time to get accustomed to having somebody new there.'

'And somebody female,' she added grimly.

'I don't suppose that helps.'

'The work isn't like I expected either. I thought you said they all worked individually on their own designs?'

'So they do.'

'Aye, well – Mr Rogers stopped me, told me to put mine away. He's given me some ancient drafts to copy. They look to me like stuff that's been abandoned.'

'Oh.' Roy gazed down at her, sorry the spirit he admired was being crushed. 'I expect he only wants to discover your capabilities.'

'But you showed him my work, didn't you?'

'Most of it, yes. But he does need to know how you get on in that environment. I can only suggest that you put on a brave front and tackle whatever you're given. For the first few weeks, at least. If things get no better, I might intervene on your behalf, but I'd rather not.'

'I'd rather you didn't, an' all.' She could imagine the reaction afterwards. 'I wouldn't have said owt to you if you hadn't asked.'

'Then just remember that I'm on your side. And I believe you have it in you to make a go of this, regardless of problems.'

'Thank you.'

Walking away to collect her bike Laura felt glad she'd had a word with Roy Lindley. As soon as he'd stopped all that silly flattery she'd begun to respect his knowledge of the carpet business. And even if she wouldn't run complaining to him, knowing he would listen was reassuring.

The following morning, Laura cycled to the mill determined to cut through the designers' prejudice. She said a bright 'Good morning' from the studio door, and made herself smile round at them all.

Wayland Rogers was the only person who replied, although

the chap who sat in front of her mumbled something.

Laura was resolved, though, that nothing they did would deter her. She had got herself into the only place where she wished to work, and was darned if their attitude would drive her out.

By the Friday afternoon, however, her resolve was ebbing. No one, Mr Rogers included, spoke to her unless there was cause. And she was still plodding through the wearisome copying of those old patterns which, she suspected, weren't even going to be used. By the time she left the canteen that dinnertime, she could think of nothing but the fact that it was Friday. Tomorrow, she only worked half the day and then she'd be free of the place until Monday.

None of the others was sitting down when she walked back into the studio. They all were standing over near the windows, grouped round the red-haired chap who was holding forth.

'We can strike of course, stand firm. We're only sticking up for our jobs, after all. Strike action is justified . . .'

Just for a minute, Laura felt immensely relieved. Their discontent had been nothing to do with her: they had some other grievance, something big – so big that they were threatening to down tools.

One of them saw her then. 'She's here.'

'I don't give a damn! I'll say owt to her face. She's no right coming from nowhere, taking our work.'

'Excuse me,' Laura began, hurrying towards them, 'I'm just about fed up of this.'

'You know what to do then, lass,' the man called Angus snapped. 'We were right enough till you came. Nothing personal, mind – but there's only just sufficient work for the five of us.'

'I don't accept that,' she argued. 'The Lindleys aren't daft, they'd never have set me on if they couldn't use me.'

'Happen he fancied having a blonde around,' one of them suggested to the red-haired ring leader. 'You know what Roy's like.'

'He certainly didn't need to take her on for owt else . . .'

'What's going on now?'

Turning, Laura was thankful to see Wayland Rogers, not that she felt he'd give her much support, but he would quell the rebellion.

'Having a bit of a squabble, are we? Now we don't want that, do we?'

Despite his effeminate manner, they evidently knew he could be firm, and everyone returned to their seats. During the afternoon, Mr Rogers disappeared for half an hour. When he reappeared, he took Laura to one side.

'I've been having a discussion with Mr Roy, lovey. He needs you in the weaving shed, just for tomorrow morning. All right?'

It will have to be all right, won't it? thought Laura, fuming. Roy was the boss, and could compel her to work wherever he thought fit – or even remove her from Lindley's Carpets altogether.

Chapter 9

Roy Lindley was very understanding that morning, explaining to Laura that he considered it wiser to remove her from the studio, for the half day, leaving the other designers to sort themselves out.

'Wayland Rogers is no fool, you know,' he assured her. 'And the men do respect him. Unfortunately, your being there is like the red rag to the proverbial bull at present. Once he's cooled them down they'll accept you all right, and that'll be for good.'

I wonder, she thought. She was beginning to realise how badly the slump had affected the West Riding, making men insecure in their jobs. They did seem intransigent, and Mr Rogers himself no more friendly towards her. What could she do, though, but carry out Roy's wishes?

The only good thing was working with Dennis again. And he worked her hard, keeping her going with fetching and carrying, looking after the coloured spools. And then, just before finishing time, he let her have a go at weaving.

Although Dennis had been friendly to her and she couldn't deny that Roy had sounded very reasonable in his earlier explanation, Laura still felt raw with anxiety as she pedalled back to Hanson Road.

It had been stifling and humid in the shed; out in the open she glanced ruefully towards the clouds gathering about the surrounding hills. Laura tried to cycle more quickly, but long before she reached 'Bien-être' she was drenched, and the rain running in rivers over the setts beneath her wheels was treacherous.

'Eh, lass, you're wet through! Come on in.' Miss Priestley had the door open for her as soon as Laura placed the bike in the shed.

'Do you want a hot bath before you have your dinner?'

'A bath would be lovely. That's very thoughtful of you.'

'You go on up then, there's plenty of water. I'll keep your dinner warm a bit longer, it's fish pie today.'

The telephone rang while Laura was dressing. When she went downstairs again Miss Priestley told her Patrick Horsfall wanted her to ring him back. I hope that isn't something going wrong with the purchase of the house, she thought, made uneasy by the week's disappointments.

'Hallo, Laura – good news. I've just received word that everything is in order now regarding the Coach House. Fix a date for moving in. In fact, if you wish, you could come over later today. Bring a few provisions and so on.'

'Oh, thank goodness for that! I've had such an awful week I was afraid something would go wrong about the house.'

'Be assured nothing will – I wouldn't let that happen.'

'I'll be there sometime after tea then. See you later.'

'You're leaving before long, aren't you?' Miss Priestley said, coming out of her sitting-room as Laura replaced the receiver. Her lips were drawn into a taut line, the pale eyes veiled.

Laura smiled sympathetically. 'Very soon, yes. I've got to make arrangements for them to deliver the furniture I've bought, but that's all that I'll have to see to. So it all depends really on how much notice you want me to give you . . .'

'I feel like keeping you here another month, but I won't do that, lass. You have your life to live, it's not your fault I'm on my own.'

'We shall keep in touch,' Laura reminded her. 'You've been a good friend to me just when I needed one, I shan't forget. Tell you what – come with me tonight, and have a look.'

'No, I – no, not tonight, I think I've got a bit of a head coming on. But don't go worriting about leaving here, make your arrangements then just let me know.'

By the time Laura had shopped for groceries and collected

154

together the utensils she could carry, she was feeling elated about her new home. She was still smarting, though, from the treatment she'd received at the mill. When she sat on the hard seat of the tram taking her into town she realised that she ached all over. But the prospect of seeing Patrick increased her happiness about the house at Arncliffe. Hearing his voice had reminded her of the added bonus of living where he'd be her near neighbour. The fact of his marriage seemed to concern her less. Maybe he ought never to have kissed her, but she doubted if that would happen again. He was in charge of the Yorkshire West Building Society, wasn't he, and he owned Arncliffe Hall. He wasn't likely ever to be more than a friend.

I'm just thankful he isn't another Roy Lindley, she reflected, changing in Halfield from the tram on to a bus. Patrick wasn't full of a lot of smarmy talk, was he? Quite the reverse. He tended to keep his feelings under tight rein, so much so that his eyes took on that distant look, locking her out.

Mrs Harrison his housekeeper answered the door. 'Mr Horsfall says to tell you he won't be long. He's trying to get through to somebody on the telephone. Would you like to take them things through to the Coach House while you're waiting?'

'Aye, thanks, I think I'd better. They're that heavy.'

Laura had brought along several pans as well as cutlery and some of the crockery she had purchased a week ago. With the weight of sugar, butter, and other provisions as well she'd hardly been able to stagger from the bus.

'You look pretty wet, an' all,' Mrs Harrison remarked, bustling beside her as they headed through towards Laura's new home. 'You might as well finish with being out in that lot, then I'll show you where to hang your stuff to dry.'

Mrs Harrison left her stowing her possessions in the kitchen. When she had finished, Laura stood for a while, gazing from the window. Recalling Beth's sudden appearance out there, she ached with longing to hold the child. To love her and encourage her, until she ceased that awful withdrawal. Today, though, she herself was drained. She doubted that she possessed any ability to get through to the girl.

Laura heard the front door opening and thought Mrs Harrison had come back for her, until she heard the footsteps. Even over the hall carpet she recognised Patrick's approach.

They reached the kitchen doorway simultaneously, from either side. Laura was so glad to see him that she could have hugged him.

He handed her a batch of documents. 'Be sure and keep those safe, they state that this place is yours. And here – your keys.'

'Thank you very much.'

She beamed at him, saw how tired his brown eyes looked tonight, the shadows beneath them. Her entire being surged with a sudden longing to draw him to her and make up for the awful problems in his life.

Patrick remained a foot or so away, placed the keys in her palm, and closed her fingers over them. Briefly, his hand enveloped hers, and was withdrawn.

'Have you much more to see to in here?' he asked.

'Not really, not tonight. And, anyway, I was just thinking I couldn't offer you anywhere to sit.'

'We'll go to my study, if that's all right with you? I'm waiting for an important call.'

'Sure, that's fine,' Laura responded, wondering what was required of her now. She wished she was accustomed to mixing with people like Patrick instead of feeling rather in awe of him.

He was pensive as they hastened through the main house again. There was too much to say to her, and no means of beginning. Their embrace the other evening had been as premature as it had been unpremeditated. Afterwards, he had thought his behaviour inexcusable. He knew, didn't he, that he was in no position even to contemplate making love to anyone but Magda, just as surely as he felt that Laura would not take kisses lightly. No amount of yearning could justify attempting to assuage this hunger.

The beige raincoat about her shoulders revealed glimpses of a silky dress, a green so pale that it reminded him of

156

tender plants newly emerged into light. Her fragrance was delicate, too, summery as the day would have been without its storms, innocent as she must remain.

'Had a good week?' he asked, trying for safer ground.

Laura snorted. 'A bit disillusioning, really. My first in the design studio. Should have been marvellous. Instead, I met a lot of resistance.' Can't you see I need reassuring? she thought, wishing he would do something.

You're hurt, my dear, he realised. Yet I must not even touch you. 'When are you moving in?' he asked instead.

Laura smiled. 'Not sure yet – when I've got them to deliver my furniture.'

'You don't have to give notice to your landlady?'

She told him what Miss Priestley had said, and how awful she felt about leaving her on her own again.

'She could always take another paying guest.'

'I hope she will. It's not good folk having so little company.'

As they went into his study Patrick took her coat and hung it to dry. Laura smiled and thanked him.

'I wish I could drive you home,' he said. 'But . . .'

'Eh, there's no need,' said Laura hastily. What must he think of her, believing she might expect that of him?

'I know,' Patrick told her, affectionate amusement sparkling in his brown eyes. 'And I would have liked to do so, just the same. But I'm waiting for someone from the Salvation Army to phone me back.'

The Sally Army? Laura was astounded.

Patrick nodded. The light left his eyes, and he sighed. He might as well tell her, he supposed, bring the matter into the open. It mattered not that he could scarcely force himself to speak *her* name. Wasn't this the opportunity he wanted – to assure Laura of his intention?

He cleared his throat. 'As you may be aware, they can assist in tracing missing persons. I have a contact there who has been making enquiries about – about Magda.'

Laura shivered. She glanced away from him, down at the lovely carpet, and shivered again. Fixing a smile on to frozen lips, she compelled her gaze to find his while he continued.

'I believe I told you my wife isn't here. I have to find out the truth . . .'

'Of course,' she said very quickly. 'I – I was only surprised it was the Salvation Army you'd asked. Wouldn't the police be more help?'

At the word 'police' he went pale and rigid like the statues she'd seen in the People's Park. She hoped he hadn't got anything to hide from the police. What had Michael said about him?

'They aren't terribly interested in an adult of sound mind who disappears – that, seemingly, is anyone's prerogative.'

The telephone rang and Laura was wondering how to respond. She offered to wait outside, but Patrick motioned her to remain.

Evidently the call was the one he expected. Laura listened uncomfortably to his end of the conversation, wishing she was anywhere but here. She tried glancing about the room, but because it was so fine everything else seemed all the more harsh. How must he feel when this fabulous home was totally spoiled because his wife had disappeared? The stress of having that happen must make you want to do something drastic. Was it any wonder that he had turned to her?

Patrick's words over the phone and his grim expression left Laura in no doubt that the outcome was fruitless.

'No luck?' she asked sympathetically.

'Not a thing. They will continue the search, but . . . Oh, let's talk of something more cheerful. How's the designing coming along?'

Laura stared. Hadn't he heard what she'd said earlier, or could he dismiss her appalling week that easily? She supposed that he would. Compared with a missing partner, her problems were insignificant.

'Haven't really got my teeth into it yet,' she said. And since he was clearly in no position to offer either encouragement or the concern for which she had longed, there wasn't much point in staying another minute. She felt disappointed in her visit to Arncliffe. Even to herself, she hadn't been able to specify what she'd expected to find here, all she did know was that she hadn't found it.

Now that he had received the telephone call, Patrick insisted on driving Laura home through the downpour that seemed worse out here amid the open countryside. Although grateful, she remained uneasy with him. His lack of attention to all that she'd said about her job had only proved how little he thought about the things that mattered to her.

Patrick felt gloom returning. Laura wasn't interested in him, he decided. As soon as she was beside him in the car, he had sensed her coolness. The traffic was very light, almost non-existent, permitting too much opportunity for thinking. She appeared distant with him now, almost as if she resented his trying to locate Magda. But how otherwise could he right the wrongs in that sham of a marriage?

Perhaps he was the one who had misunderstood the friendliness which from the first had emanated from Laura? That he had misread her seemed clear now, even to someone of his judgement – which he sensed tonight was far less astute than he had believed.

He felt diminished by his own incomprehension. Laura was an engaging young woman, that was all, with a ready smile and far more warmth than most of his contemporaries. Because she had enthused about living so near to him, had seemed so eager to share with him her zest for the future, he'd been fool enough to read more into their swift-growing affinity. But what of her response to his kiss? She had neither withdrawn from his arms nor seemed afterwards to be dismayed by its fervour.

Covertly, Laura glanced sideways at his face which might have been carved of alabaster. Why hadn't he let her go home by bus? Even the long walk down the Arncliffe drive in the rain would have been preferable to enduring his silence. I can't help it, she wordlessly asserted into the unease between them in the car's luxurious interior. The pleasing smell of good leather upholstery did nothing to make her feel at ease. All she could think was how out of place she was here – that Patrick was resenting the fact that she was around, while his wife was not. Thank goodness she had realised earlier that she ought not to attach importance to that embrace!

But despite all her rationalising, deep inside her a voice was insisting that she should cease to resist him. The impulse had been growing with every meeting, scaring her because it felt so strong. No man she'd ever met had made her feel such attraction and, inexperienced though she was, she understood how wrong it was to have this awakened by a man who was married.

Outside 'Bien-être', Patrick slowed the car and parked. Was it only earlier today that he had planned to speak of his feelings? Yet already Laura was freezing his words before he managed to form them. He must learn to stifle the longing which after years of feeling nothing for any woman had seemed like rejuvenation.

He couldn't quite contain every emotion. Before he let her go, he slid an arm across her shoulders, squeezed them. 'Goodnight, Laura.'

Her reply was swift, as were her thanks for the ride. She was out of his car and dashing towards the terraced house before the dull emptiness overtook him.

Patrick drove home by a different route, avoiding the town in order to give vent to the emotions urging him to speed. Still agonised by yearning, he parked the car and strode into the house.

Mrs Harrison met him in the hall. 'I've still got your meal keeping hot, Mr Patrick. Will you have it now?'

'No, thank you, Mrs Harrison – not hungry. You know what business lunches are.' He felt her dart him a curious look, realised it was Saturday, that he'd spent the entire day here. For once, she must think what she would. He was beyond explaining. From somewhere, he resurrected a smile. 'Give your Tom a good supper, eh? From the way the gardens are looking, he's earned something extra.'

As she turned away from him, he asked if there was anything else.

'Miss Beth wouldn't settle. In the end, I just had to leave her and hope that she would.'

Sighing, he took the stairs two at a time, walked soundlessly to the room where dread more than delight so often overtook him. He was in no mood tonight for this encounter.

Beth, however, was sleeping peacefully, her cheeks flushed now so that they appeared less waxen, pleasantly pink against the white embroidered pillow. The spread of long fair hair was soft beneath his fingers. Seeing her like this, he might pretend all was well. It seemed less likely that he could pretend anything similar about himself.

Back in Hanson Road, Laura had hurried up the front steps, then swung round to wave Patrick off. But he'd been busy turning the car, she couldn't tell if he even looked her way before disappearing.

Sighing, she fumbled in her handbag for her key. As she inserted it in the lock, though, she saw the door was already slightly ajar. Someone was standing there, with the lobby light switched off so that only the glimmer from the living-room silhouetted the dark form.

Laura's heart began hammering. It could be a burglar. There was no sign of Miss Priestley, was there? No light from her quarters.

A hand grasped Laura by the shoulder. 'I thought you were never coming home.'

'You daft thing! You frightened me to death, Michael.'

'And what do you think you've done to me? For days now, I've been wanting to see you.'

'You'll see me tomorrow in church.'

'And if that's as much use as the past few occasions . . .'

'Oh, Michael, I'm absolutely done up. If you're here to quarrel . . .'

'Anything but,' he interrupted. 'Don't be a little silly.'

'I've only been over to the house, love.'

'So Miss Priestley said.' Did she really believe that made him feel any the better? 'Did it have to be today, in that deluge?'

'I didn't use the bike. And Mr Horsfall brought me home.'

'Do you think I don't know?'

So that was it. That was why Michael was so flaming mad. He'd been watching. Somewhere inside her mind a demon labelled it spying. Nay, calling it that is sick, she thought. He's not like that.

'Would you come inside now, into the living-room?'

His voice was ominously quiet, controlled. Laura saw neither sense nor reason in arguing.

'You could have told me, Laura,' he reproached, his hazel eyes aglow with anger.

'Told you what?' she asked, winning a bit of time for thinking.

It wasn't long enough. 'That there's something going on between you and Horsfall. Don't go trying to make out there isn't – I'm neither daft nor so immature I can't recognise what you're doing.'

'I'm not doing owt. And nor is he.' Nobody would ever learn either that she had wished for that short while that the chance of a relationship between them wasn't utterly remote. 'He doesn't even care about the dreadful week I've had.'

'I wish I could be sure of that. You must realise you're asking for an affair, going to live on that estate and him on his own. You'll get yourself talked about.'

'Nay, love – Patrick doesn't even listen to half I say.'

Michael was beginning to believe her, to read in her shadowed eyes and exhaustion that he shouldn't be worrying that she'd been enjoying herself.

'A bad time at work, you say?' he asked, seizing on one way in which she seemed to need him. 'Want to talk about it?'

Laura was far too tired to face even thinking about the other designers. She shook her head. 'Not just now.'

'You don't have to work at designing, you know, love. You don't have to look any further than me for understanding either.'

He pulled her roughly against him. His body felt hard to her, demanding.

'I love you, Laura, you should know that. I have right from the start. I love you, and need you. And you're driving me out of my wits!'

His mouth clamped over hers, his arms locked about her, straining her to him. Deep in his throat he groaned.

'I wish you wouldn't,' Laura began against his lips.

Michael seemed not to hear. His tongue plunged between her teeth, explored her mouth, the intensity of his kiss threatened to choke her. His fingers stirred over her back.

'I think you'd better stop,' Laura said firmly when he paused to gasp in breath. 'Miss Priestley could come in, any minute.'

'Wrong, love – she went to bed an hour ago, with a headache.' And he was sick to death of Laura failing to understand the extent of his feelings.

But she had had enough. Pushing with all her strength, she forced Michael away from her. She might not have been out with many young men, but she'd done a lot of growing up since arriving in Halfield. If only through finding out that men could fancy her, and watching what attraction did to other folk.

Just the other day she had called on Emma Appleyard. The house had been clean enough, but such a tiny place, darkened by the overshadowing mill across the street. Emma only had a flagged square at the cellar head to serve as a kitchen, with a stone sink and a tiny gas ring.

Emma had always lived for Geoff and the carpet factory. Anybody could see there'd been nothing else for her. She'd told Laura of her father who'd been a weaver at Lindley's and had thrown her out, disgraced. There had seemed to Laura no situation more awful.

'Marry me, love, I need you,' Michael urged.

But even that wouldn't compensate for what she'd be required to give up. If ever I marry, she thought, it'll have to be for a love so overwhelming that I've got to be with that person, always. I need more than attraction, more even than what you see as love, Michael. 'I've so much still to do,' she protested. There was her work. She also needed a place where

163

she would belong. And no matter how much it saddened her, Michael didn't make her feel she would find that with him.

He sighed. 'This is how much I love you,' he told her abruptly, turned, walked from the room and was gone.

Laura listened to his footsteps departing along the silent street. As the night absorbed every last sound, she thought again of Emma Appleyard. She understood a bit more now of how Geoff might have been conceived. If a woman was reasonably attractive she was bound to evoke some sort of a reaction in a man. She couldn't think that Ainley chap would ever have had much of a conscience about taking what he wanted. And Emma, bless her, wouldn't have had the guts to stand up to him.

Thank goodness I've enough spirit to look after myself, Laura thought. But she still felt upset that Michael was the person she seemed destined to refuse. Whatever happened now, there'd be no going back to behaving as if they were the pals they'd always been.

It's not me that's ruined our friendship, though, Laura realised. And wasn't consoled. Being confronted with Michael's passion had brought her up sharp. Maybe he had been justified in always treating her as if she wasn't quite grown up. Until recently she certainly had behaved like a kid.

At least tonight's encounter had made her realise that Michael could never be the man for her. But it didn't help when all the while the person who interested her was frantically searching for his missing wife.

Laura had never been more disturbed, had never felt at the same time so exhausted and so alarmed that she could not sleep. There was only one way she knew of distracting her mind, she would have to get down to some work.

All night long she struggled with her latest design, painting in vivid colour, counting squares, trying to remove from her mind all thoughts of Michael, and of Patrick Horsfall. Patrick's image was the more resistant to her will, for with the night hours her sense of the hopelessness of their circumstances waned. She no longer tried to dismiss the idea of a future in which Patrick figured.

And the design would not come right. No matter how hard she tried, she could not get one side to balance with the other. If this was woven there'd be no pattern match. Still she pressed on, determined not to be beaten. And all the while she ached, no longer from the shock Michael had given her, but to find some means of establishing a relationship with Patrick.

The downpour had ceased by dawn. As she gathered together her paints and brushes, Laura glanced again at her design, took it to the window where the early light glistened on remaining raindrops. Yet again, she counted the squares that she had coloured in. Silently, she swore. Damn and blast it! She had calculated on twenty-eight inches not the standard twenty-seven.

The prospect of seeing Michael in church today didn't make Laura feel any better either. She could stay away, of course, attend a different church . . .

Suddenly, though, she realised that she would face him. Today. Somehow, last night's experience had admitted her to a tough new world. If she was mature enough to experience all these emotions, she'd better begin proving that she could face up to reality.

She knew in her heart that she could keep calm when she had to – could conceal her inner anxiety. By facing Michael today she would set the pattern of their future relationship.

Nevertheless she felt nervous as, wearing her navy blue costume, she walked towards St Martin's.

Smile, Laura, she commanded herself as the church came in sight. She was accustomed already to other parishioners being over-interested in her because of her friendship with their organist. Nothing in her behaviour must betray any hint of unease.

Michael was waiting for her just inside the double wrought-iron gates. She'd never felt more thankful. Didn't that mean he was going to apologise for such uncharacteristic behaviour? It would be all right. Even before she went into church, it would all be over. Forgiving him would be easy, as well as granting anything that he was likely to request. Because she knew Michael really and somehow he could again become the person she trusted more than anyone.

Poor Michael. As she drew nearer she saw how anxious he was, how sad his eyes. She was almost inclined to tell him he needn't say anything, but something must remove this embarrassment between them.

'Laura,' he began, stepping forward, bending his head with all that lovely brown hair, 'bad news, I'm afraid.'

He grasped her arm, his touch gentle.

'Your mother telephoned me so I might tell you carefully. I'm afraid your father's boat is overdue, love.'

'No!' Staring into the troubled hazel eyes, she shook her head over and over again. 'How – how long overdue?'

'She didn't say.' It wasn't the truth, but he'd be excused that. He'd never intended relaying the hysteria of the woman at the other end of the line whose only redeeming action had been speaking first to him. Laura had a journey to make, and he could not be spared today to go with her. Time enough for her to learn the truth when she arrived safely in Whitby.

'There's a train in an hour. I've arranged a lift for you. Clem Hargreaves and his sister. They know what's happened, will take you to pick up a few things, and to the station.'

Laura thanked him dazedly, watched from outside herself as she was taken by Clem and Millie, first to 'Bien-être' and then to catch her train.

Crossing the echoing wooden footbridge at Halfield station she tried to express her gratitude for their economical words of concern, for their caring. Tears tightened her throat, though, and threatened to spill over. And she couldn't do with that. Whitby today seemed much further from Halfield than she had thought. And she must arrive in a state fit for taking charge.

'Aye, lass, we know,' said Clem, leaning with one hand on his stick, the other resting on her shoulder. 'Take care now, think on. Remember us both to your mother and the girls, tell them we're thinking on 'em. And mind you let us know how things are,' he added, before limping away to join his sister who waited at the wheel of their old-fashioned Austin.

There are some lovely people who've made it easy for me to settle here, thought Laura, hurrying down the steps to the platform. I just wish I could believe that nothing would prevent me from coming back.

Chapter 10

Whitby looked strange to her already, no longer the home town where she had lived for so long. It was raining as if to dissolve the land into the grey sea thrusting and churning against the quay.

The gaunt Victorian house overlooking the harbour was empty. Laura wasn't surprised, even felt rather relieved. Wherever Mum was, their Greta, Sybil and Netta would be looking after her. Mrs Tomlinson next door generally had a key, she'd better fetch it so she could leave her case inside.

She had been seen, their neighbour met her at her own door. 'Eh, Laura lass, it's a bad do . . .'

'Any news, Mrs Tomlinson?'

'Not as I've heard. They've been down yonder since first light.'

The fishing community could never keep away from the harbour whenever there was trouble out at sea. So many times they had waited with the families of other men when boats were overdue; always believing you knew how it would feel, never acknowledging you could one day learn first hand.

'I'll have to go and join them.'

'Leave your things with me, love. I'll take 'em in next door.'

The grey setts were slithery with rain, but Laura managed somehow to keep her feet as she ran down the slope towards the quayside. She felt torn apart – aching to be with her family yet dreading seeing the anguish which, until now, in herself she had kept subdued. Getting here without giving in to the distress heaving inside her like the North Sea out there had been her only consideration. There'd be time now for thinking. Like as not far too much time.

The women were grouped near her father's boathouse. From here they appeared to be dressed uniformly in black, the older ones shrouded in woollen shawls. Only as she came nearer could Laura distinguish the browns and navy blues of individual hats and coats, eventually her mother's maroon.

Maggie Crabtree, smaller than average, seemed further diminished by twenty-four hours' anxiety. Her ashen face blurred before Laura as her own eyes filled with tears.

'I knew you'd come. Eh, love!'

Even through their substantial raincoats, her mother's bones protruded as Laura hugged her.

'What happened, Mum?'

'He were due back night afore last. When he hadn't come home by morning I knew there were summat wrong.'

'They've been late before, many a time.'

'What have I said? I knew there was summat up!' She gestured with her head towards the waves shooting twenty feet into the leaden sky before crashing down. 'That's nowt up to what it has been. Blessed weather.'

'Dad's been out in worse before now.'

'Aye, aye.'

Her mother wouldn't, *couldn't* be comforted. Laura glanced around. 'Where are the girls?'

'Greta and Sybil went for a cup of tea.'

'And Netta?'

'Over there.'

Laura saw her sister then, leaning against a wall, one hand up to her head. On either side of her were Edie and Brenda Summers, wife and daughter of Harry Crabtree's coxswain. Trust their Netta!

'I won't be a minute, Mum.'

'Don't be hard on her.'

Laura stifled a snort. Swiftly, she skirted the subdued gathering, strode through the lashing rain towards her sister.

'Netta.' The girl's dark head jerked up. Laura wasn't

deterred. 'Couldn't one of you have stayed with our mother?'

'Hallo, Laura. I did stay, only I suddenly came over faint.'

'It's her poorly time,' Mrs Summers announced.

'We all have to contend with the curse,' said Laura sharply, sickened by the dawning realisation that even this crisis hadn't made their Netta any less self-absorbed.

'You know I always have a grim time.'

Laura sighed, turned to the coxswain's wife. 'It's a bad business, Mrs Summers. I'm right sorry your Ben is out there an' all.'

'At least I have two lads. They're strong – unbelievably so for seventeen and eighteen.'

'And not in fishing.'

'Thank God,' Brenda Summers said, and turned to Netta. 'Are you feeling a bit better now, love?'

'Not so much.'

It's always her that's helpless, thought Laura, looking back over the years. Aye, and the other two were about as much use, as well. She wondered how long they had taken over having a cup of tea.

'Have you been for something to drink?' she asked Netta, trying hard not to sound as impatient as she felt.

'Not yet.'

'You'd better go along then. And take a Cephos for your pain.'

'I'll be sick if I do.'

'I'm going back to stand with Mum,' said Laura.

Her own throat was parched and her stomach churning on nothing. Being Sunday, she hadn't been able to buy a drink all the way from Halfield; her last meal was breakfast.

Mrs Summers walked back with her into the pathetic gathering, leaving her daughter to escort Netta to the corner cafe.

'The lifeboat's been out and back several times, seen nothing. And the one from Filey as well. The Scarborough lifeboat's out somewhere else, I heard tell, a wreck off Flamborough Head.'

171

'Why do they do it, Auntie Edie?' Laura asked, despairingly, reverting to her childhood name for her mother's old friend. 'It's not for the brass.' Her father never managed to make much profit.

'Born into it, weren't they? Both Ben and your dad.'

'Aye.'

Her mother seemed to have shrunk even further, lost in the stout maroon raincoat which must be heavier than ever from hours in this downpour. Laura put an arm across her shoulders and hugged her.

Tears pricked at her eyes again, and she stared into space – away from the sea. She couldn't bear the sight of that.

Over to her right, she recognised Greta and Sybil chatting to a pair of lads unsuitably dressed in cricket flannels that clung to their legs with wet, and fancy pullovers.

'They're only young, Laura.'

She didn't know her mother had noticed them. 'Some folk don't want to grow up. Have them three got jobs yet?'

'That isn't all that easy, you know. They have tried, all of 'em. Not much of a future in lots of the work round here.'

But it would bring in a few pounds. Keep them occupied, as well. If, God forbid, *if* Dad didn't come back, they'd have to buckle to and start earning. They needed a big house, with them three all insisting on having their own bedrooms: somebody would have to think about keeping what they'd got.

'How've you been, Mother, apart from this?'

'How do you think? Run off my feet, morning till night. Even the washing and ironing takes best part of a week, without cleaning or making meals.'

And them never lifting a finger. This, though, wasn't the time for saying anything.

'But we'll manage now, Laura love. Now you're here. Even if . . . even whatever.'

It wasn't the moment, either, to announce that she wasn't remaining.

'You're always so capable, Laura, always have been. I'm that proud of you. Your father is an' all – said so that time when

172

I'd been in hospital. And you know he isn't one for saying much.'

That was true enough. Laura pictured her father, hair almost as fair as her own, blue sailor's eyes, the skin at their corners crinkled by the wind and by staring towards the horizon. She loved him fiercely, always had, but he never encouraged too much sentiment. His relationship with her mother certainly wasn't nourished by words. She wondered sometimes if he had more in common with that enigmatic expanse of water.

Around them the group shifted from time to time, breaking and reforming. Crew members' wives commiserating with each other, borne up by neighbours drawn here by common concern. Except for Edie Summers, Laura and her mother seemed a little apart, maybe because of Harry Crabtree being the boss. Laura wondered, briefly, if they held him to blame.

There was no need to ask how long they would stand out here by the harbour, enveloped in the smell of fish and of the sea. She knew the answer. The women didn't go home until they had news. There could be no turning their backs on the water, on their menfolk.

When Greta and Sybil returned she would get her mother to come with her to the cafe. They'd have to force something down. If the worst came to the worst, they'd need to be strong for what must follow. If he did come back he'd need attention, feeding up, plenty of rest.

'Laura!' Her other two sisters had approached while she was deep in thought. Together, they beamed. 'Mum said you'd come back to Whitby now,' Sybil told her.

'Couldn't stay away, could I? Not with this happening.'

'You'll see we're all right, even if . . .' Greta's blue eyes filled, and she fluttered the ridiculously long black lashes possessed by all the triplets.

Again, Laura recognised that she must keep silent about the future. They all were hoping against hope that their father would come home, weren't they? No good yet upsetting everybody by discussing contingencies.

'Come along, Mother, time we dried off a bit in that there cafe.'

It was coming out of the cafe afterwards that Maggie Crabtree froze.

'I can't do it, Laura – not go back over yonder.'

Laura took her arm. 'You don't have to, not for a while. Let's have a walk.'

Without speaking, they headed uphill, battling against the wind, sometimes closing their eyes in the force of the drenching rain. The lights flickered in gas lamps. Over on the headland the ruined abbey stood bleakly silhouetted, the evening sky beyond almost as dark.

It was then that they saw them, the lifeboat and the wreck that it was towing.

'Oh, God – I knew,' the shriek came from Laura's side.

'Now, Mum, steady on. They might have saved all the men.'

Her mother started to run, an ungainly staggering lurch in the direction of the harbour. 'If your dad were alive he'd be bringing her in.'

'From the look of that boat, it'd take someone superhuman to steer her.'

But her mother was right. The lifeboat crew came ashore shaking their heads. Smashed to pieces the fishing smack had been, and nobody alive near her.

Maggie Crabtree's keening wail sliced right into Laura, the thin hand felt like a claw clutching at her arm. There was no time for even registering her own grief, much less permitting it expression. All she knew was the urgency of getting her mother back to the house. Maybe, in private, she herself would be able to let go. Sobbing loudly, Greta and Sybil pushed through the crowd, heedless of the other families distressed by the same loss.

'All right then, all right,' said Laura. 'Just stand there a minute, I'll find our Netta.'

First, though, she found the lifeboat skipper, thanked him for all they had done. Peeling off oilskins, he paused for a

174

second, studying her. He nodded, then wordlessly grasped her arm.

Further along the quay, she spotted Netta, her dark hair clinging flat to her head with the rain. She was being led by one of the Summers lads, away from the place where she had vomited.

Laura caught them up. 'Thanks, love, for looking after her. I'll see she's all right now. I'm ever so sorry about your dad – tell your mother, won't you, and that we'll be seeing her.'

There'd be other folk to see, as well, belonging to her father's crew. That would be later. Today, nothing she said or did would help, and they needed to get their mother home.

Afterwards, she couldn't have told anyone how they all reached the house. She had tried to locate somebody with a car, but few of the women drove; if any men with cars were there they were too concerned looking after their own.

Maggie Crabtree was worse than after her operation. Retreating into herself, she stared dry-eyed at nothing. And she wouldn't let Laura move more than a few paces away from her.

'I'll not go to bed tonight unless you come with me.'

Alarm surged through Laura's chest. Did no one know she needed to let go? 'All right, Mother, don't upset yourself. I'll be there.'

'What do we have to do? About a funeral and that?'

Hearing the word, the triplets wept afresh, in unison.

'I don't know,' said Laura. 'I'll find out tomorrow. We'd better make summat to eat now, keep us going.'

'Do you think I could?' her mother's voice accused her.

'I think we'll not face up to owt with just that bit of a biting-on from the cafe inside us. Happen I'd better send for the doctor.'

'What for? He can't do owt, can't fetch your father back.'

'Might have summat that'll calm us all down.'

'Calm? That's not what I need, I'm dead inside already.'

The telephone rang. Nobody but Laura seemed capable of going to answer it. On her way out to the hall, hope surged. It would be the coastguard. They'd all been mistaken thinking no one had survived.

'Laura? How are things?' Michael's concerned voice brought him very close, brought her near to tears.

'Bad, I'm afraid. The lifeboat towed in what was left of Dad's boat less than half an hour since.'

'My dear, I'm so terribly sorry. How – how are you all taking it?'

'All right. Mother – well, she's just as you'd expect: numb, lost. The girls are having a good cry. Don't know whether I wish I could, or what. Somebody has to see to things.'

'I'll come over whenever you want me to. I can now Sunday's nearly over.'

'I don't know that there's much you can help with.'

'There'll be things to do.' He pictured her registering the death, seeing the undertaker.

'Without a – a body?' Laura asked him. Her voice shook.

Michael hadn't thought of that one. 'Well, I'll ring you again in the morning. Have you thought to call the doctor. He'd give you all something, help you to cope.'

'Mother won't. And I – I'll manage.'

'Well, take care of yourself, I'll keep in touch. And, Laura—'

'Yes?'

'I'll be there for the funeral service, when the time comes.'

After she had thanked him and rung off she sat for a minute by the telephone, thinking. It had been so good to hear his voice. He'd been so caring and concerned, just like the Michael she'd known when they were both living here in Whitby. She wished, for the first time since leaving, that she could turn back the clock. There were so many problems. Michael in Halfield was a man she hardly knew and almost feared. Learning her job was more difficult than she'd imagined, and far worse now that she'd been put in the design studio only to have all the men threatening to strike. And there was that massive tangle of emotions generated every time she visited Arncliffe Hall.

'Laura, what are you doing?'

176

Here, at least, her task was quite obvious: to get the five of them through this night, somehow, and through whatever followed.

Lying rigid between humps of the flock mattress, afraid of disturbing the pitiful woman beside her who'd cried herself to sleep, Laura realised they were into Monday. She would have to telephone Roy Lindley at the mill and explain where she was and the reason. She ought to speak with Patrick Horsfall as well, tell him why she wasn't getting any further with moving into the Coach House.

Today she felt nothing but anxiety about the move. Tired like this, how would she cope with the rest of the shopping she must do, with giving her new home a thorough clean? And how, afterwards, would she manage looking after herself there when every evening after she'd finished at the mill she felt completely drained?

In the morning her mother grabbed hold of her hand as soon as the rising sun outlined the massive Victorian wardrobe.

'Laura love, you won't want to go back there now, will you, not after what's happened?'

'What're you bothering about that for already? I've only just got here.'

'I shan't be able to bear it if you leave me on my own.'

'You won't be on your own. There's Greta and Sybil, and our Netta.'

Her mother snorted. 'Aye.'

'They'll get better, you'll see, stand by you now.' Don't tempt me to stay, not while everything in Halfield seems so complex. And I'm in no state for coping.

She telephoned Roy Lindley at half-past seven, and explained.

'Oh, Laura! How dreadful – is there anything I can do?'

'Not unless you're any good at advising how to manage with a mother who just appears to have given up, and three sisters who think bawling their eyes out is all that's required of them.'

177

'You sound as though a good cry wouldn't do you any harm.'

That was perceptive of him. Despite everything, Laura smiled. 'Aye – well, I've never gone in much for luxuries of that sort.'

'And doubtless there's too much to organise . . .'

'There will be, once they . . .' Suddenly, she had to swallow. 'Didn't I say? When they found the boat it was empty.'

'Oh, no.'

His sympathy came over the line as plain as if he'd been facing her in the narrow hall with sunlight slanting through the stained glass beside its door. She thought of how distressed he'd been after that dreadful accident in the dyehouse, realised for the first time that it hadn't solely been because he felt responsible. Then there was his concern for his sister Cynthia and her defective heart.

'You still there, Laura?'

His anxiety warmed her. 'Aye – just thinking. You can be very nice, you know.'

The old Roy would have dared her to say that when he was close. Instead, he sighed. 'Not much I can do from this end. Except to tell you to take off as long as you need, your job'll be safe. Oh – and I had a word with Wayland Rogers, soon as I came in. You'll not have any more trouble from the other designers.'

'Thank you.' I wonder, though, she thought. From what she'd seen, that lot weren't above ignoring a directive, even from one of the bosses, if they felt their positions were at risk. She wasn't sure she blamed them, nor sure either that she was justified in taking work out of their hands.

Whitby had felt strange last night, and that was before they'd been told the worst. Today, the house where she'd grown up was horrible, unrecognisable almost in the gloom. In the big old kitchen she brewed tea, finding things with difficulty, perturbed by not belonging anywhere.

Her mother looked downright old, thin and pale above the winceyette nightdress that she wore even in summer. But she

178

was grateful for the tea, promised she'd get up soon and try a bit of toast.

Netta hadn't much more colour, but she sat up readily enough when she saw the cup and saucer. Laura was about to ask if her period pain was any better, but then Netta made a face, grumbled at the tea. 'Don't you make it strong! Have you forgotten how?'

Biting her tongue, Laura picked up the tray again and hurried towards Greta's room. Sybil was with her. Both seemed wide awake, neither too upset about their father.

'You're a good 'un, sis,' Greta told her. 'We haven't had early morning tea since you left.'

Laura grinned. 'Couldn't you take turns finding the teapot?'

'You know Mum doesn't like us in her kitchen,' said Sybil.

It's hopeless, thought Laura, they'll never alter. And happen that was *her* fault – who'd followed the three of them, hand and foot, just because their mother seemed to believe that was the way it should be. But couldn't they have realised that that had to finish when she moved to Halfield? Had they no eyes? How could they miss how worn out their mother was?

Her dissatisfaction with her sisters increased as the day continued. She oughtn't to have been surprised, but she was disappointed. And since her mother was incapable of doing more than sitting pensively in her chair, Laura coped with tidying the house and providing the meals that nobody felt like eating.

She was trying to find ingredients for a cake in the now unfamiliar kitchen that afternoon when the telephone rang. Greta rushed to answer it, stirring so swiftly off her bottom, for once, that Laura wondered whose call she was expecting. The man on the other end of the line, however, was Patrick Horsfall.

'Laura? I'm so sorry to hear of your loss. Is there any way in which I might be of assistance this end?' He was aching to be with her, wouldn't embarrass her by suggesting anything of the kind and couldn't, in any case, absent himself from Beth.

Laura couldn't understand how he had heard.

'Your landlady let me know.'

'That was considerate of her.'

'I think we all wish to rally round. I was wondering if you'd made any arrangements yet, about furniture being delivered and so on . . .'

'I hadn't had a chance.'

'Did you want me to contact them, have some furniture in for your return?' He felt compelled to do something to ensure that she did take over the Coach House.

'It's ever so kind of you to offer,' said Laura quickly, 'but at the moment I can't even think straight, Nothing seems real . . .'

'I know.'

He sounded as though he did. She wondered how he must have felt when his wife disappeared. And remained missing.

'I feel such an idiot,' she gulped.

'Laura – go easy on yourself. You've suffered an appalling shock. Now, have you got my telephone number with you?'

'I don't suppose so.'

'Then write it down now.' He gave it to her, along with his office number, and instructions to call him at any time, day or night.

'I don't know when I'll be back, or anything . . .'

'I understand. Just remember what I said.'

She had to hang up anyway, somebody was clattering the doorknocker. Maybe because the others knew she was in the hall, no one else had come to see who was here.

A couple of uniformed policemen were standing out on the path.

'Miss Crabtree?'

'Aye, that's me.' What's to do now? she wondered, alarmed.

'May we come inside?'

As they did so the senior officer asked if her mother was about.

Laura indicated the living-room door. 'She is, but . . .'

'Taking things badly?' he suggested.

'She's been better. Is – is it about my father?'

'Yes, we – er . . .' He eased her down on to the chair by the telephone. 'I'm afraid we've found him, Miss Crabtree.'

Laura swallowed. 'Go on,' she prompted, her voice grating.

'He was washed up on the rocks, just round the headland.'

'I see.' There was no point in hoping now, there must be no more fleeting thoughts that it had all been a dreadful mistake.

'I understand you have no brothers. Have you any close male relatives?'

'Uncles. Dad has a brother, so has my mother. Why?'

He glanced down at the hands restlessly shifting his helmet. 'Somebody will be required to identify the body.'

'I'll do that.'

She saw his astonishment.

'Mother's in no fit state. He was my father, why should anybody else have to go through it?'

'I have to warn you he's not a pretty sight.'

'There's nothing "pretty" about any of this, is there, Sergeant?'

Somehow, Laura broke the news to her mother and sisters. They all appeared resigned, anyway, to this being the outcome. There was no desperate need to remain at home with them. She asked the policemen to wait while she got her coat. It was still pouring.

They tried to make conversation in the car, imagining it would make things easier for her, Laura supposed, but wished that they wouldn't. All she needed was a bit of quiet. She had to find some way of steeling herself for the morgue.

They only showed her his poor head, but that was enough, and she'd been aware of his body beneath the sheet, distended with being in the water. He was bruised and scratched but with the waxy pallor of death the damage to his face looked unreal, like something on a cinema screen. His lovely hair was encrusted with salt, his normally smiling mouth set grimly; worst of all, because his eyes were closed the life really was absent from him.

Laura sighed, nodded. 'Aye, that's my dad. Do – do I have to sign anything?'

The younger of the officers took her for a cup of tea. She asked him if any of the rest of the crew had been found.

'Not so far. Maybe on the next tide, or the one after.'

Laura glanced at him. 'By which time they'll look – even worse.'

'Yes.' Gravely.

'I wouldn't like your job. Right now, I'm not so keen on anything, but I couldn't do what you sometimes have to.'

Leaving the place, she realised that once they had the death certificate nothing would prevent the funeral going ahead. In the centre of Whitby she went into the nearest undertakers. They were understanding about her not yet having the necessary documentation, but agreed with her that interment should be as soon as possible.

'I'm hoping my mother might begin picking up again afterwards, can't see much prospect of that until . . .' she had told the sombre-faced man who wasn't much fatter than a cadaver himself.

After he'd agreed to call at the house that evening for preliminary talks about Maggie Crabtree's wishes, Laura went to buy herself a black coat and hat. It didn't have to be today, she knew, and knew also that she was delaying returning to the house.

When she finally arrived home, she was pleased to see her mother was in the kitchen, continuing mixing the cake which Laura herself had started.

'Thank goodness you were here, Laura love,' she began. 'I don't think I could have borne to see him in a place like that.'

'Well, that's one thing off your mind. And I've asked somebody to come round tonight, about the funeral. He says he'll make arrangements tentatively, like, till we've got the certificate.'

'Who are we having?' Behind her, in the kitchen doorway, Netta had appeared.

'Glebe's, why?'

'But they're so old-fashioned!' Netta complained.

Exasperated, Laura closed her eyes. 'I don't supposed Dad will grumble on that score.'

'When Paula's grandfather died they had the new funeral directors in the High Street. The cars were really swish.'

I don't bloody care, thought Laura, and I don't know how *you* can. Was there any one of them who wouldn't be so distraught on the day that they wouldn't really see the cars?

'I ought to have known your ideas'd be stuffy,' Netta muttered, turning away.

'Pity she didn't offer to do some of the organising herself,' said Laura. And saw then that her mother was weeping again, went across to squeeze her shoulders.

'It's all right, Mum, I won't fall out with any of them.' But I'll have to get away soon afterwards, can't swallow back my words for the rest of my life.

She would have to be firm, no matter how much her mother emphasised her reliance upon her. She had struck out to have her own life, there could be no turning back. She might have thought there were problems in Halfield. All at once, they seemed slight. She'd have given anything to be at Lindley's mill, even in with those uncommunicative designers.

Coming out of the kitchen with her mother once the cake was in the oven, Laura picked up the bags containing her hat and coat.

'You haven't gone and bought black?' Maggie Crabtree snapped.

'Yes, I have, as a matter of fact.'

'Oh.' Her mother's down-turned mouth hardened. 'I thought of grey, myself, or navy blue. I've never suited black.'

'Well, all right – wear what you feel most comfortable in. Dad wouldn't have minded.'

'No. It'll have to be black now. But you might have told me what you were thinking of doing. You know, since you were away, you seem to be taking rather a lot on yourself.'

Somebody has to, thought Laura, and stomped up the stairs to her room. She could have had a good cry now, she realised, only she couldn't rely on her mother to remember the cake.

Today wasn't the day for having to cope with the recriminations if she herself didn't prevent it being carbonised.

At least she ought to sleep tonight, she was shattered, aching to stretch out on the bed in her old room. Tonight she was going to suggest one of the others take a turn if their mother wasn't up to being on her own. God, but it had been an interminable, gruelling day. And how many more would there be before Dad was laid to rest?

Naturally, having the undertaker there upset Maggie Crabtree, and when time came for bed she begged Laura to go up with her. She agreed, of course, but drank a large medicinal brandy before going up.

'Have you been drinking?' her mother asked, sniffing suspiciously.

'I'm afraid so. If the smell of it's upsetting you, I'll go in my old room.'

It seemed her mother suddenly wasn't that fastidious. 'I don't mean to pick at you, Laura love, you should know that.'

But you've had a shock, harder for you than the rest of us, he was your partner – a good partner. And you'd have been a different woman, more self-reliant, if he hadn't been away at sea so much, forcing you to face things that were beyond you. Like those three, still audibly arguing about something and nothing downstairs.

'Dad was insured, wasn't he, Mother?'

'Aye, he was that. There'll be enough to give him a good funeral.'

'I wasn't thinking of that. When – when it's over, you want to consider taking a break, a holiday.'

'Not sure there'll be that much left over, not to give all of us a holiday.'

'I'm not talking about that. I mean you on your own.'

'How could I leave the triplets? Don't talk so daft.'

'They're not tiny children any more. And Mrs Tomlinson would keep an eye on things. Is their Bessie still friendly with Sybil?'

184

'And you'd be here, anyway, wouldn't you? I never thought . . .'

Laura said no more. How could she tell her now that she mustn't count on her staying? She wished she wasn't such a coward.

The nightmares began that night, uncannily realistic dreams in which her troubled subconscious played out variations on her father's death. First it seemed he was trapped in the boat while the gales ground it to firewood, and though he struggled to free himself of the splintering timbers they shifted into piles on top of his gasping body, forcing him down on to the seabed. No sooner had she wakened in a cold sweat, reassuring herself it was only a dream, than she was back in the mortuary, identifying a corpse so horribly mutilated that the head had been placed in an oven – to dry out, the attendant told her.

In her own room, she'd have switched on her light and read a book until her mind rid itself of the pictures. Here, she could only turn over her pillow to the cooler side, and try to ease into a more comfortable position without disturbing her mother. The worst nightmare was to come, with the five of them struggling to lower the coffin into a grave. Wind and rain were soughing in the dark, surrounding trees, snatching at their clothes, and suddenly the lid slid off the oak casket. Moaning, her dad slithered into the earth.

That's enough, thought Laura after wakening with a start. Quietly, she went down to the living-room, poured herself another brandy, and sat at the table with one of her sisters' magazines until she had drained the glass. When she went upstairs again she turned a blind eye on her mother's door.

It was daylight when Laura was wakened by someone shaking her roughly by the shoulder. Sybil shouted right in her ear.

'It's for you, Laura, come on. Some chap on the telephone.'

It would be Michael, why couldn't Sybil have said? And there was nothing she could tell him yet, with no death certificate and only a provisional date for the funeral.

The voice, though, wasn't Michael's. 'Hallo, Laura – Patrick. How are you feeling?'

'Do you really want to know?' she asked ruefully.

'It is the reason I'm ringing.'

Her throat filled, and her eyes. He was such a busy man, with the building society to run, Beth . . . his sick mother.

'You don't know how much I needed to hear from you.' It wasn't what she ought to have said, but there had been no withholding. And suddenly she was sobbing, losing control. 'You'd better ring off,' she gabbled, horrified, while she could still speak. 'I – I'll call you later.'

'There's no need . . .'

'Oh, God! I want my dad . . . Daddy, Daddy!' She swallowed, gulped, choked. 'Don't listen, *please.*'

No one must witness her breakdown.

Chapter 11

For ages afterwards Laura had remained staggered that Patrick hadn't put down the receiver. It had seemed so long after her outburst that she could hardly believe it when she eventually heard him asking quietly: 'Back to normal now?'

He must have endured her shrieking hysteria, the wild sobs which had brought her mother and sisters out into the hall to stare ineffectually, and had driven them away again. She should have been disturbed that he had witnessed her breaking down, she certainly was embarrassed, but all she really knew was that clinging to the phone was like having a hand to hold.

'I don't know what came over me.' She sounded like everyone else when they'd given way to emotion. Maybe she *was* somebody else, she scarcely recognised herself.

'Something you needed,' Patrick said gently, and she could picture the sympathetic smile that was in his voice.

'But haven't you enough to put up with, without me?'

'Without you, there's nothing but problems.'

'And what do you think this is?'

'Hey – my turn now, I've listened to you!' His smile sounded to be growing. Laura couldn't imagine why, when she was making an utter fool of herself. 'You must be acutely unobservant, Laura, if you've failed to notice that, albeit gradually, you've been admitted to – to what goes on at Arncliffe. Now you know why I wish to reciprocate, if only within the limitations imposed by distance.'

'But . . .'

He laughed.

'Never thought I'd hear that sound again,' she exclaimed.

But she felt confused, because right into the heart of her black sorrow had come this man with more cares than her own, and nothing felt as bad now. Targeted deep within her, though, had come a fierce longing which the sound alone of him could generate.

'Talk to me,' she said, despite still feeling idiotic. 'How's Beth, and your mother?'

'Both no better, and no worse. But I want to know about you. Don't you need to talk?'

'Yesterday, I had to identify the – *him*. After they brought him ashore.' She paused, steadied herself. 'And I dreamed all night, horribly. Even with a large brandy to settle me. Had to take another to get back to sleep again.'

'Best thing.' It was only when there was no time limit to the anguish that alcohol proved itself merely one more burden to conquer. 'Frightened of getting too much of a liking for it?' he enquired lightly.

'Aye, something of the sort. Can't afford to, can I? Not with a home to plan and furnish.'

'Make that soon, won't you?'

'I will an' all! I've got more than a suspicion that I shall have had as much as I can take before the loose ends here are all tied in.'

Patrick promised to ring her again. Knowing that he would do so sustained her as she went to confront her family. She wished she knew how to tell them what she really intended.

'Who was he?' Greta asked. Sybil had said he sounded posh, not the kind of man you expected to be ringing their Laura from the industrial West Riding.

'The man who's selling me my new home.'

'You seemed very close, or you wouldn't have been sobbing into his ear 'ole.'

'You've done your share. We all have to show our feelings sometime.'

'But with somebody like him . . .'

'Greta – shut it! I've had enough of you three already, and we're barely into the second day. You're not sweet little girls

188

any longer who can say what they like and everybody'll just think what a caution you are.'

'Laura . . .' her mother began, alarmed by this uncharacteristic outspokenness.

'It's all right, Mum. I've said it now.'

By the time that they were told the funeral could go ahead, Patrick had telephoned Laura three more times, surprising her by his continuing concern, and becoming her one anchor. Michael had telephoned, as well, but he seemed preoccupied, making her uneasy. Perhaps what she needed was to see him face to face. She had offered him a bed for the night on the Monday following when he was coming to play the organ for the funeral, but he had made his own arrangements.

Having offered, Laura couldn't help feeling relieved that Michael wasn't taking it up. As well as the natural depression and sense of loss the house was permeated with discontent. Her mother still leaned heavily on her, and at the same time appeared to disapprove of many of Laura's actions. Her sisters exceeded her memories of their self-centredness and bickering.

Their most appalling outburst had been when they were shopping for black outfits. Laura had hoped to escape the expedition, but Maggie Crabtree had protested that she needed advice on what to wear, and Laura couldn't help but agree that the triplets would not be much use.

Choosing their own coats flared into drama because each of them had decided they had no wish to dress exactly alike. Unfortunately, both Greta and Sybil chose the same semifitted coat which did, indeed, flatter them equally. In the middle of the shop they indulged in a sudden screaming match, so embarrassing that Laura turned her back on them and marched out into the street to stand on the pavement.

'What did you want to go doing that for?' her mother demanded, when the others eventually emerged. 'Leaving me with them two fratching. You know I oughtn't to be bothered by anything, I'm too upset.'

Wryly, Laura looked at her. 'Sorry, Mum. But you'd have been more upset still if I'd started laying into them.'

'But they're your sisters, Laura. Don't you feel anything for them?'

Aye, I do an' all! she thought. I still love them dearly, but my eyes have been opened. Nobody would feel any better for being told I think their behaviour's utterly childish.

'I just wish they'd grow up,' she said mildly.

For once, Maggie Crabtree's face softened into a smile. 'And you had to, hadn't you, love – to help look after them?'

The day of the funeral was dry and bright, though the wind off the North Sea had a bite in it too chill for early September. Laura was at the door, waiting while the milkman ladled the extra milk they would need into quart jugs, when Michael crossed the road towards her.

'You're nice and early,' she said, wondering how he'd arrived first thing all the way from Halfield.

'Thought you might be glad to have me around. You're not looking too bad, my dear, how are you feeling?'

'Wanting this day over. But you're right, I'm not so bad.'

'And your mother?'

'Eh, this has fair knocked the stuffing out of her – and she hadn't much before. It's going to be hard leaving her when the time comes, she's clung to me that tight.'

'Maybe something can be done about that . . .'

'Don't see how, beyond me stopping here, and I shan't do that. It isn't as if she were left on her own. Anyway, come on in – can't keep you talking on the step.'

As he took one of the heavy jugs and walked with her through to the kitchen Laura gave him a sideways glance. 'What did you mean, about something being done?'

'Tell you later.'

She was too busy to press Michael to tell her now. Aunts, uncles and cousins would be arriving at any time, and there were sandwiches to prepare before they went to the church, and ham and salad for their tea. Her sisters were helping today. With so many to cater for they hadn't a lot of choice.

The three of them rushed to greet Michael, reminding

Laura of how good he'd always been to them – too good maybe like everybody else. She couldn't help being fond of this side of him, though, and the way he hadn't hesitated to come over here now. Despite . . . everything.

'We'll have to keep a close watch on Mum,' she had warned her sisters, 'in the church, and at the graveside.'

But it was Laura herself who cracked under the tension, weeping long and silently right through the service. It had been bad enough after Aunt Constance died; today, she began to realise how final everything could feel. A part of her was still having difficulty in accepting that her father had died, but that wooden casket, focus of their attention, was all too starkly real.

'I'll have to believe it now, won't I?' she said to Michael, back at the house. 'I've been proper daft, you know – not really crediting this has happened, even after going to identify him.'

'People often feel that way, Laura, it's a kind of – protection.'

'Well, I'll just be very thankful when I can get away to my real life again.'

'Ah, that brings me to what I was saying earlier. I've been thinking, my dear. You're not going to be very happy about living quite so far away from your family now.'

'But it's where my work is,' she asserted, and wondered how many times she'd thought that in the past few days. 'You used to be one of the first to say I had to have a life of my own. And Dad was the person who understood how much I wanted to design carpets. He persuaded me I'd got to tackle it. Now that he's gone I can't give up on what he wished for me.'

'I know. But you might be wiser to readjust your thinking. You know I'm more than fond of you, Laura . . .'

His voice seemed to fade as her head began whirling. Around them people were milling, hurrying between kitchen and living-room with plates, enormous pots of tea. And all she could do was stare, perturbed, at Michael's face which contrasted pinkly with his dark suit and tie, and a very white shirt. She had more than an inkling that he was going to suggest something that she could not accept. How in the world could she turn him down when he'd been so marvellous today?

'I was early this morning,' he continued, 'because I spent last night at Pickering. There's a vacancy there, due to the sudden death of their organist. As you know, the vicar is a friend of our family. He would gladly put my name forward.'

Laura tried to prevent her gasp. Michael didn't notice, anyway. He took her by the shoulders, his hazel eyes intense with love.

'Marry me, Laura. Living there, we'd be well situated to keep an eye on things here. I'd share the—' His tongue stuck on the word 'burden', and a fleeting smile revealed his understanding. 'The care of your people,' he added hastily.

Understanding wasn't enough, though, and nor were the kindness and concern that he had generated today. She was going to feel the ungrateful bitch of all time, but you didn't get married out of gratitude.

Awkwardly, Laura swallowed. 'Did you go after the job as organist in this new parish because of me and the situation here?'

'It was a considerable influence, yes. Of course, I haven't been long enough at St Martin's really to make my mark there, but – well, there'd be opportunities over this way. I could be invited to give recitals, maybe even in York Minster.'

'But you wouldn't have been moving this soon, and not to this part of the world.' She sighed, wishing with her entire being that he had not said one word. And most certainly that he'd done nothing about making all these changes. 'Don't think of moving because of me, love,' she said earnestly. 'I've still got a job. In Halfield. I've hardly started there. I can't give it up, not for a long while yet.'

'And there's your house, of course.' His voice was brittle.

'There is that, as well.' And I'm being less than truthful about my deepest reason for going back there, Laura realised. Hadn't coming away convinced her how much she cared about the man who, despite all the other people at Arncliffe Hall, appeared so alone there?

'Think it over, Laura, carefully. Maybe this was entirely the wrong day for saying anything. It'd be some time before I made

192

the move. And even if you can't decide now, there'd be no reason later on why you shouldn't change your mind and come to me.'

Michael's suggestion tended to take Laura's thoughts off the reason for the family gathering. She offered round plates, filled up cups, and listened to everybody letting go now the traumatic part of the funeral was behind them. And if anyone noticed that she was only attending with a quarter of her mind, not one of them said so.

'I'm going back home later today,' she announced next morning when her mother looked much brighter.

Predictably, the brightness evaporated. 'And what about me? How am I going to manage?'

'The way you managed before, love, when Dad was away at sea so much. The girls will give you a hand. If you like, I'll have a word with them before I leave.'

'I'd rather you didn't,' her mother snapped. 'You always put their backs up.'

Laura straightened her shoulders. Now that she'd decided she must go, she was determined she'd leave her mother with a fresh insight into her own techniques. 'There shouldn't be any need for me to say owt. You have a way with you, you know, love. You've always had the knack of making me do whatever you wanted, you could start on them three.'

Maggie Crabtree's eyes swivelled to scrutinise her eldest daughter. 'You do go in for plain speaking these days, it doesn't improve you.'

Before Laura set off, however, she was beginning to notice that her words seemed to be having some effect. The triplets were coming in for a range of instructions on what they might be doing to make themselves useful.

Halfield didn't look any more attractive than Laura recalled as the train pulled into the station. She couldn't have been more pleased to be back, though. All the things that had worried her about her life here had grown insignificant against the prospect of not returning. And she had brought her bike with her. That

193

seemed to her to confirm her decision of where she would settle.

The guard had offloaded the bicycle from his van and she was struggling to cope with that as well as her suitcase when a woman called to her as she came running down the last few steps to the platform. Disbelievingly, Laura gazed towards her. Inez Lindley! Why ever was she meeting her?

'Roy telephoned your home after you'd left. One of your sisters told him which train you were catching. Roy and his father are still at the mill, of course, so I thought I'd give you a surprise.'

'And a lovely one it is! Thank you ever so much.'

'You didn't cycle all the way to Whitby, I hope?' Roy's mother asked, smiling, as they stowed the bicycle.

'I was in too much of a hurry to get there for that, even if I'd have had the energy. No – this is my own bike, the other was one I was lent.'

'We all were so sorry to hear of your sudden bereavement, dear,' Mrs Lindley said, getting into the car. 'How is your poor mother?'

'Thank you. Not so good, I'm afraid. But my sisters will have to brighten their ideas up and start looking after her a bit. As a matter of fact, she's never been a self-reliant woman, even though Dad's job meant that he was away a lot. I couldn't help thinking the first time I met you that it was a pity Mum wasn't more your sort.'

'But you have your own life here now,' Inez Lindley said. 'At least Whitby isn't too far away if there are problems that need sorting.'

'I'm glad you don't seem to think I'm being appallingly selfish.'

'Anything but. And I'm very glad to see you back in Halfield. I really do mean to have you visit us again soon. I shall do something about it the minute you've settled down again.'

Mavis Priestley expressed similar delight that she had returned. Laura had rather expected her to disapprove of anything less than Mavis's own devotion to her mother.

Because her landlady hadn't done so Laura began feeling more contented.

After eating the meal laid on for her, she worked for nearly two hours on her designs. Her enforced absence and all the distress had left her afraid that she might have lost what talent she possessed. As soon as she began copying one of her original patterns on to point paper, however, she felt her work was back to normal. She had learned such a lot already, and now understood not only the basic principles of carpet manufacture, but also the intricacies of pattern matches.

These days, she was able to visualise lengths of her carpeting laid side by side, with the design repeating across the separate pieces as well as along the twenty-seven-inch width that came off the loom. The breadth this imparted to her work wasn't only in the literal sense, but made her innovative and, today, eager to get back to the mill and put more of her ideas to the test.

As it happened, Laura arrived there next morning just as Roy Lindley was parking his car.

'I was pleased to see your mother waiting at the station yesterday,' she told him. 'I'd been longing to get back, and that confirmed that I'm beginning to belong.' She went on to explain how excited she was feeling about her work.

'Jolly good! I've spoken to Wayland Rogers again, told him to expect you back. And we're agreed that you're to be given your head – to a degree. Between us, we selected one of your original designs – that York Minster window, actually. We both think you're sufficiently skilled now to be able to interpret it in a viable form.'

'Oh, that's wonderful, just the tonic I needed.'

'Naturally, Mr Rogers is there to advise you on practicalities, if there's some aspect you can't handle. But we would like you to tackle this one on your own, initially. Show what you're capable of.'

'I could hug you, you know – that's precisely what I need.'

Roy raised an eyebrow. 'Lord, but the crisis in Whitby has affected you! Grown incautious, haven't you?'

It was good to laugh with him, and more than good to approach the design studio without dreading the reception awaiting her. And even though she found that most of the other designers greeted her only grudgingly, they did at least speak, and Wayland Rogers took care to smile and spend some time reiterating what Roy had told her.

Anxious though she was to start on the work which she was determined would prove her aptitude for design, Laura paused for a second after taking out her brushes and paints. This was the moment when she would put behind her all the limitations of the past along with its disappointments. Nothing, not even her still raw grief, would be permitted to destroy her opportunity.

The day seemed timeless, so absorbed was she in her job. Only when the rest of them left their seats did she realise that lunchtime had arrived. But she couldn't be sorry to call a halt and go to the canteen when several people greeted her warmly, and Amos Kitchen gave her a thumbs up sign from across the room noisy with chatter.

Recalling that she now had her own bicycle, she went to sit beside him, and after thanking him for his condolences offered to return the machine he had loaned her.

'I'll ride over with it the next time I'm going across to Arncliffe, if that's all the same with you.'

Amos smiled a little shyly. 'So long as you check as I'll be at home. Going out quite a bit, these days.'

'Are you now? Glad to hear it. Do you mean . . .?'

'Aye, with Emma. And I've got good news, and all – have you heard her lad's back home?'

Laura beamed. 'No, nobody'd said. Well, I am pleased. And how does he seem?'

'He's doing champion. And so he ought, his mother spoils him to death. But he is healing nicely, hopes to be back here before long.'

'In the dyehouse still?'

'So I understand. I gather that Mr Robert offered him a different job, but young Geoff were determined to face the dyehouse again first. He's a gradely lad, is yon. And we get on champion. He's fond of a game of cribbage, and if I don't watch out he beats me at draughts.'

'I'm sure you must help to compensate for his own father's neglect.'

'Don't know so much about that. Any road, his dad is treating them both a bit better now, they don't want for anything.'

'Certainly that's an improvement, even if he won't acknowledge them properly.'

'Here – steady on,' said Amos with a grin, standing up ready to limp off on his way back to the scouring. 'I can't be doing with Carter Ainley getting *too* concerned, don't want my nose pushing out.'

Back in the studio, Laura was working swiftly transferring the design on to point paper. By finishing time that evening she had roughed in the outline of the pattern, and was beginning to apply colour. I might sleep a bit better tonight, she thought. And have something to look forward to when I get up again.

They were pleased with her at Lindley's. By the end of the week, Roy had confirmed that her York Minster design would be going into production. And without any alterations by Wayland Rogers or anyone else. After finishing her meal that evening, Laura got out her bicycle and rode over to visit Clem Hargreaves.

His sister welcomed her eagerly, reminding Laura how warm-hearted the pair were.

'And how are you feeling now, love?' Millie asked, leading the way through to the living-room.

'I'm all right, thanks. Glad to be back.'

Clem got up slowly from his chair and came across to take her hand in a firm grasp.

'Glad to see you, lass. How did things go?'

'A bit gruelling really. But I suppose the worst is over. I wanted to see you to say how grateful I am for the way you both got me to the station that day.'

'Only wish we could have done more,' Millie said. 'Now,

how about a nice cup of tea?'

'It's very kind of you, but I've only just had my dinner, thanks.'

'Well, sit down, any road,' said Clem, drawing up a chair beside his own. 'And are you back at work yet?'

'Oh, yes.' Laura smiled. 'That's another reason I wanted to see you. Your tuition seems to have paid off – Lindley's are actually going to produce from one of my designs.'

'By jove, that is good news! You've soon shown 'em what's what.'

'Well, I don't know about that. It's all still a bit like living on the edge of a precipice. Until I've got them interested in more than one pattern I shan't know whether this is just a fluke.'

'But you are staying on at Lindley's mill?'

'Oh, yes. I've only just begun finding my feet there.' Laura realised then what would have sparked off the question. Parishes were notorious for gossip, it would be surprising if word hadn't got around by now about Michael's possible move. She resolved that she was neither going to fuel the rumour nor pretend to deny it, and was deeply thankful when both Clem and his sister let the matter rest.

I wish Michael wasn't such a public person, though, she thought as she cycled back to Hanson Road. He had been too good a pal for her to be comfortable with the belief that his relationship with her (or the lack of it) was causing him embarrassment. And for herself she'd have preferred to choose her way of life without having this feeling that people whom she wanted as friends disapproved of her decision.

As she put away her bicycle and unlocked the front door Laura realised that yet again she was dreading seeing Michael. Ever since she had turned down his proposal she'd felt dreadful about it. He had been so kind coming to Whitby as he had for her sake. To say nothing of his thinking of becoming organist at another church because of its proximity to her family.

'Eh, lass – you look proper down in the mouth. Have you time for a bit of a chat?'

Laura smiled at her landlady's greeting, and followed her into the back room.

'Just come over you again, love, has it?' Miss Priestley said sympathetically, indicating one of the armchairs. 'That's the way of it, I'm afraid, after we lose somebody.'

'It wasn't that, as a matter of fact.' Laura paused, eyeing the anxious round face for signs of how much her landlady knew about the situation. 'Have you – have you heard anything about Michael Dawson?'

'He told me himself that he's thinking of moving on already. I shall be that disappointed if he does decide to leave. The last organist we had weren't a patch on him, and he gives us all such a lot of confidence so's we can attempt any solo he expects of us.'

'Michael asked me to marry him, did he tell you that?'

'No. And from the look on your face you didn't accept.'

'You must think I'm wrong in my head.'

'Nay, lass, why assume that? You've been straightforward with him, that's better than feigning emotions you can't feel. Specially with him being that wrapped up in the church. It would never do for him to have a marriage that didn't last, would it? No, Laura love, you'd happen have done him a lot more harm by saying nowt now, and making two of you unhappy later on.'

'I'm glad you don't think too badly of me.' She had grown to respect Miss Priestley over the weeks. And even if she didn't entirely approve of her fascination with other people's lives, she could understand that it compensated for the lack of interest in her own.

'And when are you moving into your new house?'

'Not sure yet. I wanted it to be tomorrow, but I've not done owt about it beyond making sure my furniture was delivered. And I felt I ought to see Michael again before I go.' Although she couldn't foresee that encounter as improving anything between them.

'So it's all set up then, apart from the stuff you've still got here?'

'Oh, yes.' She had telephoned Arncliffe Hall during the week, Patrick had verified that everything was safely installed. And speaking with him had confirmed her eagerness to see him. She felt as guilty about that as she had for turning down Michael's proposal.

'You could go this weekend. There's nowt to stop you still keeping in with Mr Dawson and the rest of us at St Martin's once you're living over there.'

When Laura gave her a look, Miss Priestley laughed. 'No, I'm not shoving you out! But I can't help thinking that what you want is fresh scenery and summat to keep you busy.'

Laura needed little persuading now to telephone Patrick again and enquire if there was any reason why she shouldn't move in to the Coach House tomorrow.

'Not unless you're hoping for the red carpet treatment,' he teased, 'that's still on order.'

'Carpets are my department, I thought,' Laura said quickly. 'And, in any case, I don't fancy red with the colour scheme I've got.'

'So you'll be content simply to arrive without any fuss made of you?'

'That's right. Although I shall be offended if you don't make time to join me for a cup of tea or something to christen the place. That's if you're not doing anything better?'

The rest of the evening was spent in frenetically packing all her clothes, and gathering together the items bought for her home and not yet taken over there.

'You'll need a taxi, I'm thinking,' Miss Priestley remarked, seeing how much Laura had accumulated.

'Bit extravagant, isn't it?'

'It'd have been a darned sight more so if you'd been forced to have the removal men.'

Next morning when she was ready for leaving 'Bien-être' Laura was glad not to be attempting the journey by tram and bus. And just supposing she'd dropped some of that lovely crockery on the way – that might have cost her a heck of a lot more, as well as being upsetting.

The only upset now was saying goodbye to the landlady who had grown from being rather irritating into a real friend.

'I'll be seeing you, anyway, when I come to pick up that bike of Amos Kitchen's.' There had been room only for her own cycle, and the taxi driver had grouched about that being lashed into the boot of his vehicle.

Riding up the drive at Arncliffe gave Laura a thrill in keeping with the excitement of acquiring a home of her own. She gazed up at the Hall itself then leaned forward, staring out of the cab window for her first glimpse of the Coach House. And then she was standing at its door, suitcases and boxes stacked around her feet and her bicycle propped against the side wall.

All at once, though, tears filled her eyes and the lump rising in her throat nearly choked her. She hadn't known, but she had wanted Dad to see this, he'd have been that pleased for her . . .

That sort of thinking wasn't going to do anything for her, though. She'd no need to go letting it spoil her day. There'd be many a time that she'd ache for her father, all she could do was get used to there being such a large gap in her emotional life.

Unlocking the door, Laura thrust her suitcases through into the hall, and turned to pick up the rest of her things. The china and utensils belonged in the kitchen, she would put them in there out of the way, then take her other stuff upstairs.

Passing the open living-room door, however, she felt a surge of warm air. Somebody had lit a fire in the grate. The room looked different already, homely and welcoming. Leaving her possessions in the hall, she came right inside, looking about for her new table and chairs.

Right in the centre of her table was the biggest flower arrangement she'd ever seen in an ordinary house. Grouped around striking flame-coloured gladioli were dozens of roses in all the shades from scarlet, through peach, to an exquisite gold. Leaning against the vase was a business card: 'With the wish that you may find happiness here, Patrick.'

I'll have to find him and thank him as soon as I've tidied up

201

a bit, thought Laura, then she'd make sure he came back here with her for a cup of tea. She wished she'd thought to buy a bottle of something stronger, but she didn't touch drink often enough for thinking of that to have been automatic. Maybe it wouldn't be a bad idea, anyway, for Patrick to get used to the way she was.

She had put away all the kitchen items and was upstairs admiring her lovely big bedroom when she heard a strange scratching sound somewhere at the back of the house.

Some time earlier, more annoyed than he had been in recent weeks, Patrick was striding through his home to find Mrs Harrison.

'Where is Beth this time – playing in the scullery? You know she's supposed to spend the morning reading.' Or pretending to read. When the child uttered no sound, how in the world did one establish how much she had grasped?

'It is Saturday,' Mrs Harrison began, then turned and glimpsed his expression, and was sorry. She might sympathise with young Miss Beth, but it was her father who tore your heart out. 'I'm afraid I don't know where she is, Mr Patrick. I left her in the schoolroom with her books. She certainly hasn't come through my kitchen.'

Patrick stalked into the adjacent scullery, nevertheless, and emerged scowling. Its only occupant was one of the daily women who sometimes helped prepare vegetables.

'Is it so wrong of me to want just one day to be well ordered?' he enquired of his housekeeper. 'Beth knew I was counting on her remaining where she was supposed to be.'

'Happen she did, and happen that was the reason she wouldn't.' Noting how his eyes narrowed, Mrs Harrison smiled. 'She is *your* daughter, Mr Horsfall . . .'

'What's that supposed to mean?'

'You don't want her to grow up a doormat, do you, pushed around?'

His dark eyebrows soared, but he stifled a snort. Mrs Harrison was more astute than he gave her credit for. 'I do want her literate, though, and with a modicum of obedience.'

'I know. I do know. But you can't blame the girl for growing restless. And hasn't my Tom got an uncanny knack of coming across her when she goes wandering in the grounds? If I know them, they'll be back together directly.' And if I know you, she added silently, you'll not rest until then. Whose fault was that, when he never had a chance to forget what had happened that first time young Beth was discovered out there on her own?

Unable to settle to anything, Patrick ranged through the entire house, disturbing even his parents who normally were spared the frustration so frequently generated in him by his daughter.

'I didn't really suppose she would be with you, but . . .' Shaking his head, he stood a few feet inside their sitting-room, stripped of the composure he normally assumed to shield them from his anxiety.

'Maybe it's a good sign,' his mother suggested. 'Most children love to explore when they know they're really close to home and safe.'

'And maybe it's just one more sign of the disturbance which doesn't go away no matter how much we will it to.'

'You're tired, Patrick, and it's showing. Why don't you take that holiday we suggested?'

'You know the reason.' He never left Beth for more than the obligatory hours taken up by the building society.

'Mrs Harrison is devoted to Beth, and we're here as well.'

'You could listen to us for once,' his father added quietly, his eyes reminding Patrick that unless he took a break soon his mother's health might then preclude his absence.

'I'll see . . .' said Patrick, with the vagueness which certainly wasn't characteristic, but adopted as a subconscious defence.

Leaving their suite, he sighed resignedly, preparing now to head for the gardens and begin searching.

Once outdoors, however, Patrick checked and his lips set firmly. For the first time in months he released himself from the grip of unending concern for Beth. He had wanted confirmation that she was all right before indulging himself. He hadn't yet received that reassurance but, surely to God, on one isolated occasion he might neglect putting everyone else first.

Chapter 12

'Eh, love, what're you doing hanging about out there? You'd better come in, hadn't you?'

Laura had opened the kitchen door and discovered that the sound she'd heard was Beth scratching tentatively at the window.

'Next time you come you want to knock on the door, like this.' And she demonstrated. 'Or the front door maybe.'

Going back indoors she sensed the child close behind her. When Beth saw the tiled floor she tried the first few steps of her version of a dance. She also extended both hands to Laura.

'Remembered that, have you? All right then, but only for a minute. Hang on, I've just thought of something.'

Her newly acquired wireless set was in the living-room, happen she'd find some music on one of the stations. Beth, though, wasn't releasing her hands. Overwhelmed with choking emotion, Laura edged her way along to the other room. Once there she looked down into the small solemn face.

'Now don't be daft, just let go of one hand else I can't switch on. I'm not going to run away, am I?'

Fortunately, she quickly located a lively tune which would do for their makeshift dancing. And the child's rare smile assured her that, if only for a few moments, the traumas were forgotten. Aye, Laura thought, and if losing her mother is what's done this to her, maybe that wasn't so astonishing after all. Her own sudden bereavement had left great raw areas on which she dared not dwell.

Laura was still mulling over the possible cause of Beth's condition when that tune ended and an announcer began giving details of forthcoming programmes. Beth sighed weightily and looked up at her, just like any other six-year-old asking what would happen next.

'Don't you think my new furniture's nice? I've got some more new things upstairs. Do you want to have a look?'

Coming back downstairs again, Laura wondered if someone was anxious about the child's absence.

'I was going to go across and see if I could find your daddy. Do you want to come?'

Beth shook her head, clinging to the rail at the foot of the stairs.

It was the closest to a reply that Laura had received from her. 'You can come back, you know, any time you want. I'll be living here now. Do you understand?'

And maybe Beth did, for she was certainly prepared to walk alongside Laura as she started crossing the courtyard towards the main house. The hand extended to the girl was ignored though, almost as if Beth were emphasising that contact was permissible only as a necessary adjunct to dancing.

'So that's where you've got to!'

Patrick came into sight around the side of Arncliffe Hall and quickened his pace as they waited for him to join them.

'Thanks, Laura, and hallo. You were bringing her home?'

'That, and coming to thank you. The flowers are the loveliest I've ever seen. Nobody's ever given me flowers before.'

'Oh. Well –' He felt awkward confronted with her steady azure gaze, with her youthful smile. Laura always appeared such a bit of a girl that he wondered if she could have the slightest interest in an old man like him.

'And I was going to ask if you'd time for a cup of tea? Sort of house warming.'

'Sure, fine – thank you. I'll just take Beth indoors to her schoolroom.'

His hand outstretched towards his daughter was checked by Laura's. 'Let her come as well. I've got plenty of milk if she doesn't like tea.'

'You're making a rod for your own back,' Patrick warned as they all turned in the direction of the Coach House.

'So? I shan't let her bother me, shall I, not when I've had to cope with them three as sisters.'

'But they are a little more accustomed to adult ways.'

'You don't know 'em.'

Patrick smiled, feeling easier already after only a few moments in her company.

'We'd better stay in the kitchen,' he suggested, still smiling, when Laura produced biscuits and cake out of one of the many bags she had brought with her.

'Happen so. I'll bet if Madam started dropping crumbs on my living-room carpet you'd make quite a to-do.'

'You can't seriously disapprove of attempts to turn her into a civilised member of society?'

'Put like that, no.' She was glancing over her shoulder at him as she filled the kettle. 'I hope you don't think I was criticising the way you . . . do things?'

He shrugged. 'I over-react at times, please ignore it.' But almost in the same breath he called Beth from exploring the kitchen to come and sit beside him. His glance met Laura's amused look. 'I see what you mean.'

'I'd never consciously undermine your authority, you know,' she told him, locating a packet of tea and the brown earthenware pot. 'I didn't know I was so poor at disguising my own thoughts. Happen we're going to have to make allowances.'

He smiled back at her. 'I think that might be arranged.' He would do anything to retain this relationship, to build on the foundation of her warmth.

'I'm glad you're my first guests,' Laura said lightly, after the tea had brewed and she had poured and come to sit with them. 'You've been that good to me.' Her eyes sought his. ''Specially the other day, putting up with me blubbing down the telephone.'

A hand went to his ear. 'Entirely dried out now.' And didn't she even suspect how thankful he had been simply because she had felt able to let go with him?

'You're a good listener anyway, thanks.'

One of the dark eyebrows shot up. 'Not always the impression I've been given of how I appear.' His expression seemed to close abruptly, disguising the effects of long months of stress.

Alone with him, Laura would have reached out to the hand resting on the deal table, but they weren't alone.

'Another biscuit, Beth love, or a piece of cake? And what are you going to have?'

Patrick took the proffered cake, then neglected to eat it. Almost, he'd forgotten quite how beautiful Laura was, how appealingly that froth of pale hair framed her pert face. And, vivid though memory had been, in no way had it reproduced the force of this attraction flaring between them strongly enough to make conversation tricky. How did one talk with ease of this and that while fighting against this undercurrent? He'd never been a man who relaxed into idle chatter, but anything deeper which might establish friendship required more attention than this newfound excitement permitted.

He forced himself to eat the cake, glanced towards Laura again. 'I wasn't only looking for Beth earlier. I had heard your taxi and wanted to know if you'll have dinner with me tonight?'

'Did your mother prompt you to invite me?'

Patrick shook his head. 'Despite all that she said in front of you the other week, I'm surprisingly capable of coming up with my own suggestions.'

When Laura didn't reply immediately, he continued to hold her gaze. 'If there's something perturbing about it, you needn't necessarily consider we're creating a precedent.'

She shook her head and laughed. 'It wasn't that at all – I was just thinking that you were rescuing me from some rather mixed feelings. I love having my own house, don't get me wrong – but I shall have to do a bit of adjusting to not having anybody to talk to.'

'And this isn't quite the most favourable time for beginning, is it?' he said sympathetically. If she only knew how well he understood, how often he yearned just for someone to share thoughts unconnected with business.

'What time shall I come over?' Laura asked eventually,

when she was walking with them to the door.

'Seven, seven-thirty?'

'Would it be all right if I came a bit sooner, looked in on your mother and father?'

'They'd be delighted.' And so would I. I'd like you to grow fond of them.

Aware that parting was imminent, Beth hung back, touched Laura's hand with one finger.

Going down on a knee, she hugged the girl to her, and felt her eyes filling when there was no resistance from the slight form. She kissed Beth's cheek and stood up. Her glance met Patrick's, read in the dark eyes his own hunger for affection.

'See you later,' she said.

'I don't suppose you're used to having neighbours, not that weren't family,' Laura had said as she was leaving Mr and Mrs Horsfall after twenty minutes or so. 'We've always set great store by having good neighbours in Whitby, and they've been very good to us recently. And now I'm right glad all of us here seem as if we're going to get on.'

And neighbourliness was, she had decided, the attitude she would maintain also with their son. That way, she might allow herself to enjoy the contact which promised to be near-daily. And enjoy it she would, there could be no doubting that. He was a smashing bloke when you got to know him, more amusing than she'd supposed. But then, when he was still new to folk, he didn't drop that grave wariness.

What she couldn't let get out of hand was this growing attraction. Even when she hardly knew Patrick she had felt they were drawn together. These days . . . Grimly, she sighed, resigning herself again to disregard the headiness generated just by being in the same room as he was. That time when he had kissed her it had seemed to her inexperienced mind that they had met because it was intended: despite their very different circumstances, part of a well-defined plan.

She'd done a lot of overdue growing up since then. And not only with this bereavement. Michael's feverish kisses had proved how frenzied a man could become. Resisting him had been awkward, but it had been instinctive because he wasn't the person she wanted. Here, she would have to keep her head and think, or her self-restraint would never be strong enough.

She would have to remember that she was living on her own in that Coach House. If she wasn't careful Patrick might even get the impression that she was encouraging him, being easy. That must never happen – and nor must she let him make her forget their very different backgrounds, to say nothing of his being married.

He was waiting in the dining-room tonight, a sherry already poured for her. He was wearing a dark suit and white shirt with a neat but brightly patterned navy and silver tie. Even though Patrick always looked smart, she could tell he'd made an effort because of her and the breath tightened in her throat.

Laura was thankful she'd unpacked her new frock. It was one she'd bought in Whitby. None of the things she had with her there had looked right with the coat she'd bought for the funeral, and she had felt she would wish to wear black, for a time. Not every day, that would have meant spending out needlessly, but for going anywhere that mattered. The frock was more suitable for evenings, as well. They hadn't had anything more practical in the shop.

She liked the full bias-cut skirt which reached below her knees, but was less sure about the way her waist was accentuated by the wide band of closely-fitting material into which skirt and bodice were gathered. She'd only ever seen a similar style in pictures of the pale gown Wallis Simpson had worn for marrying the Duke of Windsor.

Patrick swallowed, awed by her striking appearance, yet instinctively wishing to hold this slight girl until the sadness behind her eyes evaporated. Had her smile been more carefree, she would be ravishing. Black was the perfect foil for her light hair and porcelain complexion. The silky texture enhanced the curves of her breasts and hips, drew his glance to her narrow waist, and increased the urgency with which he ached for her.

'Hallo again, how's the move coming along?'

'Very well, thanks. But I hadn't much stuff to bring with me.'

'If you're ever short of anything, you know where to come.'

Glittering blue eyes laughed across at him. 'For a cupful of flour or something?'

'Anything. In fact, you need only pick up the telephone.'

'Aye, I meant to ask you if you realised it hadn't been disconnected.'

'Saves you walking over here if Beth turns up there again.'

'A bit of exercise never did anybody any harm.'

'Or supposing you were unwell?'

'You're not going to add me to your list of worries, I hope?'

'If I'm not to, a telephone could help you be independent,' Patrick said then paused, interpreting the look she gave him. 'And no, I shan't let you pay the bill. In this small matter *you* must be generous, and indulge me.'

'I know who the generous one is.'

'And to think I pray for the day when Beth may answer me back!'

Startled by his raising what she had supposed to be a taboo subject, Laura looked at him across the rim of her glass as she sipped. 'She's a lovable little girl, Patrick.'

'And she's taken to you.' He gestured towards the table, went to stand behind the chair at its head. 'For her, with remarkable alacrity.'

When she was seated at the place to his right, Laura sipped her sherry again, pensively. 'Is there nothing can be done?'

'Afraid I'm running dry on ideas, along with our family doctor. I used the money you gave for the Coach House, you know – to pay for a course of psychiatric treatment. It seems to be having not the slightest effect.'

'Oh, dear.'

'Some days, I believe I've reached the end of my tether.'

'I'm not surprised. Has she never learned to talk?'

'Oh, yes.' His voice faded and he clamped his mouth shut.

Laura concentrated on her drink, and was relieved

when Mrs Harrison brought in the first course. Patrick might have initiated discussion of his daughter, his disturbance had soon closed the subject.

'And I don't imagine your mother's health makes you feel any better,' she said when the housekeeper had left.

'Quite. I didn't bring you here only to burden you, though.'

'I never imagined you did. But I was just thinking – losing my dad like that was a terrible shock, but watching him in pain when there wasn't much hope would have been a heck of a lot worse.'

Her left hand was resting on the table. Briefly, his fingers closed over hers.

'How's your job going since you returned?'

'Ever so much better, thanks. Touch wood.' She told him about the design that Roy intended using, and how she was working to make it viable. 'I do believe I'm beginning to get it right. It's to be hoped so, any road, there's such a lot I want for my house.'

'Tell me.'

'Well, the living-room is that lovely and big, I'm dying to get a sideboard and some comfy chairs. Or it might be one armchair and a chesterfield. And there was a bigger wardrobe I took a right fancy to when I ordered the bed and everything. I'll enjoy saving up for them. There's the garden an' all – I'd like to put in some spring bulbs, then there'll be flowers to follow on . . .'

'Are you a keen gardener, Laura?'

She laughed. 'Me? I've never tried. We only had a little patch of lawn in the front at home, with a holly tree to one side, and a couple of drab laurel bushes.'

'And now your interest, like mine, will be limited by available time. But I'll see you have cuttings from some of our flowering shrubs. If I can't attend to that myself, I'll have a word with Tom – Mrs Harrison's husband, did I say? I'll introduce him to you. He's the proverbial fund of information, and will gladly advise you.'

Laura was frowning slightly as she spooned up homemade

asparagus soup. How would she ever repay all Patrick's kindness?

'It's quite in order, you know,' he told her, amused. 'Gardeners do help each other out with cuttings and such, without creating obligations.'

Ruefully, she grinned. 'Am I that transparent?'

'Don't consider it a fault. Too many of us spend too long behind a façade.'

She was reminded of this when it was time to leave. Patrick had insisted on walking with her through the gardens to her door. Privately, he had chosen this route, despite the late-evening chill, to avoid being alone with her in the darkened reception hall. There, with memories of her dancing with his child, he'd have failed to quell the emotions she aroused in him. The time had come for circumspection.

Laura was disturbed by the withdrawal expressed in his now solemn face and rigid body. She might decide she ought to resist him, but being resisted hurt.

'I've had a lovely evening, thank you,' she said, smiling. 'A wonderful beginning here. And thanks once again for those beautiful flowers.'

Saying goodnight, he remained a pace or more from her. As she went indoors Laura willed the tumult inside her to quiet, reminded herself of the need for restraint. The possibility of anything more than friendship with Patrick was remote. The gulf between their circumstances was too great. And until she had really mastered designing she couldn't afford to let such problems threaten her concentration.

Laura had never before forced herself to go to church. Some people might have derided her religion which was simply the continuation of regular attendance induced in her Sunday School days, and simplicity was the keynote of her church in Whitby. St Martin's wasn't quite the same, the services tended to be more elaborate, although Laura wasn't yet sufficiently familiar with them to have formed a strong preference either way.

213

She hadn't intended arriving at the last minute but she had awakened to a drizzle of rain and didn't wish to cycle all the way to church and back. The bus had been running to time, but when she reached the centre of Halfield a tram had come unhitched from the overhead wires and its crew's inability to re-connect had resulted in a stack of trams the length of Commercial Street.

Laura had decided she could be quicker walking. It was a mile or more, though, and all uphill. She was struggling for breath when she flopped down to her knees in an empty pew. A hasty prayer later, she glanced up to see the choir entering. Miss Priestley beamed in her direction.

Still uncomfortable about what she herself saw as her churlish declining of his proposal, Laura was glad Michael was out of sight in the organ loft. She couldn't know how he must feel now he'd had a few days to reflect on her decision, but she had a good idea. And it really would be goodbye to their old easy friendship.

But hadn't they said goodbye already to that? she reflected. There was no way things could have remained the same following her refusal to respond at all to his lovemaking.

Miss Priestley stood up, her face all pink while she steadied her music ready to begin her solo. Laura realised that she hadn't listened to one word of the service so far, forced her wandering attention into focus, and let the soaring notes calm her.

If she succeeded in taking rather more notice of the rest of the service, however, she became agitated afterwards when she found Michael waiting in the church porch for her.

'How're you feeling now, Laura?' he enquired gently.

'Much better, thanks. Are you all right?'

He hesitated fractionally, noticing Miss Priestley at Laura's shoulder. 'Fine, yes, fine.'

'I moved in yesterday,' she said quickly. There was no easy way of telling him. 'I was wondering if you'd like to come and have your dinner with me?'

'All that way?' he protested and Laura stifled a groan. He

was going to be difficult. She only wanted to re-establish some kind of understanding between them. She couldn't just dismiss him from her mind. Suddenly recalling a promise made some while ago, she turned to her former landlady.

'And you, Miss Priestley, I'd like you to come an' all. I've got some nice lamb chops in, there'll be plenty for three.'

'That would be a treat!' Miss Priestley exclaimed as Michael was saying he didn't think he could spare the time. 'Nay, Mr Dawson, don't be like that. Laura wants to show her friends this new place of hers. And we'll be company for each other on the way back.'

The meal began ominously with Michael conversing mostly in monosyllables when they sat round the table. His pursuit of their heels whilst Laura showed them around the Coach House had also been mainly silent.

Somehow, though, Miss Priestley's indomitable persistence in fussing over him made Michael respond. Ill-mannered he was not, and it would have taken a boor to continue being uncommunicative when faced with both her attentiveness and Laura's grace as hostess.

By the time Laura was waving them off at the door Michael had recovered sufficiently to thank her sincerely for a delightful meal and for showing them her home.

'I'll be offended if you don't come again, think on,' she said.

As she closed the door, however, and leaned against its panels she sensed that she had indeed destroyed most of what she'd shared with Michael. The only thing that made her smile was glancing through the window and seeing Mavis Priestley clutching his arm as, matching her stride to his, she set off with him down the long drive.

By Monday morning Laura's spirits were soaring. The previous night she had worked for hours on her latest design, and knew enough by now to be reasonably confident it was another pattern that would please.

Still keeping to her interpretation of light through church windows, she had worked on a range of jewel colours, with purples, carmines and blues predominating. Before beginning the draft proper, she had calculated the number of knots across the width, and saved herself time by ensuring a pattern match from the start.

Unable to leave it alone when the first draft was completed, Laura had sat up till midnight colouring in one line of the point paper to convince herself that the design would work.

Wrongly or otherwise, she was going to show this latest effort to Roy without first showing Wayland Rogers. She suspected this wasn't quite ethical, but she had no intention of being underhand. She was just scared of testing Wayland's response. Even though the atmosphere in the studio had improved, and that was his doing, she couldn't ignore her instinctive unease about this man who was her immediate boss.

Roy was pleased to see Laura anyway when she asked him to spare her a bit of time during the dinner-hour.

'Mother keeps saying that I must invite you home. When would be convenient, Laura? We're going to make it totally informal this time, and young Cynthia is dying to see you as well.'

'How about Friday night again, or Saturday?'

'I'll see what Mother says and let you know. And how is your own mother?'

Laura was confounded. She hadn't heard a word since leaving last Tuesday. Thankful to get away and to have something else to think about, she had closed her mind to much of the distress.

'You make me feel ashamed. You see, I haven't rung her up since. I've had a lot on my plate this weekend, moving.'

'Really? You'll be able to tell us all about your new home.'

'That isn't the only thing I've been busy with either . . .'
Swiftly, she produced her draft design and the beginning of its interpretation on point paper.

'I wanted you to see this before I got any further.'

Carefully, Roy scrutinised her work, checking the number of knots it would represent before smiling his admiration.

'Don't let it go to your head, but you've a real flair for colour. This could be magnificent, Laura. The only small suggestion I might make would be a somewhat lighter shade of the blue, here perhaps and here . . . to create a foil for all this brilliance. I see this in an ocean liner, or maybe one of the big London hotels. What does Wayland think of it?'

Her expression gave her away.

'Laura, for goodness' sake! All right, so you feel you're balanced on a knife edge, correct?'

'That's it. I daren't show him the stuff I've done or anything.'

'Look, love, and I'm serious about this – you're going to ruin the whole thing if you put one foot out of line. You're not stupid. You know the men in there only accept you grudgingly. Let Wayland even suspect you're by-passing him and you'll be out, regardless of your talent. There won't be a thing I can do, no matter how willing. I'll not have the entire studio walk out.'

Alarm was rocketing through her, pulsing in her head until she couldn't think what she ought to be saying.

Smiling, Roy took her by the arm. 'So you go along after dinner and show this to Mr Rogers, ask his opinion. And don't utter one word about me. If you choose to use a lighter shade where I suggested, that's an idea you've just come up with. Understood?'

Mutely, Laura nodded. Realising what a fool she'd been, she was too choked to say much but somehow mumbled a thank you.

She had reached Roy's office door when he spoke again. 'If I'm any judge, Wayland won't be able to resist this one. I hope you're ready for some hard graft. This could get the full treatment – lots of copies of the design on point paper, spread out, patterns matched all round. Could be one of the big ones – have you heard about when we have to go outdoors for space to lay the designs out?'

Laura couldn't eat any dinner. Initially, she had been exhilarated by Roy's genuine enthusiasm for her work, then immediately had felt sickened when he'd explained how wrong she had been to bring it directly to him. She could see for herself now why she shouldn't have disregarded her own initial unease. The threat of dismissal would break her heart. How would she live if she'd developed her designs to this level of acceptance only to be removed from Lindley's? There was their kindness to her, as well – she mustn't do anything to make Roy's lovely mother think badly of her.

Wayland Rogers was alone when Laura went back early after the dinner break. That was something. Would it be enough to help her overcome her uneasiness with him and put forward her work in such a way that he might be impressed?

'Hallo, Mr Rogers. I was hoping you might have time to give this your consideration. I could use a bit of advice, you see, somebody to show me whether I'm on the right lines or not . . .'

Short of really grovelling, which she didn't intend, this was the best she could think of and, fortunately, she had the right man for appreciating nervousness so obvious that it had to be genuine.

'Let's have a look, Miss Crabtree.' Affected though he might be in his general demeanour, Wayland Rogers was still a true artist. He couldn't fail to approve this design, even if produced by a woman. 'My word, lovey, you're coming on! How long did this take you?'

Laura told him. 'I was itching to get it down on point paper, I had to try a bit of it. But I was tired out by then, and I wasn't certain anyway about going much further before you'd approved what I'd done so far.'

'You may be sure I'll back this. It may require one or two minor alterations, but . . .'

'Yes, I – I thought afterwards that a lighter blue in one or two places might – er, act as a . . .'

'. . . foil for the brighter colours? Could be right, worth a try. Experiment, my dear, there's plenty of time. Let's just see what you're busy with at present . . .'

He came with her to inspect the work she had in hand. 'Better finish this one first, hadn't you?' He glanced up, checking the door. 'The others don't like it if the boring jobs don't get passed around. You've an incentive now, though, to get rid of this one quickly. I'll see then that you're given all the time you need for developing this splendid effort. And any advice you require.'

Wayland paused for a moment while Laura began breathing more steadily, still scarcely able to believe her good fortune.

'How do you fancy being our star designer, lovey?' He would come in for considerable recognition if he were responsible for a discovery, and they could make something of her being the first female designer that he personally had encouraged.

Grateful to have avoided any further contention and just as eager as Mr Rogers had supposed to be rid of the routine work under her brush, Laura worked furiously all afternoon. She was clearing away ready for leaving, and remembering with delight that it was to her new home that she was returning, when the telephone rang.

'Miss Crabtree, for you.'

Astonished and embarrassed, she hurried out to the front of the studio to take the receiver from Wayland Rogers. 'Not really allowed, lovey,' he said. 'But since you maybe didn't know . . .'

Her mother was at the other end of the line, weeping all but incoherently. 'It's our Netta, Laura. I can't do owt with her, you'll have to do summat or we'll all be taken away . . .'

'Eh, Mum – I am sorry.' Laura could just see the frail woman, her wispy greying hair awry, the desperation in her staring eyes. Her own arms grew heavy with the longing to hug her. 'Tell you what, I'll try and come over one day at the weekend.'

'What's the good of that? If I last till then, just having you home for a day won't give me a break. That lass is scriking day long. The other two are bucking up a bit, they think to help now and again.'

But Netta would be too wrapped up in herself to be any use, thought Laura wearily.

'I am trying, Laura, not – not to dwell on what happened. So's our Greta and Sybil. Then as soon as we're getting pulled together, Netta . . .'

'I really am sorry, but there's not much I can do from here, Mum. Is she there now? I'll have to talk to . . .'

'Talk!' Mrs Crabtree interrupted. 'I've talked till I'm blue in the face. She's either that dense, or plain heedless.'

'I know, and . . .'

'You'll have to come home. I can't manage, she's driving me potty.'

Laura was shattered. 'My home's here now. I can't give it up. And there's my job, I'm just beginning to get somewhere.' And what about young Beth, Patrick? Mutely, she swallowed.

'You'll have to have her there then,' her mother interrupted. 'Just for a bit, till I'm feeling stronger.'

'Nay, I'm not straight yet. I've only got one bed . . .'

'Get a camp bed or summat, I'll pay,' said Maggie Crabtree, suddenly sounding quite assured.

Chapter 13

Pedalling urgently, Laura cycled towards Halfield without seeing any of the trams or cars, much less the rows of blackened stone houses and shops. After negotiating the busy streets in the town centre, still oblivious to the traffic, she began the long uphill haul out towards Arncliffe. If she had stopped, or even allowed herself to think, she would have choked on furious tears.

She couldn't believe this was happening. Hadn't she only last weekend moved into her own lovely little home? How could everything be spoiled as soon as this? All the satisfaction of having her new design approved had been wiped out as if somebody had torn through her work.

Laura was breathless by the time she tackled the last mile up to the house. The day had been glorious for September and although she was beyond appreciating the brilliant sun, its heat was affecting her physically. Her legs were weak from staying on her bicycle even over the steepest part of the hill, and her eyes felt as if they were staring out of her head, she was trying so hard to contain her emotions.

Her one desire was to get home: maybe to seize every minute of what time remained that she could call her own, perhaps because she was driven by this irrational feeling that once there this latest blow might prove unfounded.

Laura was close to breaking, the lump gathering in her throat, her breathy gasping almost a sob. She was so disturbed that she nearly cycled past the gates of the drive.

That's the state they've got me into! she thought savagely, and turned sharply so as not to miss the drive entrance completely. Her front wheel wobbled. She tried to straighten up but was too distracted to regain control. She hurtled, head down, towards the stone pillar supporting the left-hand iron gate. Swerving hastily, she averted a collision but was hurled sideways while her cycle slithered away in the opposite direction.

'Damn and blast our Netta! Damn and blast 'em all!'

Slowly, she dragged herself to her feet. The knees of both stockings were gone, and deep grazes embedded with gravel were bleeding already. The palms of her hands weren't much better, and if she'd been panting before that was nothing now she'd had the breath knocked out of her. Aye, and the stuffing as well, she thought grimly, limping the few paces to pick up her bike.

'Why me?' she demanded aloud, beginning to wheel it up the long drive without even bothering to check for any damage.

Laura had travelled a few yards, hunched wearily over her machine with the tears she could no longer control running down her cheeks, when she heard a car behind her. Sighing, she hauled the bike closer in to the grass verge.

The car pulled up just beyond her and the driver got out.

'Laura!' Patrick came running to her. 'Where did you come off?'

'Just – just back there.'

'Come on.' He took the cycle, laid it to one side on the grass. 'I'll pick it up later. Let's get you into the car.'

'I can walk.'

'Badly.' He grinned, helped her into the passenger seat.

'If – if you'll just drop me by my door, I'll be all right.'

Patrick ignored that, driving straight to the main entrance of Arncliffe Hall. He sprang rapidly from the driver's seat and came round to open the door beside her.

'I'm all right, really. I'm not crying because I've hurt myself.'

'This way.' A steadying hand firm on her upper arm, he took her through and into the hall. Pausing briefly, he considered where best to cope. 'Up to managing a few stairs?'

'Yes, but . . . Thank you, but I'd really much rather attend to these few scratches myself.'

'Sure you're up to coping?'

'Quite sure, thanks, Patrick.'

'Just sit down for a minute then, get your breath back,' he said, indicating a chair. 'Whatever has upset you?'

'It's that family of mine, they'd make anybody upset. I know we've all had this awful loss, and I'm trying not to be selfish, but I've only just got back, haven't I, only had a few days on my own? Now our Netta's foisting herself on me. Or my mother's doing that for her.'

'You don't have to have her to stay,' Patrick said reasonably, eyeing Laura's torn stockings which she immediately covered with her skirt.

'Happen not. But how would I live with myself if Mum did give way after having to put up with so much? She has had a dreadful shock.'

'And so have you.'

'Aye, well . . .'

'What's the trouble exactly?'

'According to Mum, Netta was always Dad's favourite. Not that that were very noticeable while he was alive.' Laura swallowed. She herself had always considered she and Dad were closest. 'Any road, Netta's still sobbing up and down the place, won't join in with anything the other two are doing, won't help – not that *that's* any different to how she's always been.'

'In other words is making a confounded nuisance of herself? And now you're about to be lumbered?'

The expression made her smile at last. 'You've got it. I wouldn't care – well, not as much – if I'd had some time to myself. And the few hours that's left I'll be scuttering round like a scalded cat. I haven't even got a bed in that room. And I'll never dratted well have her sharing mine!'

'Why don't you explain all this to them?'

'I did. But, like I said, how would I feel if my mother did collapse or something because of the strain? Folk can.'

'Even the Laura Crabtrees of this world . . .'

'Nay, I'll not, I'm as strong as a horse. Worse luck.'

Patrick gazed into the blue eyes which today looked wild with agitation. 'You're decided on this, aren't you?'

'I don't have much of an alternative.'

'Right then. You need some assistance. Firstly, with the loan of a folding bed. We have several in the attics. I'll get Tom to bring one over tonight. You'll need bed linen as well, or have you enough?'

Laura gulped, shook her head. 'No, I haven't. But I can't let . . .'

'Laura, my dear, you make this very hard work. You call your sisters difficult!'

'I'm not, honest I'm not, and not with you of all people. But don't forget I bought that house so's I could be independent.'

'Does that preclude your accepting a hand just till you've coped with having your sister arrive? I swear that the minute she's gone again I'll keep out of your hair.'

'I didn't mean you were . . . oh, heck!' Her eyes had filled again, and because of a totally different emotion.

Patrick stood up and drew her to her feet.

'I'll not watch you go under, Laura, not while there's the smallest thing I might do to ease matters. It's plain your family have taken advantage of you for years. This recent bereavement doesn't excuse their continuing to do so.'

He pulled her close, kissed the top of her head. 'Do what you feel you must or, as you say, you'll not live with yourself. But don't let the girl make a doormat of you, and don't let her stay longer than you can take.'

After she had thanked him and was on her way out, Patrick thought of something else.

'And just remember while she's here if you need an escape route it's in this direction, just across that courtyard.'

Netta was arriving on Friday. Laura had arranged to meet her at the station on her way home from Lindley's mill. The only good thing about her sister coming so soon was that she herself

224

would be too busy to fret about it. Even with the loan of a folding bed and linen from the main house, she still had to stock up with provisions and do some baking in readiness.

There was her designing, too – once Netta was here there'd be hardly any opportunity to work on that at home. And the ideas had been forcing themselves to the surface one after the other, encouraged by the enthusiasm of both Roy Lindley and Wayland Rogers.

At the mill, Laura was determined that neither her mother's suggestion nor anything else should affect her chances. And once Netta arrived she would be made to understand that designing came first, no matter what.

Friday came all too quickly, and finishing time brought the familiar sinking of Laura's spirits. It was no good now wishing that she'd had the guts to refuse to have Netta to stay. She might as well put on a grin and try and convince the poor lass she was welcome.

Laura was approaching the factory gates when Roy slowed his car beside her and wound down his window.

'Tonight is all right, I take it?'

'Tonight?' She gazed blankly at him.

'You're coming to Lindley Lodge – had you forgotten?'

Laura didn't recall anything definite being fixed, had thought the date had been left in the air, but so much had gone wrong since she'd last had a word with him. And now she was appalled.

'Eh, I am sorry. I – I've had a bit of bad news from home again, I'm just off to t'station to meet my sister. I've got her staying with me for a while.'

'Bring her along, she'll be company for Cynthia.'

'No, I don't think so, thanks, I'd better . . .'

'What's wrong, Laura? We're used to youngsters around that age.'

Ruefully, she grinned. 'I'd do you a swop anytime.'

'We'll expect you both about eight then.'

On the tram lumbering down into the town, Laura reflected that, providing their Netta didn't disgrace them both by blubbing her way through the meal, visiting the Lindleys might be a godsend. It would give the girl more than a hint that Laura had made a life for herself in Halfield, with friends connected with work emphasising the importance to her of the job. Happen that might lead to her managing a few hours on her own at home to spend designing. Netta would see then that even during this temporary stay she must occupy herself.

For somebody too distraught to accept life in her own home, Netta was looking exceptionally bright. Her hair had been cut in a sophisticated style and gleamed as black as the close-fitting coat she was wearing. Her shoes were courts with perilously high heels, and from them to the neat little hat with a perky bow she reeked glamour.

'Laura!' She ran and flung herself on her sister, hugging her until Laura nearly suffocated in Californian Poppy scent.

'Hallo, love, how are you feeling now?'

'A lot better, thanks to your invite. That house was getting me down. And them two are always up to something, excluding me.'

'Well, let's hope a few days with me'll set you up again.'

As the sisters drew apart, Laura sensed Netta's surprise, read in the expressive blue eyes that she believed her stay would be longer.

'Did you bring your bike like I suggested in my note?' she asked, thinking they must get the guard to hand it down to them before the train pulled out.

'I couldn't manage it in this coat.'

Nor in those heels! thought Laura. 'Oh, well – you'll have to make do with the buses and trams.'

'There are plenty, surely, in Halfield?' said Netta cheerfully as they crossed the wooden footbridge.

'There are, yes. But wait till you see how far out I'm living.'

Netta loved the hills and valleys around Arncliffe, though, making Laura wonder if they might after all have one thing in common. Maybe they could go for a walk sometime over the weekend. There were moors in the distance, glimpses of wooded slopes. She hadn't been here long enough yet to do

226

more than have a good look around the part of Patrick's estate visible from the house and the drive that led to it.

'Is there owt good on at the pictures?' Netta enquired when they were getting off the bus and heading towards the Arncliffe gates. 'I'm sick of stopping in night after night.'

'I haven't had time to think about pictures. But we're going out this evening, as a matter of fact. The Lindleys who own the mill where I'm designing have asked us for a meal. You'll be all right, they have a daughter about fifteen.'

'Fifteen! I'll bet she's either all hockey and gymslips or a boring swot.'

'She's neither, actually, you'll like her.' You'd better try, thought Laura, or you'll wish you'd never contemplated staying here.

When Netta had unpacked, however, and was wearing a black dress which Laura hadn't seen before, the possibility of her getting on with Cynthia Lindley seemed even more remote.

'Like it?' Netta asked, twirling around so that the soft material swung out from the line where it clung about her slender hips. 'The one I had for the funeral was disgusting, like a little girl's – told Mum I'd have to have something better.'

'That's too low-cut for you at the neck. I'll see if I can find a bit of lace to fill it in.'

'A modesty-vest! Nay, Laura, don't be daft. If it's your boss's family they must be more up-to-date than that. They'll have seen more than I'm showing.'

'Happen. Certainly Roy Lindley will have. And let that be a warning to you – he's very much a ladies' man.'

'What's his wife like?'

'He hasn't got one. Which makes him all the more dangerous.'

'Are you "warning" or "warning-off"? Got your eye on him, Laura?'

'Anything but. If I'd any time for men just now I'd want somebody a lot more subtle.'

'What time are we setting off?' Netta asked, re-applying

lipstick then patting her already immaculate hair.

'We've just missed one bus, we'll have to make sure of the next,' said Laura, and gently pushed her sister out of her bedroom. 'You'll have to wait in your own room, or downstairs.'

She didn't want an audience, and would have to find some other frock to wear instead of relying on the black she'd planned. She wasn't going to have anybody imagining she wanted her and Netta to look alike! She put on a silky lavender print that she'd bought last summer for the church fête. It was rather too summery for the September evening, but she'd always liked its puffed sleeves and round neckline. Glancing towards the clock, she decided they must set out.

As soon as they'd arrived Laura smiled to herself over Roy Lindley's predictability when she introduced Netta to him. If his eyes were less firmly anchored they'd have dropped out into her sister's cleavage. He soon took charge, however, disposing of their coats and conducting them through to the sitting-room very smoothly. Cynthia was with her parents and, to Laura's relief, she and Netta seemed to take to each other instantly. She could see Cynthia's eyes widening in admiration of the sophisticated black dress, and their Netta was the last person to fail to notice admiration.

Robert Lindley and his wife, being used to teenaged girls, allowed them both to drink wine with the meal, but kept an eye on how much they consumed. And that was as well, Laura silently observed. Netta was growing gregarious: so far, this made her appear vivacious, any more would have indulged her craving for attention.

'You don't have to watch her like the proverbial hawk,' Roy's father confided softly from his seat to Laura's left. 'We'll ensure that she doesn't have enough wine to go to her head.'

It's not only the wine as will do that, Laura thought, unable to ignore Roy's blatant fascination with a pretty face and figure.

'And what is your work, Netta?' he was enquiring, leaning sideways until his head nearly touched her glossy black waves.

'Oh, I'm going into an office, when I find the right place.

Unfortunately, in Whitby there isn't too much of interest on offer.'

'So that's why you've come to Halfield?'

'I'm certainly going to look around, see what's going.'

Heaven forbid! thought Laura. She would do almost anything to escape having Netta living permanently in the Coach House.

'Have you considered a temporary position, to gain experience and judge what sort of office work is best suited to you?'

Laura began holding her breath, wondering what in the world she could do to avert the catastrophe that Roy seemed about to suggest.

Netta beamed up at him, fluttering her long dark lashes. 'I would really appreciate that,' she said breathily. 'Are you thinking what I'm thinking?'

'We definitely could find a job for you at the mill, see how you got on there . . . How good's your typing?'

'Needs a bit of polishing up,' Netta admitted coyly.

Laura swallowed, suddenly seeing the funny side of it all, but determined not to betray any emotion, even a laugh. If Roy took their Netta on, the girl would prove her own hopelessness, she'd not need to throw a spanner in the works for her. *Typing that needed polishing*? Give her one of them machines and she'd not know where to start. Maybe it wouldn't do Roy any harm to find out the hard way what lay behind that glamorous little face.

But Inez Lindley was claiming Laura's attention, mentioning that she'd been told how her designing was improving. 'Both Roy and his father have come home singing your praises. I'm very pleased. We can't let these men think they are the only ones with any flair, can we? And I understand you've moved into your own home as well, that's quite an achievement.'

Laura grinned, and reminded them that it wasn't because of money that she had earned. 'I used some brass I was left by an aunt.'

'And used it to good effect,' Robert Lindley put in. 'Lots of lasses, these days, would have frittered it away on clothes and suchlike.'

His gaze rested on Netta and, again, Laura smiled. Maybe having her sister in Halfield wouldn't be too unendurable, so long as some people recognised that they weren't a bit alike.

'And how are you getting on?' she asked, turning to Cynthia beside her. 'I'm glad this is an occasion when you're joining us for dinner.'

'I'm all right, thank you, getting over the disappointment a bit now.'

'Disappointment?'

'Haven't they told you? I'm not going to be allowed to study medicine. No one thinks I'm going to be strong enough.'

'Oh, dear. What are your plans then?'

'College, providing I get good results in my School Certificate and the next lot. I'm going to study mathematics, it's something I'm good at, might as well use it.'

'Then she'll be coming into the firm,' her father told Laura. 'Unless by then her ideas are too grand.'

'Oh, Daddy, you never take me seriously. You know if I can't be a doctor I dream of running Lindley's. The only trouble is him,' she finished, looking across at Roy.

Laura smiled at her. 'I suppose having an older brother in the firm does rather cramp your style.'

'*Rather?* If I wasn't quite fond of the old thing I'd be finding some scheme for disposing of him.'

'Grow up, brat,' exclaimed Roy affectionately, 'we need more mature people in administration at the mill.'

His glance swung back to Netta who inhaled deeply and returned his burning gaze.

He's no better than that sister of mine, Laura thought, wanting to laugh again. When Roy had turned his overt sensuality on *her* she'd been too annoyed to realise how silly he seemed. Happen he and their Netta were well-matched; might unwittingly teach one another a lesson.

After they all returned to the sitting-room, though, Laura began feeling so irritated by Netta that she resolved to give the girl a good talking to once she got her on her own. When they were leaving, however, her feelings altered yet again. The interchange of prolonged glances between the pair had Laura suppressing amusement. She could only warn Netta to be careful. How could she condemn her young sister for behaving ridiculously when a grown man was no less entranced?

All the way home in Inez Lindley's car Netta followed one question about Roy with another. Laura could tell from his mother's answering voice that such keen interest was going beyond a source of laughter.

'I'm sure you're sensible enough to realise, Netta, that Roy's feet are clay, if not veritably cloven. He loves to tease young girls into making eyes at him.'

'At least he doesn't ignore them,' said Netta swiftly. Nothing anyone said would dim her opinion of this glamorous man who'd hardly talked to anyone else all evening.

'You heard what Roy's mother said,' Laura cautioned as they went into the Coach House. 'I only hope you're not as daft as you sometimes appear.'

Netta laughed, and ran her hands through her hair. 'Don't be such a stodge, Laura. I was only having a bit of fun, so was he, right? When I come to work there it'll be different. I'm not stupid, you know — I can understand that they won't keep me on if I don't prove myself useful.'

'Keep you on? Netta, this is just a temporary job, for a short time, don't go banking on it being more.'

Netta gave her a look then shrugged, hugged her impulsively, and went up to her room.

Laura had expected that she would hear nothing else but Roy Lindley's name over the weekend, but Netta evidently possessed more sense than her sister had credited and only mentioned him once or twice. The Saturday morning turned out quite agreeably with Netta offering to dust and go through the house with the carpet sweeper while Laura got on with washing and ironing.

The day was another warm one for a Yorkshire September.

231

Laura suggested a walk when they had finished their afternoon cup of tea. They came across Patrick as they began strolling through the extensive gardens surrounding the hall. Netta was introduced and he enquired where they were heading.

'Just for a walk, exploring,' Laura told him.

'Have you been as far as the new reservoir yet?'

'Didn't know there was one, whereabouts is it?'

'Couple of miles away, over towards Moorland Road. Like me to show you the way?'

'That'd be lovely,' said Laura, delighted to be having his company, if somewhat apprehensive of how her sister would behave this time.

Patrick, however, prevented any silliness on Netta's part, keeping them fully occupied by pointing out landmarks as they passed through his estates then out of a side entrance which gave on to an exposed hillside with woods beneath them on the slopes of a deep valley. Approaching the reservoir he told them something of its construction.

'It's nearing completion now – a massive project, but more tastefully in keeping with the countryside than some of us originally feared. Wolf Richardson – he's the civil engineer responsible – is perspicacious enough to . . .'

'What's that?' Netta asked.

Laura could have hit her for airing her ignorance, Patrick merely concealed a smile.

'Clear-headed. He foresaw most of the potential causes of opposition, and removed them. By re-housing those who lost their homes to the scheme – and, I believe, continuing his concern for them. And he ensured that his plans took account of the nature of the site. I think you will agree that when the construction is filled with water it should enhance more than detract from the vicinity.'

'I'd certainly love to see it when it is finished,' said Laura as they came close enough to view the enormous concrete dam bridging the valley.

'And so you will, won't you?' Patrick said, smiling, picturing how they might walk here together on summer evenings, or when snow covered the ground. And walk here alone.

'Could well become one of my favourite places,' Laura agreed, and wished her voice were steadier. All the way from the house, just being beside Patrick had induced the familiar pulsing of attraction. She often wondered if he could be aware these days that this was her reaction to him. Today she had the additional problem of guessing whether Netta also could be conscious of his effect upon her.

'I'd like to see it an' all,' Netta asserted. 'How long will it be before it's ready?'

'Can't be sure, I've rather lost track now. I do know that Richardson is anxious to complete before things hot up in Europe.'

'Hot up?' Suddenly Laura felt about as ill-informed as young Netta.

Although Patrick smiled, his dark eyes remained grave. 'Those of us who need to consider long-term investment and such solemn matters are obliged to keep a wary eye on what Hitler is about.'

'Oh, that,' said Netta, so dismissively that both Patrick and Laura waited to see what she might add. 'We were told all about them and their Hitler Youth at school. But they're a long way away, aren't they? They can't affect us over here?'

I wonder who's indoctrinating our young people with that bland notion? thought Patrick, but Laura was looking anxious even if her sister was not, and he'd no wish to mar their day.

'Let us hope that that's where they remain,' he said, far more lightly than he reasonably supposed justified. The lengths to which he might go to protect Laura hit him quite forcibly. And from fears as much as from any more substantial threat. Well, she'd had a rough time, hadn't she? There was the aunt she'd lost, and then so recently she'd suffered the second, deeper, bereavement which in turn had resulted in her assuming responsibility, however temporarily, for this flashy young madam who dressed for the kill.

If we were on our own, reflected Laura, I'd ask him to tell me all about what's going on in Germany, and why he dreaded its effect on England. Aye, and he would explain it all to her, as well, not alarming her more than was necessary but acquainting her with facts.

Happen I've been as bad as Netta, she thought, in my own way. I've been ignoring world events as if that could make them go away. She glanced towards her sister who was wearing a plaid kilt and white jumper, standing outlined against the distant heather of the moors, her head erect because she was that sure of her own beauty she only neglected to hold herself well if she was poorly. Or, of course, indulging in a bad mood.

'How's it going?' Patrick asked Laura quietly, with a glance towards Netta.

Laura grinned at him. 'Today, she's not so bad. Last night I could have strangled her – when I wasn't trying not to laugh. We were invited over to the Lindleys' for a meal. You should have seen her lapping up all the attention Roy was giving her. And what do you think he went and did? Only offered her a job, didn't he, in the office.'

'But she won't be here long enough . . .'

'That's what I was banking on. Till he had to go and put his two penn'orth in. Called it temporary work, but I don't know.'

'Will she be any good?'

'Your guess is as good as mine. I'd have thought not, but I do have to admit to being prejudiced.' She laughed wryly. 'It'll all come out in the wash, I suppose.'

Before they strolled over to join Netta, Patrick briefly took hold of her arm. 'Just remember what I said. Don't let her spoil your life, and you know where to find me, even if you only need to let off steam about Madam over there.'

'I'm just hoping and praying that if she does stay on any length of time at Lindley's she'll make her own pals in the firm.'

Before the following weekend Laura began to believe that was indeed what was happening. She had gone reluctantly to the pictures with Netta on the Tuesday evening straight after work. When it came to Thursday and Netta began making her face up to go out, Laura gave her an awkward smile.

'Didn't I say, love? I can't keep going out with you two and three times a week. I'm afraid I'm saving hard to get the things I still need for this house, I'd barely moved in when you arrived, had I?' There were chores requiring attention as well, of an evening. She'd die rather than see her home grow neglected.

'Oh, that's all right, Laura love. I'm going out with somebody I've got to know at work.'

'That's nice. Are you and this lass going to the pictures?'

'We haven't decided exactly. Might go dancing . . .' She was eyeing Laura, weighing her reaction.

'Oh, I don't know about that, Netta.'

'Why not? Because of Dad?'

'Nay, he'd not expect you to make yourself proper miserable. But you are only sixteen, love.'

'Nearly seventeen. And – and we'll be brought home by car, this – this girl's brother has promised.'

'All right then, just see it isn't too late. Don't forget it's work tomorrow.'

As soon as Netta had slammed the front door after her Laura inhaled deeply and smiled. Slowly, room by room, she went through the house, pausing to glance beyond its windows to the hills, now quite beautiful in the gathering dusk. Only at the door of Netta's room did she hesitate and turn away sharply after one glimpse of scattered garments and a dusting of talcum powder on the carpet.

She was wasting time, anyway; she'd not touched designing at home for days, and in the factory studio she was busy on making existing patterns viable rather than thinking up fresh ideas.

Laura set out her paints and brushes on the oilcloth covering her living-room table, switched on the wireless for a nice bit of dance music, and settled down to work.

Although the stained glass inspiring her early work had captured Roy's attention as well as his father's, she sensed already that she must be searching ahead for a different source. She needed to experiment, with colour as well as shapes.

She had learned a lot about shading this week. Hearing that she hadn't yet studied colour matching, Wayland Rogers had taken her along to see the process.

Fascinated, Laura had watched while the ends of the dyed wool were matched for the exact depth of colour required. Seeing the cut ends of the yarn like this had helped her to visualise how they would appear in a finished carpet. She had enjoyed examining the varied shades, could recall now those that she had longed to use. One was a deep blue just a touch lighter than navy, another brilliant red, there was gold also and a rich purple.

All at once, gazing pensively across and through the window, she pictured the sky as it had been the night of the storm. There's my idea, she thought. It might not be entirely original, but it'll be up to me to create something unlike any carpets I've ever seen.

Working swiftly now, Laura played around with colour, slashing the flame and gold in daring streaks across the width of her paper, filling in around them the midnight blue and swathes of purple. She wasn't certain at this stage that her experiment would prove acceptable, but one advantage of working at home was this indulgence of her urge to create unusual effects.

So long as she provided Lindley's with enough practical designs to justify her place in their studio, she could continue this in private. And if she studied really hard until she understood how they decided what made a particular design acceptable, she ought to be able to convert every idea that she came up with into something saleable.

Today, despite having had Netta travelling with her to and from the mill, Laura had felt happier than any day since her father's death. And she'd also been cheered by something in the colour matching department. She hadn't been alone during the demonstration, and was especially pleased that young Geoff Appleyard was being trained there. He told her that since his return to work Mr Roy was taking a personal interest in his progress.

'I went back into the dyehouse, made myself face it. But then he had a talk with me, said I ought to try and better myself. I was good at painting at school, he seems to think I've a decent eye for colour.'

Laura was very thankful that Geoff had a more promising future in front of him. At the time of the accident and Carter Ainley's threats, she'd thought of little but avoiding trouble for Lindley's. Since then, though, she had been rather uneasy, wondering if the firm had got off too lightly and hating the feeling that they had covered up that accident.

Knowing that Geoff might end up better off for what had happened, together with the prospect of his mother and Amos Kitchen also enjoying happier lives as a result, suited her sense of justice.

Thinking about Lindley's Carpets gave Laura quite a warm feeling now. She appeared to get on reasonably well with Roy these days, and with his mother as well as Robert Lindley. And she liked some of the ordinary working folk – Amos, and Dennis who'd taught her such a lot about weaving. Her only regret was that she had no close female friends of her own age while their Netta seemed to have palled up with somebody after two or three days. But then, where would she herself find the time for gallivanting off so much? That could wait until she'd got everything she wanted for this house, and had really got herself properly established designing.

I could do with a bit more energy for this, never mind for dancing and suchlike! she thought ruefully an hour later. Her eyes felt sore and her head heavy as she struggled to complete the initial draft at least to her own liking.

Laura wakened with a start, shivering in a room grown cool with the night. Yawning, and wriggling her stiff shoulders to ease them, she looked at the clock. Half-past twelve! And where was their Netta? She hadn't heard her come in.

Maybe the clock was wrong, she didn't seem to have nodded off for that long. Laura glanced down at her wrist and realised she had left her watch in her bedroom. Still yawning, she ran upstairs.

The door of the spare room was ajar, and Netta was in bed with the covers drawn tightly up around her chin.

'I thought you'd gone to bed, Laura. There was no sound from anywhere when I came in.'

'What time was that?' she asked from the doorway.

'Ooh, ages ago. Never looked at the clock.'

'Did you have a nice time?'

Netta smiled, her doll-like features innocent. 'Yes, thanks. What about you?'

'I was enjoying myself working on a new design, till I dozed off.'

''Night then. Do you mind closing the door? Don't seem to be able to get off to sleep with it open.'

When Laura had left Netta waited, listening, until her sister had been into the bathroom then crossed the landing to her own room. As silently as she could, she eased back the covers and slid out of bed. Still quietly, she slipped out of her dress, discarded her petticoat and bra, and found her nightdress. Even when she got back into bed again her heart was still pounding like a massive hammer. Lord, but she'd been lucky! As soon as she'd seen it was gone midnight after the car had dropped her off at the entrance to the drive she'd been petrified, anticipating a big row.

Believing her sister to be in bed hadn't reassured her. She'd expected Laura would be lying awake, listening for the door. Hearing her coming upstairs had really flummoxed Netta. She'd instinctively shot under the covers fully dressed. It was a pity, but she couldn't risk such a close thing again. She'd have to say that she ought to be home sooner next time. Nothing was going to make Laura send her back to Whitby.

Chapter 14

By Saturday of that week Laura was still feeling tired from falling asleep over her work on Thursday night. She turned over and switched off the alarm clock, snuggling down again under the covers. Another hour wouldn't hurt. If Netta felt like getting up, having to make her own breakfast would do her no harm.

Somehow, though, despite her tiredness, Laura could only doze. The birds in the garden were obtrusive today instead of pleasing her, and somewhere a door was banging in the wind.

The shouting began suddenly, startling her fully awake. That it was Netta's voice didn't immediately surprise her, she was inured to the noise her sisters made. All at once, though, she wondered who could be there to spark off Netta's temper.

Puzzled more than irritated, Laura thrust on her dressing-gown and ran downstairs. Following her sister's screeching, she hastened into the kitchen.

Netta was at its open outer door, her back to Laura as she confronted the small person on its step. 'Answer me when I speak to you, do you hear?'

Appalled, Laura hurried across just as Netta leaned forward as if to shake the child.

'Don't you dare.' Seizing her sister by her arms, Laura flung her aside. She then went down on one knee, both hands extended. 'Beth love, come on . . .'

Shaking her head, Beth stepped backwards, stared apprehensively past Laura to Netta.

'It's all right, Beth.' Reaching out to grasp one thin wrist, Laura drew her gently to her.

239

'She's insolent, that's what,' Netta asserted, recovering from the shock of having her sister turn on her.

'Please, Netta – hold your tongue till you know what you're talking about. And get into the other room. She'll not come in here while she can see you there.'

Netta refused to move. Sighing, Laura sat on the kitchen doorstep and pulled the child down beside her. How small and frail Beth was, more like a four-year-old than six. But she appeared to have recovered from the alarm generated by Netta's abuse, hadn't shrunk from the arm around her; she even glanced up shyly into Laura's eyes.

'What have you got there?' she asked gently, noticing the slate and slate pencil which Beth was grasping in her right hand.

The girl hesitated, considering, then pushed the slate on to Laura's lap.

Amazed and suddenly moved, Laura gazed at the sketch which, however childish, was a remarkable likeness of herself.

'Aren't you clever! You are good at drawing . . .'

The clattering of the front door knocker interrupted. Netta stomped off to answer it.

'I'm sorry to disturb your Saturday morning, Netta, but I wondered if either of you had seen anything of my daughter?'

'She's here, Patrick. Come through, will you?' Laura called.

Entering the kitchen he was immobilised, his throat disturbingly full when he saw the lovely young blonde woman sitting with an arm holding his child against her.

'Come and look at this, or have you seen it?' Laura said over her shoulder.

Patrick swallowed, took a deep breath. Walking the length of the small kitchen felt like tackling a route march. His eyes seemed glazed, and deep in his chest emotion hammered for release.

Unable to speak, he took the slate and stared down at it. There was no denying that Beth had captured that froth of pale hair, tousled the way it now was. The eyes hadn't quite been rendered as a pair, but even so something of their beauty was represented. And there could be no mistaking the dauntless tilt to that chin.

Beth had wriggled around on the step, her apprehensive glance latching on to her father.

'This is very good, Beth love.' He looked at Laura. 'I didn't know she managed more than childish scribbles. And before you go telling me that I should have known, I am aware of that.'

Laura got to her feet, bringing the girl with her to stand near the kitchen table. 'It's none of my business what you do, is it? Not that I see owt to criticise, any road. You're a busy man with a lot on your plate.'

'If not literally at present. I skipped breakfast to search.'

He was hankering for an invitation, and Laura had no intention of sending him away.

'I'm famished,' she announced, 'and could murder for a cup of tea. I'll get the kettle on. Why don't you two sit down here? Oh – you'll have to excuse the way I'm dressed, or not! I was just thinking I'd put something decent on and bring Beth over when you arrived.'

'I really think perhaps we oughtn't to be causing you so much trouble . . .'

'Trouble? That's what there will be if you decide we're not good enough here. Just a second, I'll give our Netta a call, see if she's had owt to eat.'

Netta, sounding subdued, called back that she wasn't hungry.

Laura shrugged. She'd find out in time whether her sister was going to condescend to eat anything. And cooking for the three of them would be enough.

'Has Beth had her breakfast?' she asked Patrick.

He grinned. 'Not unless she wheedled something out of Mrs Harrison. Officially, we breakfast together at weekends.'

'I'll do enough for us all then.'

Laura felt quite dizzy standing at the stove, cutting rind off the bacon and placing it in the pan. She told herself she'd gone too long since her meal last night, but suspected it might have

241

rather more to do with the man whose gaze was devouring her.

'Do you like your eggs scrambled or fried?' she enquired, over her shoulder. Suddenly she felt as shy as Beth.

'Whichever's easiest.'

'You're a good one to cater for, you can come again.'

And never leave, Patrick was thinking, acknowledging how right this seemed, and that the hopes which had remained unvoiced even to himself were culminating in an experience that shattered his composure.

It could, perhaps, be seeing her so vulnerable in that soft blue dressing-gown which invited his touch. Or wasn't it more her tenderness with this child of his who'd caused him so much heartache?

'Have you a lot to do today?' Laura asked, cracking eggs into the pan.

'Quite a bit of correspondence this morning, why?'

'I was only going to suggest another walk. While Netta's here she might as well see all there is to see. You could show us around. Beth could come an' all.'

Patrick frowned. 'She doesn't normally go beyond the estate.'

'Up to you.' She wasn't going to make him uncomfortable. 'For a start, though, you can leave her here this morning. She can draw summat else, and I've got some paints she can mess about with.'

'Mess might be the operative word.'

'You don't need to tell me. I grew up with three of them. Became adept at clearing up.'

'She does seem to like finding her way here.'

'And not like much else?' Laura smiled sympathetically as she set a plate before him. 'Don't take on so. We'll see she's all right, one day. Won't we, love?'

Beth was too busy gazing longingly at her father's plate to notice.

Laura laughed. 'We haven't forgotten you, Beth love. I'm just learning you that grown-ups get served first.'

Patrick left them reluctantly, and only when he could

consume no further cups of tea. Noticing the hesitant way in which he headed towards the door, Laura felt her already quickened pulse accelerate. He was just as pleased as she was to spend time together. Maybe he also felt this same delight because young Beth had taken to her?

At Laura's suggestion, Beth dried the dishes for her, her small face set in concentration, every movement careful.

'And now shall we make the beds?' She didn't want to leave the child unsupervised for longer than it would take to wash and dress, and that would be safest if it could be managed when Beth was settled with paints and brushes.

They met Netta at the top of the staircase as she came out of the spare room. Appalled, Laura realised that she'd forgotten her sister's existence.

'There's plenty of bacon left if you want some, Netta love,' she said hastily.

The second thing that was wrong was Netta's being dressed for going out. Laura couldn't let her go off because of being made uncomfortable. 'Eh, you don't have to take no notice of our ups and downs, love – we can't cut them out altogether.'

She was relieved when Netta smiled. 'I know. It's nowt to do with that. I'd arranged to go out for the day, anyway.'

'You never said.'

'Should I have?'

'Well, yes – if only out of politeness. You're my guest, aren't you? I could have arranged summat else.'

'Have you done?' From the look on her face, Netta would have let that make no difference.

'Nothing that'll be spoilt by your going somewhere else. Are you seeing them that you went out with on Thursday?'

'That's right.'

'And where are you off to?'

'I don't know. Does it matter? I'll be taken good care of – and brought back home.'

'Not too late, I hope . . .'

Netta was trying to make a good impression, but this was

more than she could stand. 'You're not my mother, you know.'

Laura smiled. 'It's only that I feel I've got to deputise for her.'

'But *you* came here to stand on your own feet.'

'I was in my twenties.'

Netta groaned. 'And how will I grow up if you don't let me show I can behave responsibly?'

She sounded this morning as though she actually was capable of being reasonable, and Laura didn't wish to antagonise her. It hadn't been Netta's fault that she didn't know Beth couldn't communicate.

'Go on then – enjoy yourself. And just make sure they do see you get back all right.'

Netta grinned. 'You're a love. And you need have no fears on that score. I've never been looked after better.'

As soon as her sister had dashed down the stairs and darted, almost skipping, out of the front door, Laura turned to Beth who had remained as motionless as she was silent for the past few minutes.

'You are a good little girl – you make me wonder if you're still here you're that quiet. Are you going to be all right painting on your own after we've made the beds?'

Laura found paints and brushes and several sheets of paper, then spread them out on the kitchen table where it wouldn't matter if Beth had an accident with paint or water. She was surprised to discover the child didn't understand what to do with either the brushes or the bright colours. Moistening a brush, she pulled up a chair beside Beth's and began to demonstrate.

The sight of great splodges of red and yellow thrilled the girl who needed no second prompting when Laura offered her the brush.

'Now you do me a nice picture,' she said, 'while I pop upstairs.'

She had the swiftest wash of her life, and ran down to the kitchen again with a towel wrapped around her.

Beth turned her head, smiled in amusement, and returned

to her painting. By the time Laura was dressed, the second picture was in progress.

Patrick's daughter possessed immense concentration for so young a child. She sloshed on paint uninterruptedly, creating her versions of houses, trees, and an exotically coloured revision of the sketch of Laura.

'I'll have to take you back home in a minute, love,' Laura eventually announced, looking at the clock. She had promised Patrick she would do so before midday.

Beth took no notice, reached out and snatched another blank sheet of paper.

'No, love, not today. I'm sorry, but I did promise your daddy.'

Beth scowled, dipped her brush in water and scrubbed it furiously into the block of purple.

'I said no,' Laura persisted, determined not to be overruled by a six-year-old, no matter how much she sympathised.

She went to take the brush from the small fingers, and Beth held on.

'You can come back another day. Now give that to me . . .'

Beth screamed, hunching her shoulders and clutching her arms across her chest as she had the first time they had met. The screaming continued, louder than anything Laura had heard when the triplets were small, and infinitely more protracted.

Horrified, Laura attempted to hug Beth to her, but the frail body seemed to go into a spasm, rigid and shrinking. She was afraid to leave the child in this state, and appeared powerless to stop her. Each time she tried to speak, calming her, her voice vanished beneath the volume of Beth's yelling.

Mrs Harrison appeared at the kitchen door just as Laura was thinking she would have to pick Beth up and carry her bodily to the main house.

'Eh, dear,' the housekeeper began, her voice matter-of-fact and relaxed. 'It'll be the first time you've seen her like this. You'll find it alarming. There's nothing will stop her but leaving her to scream it out.'

'But I . . .' Distressed, Laura was incoherent. 'I – only asked her to stop painting because it was time she went home.'

'Aye, aye – sometimes it takes less than that. You'd best not let it get you down if you mean to see much of her. I'll be on my way with the lass now.'

'But how?'

Mrs Harrison smiled rather grimly. 'Watch this.'

She bent down, lifted Beth, still screaming and rigid, and holding her by the elbows rammed against thin sides, carried her outside.

'Do you need a hand?'

The housekeeper still had breath to laugh. 'If I had a shilling for every time I've done this I'd be a rich woman. She's never quite bested me yet.'

'How is Beth?' Laura began anxiously, later that day. 'I'm ever so sorry I made her scream.'

Patrick had arrived, as arranged, to go walking. 'You didn't. It's frustration triggers the screaming. What no one can comprehend is why the hell she doesn't express that frustration verbally. If she'd never been able to speak . . .' He shrugged. 'Come along, put her out of your mind.'

'But I thought we were getting on so well.'

'And you are. Laura –' He took her by the shoulders, gazed down at her, his brown eyes affectionate. 'Laura, don't you know? You have achieved a great deal already. If you'd done much more this soon, I'd feel you were taking over from me.'

'I wouldn't,' she said breathily, aghast that he might ever suppose she might.

He hugged her close. Laura's anxiety about Beth was superseded by the overwhelming excitement inside her. She'd read about attraction, had seen it represented at the pictures, but nothing had ever warned her that it could be so compelling.

His kiss, though, was on her forehead, and reminded her that she shouldn't be longing for more from this man who still had a wife somewhere.

'Where are you taking me today?' she asked lightly, easing away from him. 'There's only me, by the way. Our Netta has arranged to go out with somebody from work.'

'So she's making friends already? Good.'

'Gives me a bit of breathing space. Hang on a second, I'll just lock up and get my key. We might as well make the most of this lovely sunshine.'

They took their time wandering out through the estate. Patrick stopped every few yards to show her some colourful shrub of which he was fond, or the fine display of dahlias and chrysanthemums.

'I wish I had more time,' Laura sighed. 'Don't know when I'll fit in all the gardening I planned.'

'I'll loan you Tom Harrison if that'd help.'

'No, you mustn't do that. Thanks all the same I want to do it all myself. And I suppose I'll make time when I've got things sorted out.'

'And your sister's future settled. How is she shaping up at Lindley's?'

'*She* says all right, but that's not much to go by. I've not had a chance to ask Roy Lindley. If I do get to see him, it's about my own work.'

'And that's going more smoothly now?'

Laura smiled at him. 'I think so – nothing's been said for a week or more, but I suppose they'd soon tell me if it weren't up to scratch.'

She felt guilty, though, for not making enquiries about Netta's progress. And after Thursday night she'd meant to find time to call in at the office and meet the girl Netta had made friends with. The only office staff she knew were those who paid out wages on a Friday.

Once the gates of Arncliffe Hall were behind them Patrick indicated a narrow lane leading along the hillside.

'It's quite some while since I came this way, except by car en route elsewhere.'

'Aye, I don't suppose you give yourself a break often enough either.'

'Perhaps what I need is some encouragement. Company does make a difference.'

Laura didn't know what on earth to say. She was still very aware of his being the owner of Arncliffe Hall. And married.

A narrow pathway led off uphill between the trees which were such a feature of this hillside. Oak and sycamore, ash and beech, they were bright with autumn shades, and filtered the sunlight into slanting rays.

'Happy with your new home, Laura?' Patrick enquired, as they began climbing the sandy path. 'Or were you – until your solitude was invaded?'

'Very happy, it's a lovely little house. Happen I oughtn't to be so selfish, wanting to keep it to myself.'

'From what you've said, you've sacrificed enough to your sisters. Are they all very alike?'

'In looks, yes. Can hardly tell 'em apart. Thinking back, though, maybe Netta has always been rather excluded by Greta and Sybil. I just wish I knew what to do about her.'

'She seems to be taking care of her own interests.'

'Aye, and if she's with a girl out of the office, she must have something about her. Happen it'll all work out.' She glanced sideways at him. 'I do go on, don't I? Habit, I suppose. My mother's the sort that tends to lean.'

'And by the time Netta returns to Whitby the girl could well have matured sufficiently to become the necessary prop. She is finding her feet, you can't say she's depending on you.'

No, thought Laura, and I'm proper daft wasting all this – dwelling on my sister while we're walking out here surrounded by trees, birdsong and the scent of good earth. There was one matter, however, which she wished to clear between them.

'When I have the opportunity, I will explain to her that Beth doesn't talk. I can't just leave it. Our Netta looked as though she could have hit her this morning.'

Patrick's laugh startled her. Laura's blue eyes were bewildered when she focused on him.

'I can't help but sympathise!' he said. 'Many's the time I've itched to give Beth a slap. Or to shake her until she speaks.'

Laura didn't laugh with him. She was compelled to swallow, distressed by what the situation was doing to Patrick as well as to the girl.

'Now, don't,' he said gently. 'You're letting yourself spoil the few hours we've got. I'll have to teach you to use the countryside here as an antidote to problems.'

'Is that what you do?'

His grin was rueful. 'In truth, rarely. Good intentions are liable to be crowded out.'

They walked for miles, up through the woods until they emerged to a magnificent view over the treetops towards grassy hills and moorland. Somewhere along the way the going had been steep, rough as well. Patrick had taken her hand which still remained in his.

Laura felt drunk with his touch, exhilarated by him until she feared her conversation had grown desultory. How could anyone think when their senses whirled and rocketed so continuously?

'My parents are asking to see you again before too long, Laura. Have you anything planned for later today?'

'Nothing that won't keep.'

'You'll dine with me then, this evening?'

'Aren't you afraid that's becoming a habit?'

'I was rather hoping that it might . . .'

His fingers were tightening around hers. How could she deny her longing to believe she meant something to this man? And how deny that she had felt more alive than ever since the day that they had met?

'Well, I'll have to make sure that Netta isn't left at home on her own.'

Netta, however, had not returned when Laura arrived back at the house. In case she reappeared to find the place empty, Laura left her a note. Bathing slowly and selecting something to wear was enjoyable rather than the usual chore. Brushing out her fair curls which had been tangled by the afternoon's breeze, she smiled at her reflection.

This life suits me, she decided, and turned from the mirror

to slip on a pale yellow dress. The crêpe-de-Chine felt deliciously silky, delighting her by its touch, and making her conscious of her own body. Even apart from Patrick today she remained aware of the yearning he created within her. She was aware as well that this desire was merely one small facet of the need drawing her to him. I'll have to remember about being careful, she thought, locking the door behind her, and walking briskly across the paved courtyard.

Her care, nevertheless, was directed elsewhere from the moment that she entered the suite occupied by Patrick's parents. Was it imagination or did Mrs Horsfall really seem even less substantial than at their previous meeting? Were the lines sketched across the once beautiful forehead more clearly defined, was her voice weaker?

'Patrick tells us you've had a long walk, Laura,' she began while her husband found Laura a chair.

'You're doing him the world of good, you know,' Mr Horsfall added, smiling. 'Desk-bound all week, and many a Saturday as well. Nobody'd believe he trained people to accept responsibility.'

'Can't remember when he last took Saturday off,' his wife confirmed. 'I only hope you enjoyed the exercise as much as he did.'

'It was wonderful, and the views – I love it here. The expanse of countryside stretching towards the moors. And some of the fields and woods we saw today looked perfect. But what have you been doing?'

'There was a very good production of Macbeth on the wireless,' Mr Horsfall told her. 'We've never thought it an unlucky play, despite superstition.'

'And there was an exquisite broadcast of orchestral music,' his wife continued, her tired eyes lighting. 'We enjoyed one of the pieces so much that we're getting Patrick to obtain a record for us. Do you enjoy music, my dear?'

'I don't know much about it, I'm afraid, not classical, that is. Except for church music.'

'I don't suppose having a house full of sisters allowed much opportunity for sitting and listening.'

'Not really. The music I know best is dance bands. At one time I spent all my spare time dancing.'

'But you gave it up – why ever was that?' Patrick's mother enquired.

'I – my aunt was my teacher and she died. Somehow I hadn't the heart to let anybody else continue teaching me . . .'

'We don't want you looking all downhearted,' Mr Horsfall said, with an encouraging smile. 'You evidently have plenty of interests now, maybe they have prevented your returning to dancing?'

'I certainly don't know where the days go, never mind the hours.'

'Speaking of which, we don't wish to appear excessively greedy for your company, keeping you to ourselves,' Mrs Horsfall said.

Laura glanced at the marble clock. 'There's no rush yet.'

Not even Patrick himself would keep her from his parents. She admired their spirit. Despite their incarceration in their own part of Arncliffe Hall, they still inhabited a far wider world.

'And what have you been reading since I saw you before?' she asked.

They showed her their latest books, opening one of them to reveal beautiful reproductions of paintings.

'These are in the Uffizi – in Florence, you know,' Patrick's father told her. 'We like to relive our visits there. And to learn a little more about artists we've long admired.'

The door opened and Patrick walked in. Although greeting his parents it was to Laura that his dark gaze immediately sped. His smile began in his eyes, warming her with its sincerity.

A short while afterwards, part way along the corridor leading to the rest of the house, he paused and drew her to him.

'Bless you, Laura, for everything you've become to us all,' he murmured, and his arms locked around her, holding her against him.

Through the thin silkiness of her dress he was warm,

251

powerful for all his lean build. Against her, he felt taut, insistent.

I'll never move away, thought Laura, never withdraw. She was weak with the need for his love, yet at the same time stirred into more life than she'd ever experienced by the emotions that he awakened.

His kiss was so light that she couldn't be certain it occurred. And it was on her forehead.

Far away in the dining-room the brass gong sounded, summoning them to their meal. Laura started, and Patrick laughed gently.

They hurried hand-in-hand to appease Mrs Harrison's impatience.

'You said you'd not be long, sir, when you went to fetch Miss Crabtree . . .'

'So I did,' he agreed amiably. 'And, knowing your professionalism, you'll have created another delicious meal that won't spoil with waiting.'

Mrs Harrison raised an eyebrow but said nothing. For once her boss was past caring how he appeared, it'd take somebody far less observant than she to know what he'd been about. And if that was how the land lay she, for one, wouldn't be sorry. With Mrs Horsfall senior in such a bad way, the place had been too long without someone to hold them all together.

Really aware of her host alone, Laura couldn't have told anyone afterwards what they had eaten that day. The brown eyes that she'd noticed all those weeks ago dwelt repeatedly on her, willing her to recognise that their relationship was deepening. Patrick talked, easily, readily, of Arncliffe, Halfield, and of his work. And all the time she knew he was surrendering to her the final vestige of his innate reserve.

He offered brandy with their coffee. Even after the wine they'd drunk, Laura accepted. She must try anything that might steady her turbulent emotions.

And Patrick had other matters in mind, to disturb and elate her in an altogether different way.

'I'd like to see some of your work,' he announced suddenly.

'From the way you seem to be settling at Lindley's, I suspect you possess above ordinary talent. I wasn't entirely joking some time ago when I said I wanted to improve our London office with carpeting, and that I'd like to see what you come up with. It's got to be synonymous with our Yorkshire roots – did we discuss something about incorporating the white rose with our society cypher?'

'That sort of thing, yes. Do you really want me to have a go?'

'I've always believed in utilising local talent. Would you like to show me what you can do?'

'Oh, wouldn't I just! I'd love it, more than anything. What shade of background have you got in mind?'

Patrick grinned. 'Haven't got as far as that, I'm afraid. It ought to be fairly light, though. Did I mention there's a lot of dark panelling?'

'We've got a lovely deep gold that could look champion. You'll have to let me look at your building society cypher. Oh, I am enjoying this! Of course, if this did come to anything we'd have to talk to my immediate boss, Wayland Rogers.'

'But I'd insist you should be the designer involved. Glad you don't object to being reminded of work tonight. We could adjourn to the sitting-room, though,' Patrick said, taking their glasses.

He set them down in the other room and turned towards her. His expression was suddenly serious. Having received such a warm reception to his idea, he was determined this must be the time for putting her in the picture more fully.

'You will recall, Laura, that I was in touch with the Salvation Army, attempting to trace my wife?'

His words were a complete shock. Her face stung as it might from a physical blow. Why didn't you hit me? she thought wildly. That would have been preferable. Grimly, she nodded.

'Unfortunately, they were unable to help,' he continued. 'I'm trying other possibilities now.'

Laura wasn't going to suggest the police again, she could have done without this reminder of how he'd reacted when she'd mentioned them before. Then there was the way that

Michael had warned of something wrong in Patrick's past, and she certainly hadn't wished either to recall how determined he was to get Magda back.

'Medical records may throw some light,' he went on. 'This lack of any information is intolerable.'

'I suppose it must be,' Laura said coolly, and realised she was even colder than she sounded.

Patrick saw her shiver. 'Are you feeling a draught? Let me find you a wrap or something. I'm sure Mother . . .'

'I'm all right, thank you. I'll have to be going in a minute or two, anyway.'

Disappointment replaced surprise on his face.

Laura tried her hardest not to be influenced by it. 'Netta'll be home before long. I – I want to put things right after that bit of a tiff this morning.'

If it sounded as glib to him as it did to her, he'd never believe that was the reason. So what? she thought savagely. He was the one that kept hugging her, and then thought better of it and started on about his wife. Had she been completely wrong about him? *Could* he be another like Roy Lindley, unable to keep his hands to himself? And worse than Roy really, because Patrick wasn't single.

'Won't you sit down and finish your drink?'

Laura took the glass from him, but went to a chair, not the sofa that he was indicating. She might be inexperienced but she wasn't born yesterday. She knew better than inviting him to continue where they'd left off before dinner. Suddenly, she didn't even want to return to discussing the carpet on which he'd consulted her.

Laura just wished she knew more about men. She'd been so sure today that Patrick felt the same as she did, that there was more between them than mere attraction. Why *was* he reminding her about his wife? And what must he think of her for letting him hold her like that when he wasn't free? Did he believe she was one of those common lasses that didn't say no? Especially to somebody in his position.

'As I say,' Patrick continued, 'I'm attempting to locate her through doctors' records, but the process is abominably slow. Meanwhile . . .'

Laura couldn't bear this. 'I'm sure I hope you're successful,' she said sharply, and stood up so quickly that her head reeled. 'Thank you for the dinner, it was lovely. I'll see you another day.'

'Laura, please.' He crossed swiftly from where he'd been standing, his back to the fire. Grasping her arm, he tried to make her sit down again. Even that touch of his fingers fanned the longing deep inside her. Heavens above! If she could trust him, she certainly neither knew nor trusted herself now.

'You're not really listening to me. I'm trying to explain . . .' Patrick began. But maybe that had been his mistake, he realised. He wasn't much good at putting feelings into words. This was disturbing. He knew how badly he reacted under stress. When things had gone so sorely awry in the past, he'd let his anger overflow. Regretting the way he'd taken it out on them had made no difference since. He'd never seen Magda after that day; and Beth had changed into this withdrawn creature.

'I heard you,' Laura responded fiercely. 'And that doesn't alter the fact that I – I've got a terrible headache, I'll have to get home.' Hadn't this entire situation perturbed her previously, spilling over into the rest of her life until she made a mess of her work? That wouldn't happen more than once. She must not let it.

She freed herself of his hold and darted for the door. Behind her, Patrick was saying he was sorry, but Laura was hurrying away, along to the huge dark ballroom then out through the far door which, mercifully, wasn't locked.

Gasping in air with painful sobs, she staggered the last few yards across the courtyard. As she did so, she heard a car passing the far side of the Hall, wondered irrationally if it could be Patrick choosing that means of following her. And then she noticed the car sounded to be driving away towards the main road.

Inside the house, she shut the door behind her, leaned

against its panels, her chest searing with each rasp of breath. She'd never been more upset. No matter how she tried, she couldn't obliterate the pleasure of their walk that afternoon, nor the warm feeling she'd experienced talking to his mother and father, nor afterwards the thrill of learning Patrick really did want her to design for him. And nor would she forget *ever* one moment of the feelings experienced close in his arms.

Behind her shoulder she heard a key scrape into the lock, felt the door move against her weight, as the knob was turned. And she knew that what she had felt for Patrick while he was holding her to him was something far too powerful to be resisted. If she saw him again before she had mustered a bit of sense from somewhere she'd never withstand this longing.

'Don't think you're coming in,' she shouted, pressing all her body against the door. 'Somebody's got to put a stop to this!'

Chapter 15

It was Netta at the door, and for weeks afterwards Laura felt upset each time she recalled the reproachful look in her sister's eyes when she finally let her in.

'Eh, Netta love, I am sorry,' she said swiftly. 'You must think I'm proper daft. Come on in . . .'

'Were you shouting summat about the time? It's nobbut just turned ten.'

Laura swallowed, staring bewildered at her, able to register no more than relief that Netta hadn't heard everything that she had been yelling through the door.

'Eh, love,' Laura finally exclaimed again, and flung her arms round her sister.

'Have you had a good day out?' she asked at last, when she'd regained enough composure to release Netta and risk her scrutiny.

'The most wonderful day of my life! I've never been so happy.' Briefly, Netta paused, staring at Laura until she made her afraid that questioning was going to start concerning the strange reception she'd been given.

But Netta was too carried away by her own excitement to wonder more about that for very long. 'I'm glad you didn't think I was late coming home. We were that careful making sure I shouldn't be.'

'All right, love. I'm pleased you've had a nice time.'

Laura was heading towards the stairs, desperate to be alone with the distress Patrick had caused. Her only conscious thought, running towards the Coach House, had been getting away to think things through on her own. Having Netta appear had set her back so much she didn't know how to talk to her and make sense.

'Aren't we having any supper?'

Laura quelled a sigh. 'I've only just eaten a big dinner, but you have something if you want. Can you find things for yourself? I've got a splitting head.' It was the second time she'd made that excuse, and she realised that it was quickly becoming the truth.

'Yes, of course,' Netta responded cheerfully. 'I only want a hot drink and a biscuit or two.'

Laura was in bed, trying to calm her mind enough to be able to rest if not to sleep, when her sister rapped on the door. What now? she thought. Am I never going to be allowed to be alone?

'You don't mind if I come in for a minute, do you?'

Netta, her cup and saucer held precariously over the bed, was already in the room. 'Are we going to church in the morning?' she asked, beaming. 'We've not seen Michael since I came to live here, have we?'

Live? But Laura was in no condition for emphasising the impermanence of her sister's stay. Enduring her company at this moment was more than enough.

'If you like,' she said, without wondering about the girl's uncharacteristic eagerness to attend church.

Netta's smile had, if possible, widened. She had been determined to get on the right side of their Laura, was congratulating herself on her ingenuity.

'Have you made any plans for next weekend, Laura love?' she enquired next, apparently concentrating hard on sipping her tea.

'Haven't even thought about it, why?' Wasn't life bad enough now, with the prospect of awkwardness and nothing else between herself and Patrick, without being expected to keep coming up with ideas for entertaining their Netta?

'Then it won't put you out if I say I'm going away for a couple of days?'

Going away? 'Back home to Whitby, you mean?'

Netta's horrified expression answered for her. 'No – I've

been asked to go to the Lake District, just for a bit of a break.'

And a break was what it would give Laura, wasn't it: opportunity to devote all her attention to bringing herself back into line. Thought and will-power were all it needed. She'd soon be her usual self, be rid of this person she'd become who seemed far too aware of her feelings.

'You go off and enjoy yourself while you can,' Laura began, managing a smile now that it seemed respite was imminent. And then she remembered her sister's age, that she wasn't really so mature as she appeared today. 'Just a minute, though. Are you and that girl going on your own? Is somebody grown up going to be there?' Netta would flare at her now for that, would protest that they didn't need anybody to keep an eye on them. But she was only sixteen.

Her sister's smile didn't falter. 'Of course somebody grown up will be there, all the time.'

'Well, you did say the other night how well they looked after you. I don't think even Mother could object, do you?'

'We'll be setting off on Friday night,' Netta told her, then left Laura wondering how she would survive until then whilst continuing to pretend this great lump of sadness wasn't lodged in her throat.

The following morning Patrick set out for the Coach House, leaving the Hall by the main entrance, cursing himself already for being so inhibited. Until today, he'd never have considered that he might be wiser to avoid approaching across the courtyard where he could be seen.

Laura wouldn't refuse to listen, surely? He couldn't have been that wrong about her? Despite the way in which she had sped from him last night as though she thought him the devil incarnate, he couldn't have interpreted their relationship as other than warm?

He had been ham-fisted, he now knew, expecting her to understand that he must clear the air by speaking of this intention of tracing his wife. Regardless of yesterday's misgivings about his own ability to conduct a stable relationship, he'd

259

come to see that whatever else he must finally rid himself of the past.

His train of thought was broken abruptly by the sight of Laura and her sister, hurrying towards him around the corner of the Hall.

'Good morning,' he said brightly, and tried not to react to Laura's face which seemed far paler than her hair, about as animated as that old dead tree silhouetted against the sky.

'We're just off to church,' she said hastily, 'can't stop.'

'Why don't you let me drive you there?' he suggested.

'Oh, that would be lovely,' Netta exclaimed. 'What sort of a car is it?'

'Thank you, but we're going on the bus,' snapped Laura, seizing her sister's arm and hauling her along.

Patrick didn't persist. Where was the purpose in doing so, when there would be no hope of speaking with Laura alone?

'What's up with you, Laura?' Netta's voice floated back to him. 'You can't seriously prefer the bus and tram to riding in his car?'

I'm very much afraid that she does now, Patrick thought gravely. And until he could see Laura alone he must resign himself to that.

Today's being Sunday didn't help. Last night, worrying about his inability to find Magda, he had decided to have another go at the banks who might be persuaded to yield information. Bank Trust companies held details of persons becoming beneficiaries under a will. Magda had had innumerable relatives, many of them aged. During the two years and more since her disappearance she could have inherited at least once. Waiting for the banks to open tomorrow did not improve his humour.

If only there were some lead to work on, however slender. He'd not spare himself if there was hope that the outcome might be the address needed before he could even begin to initiate proceedings.

Laura, sitting in the bus, was no less exasperated. If only Netta hadn't been there, she'd have told Patrick what she thought of him for making up to her while he was still hankering after his wife. His being married was problem enough without that! Her mother would have a fit if she learned her eldest daughter was keen on somebody who wasn't free. It was only a couple of years since her half cousin had left her husband, scandalising all the Crabtree family. But *she'd* lived down London for years, was known for being fast.

'Did you go for that walk yesterday?' Netta asked her, wondering why Laura was so crabby. 'Wasn't it nice?'

'It was beautiful, if you must know. Very lovely.' And even thinking about how happy we seemed together earlier that day does terrible things to me, thought Laura.

'Don't talk about it if you don't want to.' Netta didn't care, she was too excited about her forthcoming visit to Lake Windermere to give Laura's mood lasting attention.

Seeing Michael at the far end of the church didn't make Laura feel any better. She was only reminded of how she'd managed to get on the wrong side of him as well. Was there something up with her where men were concerned? The last time she and Michael had met had only proved how effectively she'd damaged their friendship.

After the service Laura was sure Michael was relieved to see that Netta was with her. She tried not to feel slighted by his casual nod in her direction while he fussed over her young sister, and reminded herself who was to blame. She could have all the attention she wished from Michael, for all time, if she had only agreed to marriage.

'You two've quarrelled, haven't you?' Netta observed, scrutinising her while the tram rocked and racketed back into the town centre.

Laura sighed. She might as well tell her now, it would save any further embarrassment.

'Michael asked me to marry him, in Whitby, after Dad died.'

'And you're not going to?'

'No. I'm not in love with him. And I've too much to do in my life for settling down with anybody yet.'

'Good for you! You don't want a man who'd expect you running round in circles looking after him.'

'Oh, you know all about it, do you?' said Laura dryly, hopping off the tram and walking briskly towards the bus for Arncliffe.

Staggering over the lumpy setts in her high heels, Netta still managed to sound assured. 'When I marry it'll be somebody as knows how to take care of me.'

'Oh, aye – in a life of luxury, I suppose?'

As they clambered aboard the bus, Netta grinned. 'Well, I don't plan on scrimping and saving all my life.'

She's got fancy ideas, thought Laura, sorting out change for the conductor. Still, that's how it is when you're young, if you've not had to face many problems.

'We'd better ring Mum up today,' said Laura. Maggie Crabtree had written just after Netta's arrival to say she hoped she was settling. After repeated admonitions from Laura, Netta had written back but they had heard nothing since.

'All right, but *I'll* tell her about my weekend off next week.'

'You can tell her everything there is to tell while I'm getting the dinner going. Give them all my love.'

Laura would be thankful to have the kitchen to herself for a while. Netta always wanted to talk, and all about summat and nowt. Laura hadn't waited this long for her own place to put up willingly with not being allowed to think her own thoughts there.

Not that they were worth much today, she reflected dejectedly. Trying *not* to remember how last night had ended was nearer the mark. The best she could hope for was that Monday morning wouldn't be too long coming. At least Lindley's Carpets kept her occupied.

Laura had just said cheerio to Netta inside the factory gates on that Monday morning when Roy's car drove in. He caught her up as he headed towards the design studio.

'I'm glad I've seen you,' Laura began. 'I've been meaning to ask – how's our Netta framing?'

Roy glanced sideways at her through his long golden lashes. 'Oh, you know, settling in all right. Her typing's worse than useless, but there's plenty for her to do without it. None of the other girls like filing, Netta's willing to do anything.'

'That's all right then. I just wondered.'

'You can stop worrying, Laura. She's got a job here as long as she wants one.'

'I see.' *That* wasn't quite what she'd wanted to hear. At the moment, though, she'd too much on sorting her own life to spare much thought for where Netta would end up living. And certainly since the girl had made friends so quickly Laura herself couldn't grumble that she had her round her neck all the time.

'It was to discuss your work, actually, that I caught you up, Laura.'

'Oh, yes?' Her spirits plummeted. The way things had gone this weekend, it'd be the final straw if Roy complained.

'That first design of yours is going into production. Father and I both think it'd be good for you to have a go at weaving on it.'

'Eh, that would be lovely!'

'I'm coming with you now to see Wayland Rogers – but I've had a word already. It's just a matter of deciding how much time you'll spend in the studio this week, and how much in the shed.'

The noise of the looms seemed more tolerable when she had the thrill of watching her own design beginning to take shape. It was Dennis Jagger who had been given the task of this first trial run.

'We can only do so much, you see, before checking the pattern's been set up right. If it hasn't been done proper and there's mistakes show up, we have to stop the loom before there's too much wastage.'

He demonstrated how everything was in place ready to start weaving. 'I'll have to do the first few inches myself, but once it's going steady like, you can take over.'

'I'll be scared of doing something wrong.'

Dennis grinned. 'I shall keep a sharp eye on you, don't you fret. And these Jacquards do the hard bit for you.'

'It's to be hoped so, an' all.'

Laura was fascinated, anyway, watching the pattern beginning to emerge after the first few rows while Dennis was weaving. By the time she took over she was too thrilled by seeing her design turning into carpet to worry about the danger of doing something catastrophic.

That week became the most exhilarating so far. And there had been other good times there since beginning her career. Whenever Robert Lindley or his son passed through the shed now they paused to chat with her, complimenting her on the emerging carpet. Laura herself felt very pleased. There had been no flaws in the way the loom was set up, and none either in her initial contribution.

'I've never known a new line go more smooth,' Dennis told her, beaming. 'Let's hope they give me all Laura Crabtree's stuff from now on!'

'You might be under-employed for a while,' she told him, smiling. 'I haven't quite mastered the knack of keeping ahead on designing so's there's another pattern accepted once the first's in production.'

That aspect would come with time, she was sure. She'd never felt so confident, and even the attitude in the studio changed. Later in the week she spent afternoons at her desk. News of her work's proven viability had spread. Without exception, her colleagues were acknowledging her existence. And if in some of them she still recognised concern for the security of their jobs, she now sensed that time would convince them there was room for everyone in the team at Lindley's.

Laura was getting ready to go home on the Saturday morning when Robert Lindley came up to her. They hadn't worked every Saturday this month, production was well ahead, and nobody in Yorkshire wasted either steam or wages if there was no need. But this week there were new orders for fitting out a big hotel on the South Coast somewhere.

'Looks likely business'll be booming again, eh?' said Laura, smiling. She was pleased for Robert Lindley as much as for herself that the future looked even more stable.

'Aye, can't grumble – while it lasts.'

She grinned. Nobody in this part of the world was given to over enthusing. Caution was the byword, even when prospects were good.

'I've got something for you. Call round by my office as you leave, will you, love?'

Love? That was nice, Laura thought, as he strode off. She might have disliked Roy's overt flirting when she first arrived, but she had taken to his mum and dad instantly and it seemed they had taken to her. And to their Netta, for what that was worth. She supposed that was something in her favour. At least Netta hadn't muckied her ticket.

If Roy was around today she'd think on to ask him about that girl in the office with whom Netta had become pally. She had decided against asking her sister herself. Netta did seem to be trying to stand on her own feet; she wouldn't want folk coming heavy-handed, checking up on her, deputising for their mother.

When Laura reached Robert Lindley's office he was alone, anyway, and appeared to be in a hurry to get off home.

'Just wanted to give you this, Laura.'

It was a square of her carpet. She gazed and gazed at the glowing colours, thrust fingers deep into the closely textured pile, and recalled how carpet had felt beneath her fingers all those years ago, when Clem Hargreaves had shared with her his enthusiasm – and had inspired her to design.

'Thank you ever so much, that is a nice thought.'

'I daresay you'll give it pride of place somewhere. And just think on – if you hit a bad patch, and nobody's immune to those, this is the proof that you have it in you.'

There'd been brown paper to wrap the carpet, but all the way in the tram Laura had been just as delighted as if she were sitting gloating over the pattern. She wasn't going home, not yet. There was somebody who had to see this, before anyone else.

Clem came to the door himself, told her as he invited her in that his sister was still out shopping. 'Always goes down to the market every Saturday, regular. Says if she didn't every day'd be alike.'

'I've something to show you,' Laura said, her blue eyes glittering with excitement.

When she sat down and turned the parcel to get at the knots in the string, she discovered her fingers were trembling.

'Oh, what the heck!' She handed the parcel across. 'You open it for me.'

Clem glanced from her to the rolled up carpet, felt in his waistcoat pocket for his spectacle case.

'Oh, now that's fair grand!' he exclaimed, smoothing out the woven square, and scrutinising the design. 'That is a beauty. Your first one, is it?'

Laura nodded. 'Just come off the loom this week. I even made some of it myself. They've got me weaving an' all sorts, you know.'

'And you're loving every minute. I'm right pleased, lass. D'you know what? Your doing so well makes it seem as if my mill burning down weren't just sheer waste, after all.'

They exchanged a smile. Clem returned to examining the carpet, curving it to study the density of the knots, inspecting the backing.

'I meant what I said just now,' he went on. 'All the time I ran the mill I felt I were providing some sort of continuity, passing on all that I'd learned. When all that went, I felt awful. Not now, though. You'll do, lass, you'll do. This isn't bad at all – considering it's not one of mine!' He glanced at her and winked. 'If you ask me, this calls for a bit of a toast.' He rose slowly and crossed to the sideboard. 'We've got port or sherry. Can't offer you owt else, we've never been drinkers.'

Sipping sherry with Clem, Laura felt contented. Their Netta had gone off, full of herself, last night after work. The girls in the office didn't have to work Saturdays as a rule. She'd said they were setting off for the Lakes after they'd had something to eat, and had taken her weekend stuff with her to work. Not having a dirty job, she hadn't needed to come home first for a bath.

As for herself, Laura had come to terms with the limitations of her friendship with Patrick Horsfall. And limitation was to be the word, from now on. She'd been brought up sharp by learning he was still trying to find his wife, she'd not need reminding again. Now she'd proved that her carpet designs worked she was even more ambitious. She couldn't afford to be side-tracked by eating her heart out over somebody whose ideas were so different from her own.

When she eventually arrived home after visiting Clem Hargreaves Laura felt hungry, which was an improvement on how she'd been feeling ever since the previous weekend. She fried up eggs, bacon and tomatoes, and cut slices of new bread from the loaf she'd bought at the bakery on the street corner by the mill.

She had decided to get the washing and ironing out of the way over the weekend. She had bought new single sheets for the folding bed and meant to return those borrowed from the Hall to Mrs Harrison. She had a shrewd idea by now of the time when Patrick dined, and should be able to avoid him.

Laura was hanging her first lot of washing on the line in her tiny garden when she experienced the strange sensation of being watched. Oh, heavens, she thought, Patrick? And hardly dared turn to look.

'Eh, Beth, I didn't know you were there, love!' she exclaimed. 'Just wait there a second till I've finished this, then we'll see if we can find a biscuit or something for you.'

Beth, however, was not interested in anything to eat. As soon as they were inside the kitchen she gazed up at Laura and extended her arms, indicating that she wished to dance again.

'All right then – do you remember where the music is?'

Smiling, the child turned around and scampered across the hall to the living-room. She was standing before the wireless set when Laura caught her up.

'You're learning fast, young lady. Well, let's see what sort of music they've got today.'

The only station playing music was devoted to classics. Frowning slightly, wondering what to do with the child, Laura was about to switch off. Beth, however, was tapping one foot in time to the polka, her expression eager as she again extended her hands to Laura.

'Go on then, we'll have a go. But I don't know the proper steps to this one, we'll make it up as we go on.'

The piece was far longer than dance music, and Laura had had enough long before the child was willing to give up. Still, Beth had discovered something she loved doing. Laura hadn't the heart to discourage her.

It was as the piece eventually ended and Laura flopped on to a chair and grinned at the girl that she noticed for the first time that they were observed. Patrick was outside the window.

'Look who's here,' she remarked to Beth and went to open the front door.

'Hallo, Laura – I suspected my daughter might be running away with your time again.'

'Doesn't matter.'

'I did knock, but you obviously didn't hear.'

'Because of the wireless, sorry.'

'Don't be. We're the ones who owe the apology if any.'

'Nay, don't talk like that. Are you coming in?' In front of Beth, there was no possibility of maintaining the awkwardness she had felt about him for the past week.

At first, Beth seemed to shrink from her father. Laura sympathised; he sometimes intimidated her also. But he smiled in his daughter's direction. 'I shall only take you home if Miss Crabtree says you're in the way.' Still smiling, he faced Laura. 'You're doing wonders. I've not seen her so animated for long enough. Dancing doesn't do you any harm either,' he observed. Before she could move away he caressed her cheek with the back of his fingers.

She hadn't needed his touch to reawaken attraction – that had resurrected simply by seeing him at the window. Whatever

268

am I going to do? she wondered despairingly while she heard herself actually offering tea.

Patrick beamed. 'Only if that won't create too much of an interruption.'

Beth might not communicate, but she was fully aware of what was going on. When Laura set off towards the kitchen the girl was skipping along ahead of them.

'You can sit in the living-room if you like,' Laura told Patrick.

He shook his head, sat at the kitchen table as if totally at home there. 'I'll feel easier with Madam here, if she isn't in danger of ruining your lovely room.'

Laura had made a pot of tea and was pouring when Patrick asked her to have dinner with him again that evening.

'I'm sorry, I can't — thanks all the same, I've got a lot to do.'

She heard him sigh, felt awful about refusing, but what could she do? It wasn't fair to either of them to plunge on, getting deeper and deeper into something that would have to end. Her awareness of him now was making coherent thought difficult, filling her with insistent longing that made her want to sit on the chair at his side, as if being separated by these few paces were intolerable.

'I've got to talk to you, Laura. After last weekend, I'd hoped to come across you during the week. You know the reason.'

His brown eyes seemed darker, filled with concern. Laura couldn't look at him without being seared by her longing to put things right.

Again, her own suggestion was out before she weighed it thoroughly: 'Tell you what – you come over to me for Sunday lunch if you've nothing planned.' At least meeting on her territory like this gave her a little more composure. Delaying until tomorrow might allow her to think up some means of continuing to see him without increasing the difficulties.

'I can't say all the things I need to in front of your sister.'

'She's away, gone to the Lakes for the weekend.'

Waiting was not a good idea. Although Laura kept busy with

all the work she had planned for Saturday afternoon and evening, none of the jobs occupied her mind. Even though she worked until eleven that evening preparing a cold pudding for lunchtime, when she went to bed her mind and body alike were too alert for sleeping.

She had been too agitated to tell Patrick a time for lunch. She got up early in order to have everything prepared well ahead, then tried fruitlessly to fill the minutes until, at long last, he arrived.

He was wearing immaculately pressed fawn slacks, a cream-coloured shirt and a diamond-patterned pullover which combined the two shades. Despite his unease, which appeared to match her own, Laura felt so overwhelmed she could scarcely utter the greeting she had rehearsed. And she failed to notice the bottle he was carrying until he pressed it into her hand.

'Just some wine to have with our meal. I rather thought we might need it.'

Laura was compelled to smile. 'Thanks. I suppose you're right.'

She suggested he sit in the living-room while she completed preparations. The table was laid already, the meal almost cooked. But Patrick was quick to point out that he ought to open up the wine, let it breathe.

And how can I breathe, thought Laura wildly, while you're in here with me again? Why did kitchens feel so intimate?

Working swiftly, she soon had the meal served and on the living-room table. Patrick poured the wine, and Laura took several sips before beginning to eat. I don't think I'm going to like what he has to say, she thought grimly. I shall have to steel myself to accept it.

Until they finished their main course they talked in general terms of the working week, and Laura was glad to be able to tell him about the weaving of her first design for Lindley's.

'I'd be very interested to see that.'

'You can after dinner. Robert Lindley gave me a square to bring home.'

'I felt sure I was justified in entrusting my ideas for our London office to you. You must be delighted by how much you've achieved within a few months?'

'Seems far longer. And I haven't done all the designs from scratch. I had some drafted out, even before I came to Halfield. Not that many of them have passed beyond that stage yet.'

'It does seem a lot longer than those few months since we first met, Laura,' he said seriously, seeking her gaze and finding her glance lowering. 'You know my wife disappeared? Until I trace her there isn't a hope of putting my life in order.'

For once she said precisely what she'd intended: 'And I hope you manage that before long. You need to be a family again, especially for Beth's sake.'

'If you only knew! It's because of her mother that Beth's the way she is.'

'Are you sure? All children need both parents.'

'Until the day Magda vanished Beth was a normal garrulous youngster.'

'Then surely she'd recover if her mother returned?'

'How could she learn to accept that length of absence, all those months of not knowing?' His voice dropped. 'How could I?'

'Before – before it happened, did you get on?'

'As well as many couples, I thought. I was busy, naturally. Could have given her cause to feel neglected, I suppose, but . . .'

'Not enough to justify her walking out on you?' Uneasily, Laura stood up, went to look out of the window.

She sensed Patrick behind her, felt his fingers on her shoulder.

'I wish to God that I were free,' he said, and his arms slid around her.

'But you're not,' she said firmly. 'If so little was wrong between you, I'm keeping out of this. I'm pleased we're friends, but that must be all.'

Patrick sighed again and returned to the table. When she joined him there Laura resisted the urge to meet his gaze. She knew well enough how readily he affected so many of her emotions. She could remain resolute only by cooling this whole situation.

'You're wonderful with Beth, Laura, with my parents as well,' he reminded her as she began serving their dessert.

Laura couldn't help smiling. 'I'm not going to stop seeing them, am I, love? Just – oh, I don't know . . .'

'Leave you alone?'

It's what I ought to say, Laura realised. I don't know if I can find the strength. She drew in a deep breath. 'Look, I came to Halfield to work. I'd waited years before I could even begin. I've got to ensure that nothing prevents me getting somewhere with it. You say you have things to sort. Where's the harm in simply leaving everything else as it stands?'

Patrick did not answer. He topped up her glass and then his own. The attempt to make Laura understand had been a disaster. She had left him no space to manoeuvre. His only hope was to find Magda, divorce her, and pray that Laura hadn't gone out of his life by then.

The only good thing about today was its capacity for concentrating his mind. For some time now he had ceased to blind himself to what his wife really had been. Nothing must prevent him from issuing divorce papers. Maybe his solicitor might have some idea how to locate Magda and serve her with them.

He thanked Laura for the meal which had been delicious, and sat on at the table deep in thought while she cleared away the dishes. He had known for some long while how grossly Magda had deceived him, bleeding their joint account until only that few pounds remained. And in the process making him look incompetent before his own board. If he lived to be a hundred, he'd never erase from his memory the embarrassment she had caused. To say nothing of the crisis.

The fact that the money involved had been personal funds rather than the building society's had been irrelevant. The shortfall had only come to light when he'd been unable to provide the injection of capital he'd promised his fellow directors. Instead of the expansion which he had been advocating, they had been obliged to economise, and at the next Annual General Meeting worse had followed.

Disquiet roused among some members of the board had sparked questions regarding his ability to lead them. After all, they had pointed out, he seemed incapable of handling his own finances. Word had also got around regarding the fact that he'd recently been interviewed by the police. At that time, he'd been unwilling to reveal that the questioning concerned Magda's sudden disappearance. It had been bad enough when that heated meeting had revealed that before leaving she had sold her entire shareholding. If she had set out to ruin him, she couldn't have made a more thorough shot at it!

'Why, though, why?' he muttered aloud. 'I provided well for her, from the day we married . . .'

Wearily, Patrick glanced up. Laura was staring bewildered from the living-room doorway. He understood so little himself – how would he ever help her to comprehend?

Chapter 16

Quite shaken by the conversation with Patrick, Laura was sitting near the window of her bedroom when Netta returned at nine-thirty that evening. She had heard a car somewhere in the drive, but it had come no nearer than the far side of the main house. I hope she hasn't got anything to cover up, she thought uneasily as she ran down to open the front door.

'Hallo, love, have you had a good time?'

'Marvellous, thank you, absolutely marvellous.'

'I'm glad. Well, come on through. Leave your case there for a minute, you can take it up later. Have you had something to eat?'

'We had a huge lunch before we left, and a smashing tea in Skipton. I wouldn't mind a drink of tea, though.'

Laura went to put the kettle on. 'I thought I heard a car. You didn't want to bring your friends in then?'

'No, it's all right.'

'You could, you know.'

'They have to get home, as well.'

'They could have brought you up to the door.'

'There's more room to turn the car outside Arncliffe Hall, isn't there? And there were lights in most of their windows, and shining from here soon as I turn the corner.'

'I'm fussing, aren't I?'

Netta smiled. 'You are rather, old love. And here am I, all nice and early. Even Mum wouldn't be able to create. Now, what've you been doing? Working all the time? The house always looks nice, a credit to you.'

I've no right to question her about what she's up to, thought

Laura, startled. Not when I've been sitting here trying to control this longing that I feel for a man who's married.

'This is for you,' Netta announced later, coming into Laura's bedroom after she'd unpacked. 'For your new home, and to say thanks for putting up with me.'

'Thank you, Netta love.' Smiling, Laura unwrapped the small package and discovered a neat thermometer mounted in some sort of grey-green stone.

'I think it's slate,' her sister told her, 'there was a lot of it in the Lake District.'

'It'll look beautiful in the hall.'

Laura wished she wasn't so exhausted. She ought to be showing interest in Netta's weekend away, but the encounter with Patrick had drained her. 'What did you do then?' she asked. 'What did you see?'

'Oh – you know . . . toured about a bit, saw most of the lakes, I suppose. But yesterday it rained in the afternoon.'

'Did you go to the pictures then?'

'No, we – just stayed around the hotel.'

'Was it a nice one?'

'The most beautiful place I've ever been to.'

Happen that's what I need, thought Laura, to get away for a day or two. It certainly had done wonders for Netta.

'You'll have to tell me all about it tomorrow. If we don't get to bed now, they'll be missing two of us at Lindley's in the morning.'

Laura was surprised that Netta appeared equally lively at six o'clock the next morning. She herself might as well never have been to bed. If she had slept, it couldn't have been for more than twenty consecutive minutes throughout the long night. The discussion with Patrick certainly hadn't made her any happier.

Whatever she felt for him – and she was resisting analysing that – she loved young Beth and yearned to look after her. Not that she'd be able to do that properly either, not without sacrificing the career she'd only just begun. And in any case the child's father disturbed her so much with his fixation about

276

finding his wife that Laura felt she couldn't be a lot of use to either of them.

Fortunately, the mill was as demanding as ever. Now that her first design was being produced both Wayland Rogers and Roy were insisting that she must ensure that her second should soon be ready for setting up.

'Getting the Jacquards set for a new pattern takes ages, you know,' Roy reminded her, smiling. 'And I want you to have a new pattern to hand each time we begin weaving its predecessor. Think you can manage that?'

Laura grinned. 'I'll have a darned good try.'

'I should make this next another of your church window styles, then we'll have a change for a while. What about that one you said was based on a sunset? That had plenty of colour.'

Aye, thought Laura, and so far I've only really been experimenting with that one. She would need to work day and night to keep up.

It didn't feel like work, though, she decided that evening when she set out her paints and brushes. And she was secretly glad to concentrate on something other than Netta's exuberance.

Her sister's elation about her weekend away had not dimmed during the day at the mill. All the way home, in first the tram and then the bus, she had chattered on about how lovely the Lake District was.

'I'm going there again,' she announced, 'I can't keep away.'

'You'll have to save hard, if you're expecting to gallivant off like that very often, lady. How much did it cost you this time?'

Netta gave her a sideways look. 'Oh, not very much. The – the folk I went with have pots of money.'

'Oh? I'm not sure I like the idea of being beholden to anybody. Crabtrees always pay their own way, you know.'

Netta smiled. 'I was assured it was quite all right, really.'

'And you say there was a few of you staying at this hotel?'

'Yes. Now, do stop going on at me or I'll believe you're jealous.'

'Nay, I've too much on my plate just now to be hankering

to go off like that. And oughtn't you to think about a trip to Whitby to fetch your bike, if you are intending to stay here for a while? That'd make more sense than tripping off to t'Lakes.'

'Don't fancy riding up and down these hills. The tram and the bus suit me well enough.'

'Happen so, but spending out on fares when my bike's there doing nowt doesn't suit me.'

'I'm not stopping you using it, Laura. I'm not a kid, I can find my way to Lindley's on my own.'

'Aye, well, you might be doing that soon. When winter really sets in I shall have to lay my bike up. I want to use it while I can.'

From that day, Laura began doing just that, and only used public transport with Netta when the day was wet. Not seeing quite so much of her eased the pressure of having her sister living at the Coach House. So long as it isn't permanently, she reminded herself when she felt afraid that Netta might come to believe there was no limit to her welcome there.

Since Netta went out quite frequently of an evening and both days at the weekends, Laura had plenty of time available for designing. On occasions, Beth joined her at the table, dabbling contentedly with paint, her eyes lighting with animation when Laura let her inspect what she herself was doing.

Patrick she saw only rarely, mostly when he was somewhere in the grounds of the estate. After the Sunday when he'd lunched with her, Laura hadn't invited him again, and if she went into the main house it was either to return Beth or to visit his parents.

Seeing them inevitably made her feel guilty about her own mother, but their letters and telephone calls confirmed that she was coping, if with a degree of reluctance. There was no sign of work for either Greta or Sybil. There had been one tentative suggestion that they also might find something in Halfield.

Alarmed, Laura had smothered that idea before it could develop. 'Well, I've no more room, and when they're not yet

278

working they couldn't pay for lodgings,' she said, thankful that being distanced by the telephone gave her the guts to stand up to her mother.

'No, I suppose not,' Maggie Crabtree agreed dejectedly. 'It's such a pity we're not all together. You'd know what to do.'

'Nay, Mother, don't exaggerate. Any road, it wasn't me that found our Netta a job. And it is only temporary.'

'Are you sure? That isn't the way she talks. And the other two are missing her, you know. They are triplets, after all . . .'

'I'll tell her what you've said. She's not in just now, spends most of her time out with her pals.'

'No need to sound waspish about that, Laura. You never did know how to make friends.'

Never had time, you mean, she thought and stifled a sigh. Her mother's words, true or otherwise, had drawn blood. Hadn't she ruined the friendship with Michael Dawson, to say nothing of the sow's ear she was fashioning out of the acquaintance with Patrick?

Maggie Crabtree went on to complain about the length of time taken over settling her husband's affairs. The trawlers were being sold piecemeal, but the sons of Ben Summers, the coxswain who'd been lost in the wreck, had offered to see they fetched a fair price. Naturally, Maggie bemoaned Laura's absence when *she* might have taken control.

I'm not going to let her get me down, Laura resolved. She had taken Netta to live here, that was more than enough distraction from her work.

The weeks began flying past, so swiftly that the increasing cold as the winds stiffened, sweeping down off the moors, kept taking her by surprise. No sooner had she changed into blouses and skirts and found her thick cardigans than she was looking out jumpers instead. Her heavy winter coat was hung on the line one fine Saturday to rid it of the pervading smell of mothballs.

Laura felt really warm only when she was sitting before her living-room fire, or on her bicycle pedalling for all she was worth despite the cumbersome thick garments.

The cold mornings didn't seem to suit their Netta. Once or twice Laura had gone up to the spare room to get her out of bed before she set off for Lindley's. 'You'll never be on that bus, lady. And if you miss that one the next doesn't connect with the tram.'

Netta had eyed her pathetically from behind the edge of bedcovers drawn up to her nose. 'It's all right, Laura, stop fussing.'

In the end, she had decided Netta was old enough to get up on her own. And, after all, if she lost her job she'd have to go back to Whitby. But it would be with one lesson learned.

Weekends now seemed to be the same. If Netta was going out, she set off at a much later hour, and if she had nothing planned there was no telling what time she would emerge from the bathroom to mooch about the house.

The person who sympathised, astonishingly, was Michael. He had asked if Netta had left Halfield when Laura repeatedly appeared alone at St Martin's.

'She's still with me, she just seems to be hibernating.'

'While you do all the chores?'

'Happen so. But it is my house.' She didn't want interference.

'Still happy there, Laura?'

'Yes, thanks. It's a grand little place.'

'Will you promise me something, though?'

'Depends what it is.'

'If anything makes you miserable, either your Netta's antics or anything else, get in touch. Doesn't matter whether it's here or even if I do move on.' He hadn't yet made a firm decision.

Laura had promised, but only because she still felt indebted to Michael for introducing her to Halfield and quite wistful about the way they no longer got on nearly so well.

Laura hardly felt like turning to Michael when the crisis arose. It was the third Sunday in November. Netta had been away again for a weekend, to Blackpool, she had said. She returned earlier than expected, though, full of cold and decidedly seedy.

'Were you frozen daft at Blackpool? I expect you would be

this time of year,' said Laura, unable to feel more than annoyance because you couldn't sympathise with folk who went seeking trouble.

'Actually, that wasn't where we went in the end. We've been down to London. Only we had to come home.'

'Because you felt that bad?' Laura was trying hard to understand just how ill her sister was.

'No, no – he had to see somebody on business.'

'*He*? Do you mean that lass's father?'

'Yes. Yes, that's right,' said Netta hastily.

'I think it's time I met these friends of yours, you know,' Laura began, wondering again how the weeks had slipped by while she had done nothing about even getting to know Netta's pal. 'I take it one of them is still this girl who works in the office with you?'

'Oh, yes. Yes, of course.'

Without knowing the cause, Laura felt troubled, but dismissed that in favour of doing something practical.

'What you want is a hot meal inside you. I haven't much in, being Sunday night, but I'll fry you a couple of eggs and do you some chips.'

Before she had finished speaking Netta tore out of the room and ran for the kitchen. Laura heard her vomiting into the sink.

'Eh, dear,' she said afterwards when Netta was sitting at the kitchen table sipping water. 'Is it the flu? Let's feel at your head . . .'

Her sister's head was no hotter than her own hand. Maybe the journey had been too much for her, or something she had eaten?

'Have you had a lot of rich food while you were away?'

Netta shook her head, but smiled slightly to herself.

'Is it your poorly time then?' Laura enquired sympathetically, recalling what a bad few days Netta had had after their father was lost at sea. 'I've got some Cephos somewhere.'

'It's certainly not that. You can stop your guessing games, Laura, you'll have to know some time. I shall be getting married soon – very soon. I'm having a baby.'

Laura clutched at the table, sank on to the chair next to her sister. 'You're having me on, you've got to be! Please tell me you're having me on.'

'I knew you'd be like this. Can't you be glad for me, that I'm going to have a family, going to be a mother?'

'At your age? You're not old enough, not to be wed, not to . . . Oh, my God, Mum will have a pink fit.'

'Not when she knows how well looked after I'll be.'

'Well looked after? *Well looked after?* Nay, dammit all, lass, if he'd been looking after you, you'd never have fallen for a kiddie. Even if you hadn't sense yourself to stop him.'

'It's not been like that, he's not . . .'

'And who is he then? I'll kill him when I get hold of him. Doing this to you when you're nobbut a bit of a kid yourself.'

'I don't think you will feel like doing that.'

'You've been carrying on with some lads, haven't you? You and this girl, whoever she is, that you palled up with.'

'No, Laura, no.'

'You've lied to me, haven't you – right from the word go?'

'The only time I told a fib was the first time I went with him, and if I'd said who it was you'd have thought he was too old.'

'Doesn't sound old enough to know what he's doing.'

'He knows all right, he's the most romantic man I've ever met.'

'Well, I hope you'll still think so when you're living in a one up and one down at t'bottom end of Halfield, and sharing an outside lavatory with everybody in t'row.'

'You needn't worry, we shan't be living like that.'

'Oh – posh off, is he? And how do you know his mum and dad will allow you to get wed?'

'He's over twenty-one, quite a lot over.'

'And where did you meet him?'

'You introduced us, as a matter of fact,' Netta announced, that maddening smile of hers erasing all trace of sickness from her face.

'I've never . . .'

'You're no good at putting two and two together, are you? It's Roy, of course.'

'Oh, my good Lord!'

For what felt like an hour or more Laura sat stunned, pondering. How had this come about? How in the world had Netta fallen for his daft claptrap? How could she believe Roy would marry her? And how had Laura herself never even suspected what was going on?

'I suppose you fell for a baby when you took off to the Lake District?'

'Who's reckoning up the dates?'

'But you told me you were going with that girl . . .'

'I might have let you think that.'

'Aren't you ashamed? Having me believe you were with another lass! And you definitely said there were other folk there.'

'So there were. Hotels don't open up for just one couple.'

'Don't be smart with me. So you two left Halfield on your own, stayed on your own?'

'He was kind to me, Laura, understanding. From that first day. He has a way with him, has Roy.'

And don't I know it! thought Laura, but was too sickened to say.

'He's everything a man should be – protective, clever. I can never have enough of listening to the way he talks.'

And who was better geared than Roy for thriving on adoration?

'He could tell I was needing a lot of reassurance and affection after losing my dad.'

And you weren't getting that here, thought Laura grimly.

'I've never had so much love, never just for me. And to think it's *him* that wants me – Roy could have had any girl in Halfield.'

And if he *hasn't*, it won't be for the want of trying, Laura sighed inwardly. Half of her wanted to open Netta's eyes, show her what an opportunist Roy was. What good would attempting that do now, though? Netta evidently knew all about his sensuality if not his playing around, and wouldn't believe anything worse about him.

'We'll have to be extremely careful how we tell Mum this, the shock could be the finish of her,' Laura warned her.

'I knew you'd want to help.'

'Oh, no. I've finished with you, Miss Glitter Knickers. I'll do all I can to spare Mum further distress, that's my limit.'

'But you will tell her?'

'Somehow, happen. But only because I don't think either you or Roy have it in you to be gentle with her. You'll be there, though, both of you.' She prayed Roy wouldn't wriggle out of it. 'You'll say what I tell you to say, nothing else. You're both that daft you'll let her see how he's swept you off your feet and between the sheets as if he'd invented sex and held the patent. There's thousands of other young men, Netta. Couldn't you have hung on for a few years?'

'You have to degrade everything, don't you?' Netta pouted. 'It's obvious you've never loved anybody but yourself. I *love* Roy and he loves me, and I'm thrilled to bits that I'm going to have a baby that'll grow up to be lovely and generous and kind the way that he is.'

'Don't forget that the poor little beggar will have a lot of you an' all. You'll have to watch it every minute of the day – it'll not have the sense of a pet rabbit!'

All that week Laura could think of nothing but the mess Netta was in. She blamed Roy, naturally, he knew what he was up to. At first, she had intended tackling him, giving him a piece of her mind; but he had promised to wed Netta. Any disagreement might cause him to change his mind. For Mum's sake, the three of them would have to get together to convey the news to her in the least painful fashion.

There would be the future, as well, with Roy and Netta living somewhere round Halfield. She couldn't bear the prospect of there being lasting animosity between them. If only it hadn't been Roy, she thought, then realised that was unjustified. Any fellow that had got one of her sisters in the family way would have been subjected to her disapproval. And

284

maybe she ought to have anticipated this, and have kept him and her sister apart.

During those next few days Laura began worrying about the practicalities of the forthcoming marriage. Would Netta even be permitted to get wed so young? When she mentioned this to her sister, however, all she received was a smile.

'That's all sorted out long since, Laura. We had a word with the registrar. So long as Mother gives her consent everything will be all right.'

Would it? It seemed to Laura that the match couldn't have been more inauspicious. A chap like Roy who contrived all sorts of potty ways of getting a girl on her own, and a silly young lass who swallowed everything he said and did! A lass who seemed to think he was a cross between Prince Charming and Father Christmas.

Laura could have liked Roy considerably, however, on the day that he, Netta and herself set out for Whitby. He had insisted on their using his car, and beside Laura on the back seat was an enormous bouquet of chrysanthemums for her mother.

'That's just like you, Roy,' Netta had exclaimed, seeing the flowers when he picked them both up at the Coach House.

'We'll be guided by you, Laura,' he announced. 'On how much or how little to say. You know your mother better than anyone.'

'Has Netta told you I didn't elaborate on the telephone? I simply said we'd like to go over for Sunday dinner, and that we'd have a young man with us.'

'I hope you're not going to spoil our dinners by telling her why Roy's there as soon as we get in,' snapped Netta, rather less happy today about her situation.

'Depends what she has to say. If she makes a fuss of Roy it'll do no harm to explain he'll soon be one of the family.'

'I'll be relieved if we can clarify matters early on,' he affirmed.

'There's clarifying and clarifying,' Laura said wryly.

'Speaking of getting wed's one thing. More than that's inadvisable.'

'Hang on a minute, though,' he persisted, over his shoulder, as he drove up towards the moors and Bradford. 'I mean to have everyone understand that I shall take full responsibility for ensuring my child is brought up secure – not only in everything my means can supply, but also in a great deal of love.'

'I'm glad to hear that's what you intend for the youngster,' said Laura. 'But you'll muck everything up by telling Mother that today. The wedding'll be soon enough for that. Let her get used to you first. Or, ideally, keep quiet about the baby till it arrives.'

'I knew you'd come to see things my way, Laura,' Netta burst in. 'I said to Roy we needn't tell her I'm expecting.'

'It's not to save your face, think on,' Laura retorted. 'It's for Mum. She's had enough shocks for one year.'

The day was pleasantly sunny for so late in the year, and travelling in a comfortable car an agreeable alternative to the train. By the time they had passed through York and Malton and were heading on towards their destination, Laura had relaxed sufficiently to be enjoying the scenery.

In the front of the car Roy was demonstrating his concern for Netta which appeared to be genuine enough. Every few miles it seemed he was enquiring if she felt all right or if she was comfortable. And Netta was confirming Laura's supposition that all the girl wanted was a man who would look after her. Happen it was a good thing there were some lasses who were so easily pleased.

Mrs Crabtree opened the front door while Roy was still parking the car. On either side of her Greta and Sybil appeared, all but dancing up and down with excitement.

Seeing her sisters, Netta flung herself out of the car, up the few steps and at them. Giving them and her mother a joint hug, she giggled and shrieked as if her weeks in Halfield had been spent pining for them.

Maggie Crabtree disentangled herself as Roy opened the

car door for Laura then exchanged a smile with her as they walked towards the house.

'Mother, this is Roy Lindley,' Laura began. 'Roy, I want you to meet our mother . . .'

'Your young man!' their mother exclaimed, sounding about as mature as her triplets.

Laura shook her head. 'We'd better have this straight from the beginning. Roy isn't . . .'

'But you said it was important, that we'd something to discuss.'

'Aye, we have an' all. But let's get inside, you don't want to be telling the whole of Whitby.'

Somehow, though, it seemed that telling the whole town was precisely what Mrs Crabtree would have done as soon as she understood that Roy wished to marry Netta. There was no curbing her enthusiasm for what she called the most romantic thing she'd ever heard of.

'Thanks, Laura,' Roy murmured later while Netta was tearing through the rest of the house with her sisters, reacquainting herself with every room. 'You made it easy, far easier than I deserved.'

'Better not let Mum hear you talk like that. We were lucky the way it turned out, for a start. There's only me going to say you should have minded what you were doing if you couldn't behave. And I'm only going to say it the once. Keeping on about it isn't going to change owt.'

The rest of the visit to Whitby was clinched as a success when Roy issued an invitation for Maggie Crabtree, Sybil and Greta to spend a weekend at Lindley Lodge.

You're not as daft as I thought, Laura reflected, and was cheered by the knowledge that Roy's parents would lay on a memorable occasion.

'You'll love Mrs Lindley,' she told her mother. 'I hope, though, that they'll spare you long enough for me to show off my new home.'

Roy's expression tightened. 'I don't see why not. Don't count me in on the tour, though, a certain amount of work

287

has to be fitted in at weekends.'

'Up to you.' Fleetingly, Laura recalled that he'd striven previously to remain unobserved in the vicinity.

'Have you ever been to Whitby, Roy?' Greta asked during the afternoon. 'You can't go back without us showing you around.'

'I know all the best views,' Sybil asserted, while Laura watched him becoming almost as besotted with the other triplets as he so evidently was with Netta.

'It's only because they're dark-haired editions of you, you know,' he told Laura as he waited for the other three to pretty themselves up. 'In the beginning that was what fascinated me about Netta.'

She snorted. 'Oh, aye – happen that, and the fact that she didn't put you in your place.'

When they eventually left for the drive back to Halfield, however, both he and Netta surprised and touched her.

'We've talked it over and we want you for the chief bridesmaid, Laura,' Netta announced.

'Are you sure – won't the other two trailing after you down the aisle be more than enough?'

'We're sure,' Roy added. 'And I know you've just had the expense of moving house. If there's any difficulty obtaining the dress you'd like for this wedding that's been sprung on you, let me know.'

'I'll manage, but thanks anyway.' Suddenly, though, Laura recollected. 'Hang on a minute – you're not planning a big white wedding?'

'I'm not having a hole-and-corner do,' said Netta. 'We've neither of us been married before, have we? We've no reason to get wed without all the trimmings, like the Duke and Duchess of Windsor last June. I felt sorry for them, I'll not . . .'

'But white – you're not entitled.'

'It was you said we hadn't to tell my mum owt about that. You don't want her to start putting two and two together now, do you?'

Laura could only agree but, despite the smooth-running of

that day, she felt uneasy after saying goodnight to Roy as she got out of his car. She had the distinct impression that from now on he and Netta would contrive their own way over everything.

'You have been a love organising such a wonderful day,' Netta enthused, hugging her as soon as they were inside the Coach House. 'I was that scared that Mum would take against Roy, and begin asking searching questions. Instead of that you've got her thinking along the same lines as us about it all. I never appreciated before how clever you are.'

And I never appreciated how quickly folk's ways rub off on others, Laura thought. You've been with Roy no time yet, and you're getting just as smarmy.

Chapter 17

Laura had thought earlier that she was busy. Now there was
never a spare moment in any day and each week ended with
frenetic efforts to complete tasks planned seven days ago.
Strangely, though, she was happy. Her work for Lindley's was
going well. Maybe she functioned better under pressure. As
soon as she completed one design the next was forming at the
back of her mind. And she was pleased for Netta.

There could be no doubting the girl's delight which soared
above the circumstances, and the haste, of her marriage. Two
weeks after the visit to Whitby, they were welcoming Maggie
Crabtree, Greta and Sybil at Halfield station. Both Roy and his
father were there with cars and the entire Crabtree family was
enveloped in Lindley hospitality.

Virtually the whole weekend was devoted to wedding
arrangements, with a short break to enable Laura's mother
and sisters to be shown around her home. By the time Sunday
evening came no detail of the ceremony had been omitted
from the discussions.

The wedding was to be by special licence, in Whitby on the
following Saturday, with Roy's brother Alan as best man.
Netta was returning home with her mother and sisters. Laura
would travel over there with the Lindleys on the day of the
wedding.

'We'll have nobody working that Saturday in the mill,'
Robert Lindley had asserted, beaming. 'We've waited long
enough for our Roy to find a wife, there's going to be no one
doubting that it's an occasion.'

Occasion was the word, too, Laura had thought more than

once during those few weeks. The four of them had chosen dresses which would have graced a royal wedding. Her own, in the uncrushable velvet to be worn by all the bridesmaids, was of a subtle green. Greta and Sybil had plumped for a peach shade which complemented their dark colouring. While their dresses were quite elaborate, in the style of their favourite Hollywood movie queens, Laura's was more classical in cut with long sleeves caught into a tight cuff and a flare of material around her ankles accentuating the simplicity of bodice and skirt.

Netta's dress required considerable care. She had insisted that Laura rather than their mother should shop with her – a fact which Laura had found pleasing until they were in the store. Then she had recognised that her sister's already thickening figure needed concealing from Maggie Crabtree's eyes.

'Better make sure you've plenty of room in it, or with a week or two to go yet we'll be needing a shoehorn to cram you into the thing on the day,' Laura murmured when the salesgirl left them alone.

Netta only giggled. 'I never realised how fast you put weight on in my condition.'

'You needn't sound proud of it. How far gone are you, anyway?'

Her sister grinned. 'Your doctor seems to think I fell for this the very first time.'

'And . . .?'

'When we went to the Lakes, of course.'

Conversation was interrupted by the return of the assistant with several dresses draped over her arm.

Afterwards, in the bus out to Arncliffe, Laura decided she'd better caution her sister on the subject.

'You won't ever hang on to Mum that you let Roy go the whole way that soon, will you, Netta? She'd be ever so upset. 'Specially now Dad's gone. He might have convinced her it wasn't because of any neglect on her part. As it is . . .'

'Neglect? What're you talking about? It was just the opposite, most likely – never being allowed any freedom at home. But it doesn't matter, any road, not now.'

Laura quelled her sigh. If that truly was how her sister felt, she would have to stop minding that this had happened. Certainly when Netta again tried on the creation of white crêpe-de-Chine in the spare bedroom there could be no denying that she looked lovely. The style resembled a favourite of the new Queen with soft draping over the bodice and a full skirt flowing out into masses of flounces. The sleeves were full as well, just to the elbow.

'I hope you don't catch your death,' Laura exclaimed. 'Remember it's hardly the middle of June.'

'I've got my eye on a gorgeous pair of long gloves. And I haven't told you yet what Roy's buying me.'

'Go on.'

'The most beautiful short white fur that you've ever seen.'

'That's all right then.' Laura only hoped he'd budgeted as well for a pram and a cot. To say nothing of a home.

'Do you know where you're going to be living?'

'Oh, yes. Roy's renting a place, temporarily, near his parents, just till we find a house to buy.'

Where was the sense in Laura feeling upset when the pair of them were so evidently well-pleased with themselves, and with their future?

There wasn't going to be much space in Laura's mind, anyway, to accommodate more than practical arrangements for going to Whitby. There could be no putting off to the last minute of even the smallest task. Travelling over there in one of the Lindleys' cars, she wasn't going to be a nuisance by being anything less than well organised.

A few days ago, however, she had spared a bit of time for Beth. Well aware that she might have neglected the little girl for a while Laura had decided to find her a small gift of some kind, preferably something that might keep Beth occupied.

It was while she was wandering about in a toyshop that she spotted a whip and top. Immediately, she remembered how much fun she herself had had playing with them as a child. More recently she had watched youngsters colouring the tops with chalks, then exclaiming over the effect once they set them spinning.

It wasn't really the right time of year for playing out, but the paved courtyard between the Coach House and the Hall was reasonably sheltered. And she could watch that Beth didn't spend long enough out there to grow chilled.

Laura had given the girl her whip and top in time snatched during the weekend devoted to planning Netta's wedding. Early one morning Beth had appeared at the kitchen door and, for once, had been dressed for outdoors.

Finding the chalks she had bought, Laura had demonstrated how the top might be coloured before showing how winding the whip tightly around the top sent it spinning.

Beth's first few attempts resulted only in a wobbly spin or two before the top keeled over. But the child was persistent, and after only a quarter of an hour had it spinning more steadily.

Laura smiled at the girl's gleeful expression. 'That's right, you're coming on champion. Just practise for a minute or two, love, then it'll be time for a hot drink. This is really for warmer weather, you know, but I wanted you to have it now.'

Laura had been so pleased with Beth's delighted reaction to the whip and top that she had felt rather reluctant to be going away to Whitby so soon.

The journey, however, actually proved to be fun. Netta had also asked Cynthia to be a bridesmaid. A dress had been chosen, similar in colour and material to Laura's but of a less sophisticated style. And Cynthia was so excited she seemed younger than her fifteen years.

They were travelling in Roy's car, but with Alan at the wheel. The family had vetoed Roy's driving, determined any possible pre-marital nerves would not be permitted to endanger anyone. To Laura's surprise, Roy had indeed appeared somewhat preoccupied as he set out with his parents in the car they were following.

Alan was lively company, keeping both Laura and his young sister laughing with tales of medical school and hair-raising experiences on the wards.

They were more than halfway to Whitby before Laura noticed Cynthia's laugh sounded forced now and her expression was wistful. I'll have to get them talking about something different, she thought. The poor girl must ache with longing for the medical career that her frail health was denying her.

'What are you doing at Christmas, Cynthia?' she asked. 'Lots of parties with your friends from school?'

'There'll be quite a few. The dress I've got for today will come in handy.'

'And she's persuaded the parents that she can behave for long enough to join the adults,' Alan added patronisingly.

'Listen to him!' Cynthia exclaimed. 'I don't quite have to have a bib tied under my chin. And I'm not wearing pull-ups to keep my legs warm, even today!'

'But you are glad you won't be excluded from anything,' said Laura, and Cynthia grinned.

'Naturally. 'Specially now. Your Netta's already planning to do a lot of entertaining.'

Our Netta hasn't considered the hard work that will entail, Laura realised. But she kept the thought to herself. 'You'll enjoy that.'

'And so will you. She is your sister, after all. You'll be included in everything they plan.'

Inwardly, Laura groaned. She could just picture herself turning up for every gathering Netta and Roy laid on! Did nobody realise that she had her own life, her own interests?

'Don't tell me you won't be joining in?' Alan exclaimed. 'I shall be home over Christmas, thought I could count on having you around?'

'We'll have to see, won't we?'

If she dared only admit it to herself, she had visualised any time she could spare being spent in and around her own home. After all, from this weekend, she was having restored the freedom that had been so short lived.

The Lindleys had a game for enlivening long journeys, Cynthia explained. A colour was chosen and within a given time there was a contest to observe the most vehicles, clothing of passersby, anything of the selected hue.

'Red,' Alan announced. 'You're playing as well, Laura.'

The rest of the way to Whitby passed loudly and hilariously, as arguments developed over items spotted or otherwise.

The other car had pulled ahead, and Roy and his parents were already installed in the front room of Laura's old home when Alan parked outside.

Mrs Crabtree had insisted that the Lindleys should come here to change for the wedding, even though that involved complex manoeuvring to ensure that bride and groom did not meet too soon.

'Is our Netta in her room?' Laura enquired, giving her mother a hug.

'Aye, and the other two an' all. You're changing up there with them. That'll leave the other rooms free for everyone else. I'm ready.'

'So I see.'

Laura stepped back a pace, holding her mother by the shoulders while she inspected her navy blue costume with a fox fur collar.

'It's very nice, Mum.' Smiling, she tilted the jaunty little navy hat so that its satin flower was over one eye. 'That's quite saucy, you know.'

'Yes, well – it had to be navy, 'cos of your dad, but I didn't want to look dowdy.'

'And you don't, you've got it just right.' Maybe she had more than her outfit under control, as well, thought Laura, feeling very thankful. She'd never known her mother be ready for any occasion ahead of time before, and never to avoid fussing.

Greta and Sybil were already in their peach velvet, and hurried to greet Laura in the bedroom doorway.

'Come and look at this one . . .'

Dressed only in white silk brassiere and panties and very

fine silk stockings, Netta was parading about in front of the long mirror.

'She won't put her frock on,' Sybil announced.

'There's time yet.' As she said hallo to Netta, though, Laura wondered how her sister dared show herself off like that. How could the other two fail to notice her figure?

'You look gorgeous, you know you do,' Greta exclaimed. 'Stop fancying yourself now and finish getting dressed.'

'Can't see why you're so particular about your undies anyway, it isn't as if he hadn't seen it all before,' Sybil added.

They knew. Carefully laying her bridesmaid's dress on the bed, Laura went to close the door. She faced Netta who, sensing the severity of her gaze, stopped promming up and down and raised a questioning dark eyebrow.

'You've told them, haven't you, Netta? Does Mum know an' all?'

Smiling, Netta shook her head. 'And I didn't have to tell these two either.'

Moving instinctively, Greta and Sybil had closed in on either side of the sister who suddenly looked vulnerable in her underwear. They'll always be triplets, thought Laura, even if they all wed blokes who take them to the opposite ends of the earth. And she was the elder sister, very much so.

'You are sure Mum doesn't know?'

Three pairs of blue eyes sparkled with amusement. Simultaneously they chuckled. After a moment, Sybil came to Laura and thrust an arm through hers.

'Have you been away that long you've forgotten how naive Mum is? She doesn't even think about sex and all that. She's that old-fashioned she used to undress in the dark so our dad didn't see her.'

Joke or not, Laura suspected that might be very near the truth. But Maggie Crabtree's awareness or otherwise of Netta's condition surely depended on nothing more or less than her possessing eyes?

Netta smiled at Laura, then spoke to the other two. 'You'd better help me on with my dress, or Madam here'll be so busy scolding she won't be getting into her own.'

Laura nodded, and made for the bathroom before the Lindleys came upstairs to get ready. Alone, she warned herself to stop fussing. She would be off back to Halfield tonight, anyway, it wouldn't be her misfortune to contend with her mother's possible suspicions. And if *she* kept on about their Netta expecting, she was the one who would ruin the day.

The church was nearly full, and the big old boiler steaming away to try and counteract the winter chill. The vicar smiled at them all, and murmured that he was glad to see Laura again as he met them at the porch. And then he was leading Netta on the arm of her uncle all the way to the front where Roy and his brother were waiting.

Whatever else, Roy looked magnificent today, tall and straight, and his smile as Netta reached him would warm anyone's heart. His hair and the slightly darker gleam of Alan's seemed to glow and, with Netta's white and the other triplets' pale dresses, lit the sombre winter interior of the church.

Everything's going to be all right for them, thought Laura, and felt relief in waves washing down over her, removing the burden so that now her shoulders straightened. She took Netta's bouquet and listened intently to the age-old words binding her sister to the man who'd given her his child.

On Alan's arm as they retraced their steps down the aisle after the signing in the vestry, Laura felt good, more contented about her family than she'd believed possible after her father was lost at sea. Mum did appear to be learning to cope, and hadn't shed more than the customary odd tear during the ceremony. And now Netta was wed, however young she might be. There was hope also of this kind of a solution to their sisters' future. Perhaps she needn't worry too much about them all from now on.

Outside the church, Maggie Crabtree bustled around, introducing the Lindley family to her own friends and relations, and further convincing Laura that she had found new reserves of energy. While they were standing together for one of the many photographs, however, a sudden remark startled her eldest daughter.

'Doesn't our Netta seem well? Must be the way you've looked after her, else being in love suits her. Her face seems to have filled out somehow.'

Laura nodded, not trusting herself to speak. Her other two sisters were standing nearby, she willed them to say nothing in their mother's hearing. But Maggie spoke again, and to them.

'I hope you two aren't getting any ideas about leaving home, not yet awhile. What suits one won't necessarily suit another. And just because our Laura fixed Netta up with somebody doesn't mean she could do it again.'

Together, Greta and Sybil laughed. 'Mum wants us at home, would you believe that! We're not the nuisances she always says.'

'You're good girls, all four of you. I've always maintained that.'

Not always to me, you haven't, thought Laura, but cared hardly at all. Tonight she was going home. She could love her family without wanting to live in their pockets.

Wedged between Cynthia and Alan in the back of the Lindleys' car, Laura realised the day had drained her. She drowsed repeatedly, wakened ashamed, and drowsed again.

'Sorry I haven't been much company,' she said ruefully as she thanked them when they dropped her outside the Coach House.

Roy's mother, who had got out with her, smiled. 'I know just how you feel, love. It's been a very long day. A lovely one, though, as well. It was time our Roy settled down, and if your sister's anything like you he'll have no regrets.' Moving a yard or so from the car, she lowered her voice. 'I think it's going to work out, you know – despite their getting off to a less than ideal start.'

'I was worried most in case Mother suspected. She's had enough to bear this year. But by the time the kiddie arrives she'll be thinking of Roy as the son who's helped her cope with so many girls.'

They said goodnight and Laura turned at her front door to wave them off. It *had* been a good day, everything had been champion. And tomorrow, thank heaven, was Sunday. She was going straight up to bed now, and she would have her sleep out. There'd be no strident alarm disturbing her while it was still dark.

Before going upstairs, however, Laura felt compelled to have a quick look right through the house. The living-room seemed cosy, even though there had been no fire in the grate since the previous evening. And the kitchen was nice and tidy. She took pride in keeping it that way, still hardly believing that it was her own.

Turning from the kitchen to go to the foot of the staircase, Laura heard the rattle of a door. Mystified, she hesitated, listening. For several seconds there was no further sound, but she was uneasy now and went back into the kitchen. She hadn't switched on the light again but the glow from the hall was sufficient to reveal the movement of the handle on the outer door.

'Who's there?' she called, trying not to panic for the usual explanation of Beth's appearance seemed most unlikely at this hour.

There was no reply, and one means only of satisfying herself in order to sleep. Trying to control her ridiculously unsteady pulse by breathing deeply, Laura hurried towards the door. Again she called to ask who was there. Again there was no answer.

Standing so that the door at least would protect her, she turned the key in the lock and drew back the bolts. She opened the door just an inch or two whilst remaining ready to slam it shut. On the step was a slight figure with long pale hair.

'Beth! Don't you know it's round about midnight? You gave me the fright of my life.'

The child looked to be smiling unconcernedly. When Laura opened the door wider she stretched out her arms in the familiar invitation to dance.

'Oh no, you don't, young lady. You're going straight home this very second.'

Pausing only to check that she had her key, Laura came out on to the step and secured the door after her. She made a grab for one of Beth's hands but, sensing that it wasn't playtime, the girl withdrew, clasping her fingers resolutely behind her back.

'Come on then . . .'

Grasping Beth's shoulder, Laura began urging her towards the main house.

She had heard the girl's scream before. At this time of night it sounded fifty times louder and more horrifying.

'You can stop that nonsense,' she told her firmly, trying to haul her along.

Beth went rigid. Although still moving, she was digging in her heels with every step. Laura was thankful the paved courtyard offered little purchase.

'Now just stop that silly yelling.'

Her command made no difference. She didn't know whether she was glad or sorry that there were still lights in the Hall. Whoever was up might come to her assistance, but what would they make of the way she was compelled to manhandle the child?

The door from the large reception room opened when they were a couple of yards from it.

'How the blazes did she leave here?' Patrick demanded.

'Don't ask me. I certainly didn't encourage her. I've been out since the crack of drawn. I've just arrived home, exhausted. She scared me half to death rattling the door. And if I hadn't been around she could have wandered off anywhere. It's time somebody became responsible for keeping Beth indoors, 'specially at this hour.'

'For all I knew, she was in bed and asleep. That was how I left her long before nine o'clock.'

He was wearing a maroon silk dressing-gown and matching pyjamas, but looked too wakeful to have been in bed. Seeing her father, Beth's rigidity had increased. Laura gave up the struggle and left her a few paces short of the door. She wouldn't have been human if she hadn't felt satisfied witnessing the struggle Patrick was having to win Beth's co-operation. Finally, he lifted his daughter bodily and carried her through the door, up the steps to the minstrels' gallery and away out of sight.

About to return to her own home, Laura checked, aware now of her own sharpness with Patrick. If what he said was true, he could hardly be expected to keep guard on Beth's door to prevent her emerging. He had looked tired as well, and nothing she knew about him made her suppose he'd have spent the day celebrating anything.

Patrick returned more swiftly than she'd expected.

'Mrs Harrison had heard her too,' he announced, coming down the stairs. 'She'll sit with her until she's asleep again.'

He looked at Laura, sighed, gave a shrug. 'Sorry. Beth must have startled you, arriving at your door this late at night. Sorry as well about her yelling. As you will realise, that's something we still have to conquer.'

'And I'm sorry I was a bit sharp with you. It was just . . .'

'Again, all the apologies should be ours. Look – this must have disturbed you as much as it has me. Let's find a drink.'

Patrick led the way across and through the long echoing hall and into a smaller room, furnished with antiques together with several velvet-upholstered sofas and chairs.

'You'd better sit down before you drop.'

He went to a carved sideboard, located glasses and decanters. He poured for her and brought the glass over without enquiring what she would like.

'Not sure I should be accepting this,' Laura said, her smile wry. 'I've been drinking more than usual already.'

'Some sort of celebration obviously. I was thinking you look very splendid.'

'Netta's wedding.'

'Netta's? *Netta's?* Isn't she a trifle young . . .?'

'Yes. She's also a trifle pregnant. Though I'd prefer it if you kept that to yourself.'

'Of course.' Patrick sat beside her, sipping his own drink. 'Somebody in Halfield?'

'One of our bosses – Roy Lindley. Evidently, I didn't keep a sharp enough eye on her.' She checked herself, grinning. 'And there am I – telling you you should keep tabs on Beth. No one can, can they?'

'It wasn't expected of you, surely, or only within reasonable bounds.'

'Go on saying that, I'd like to believe you. The only good thing is that Mother doesn't suspect Netta's condition.'

'And Lindley has married the girl then?'

'Yes, they seem surprisingly well-suited too. I just – well, wish I'd stopped the daft hap'orth before it came to this.'

'You have your own life.'

'Aye. And happen if I hadn't been so floored by having her thrust upon me I'd not have been so eager to let her go off out without me.'

'Laura – stop blaming yourself.'

Slowly, gazing earnestly into her eyes, Patrick rose. He drew her with him, held her.

'You're only a bit of a girl yourself.'

'I'm twenty-six.'

He chuckled into her hair, pulled her closer against him, savouring the fragrance of her, the velvet of her dress beneath his fingers.

'You're very lovely.'

This near she couldn't ignore the hard tension of his body nor could she pretend to dismiss the sudden pulsing awakening in her own. Minutes ago she could have cursed him soundly. Now she knew only that she was where she needed to be.

His lips were gentle at first. Beneath them, though, her own stirred and parted.

'I was tired out,' Laura murmured, half in protest.

'So was I – desperately, after an appalling day.'

Looking at him, she read the sadness in his dark eyes, saw the lines etched at their corners and deeper lines to either side of his mouth. Easing herself out of his arms, she sat down again and faced Patrick as he joined her.

'Want to talk about it?'

'In a minute. So – now we know why Beth couldn't find you today. She kept trying, you see. Straight after breakfast she put on her scarf and coat and found that whip and top you gave her. I was watching from upstairs. She seems to have got the knack of it all right now, but she was missing your approval. Each time she got the top spinning well she glanced towards your windows.'

Laura smiled. 'Poor little Beth. Still, it'll do her no harm to play on her own.'

Patrick was nodding. 'Playing isn't something she's very good at, I'm afraid.'

'But she will still draw and paint contentedly for hours. Is she artistic in other ways?'

His grin was rueful. 'Don't ask me. Afraid I've always tended to be wrapped up in more practical matters.' He paused, then looked at her. 'I do appreciate your interest in her, you know. You're becoming a marvellous influence.'

'Well, you'd do more yourself if you hadn't so much on your plate.'

He glanced down at his hands. 'Certainly there are times when I can't give Beth my undivided attention. Even at weekends. My mother has had a dreadful day today. Couldn't even keep water down. And you know how every bit of food is specially prepared for her.'

'Can't they do anything, Patrick?'

'Operate?' He sighed. 'They did. The tumour was too extensive to be fully removed. Shouldn't be surprised if it's increased in size again. We can only wait.'

'And hope . . .'

He shook his head. 'Not that, not any longer. And watching her starve is torture.'

'I'm so sorry.' She kissed him tenderly, full on the lips. She was desperate with the need to make him forget. To make up to him for the succession of anxieties which robbed him of all joy.

Patrick would have drawn her into his arms again only Laura resisted. But when she spoke her voice was warm and sympathetic.

'You don't have to bear this on your own, do you?'

His expression was rueful. 'Nor to keep the rest of the family in the dark. I did telephone my sister this evening. It was Ted who answered. Jenny had just gone into labour a week early, they were about to call the midwife and doctor.'

'So now you're wondering how she's going on as well, eh? You've not heard any more since?'

He shook his head. 'And it sounded as though we shan't before morning. In any case, they wouldn't ring with the news this late.'

'At least another grandchild will give your parents a new interest.'

Patrick didn't wish to think about them any longer, nor even to think at all. He ached to submerge despair along with himself. And knew that he must not, that he would not. If he could still manage to restrain the heartbreaking worry about his mother, about Beth, he would certainly clamp under control this fierce urgency to love.

'Don't even think about them now,' Laura murmured, and her hand covered his.

Patrick stifled a groan, willed himself not to pull her into his arms. Against his side she felt enticingly warm, the velvet of her dress so soft it stirred thoughts of her yielding. And then he remembered.

Today, he'd felt as bad as ever in the past; short-tempered, resentful of the hand fate had dealt. Why me? he had thought, just as he had when he was under so much pressure before. Why us? Yet he knew himself – he would have destroyed anyone who cared enough to stay around. He must never expose Laura to all that. He would always remember how anger had made him react that time with Magda, and with Beth. The way he had turned on them.

'Is there something else?' Laura enquired gently. 'Something else that's wrong?'

Patrick shrugged. 'No more than usual.'

In a way, he ached to tell her, to lay bare his abominable loss of control. He would be free to explain then perhaps, to set out the reasons for the fury Magda had induced. And he might bring himself to express the hope that his bad temper hadn't been the sole cause of his wife's leaving . . . of Beth's protracted silence.

If we could only be like this, Laura was thinking, if we could just sit and talk things through, I could help prevent him being quite so disturbed by Beth, and so sad about his mother. There'd be *us* from now on – he wouldn't be alone any more. Inwardly, she murmured his name and looked into his dark eyes, her own hazed with longing.

'It's seemed such an age since I've even seen you,' he told her, smiling at last. 'Suddenly, that's of no consequence.'

Laura smiled back. 'Now Netta's wedding's over I'll never be further away than Lindley's mill. And that'll only be when you're at work as well.'

'You must have other interests . . .' he said, and realised he'd no wish to hear of any. He was glad when she merely shrugged.

Patrick caught himself wishing away the months, yearning to have his past life sorted in such a way that he might truly put it behind him. Yet there seemed even less hope of that than during his last meeting with Laura. Attempting again to contact Magda, he had tried every means that had come to mind, and the result was still the same. No trace of her. Nothing.

His inability to achieve anything had generated the same feelings of inadequacy that he'd experienced at the time of all that trouble. This certainly was no life which any woman would wish to share. He grew aware again of the need that remained insistent beneath all his difficulties. Grimly, he recognised that he must send Laura home, at once. Like this, they were both too vulnerable. He surely was in danger of surrendering to the temptation to find the warmth he needed.

Almost as though she might have shared his misgivings

about the emotions this proximity induced, Laura rose, and smiled down at him.

'There's always another day,' she said. 'And it really is time we tried to get a bit of sleep.'

Nodding agreement, Patrick also stood. 'I'll see you out.' He realised suddenly that just watching her unlocking the Coach House would give him the reassurance of knowing she was only that short distance away.

The night air had cooled considerably with a strong wind beating down from the moors, bending bare-branched trees that were silhouetted against a sky paled by moonlight.

Frost sparkled on sandstone walls and from the paving that struck cold through their soles. Garden shrubs and the grass of the lawns were blanched by particles of ice.

'Lord, but that's lovely,' Patrick exclaimed, making her thankful that he'd been spared one moment from his cares.

After saying goodnight, Laura hurried towards her home, her feet light despite her tiring day. Tonight Patrick hadn't seemed a bit like the owner of a place the size of Arncliffe Hall. He certainly wasn't as intimidating as she used to find him. And she had hardly ever noticed that he was so much her senior – in experience as well as years. He had confided as he might to an equal, and she was glad.

But she was glad also that these few months in Halfield had taught her such a lot, and not least about her own feelings.

She wasn't a bit of a lass who'd give in to her emotions any longer. She could hold them in check. No matter how much she cared about somebody.

For once, she felt satisfied with her own behaviour. She believed she had managed to be warm and sympathetic without yielding to the urge to be more than that.

Laura smiled, picturing herself and Patrick through future years, being there for each other. Someone to turn to when life was hard. So long as she steered this kind of a course, she need never worry that she'd be like their Netta, with a hasty wedding and the early months of marriage spoiled by folk counting up the weeks.

As she was nearing the far side of the courtyard still acutely conscious of Patrick watching from the Hall, everything changed. Laura realised suddenly that marriage *was* what she wanted. And there wouldn't be a wedding for them. There couldn't be, ever. Patrick was committed years ago to the woman he was seeking so desperately. The one whose absence was causing Beth's disturbance. How could she even think of her own happiness, when that could mean depriving his child of her mother?

Chapter 18

Laura saw Patrick the following day. He arrived while she was trying to waken up with a cup of strong coffee. He was smiling, full of his nephew's arrival in the early hours.

'Ted telephoned me at seven – they're both well, and Patrick's to be one of his names. They haven't finally decided on the others yet.'

'And when will you see him?' she asked, offering coffee.

'Pretty soon. Once Jenny's fit they'll bring him over for the parents to admire.'

'How is your mother today?'

'Not too bad, thank you. She had a reasonable night, has managed to keep down what she's had so far.'

'Good. And how are you?'

'All right, thanks.' He was rather perturbed, remembering his firm decision to sort his own life before making any move to involve Laura seriously with him. But he needed her company. Surely they could go out together occasionally, especially over Christmas? He suggested that to her. It was the season he most dreaded since Magda's disappearance. Not that Christmases with her had been more than excuses for materialistic indulgence. But at least, with Magda, time had never hung heavily.

Laura seemed anything but enthusiastic. 'I'm not sure, I'll have to see . . .'

Her evident caution felt like a slap. Patrick paled and stood hastily. But then Laura smiled and motioned him to sit down again.

'I'll see you around home, remember,' she said quickly.

'And Beth as well, of course.'

'You're afraid of people talking, is that it?'

'Happen so. I don't know.' She could hardly announce her fear that she might end up in bed with him.

And, Patrick realised, Laura could still feel afraid of criticism even when I've located and divorced Magda. Whatever happened elsewhere, the people around Halfield believed in marriage. They also believed in enduring, no matter how unsatisfactory the partnership might be. He was beginning to understand how difficult he would find persuading Laura to think otherwise.

The ensuing months seemed to prove, however, that remaining close to Patrick was not only still possible for Laura, but very enjoyable. She was invited across to the Hall when Jenny and Ted arrived with their infant. Again, on Christmas Day, the Horsfall family wouldn't hear of her going anywhere else.

Laura was glad that she might be able to help Beth enjoy Christmas, and felt quite happy to accept an invitation that excused her joining the gathering organised by Netta and Roy. She saw her mother, Greta and Sybil when they arrived to stay with Netta on the Saturday before the festival, and was content in the knowledge that they would all meet up at Lindley Lodge on Boxing Day. Since coming to live in Halfield she had grown to value the freedom to make her own friends. Now that Netta was married to Roy, Laura had begun to realise that she was in danger of having her interests submerged in theirs if she visited them every time she was invited.

Giving her attention to Patrick and, of course, to Beth was what she most desired. Choosing presents for their family had been the only difficult part, and she was soon reassured that she had chosen well. Beth was very happy with the box of water colours and thick pad of paper, and Mr and Mrs Horsfall enthused over the classical records only released just before Christmas. For Patrick himself, after much searching, she had bought a silver inkstand.

'You probably have several,' she began, as she handed it to him.

'But only this one will now be kept on the desk in my study.'

He had given her pearls – real ones, she could tell – and moved her almost to tears by the tenderness with which he fastened them for her. It had been wrong of him, she knew really, to buy her something so costly when there could be no more than friendship between them, but Laura had been unable to feel anything but delight.

She became more thankful than ever for all her Halfield friends when, early in the New Year, Michael went to his new church. She was badly shaken when shortly before leaving he suggested yet again that she should marry him.

Embarrassed, and torn between being downright adamant and letting him down gently, she was afraid he'd gone away with the impression that she might some day reconsider.

It was in her old landlady that she confided. She had heard from Clem Hargreaves that Miss Priestley had been laid low with bronchitis and went one Saturday to 'Bien-être'.

Mavis Priestley was up and about, but only just, and Laura insisted on making the pot of tea to go with the homemade cake she had brought.

After she had listened to all the symptoms of her friend's indisposition, Laura was treated to a penetrating look.

'You didn't change your mind then, before Mr Dawson went?'

'I'm afraid not, he still isn't the man for me. I wish I'd had the courage to be more definite about it, an' all. I've got a nasty feeling he might think he's justified in going on hoping.'

'And isn't he? You could look a lot further, you know, and fare a heck of a lot worse.'

Sadly, Laura smiled. 'I do know that. But I simply don't love him, not in that way.'

'Might there be somebody as you do?'

'There might.'

'But there's summat up, isn't there, love?'

Laura sighed. 'Aye. Nothing's ever straightforward, is it?'

311

Despite these private difficulties, somehow Laura remained happy. Her work grew increasingly satisfying as she watched more of her designs coming off the looms. And she was happy also for Roy and Netta who so evidently were well-matched. His wife might be extremely young, but their relationship matured him, ridding him of the need to flirt and endowing him with a seriousness which earned him Laura's respect.

'You didn't like Roy at first, did you?' Netta surprised her by remarking one day in February when they had gone into town shopping together. 'I'm glad you've got over that. We both want you to be godmother, you know.'

'What about Greta and Sybil? They'll be upset if neither of them gets asked.'

'One of them might, if it's a girl. Don't know how I'll choose between them, though, they'll have to toss for it.'

'Has Mum guessed yet – that it wasn't a honeymoon baby?'

''Course she hasn't. Mind you, I did have to add a few weeks when she wanted to know when it's due.'

'You'll not be able to pull the wool over her eyes when it arrives.'

'Happen not. And happen she won't care.'

'Aye, well – there's time enough.'

'Too long if you ask me.'

Netta was counting the weeks, and Roy was no less eager to see their child. But he, together with most business people, was also occupied with events in Europe. When Hitler's forces marched on Austria in that March of 1938, the pace at Lindley's accelerated.

Wayland Rogers gathered the design team around him first thing one morning. 'We're working overtime from now on through most of the mill,' he announced. 'Ourselves included.'

There were a few surprised comments. Normally any working of extra hours by designers was expected as a part of their rather privileged position, not planned long-term, and not guaranteed remuneration.

'Mr Robert tells me we've a full order book, and nobody's

going to say Lindley's never tried to meet those orders before a stop's put to production.'

'A stop?' Laura couldn't help exclaiming. 'Why ever would . . .?'

'War, you ninny, what do you think!' one of her colleagues hissed into her ear.

Wayland Rogers nodded. 'Unfortunately for us, the government'll not believe carpets are vital then. So, that's why every effort will be made to get out every yard we can before hostilities commence.'

Laura felt an idiot because of failing to admit in the same way as other people that war was inevitable. She had tended to blind herself to the signs. And all because she needed so desperately to cling to this opportunity to establish her career more firmly. Suddenly she felt profoundly upset. She couldn't face the prospect of a halt being enforced in her work. There was so much she hadn't even started on, including that carpet for Patrick's building society which, although never discussed in detail, had become a part of her future plans.

The next time that she saw him she sounded him out about the international situation, and was anything but heartened by his reply.

'I'm afraid, my dear, that we can only conclude that it'll be months rather than years now before we're forced into a conflict.'

'Oh, no. Whatever shall I do?'

He longed to hug and to reassure her. But since that occasion in early December he'd hardly trusted himself to show her any warmth.

'There'll be some work available surely at the mill, if it's requisitioned. Try not to let it get you down. There's no sense in brooding now, spoiling what's left of this uncertain peace.'

The threat of war seemed to encourage some people to settle their domestic situations. Amos Kitchen and Emma Appleyard announced they were getting married, and invited Laura along to the ceremony one Saturday in April.

She was delighted to attend the simple service in a local Methodist chapel, and was especially pleased to see how strong Geoff appeared as he escorted his mother.

Afterwards, over chicken and ham sandwiches in the Sunday School, he told her how complete his recovery was, and of his progress at the mill. 'I hope you've noticed that I've done a lot since we met up to learn colour matching. I've had a spell in the winding department, and they're promising me a stint creeling.'

'As a prelude to weaving?' she asked, smiling.

'You bet! I'm going to cover every process in that mill. It's becoming a foreman of some kind that I've set my heart on. There's other mills, tha knows, if we reach a point where Lindley's can't offer me further promotion.'

And if the war comes? thought Laura, but would not quash Geoff's enthusiasm with the anxieties forced upon her. And certainly not like this, on the day when his mother was looking forward to happiness and security.

Emma appeared different altogether these days, no longer the nondescript little woman who'd fretted over the difficulties of feeding her son and herself. She had filled out quite a lot, and smartened up a great deal. Today she was wearing a dove grey costume and hat with a beautiful pink crêpe-de-Chine blouse.

'Doesn't she do me proud!' Amos exclaimed, coming over to have a word with them.

'You're not so bad yourself,' Laura told him, grinning.

In a good dark brown suit and a brilliant white shirt, he'd stood at the front of that chapel so straight that nobody remembered the shrapnel in his leg which made him limp. Even coming down the aisle after the service his gait had looked steadier.

He had invited his old employer, Clem Hargreaves, along and it was with Clem and his sister Millie that Laura left the reception.

'Would you like a lift home, Laura love?' Millie suggested, as they approached the old Austin.

314

'Nay, it's too far for that, surely, thanks all the same. You haven't forgotten I live out at Arncliffe?'

They hadn't forgotten, and when they insisted that the journey would take no time by car Laura realised this would be a good opportunity to show them her home.

Sitting at her living-room table following the tour of her Coach House, Laura was feeling contented, until Clem Hargreaves alarmed her so much that she nearly spilled the tea she was pouring.

'You're all right here then, lass? You've not had any trouble with him, I take it?' he began.

'Trouble? Who with?'

'Him in the big house, Patrick Horsfall.'

'Clem . . .' his sister said warningly, but he was intent on having his say.

'I suppose if there'd been owt really wrong the sale of this place wouldn't have gone through, your solicitor would have seen to that. But he's not a man I'd have confidence in, I'm afraid, not since . . .'

'Clem,' Millie protested again, and this time won a few minutes' silence from him in which to voice her opinion. 'Nothing was proved against him, never. And you've no decency coming out with it, after all this time.' She turned to Laura. 'There was a bit of bother, once, a long while back, folk said as how the police were questioning Mr Horsfall. About what, nobody ever did say, and it didn't come out.'

'Aye – and we all know he's always been capable of *making* folk keep quiet,' Clem interrupted, still hotly.

'How much do you know?' Laura asked quietly. 'Michael Dawson once said about as much as you have just now. I don't like rumours, especially them that mightn't have a great deal of foundation. But we've been friends since the old days in Whitby, I'll listen to you.'

'Happen it's best that you should know as much as I do, so's you can form your own opinion,' Clem continued gravely. 'And there were a bit more than gossip to this, at the time. I've invested with one of the Yorkshire West's rivals ever since I

315

came out of business when the mill burned down. In fact, I wouldn't have owt to do with Horsfall after he said he couldn't lend me enough to set up again, even though I were going to pay in all I got from t'insurance.'

His sister sniffed. 'And that's just about it, Clem – you've never forgiven Horsfall, that's allus made you ready to believe the worst.'

Clem gave Millie a look before turning back to Laura. 'Any road, the chairman of the building society I use turned out to be an old pal of mine from when we were lads together.'

'Clem, I don't think you ought to say owt,' Millie began again, but was cut short by her brother's voice.

'Now he *knew* no more nor anybody else at the time, but he reckoned the police were interrogating Horsfall about some funds that went astray. Happen they weren't belonging the building society, but he said a tidy amount was involved. And what's become of Horsfall's wife? Certainly, nowt no more's been seen of her from that day to this. Alive or dead.'

'Oh, if it's her disappearance that's causing you concern, there's nowt to worry about, Mr Hargreaves. To this day, Patrick's still trying to trace his wife.' Laura smiled. 'If what you're hinting at was right and he'd been implicated in some way in her disappearance, he wouldn't be doing that, would he now?'

'No. No – I don't suppose he would.'

'You see.' Millie sounded triumphant. 'You didn't ought to have said owt. You men talk about us gossiping, you're ten times worse.'

'There was the brass that went missing, an' all,' her brother reminded her. 'And I am sure there was quite a to-do at one of their annual meetings.'

'You're just prejudiced against him,' Millie stated, and turned to Laura. 'I'm afraid he's allus been that way since he was refused that loan. And I expect it'd only be because Clem were too old for starting up in business again.'

'What're you talking about?' snapped her brother. 'I were nobbut sixty-six.'

'Well, love,' said Millie, 'he weren't to know you still had a lot of go in you.'

'Anyway, you thought to protect me now,' said Laura, feeling better because she was sure there could be nothing really wrong about Patrick. 'I'm grateful, you know, even if there was no need.'

Somehow, having Clem Hargreaves remind her of how he had faced accusations, however unfounded, made Laura determined that Patrick must never doubt her loyalty. He'd had such a lot to put up with. She could only marvel that he'd survived. Hadn't the anxiety of his wife vanishing and Beth becoming disturbed been enough?

Despite her own earlier doubts about their relationship, Laura relaxed her intention of limiting their meetings so strictly. By the time she had saved up and purchased a beautiful three-piece suite in a sage green uncut moquette, she was planning a celebration. She invited Patrick first, making certain of choosing an evening he could manage, and then she telephoned Netta and Roy.

It was Roy who answered, sounding perturbed. She rarely contacted them away from the mill.

'Not some family trouble, I hope, Laura?'

'Eh, no – it's nowt like that. I'm having a bit of a do, that's all, and I want you and Netta to come.'

Briefly, Roy seemed to hesitate, then when he spoke again it was quite loudly. 'Why not? Why not indeed. When's it to be then?'

Laura told him the day and the time, then asked to speak to Netta.

Her sister was bursting with her own news, would hardly listen.

'Guess what Roy's bought me, Laura – a car! It's only little, but it's a beauty. I'd been reading about women needing cars in an old copy of *Good Housekeeping* that Roy's mother gave me. As soon as Roy knew I wanted one, he got it for me.'

'But I didn't know you could drive,' said Laura, then

317

realised how disapproving she sounded. Netta might even think she was envious.

'I'm learning. Roy's been taking me out, and his mother.'

'Well, you be careful, think on. There's that bairn to consider as well as your own skin.'

'I know that, don't I? Oh, you are stuffy, Laura. It's partly because of the way I am that Roy's got me a car. When he's at work I'm stuck at home, and buses and trams make me feel poorly.'

Pity you didn't keep on your job, thought Laura, there'd have been less time for boredom. 'Anyway, how're you fixed for coming over here, did Roy tell you what day?'

'Oh, it'll be all right, yes. Be nice seeing you. I'll be able to drive us over to Arncliffe,' Netta added, her voice shades brighter.

Laura prevented further words advising caution. Netta was a married woman now, should have the sense to drive a car safely.

'Who else will be there besides us?'

'Patrick Horsfall, that's why I wanted a word with you. Please try not to be as tactless as sometimes, love. Be nice to him. He does have a lot to put up with.'

'That girl of his, you mean.'

'Well, yes – Beth does cause anxiety. And his mother's seriously ill.'

'Don't worry about a thing, old love. I'll be as nice as pie, make such a fuss of him that Roy will be jealous.'

'I don't want you going proper daft . . .'

Netta's giggle interrupted her. 'I know – I do, honest. Roy's learnt me a lot about getting on with folk, you know.'

On the Saturday evening Patrick arrived ahead of her other two guests. Laura couldn't feel sorry.

'I'd better warn you about our Netta,' she said, with a grin, as she saw him settled into one of her armchairs and handed him a glass. 'Roy's only gone and bought her a car, hasn't he! I always knew he was wrong in the head. I'm afraid you'll hear nowt else all night.'

Patrick smiled. 'Doesn't sound like she's matured very much.'

'According to her telling, she has – I'll believe that when I see it. Still, they're both happy, and they're not spoiling two houses.'

Patrick appeared to choke on the sherry he was sipping. 'You Crabtrees have a marvellous respect for each other, haven't you?'

'We are close, really – when there's any upset.'

'I know. And when that child arrives, you'll be the proudest auntie ever.'

'You reckon?' Taking up her own glass, she went to sit in the chair across the hearth from him. 'Haven't thought about it much, except to hope everything's all right. And I suppose it ought to be – that's one good thing about having plenty of brass.' Reading the amusement in his brown eyes, she groaned. 'Oh, heck – I'm doing it again, aren't I? Any road, you folk that have money *are* able to get medical treatment and such without thinking twice.'

She was interrupted by a car horn outside the drawn curtains and the slam of a car door.

'Excuse me a minute, that'll be them.'

Netta straightened up from locking the car as her sister opened the front door.

'Where's Roy?' Laura enquired quickly, gazing into the night.

'Oh, he cried off – said to tell you sorry. He's got a frightful head, poor love.'

'And he let you drive all this way on your own?'

'Don't start that. He tried to stop me.'

And nothing could, short of a road roller stuck in front of that car, thought Laura.

'Come on in.'

In the hall Netta swung her white fur away from her shoulders with a flourish, and handed it to Laura. 'Thanks, love. Now, where's the phone? Roy made me promise to let him know I've got here safe.'

'Say hallo to Patrick first, will you? He's in there.'

'Hallo, Patrick.' Belying her now considerable bulk, Netta whirled into the room, straight to his chair, then leaned over and kissed him lingeringly on the cheek. 'How are you, love?'

'Very well, thank you. And you?'

'Fit as ever, and twice as big!' Her laugh trilled through the room. 'See you in a tick.' She flounced out again to the hall telephone.

Laura returned to the living-room as Patrick was scrubbing savagely at his lipsticked face. He met her laughing glance, raised his eyes heavenwards.

'Told you I'd be all right,' Netta's voice drifted in to them. 'No need for you to fuss. Just you take your nasty headache to bed, darling. Soon be better now . . .'

'Nobody'd guess he could run a mill,' Laura muttered, then realised she was criticising Netta again. 'Oh, well – if it suits them.'

'So how's your pretty little daughter, Patrick?' Netta effervesced, coming back in and perching precariously on the arm of his chair.

'Not too bad, thank you,' he responded cautiously. 'She really does seem more animated, these days, especially with Laura here.'

'Laura's always had a way with youngsters, look how she put up with us lot.' She glanced across at her sister. 'Not so good with the hospitality, though. Where's my sherry?'

'You're having lemonade or dandelion and burdock, nothing any stronger than that.'

Netta groaned. 'You're as bad as Roy and his family.'

'I should think so an' all – you don't want that kiddie born with something wrong with it. And you are driving as well.'

'I know – I do know really. You'd be surprised how sensible I am.'

Surprised is an understatement, Laura thought, but was growing adept at not voicing her thoughts. Instead, she poured Netta's lemonade and placed it on a small table beside the sofa. 'Here you are then.'

'My sister's splitting us up, Patrick.' Languorously, she strolled away from him and took her time over sitting. Laura contained a smile. Despite the unmistakable lump scarcely concealed by a voluminous silky grey suit, Netta was still glamorous. Laura could understand Roy being smitten, was glad it seemed to be permanently.

If Patrick missed the company of another male, nothing in his demeanour during the entire evening gave that away. He was coaxed by Netta into relating some of the history of Arncliffe Hall and its surrounding area, and seemed to hold Netta enthralled as well as Laura. He didn't leave until they had waved the girl off with joint admonitions to take care.

'Do you wish me to wait with you until you get her call to say she's safely home?'

'It's all right, thanks, Patrick. Unless you want to hang on.'

'I should look in on Beth, check she's sleeping.'

'You do that then. Leave me to cope with my responsibility.'

'Is that how you still see Netta?' He was gazing intently into her eyes.

'Suppose I must do. Daft as a brush, aren't I?'

Slowly, he shook his head. His eyes closed as he bent to kiss her. The kiss was sweet rather than sensual, and very brief.

'See you,' he said, and walked away towards his own home.

The tiny house seemed full of his scent, the masculine tang of a piney soap, the new fabric smell of a shirt freshly purchased. You haven't really gone away, thought Laura, not while this remains here.

She sat in the chair where he had been sitting, rested her hands where his had lain, leaned back her head. Eyelids lowered, she inhaled slowly, savouring his recent presence, willing it to ease the excited tattoo deep inside her which had grown and increased all evening, despite their being accompanied.

She pictured him with Beth, visualised his fingers in that silk-fine hair, felt them in her own hair . . . longed . . .

'Soft, that's what I'm getting!'

Abruptly, she rose, thrust the fireguard in front of embers

now shifting as they died. When the telephone startled her back to reality she was glad, thankful as well that she was too tired to lie awake for long afterwards.

'Is your head better now?' Laura enquired on the following Monday when she bumped into Roy as they arrived in the factory yard.

'Head? Oh, yes – perfectly all right now. Sorry about Saturday. Netta enjoyed herself, though.'

'She certainly seemed to – and the drive over. You do know what you're about, I hope, giving her a car?'

Roy nodded seriously. 'I understand your concern. It's unfounded, though. Much to my surprise, I'll admit, she's a natural behind the wheel. And she is careful. A bit like my mother – when driving. Maybe because Netta's taken quite a shine to her.'

'Has she? I'm glad. I liked your mum from the start.'

'If I'd been able to make it on Saturday, I was going to have a word. Not that I believe in talking shop on social occasions.'

'Oh, aye – and what would you have said?'

'Just to tell you your designs are going down very well with some of our best customers. Even in London. The proprietor of one of the big hotels has suggested you come up with something 'specially for them. On the lines of your stained-glass interpretations, but incorporating their monogram. It's an independently owned hotel. The boss is an old chap, bit of an autocrat, has no family. Wants his name preserving this way, maybe.'

'Does that mean I'm going to get a trip to London?'

'Oh. We'll have to see. If you can be spared. We're that busy, aren't we?'

'Trying to keep ahead of the Hun.'

'Aye.'

'How bad do you think things are, Roy? Is war unavoidable?'

'You can see how we're working . . .'

'You think it will come to that?'

'Be a nice surprise if it doesn't.'

322

'How do you want me to tackle this job then?'

'Discreetly, for a start. You know what the others in the studio are like. Wayland Rogers knows what you're going to be doing, and that's all. I want you in my office at ten sharp this morning, Laura, I've told him as well. Between us, we'll get down to giving that hotel exactly what they want.'

She had never been more excited. She was nervous too, though, and had to place her pencil on the table in front of her because she couldn't hold it steady. Roy was showing her some photographs of Netta while they waited for Mr Rogers, they couldn't begin without him.

When he walked in he was carrying some of Laura's early designs, one of which hadn't yet been utilised. After he had seated himself beside Roy and across the desk from Laura, he began expressing his conclusions.

'This one here's the sort of shades we're after, I think, but the pattern's all wrong somehow. What we need is something on the lines of this other that's gone into production, but on a bolder scale.'

'Do you mean a bigger pattern altogether?' Laura asked.

'Or stronger colour?' Roy suggested.

'Not sure. Need to see a few designs worked out. You enjoy experimenting, do you?'

'Very much.'

'Better get on with it then, hadn't you?' Wayland Rogers said, his smile for once quite genuine.

'And sharpish, Laura,' Roy added. 'We want this carpet finished and fitted before anything stops us.'

'What'll be the completed size?' she enquired. She would need to know in order to consider the proportions and how bold the pattern might be.

Roy handed across one of the documents in front of him. 'All the dimensions are here, Laura. We shall be manufacturing in twenty-seven inch, of course. You'll see I've calculated the number of widths and so on.'

'It's a lot of carpet,' Mr Rogers asserted. 'Just you watch you get it right.'

'I will,' she said. And marvelled at her own confidence.

'You can start letting us see your ideas as soon as you get them down on paper,' Roy told her.

'We shall reject some, be prepared for that,' Wayland warned her, straightening his purple velvet bow tie.

Laura asked a few more questions about specifications then hurried back to the studio. She had finished a design the previous Saturday morning so was able to begin straight away.

Calming herself sufficiently to produce her best work was the first hurdle. Throughout that week, she experienced surge after surge of adrenalin because she had been chosen for this important job. By Friday evening, however, she had several patterns drafted and passed on via Wayland Rogers for Roy's approval.

She was clearing her desk ready for going home when Roy appeared in the studio. He called her over to Wayland's desk.

'You're doing very nicely, have grasped the general idea. Unfortunately, what we're most enthusiastic about is the colour scheme of one design, and certain features of two of the others.'

'All right,' said Laura quickly. 'I'll incorporate them over the weekend.'

'Work at home tomorrow morning then,' Roy told her. 'It'll be easier to concentrate there than here in the studio. And the others won't wonder what you're about. I'll see you're paid for the hours you put in.'

'I want to get this right. I'm not so bothered about the pay.'

Laura was gathering up the designs ready for walking away when Roy called her back. 'Here – I say – you *are* Yorkshire, are you?'

She set off for Arncliffe with their laughter echoing in her head.

She stopped to buy fish and chips on the way, and as soon as she'd eaten set out her paints and a stack of point paper. At first, as she often did when designing at home, she listened to the wireless. But even music intruded on the job and she got up, stretched her aching shoulders, and switched off the set.

Beyond the Coach House windows the sky was darkening over the valley where the trees now were almost in full leaf. Time seemed to be scurrying. She might be happy about her career, more so this week than ever, but she hadn't done half the things she'd intended since moving in. That steep-sided green valley out there and the surrounding moors were largely unexplored by her. She had never revisited the reservoir, and longed suddenly to walk there.

Back at her designing, Laura reimmersed herself in combining the different aspects of the three patterns. The task was fascinating, however slow and tedious, and she revelled in the challenge.

Fifteen minutes later the telephone rang and, sighing, she hastened into the hall.

'Laura? Patrick here, how are you?'

'All right thanks, busy. And you?'

'Fine. I wondered – if you're not planning anything tomorrow, we might take a walk as far as the reservoir . . .'

'Well, I never! I'd just been thinking I hadn't gone back there.'

'That suits you then?'

'Oh, love, I'm sorry. I've got that much on my plate this weekend, I'm afraid I can't.'

'Oh.'

'I've got point paper all over the place. I have to get this design right by Monday.'

There was no mistaking Patrick's disappointment, nor was there any way that Laura could see of making time for him as well as her work.

Returning again to the table, she found getting back into the task more difficult. With her subconscious divided between the pull of the surrounding countryside and the attraction of her near neighbour, her brush seemed to do its own will ungoverned by her head.

She ruined one sheet of point paper, began again, and noticed the pain which, intermittently, gnawed away above one eye. Maybe she needed her glasses changing. She couldn't recall when she'd last seen the optician.

By eleven that night the pain had spread right around her skull. Laura took a couple of Aspros and, leaving everything all over the table, went heavily up the stairs.

The following morning, she was thankful the headache had departed. She had slept soundly, for once, and felt refreshed. At eight-thirty she went back into the sitting-room, eager to get on now that she had bacon, eggs and fried bread inside her.

Perhaps because of being less tired, inspiration seemed to have reappeared. After studying the three designs side by side for only a few moments, Laura could see how they might be amalgamated to best effect. It would mean starting from scratch, none of the ideas she had worked up so far contained all the desired elements. But she finally felt she was getting somewhere, and quickly filled her brush with the glowing claret red she was daring to use as her outline.

Somebody clattered her letterbox, repeatedly, agitatedly, making far more fuss than any postal delivery.

I'll bet I know who that is! Laura rose, smiled ruefully, and went through to answer the door.

Beth's long fair hair was caught back in a ribbon, making her thin face appear especially piquant. She was beaming. She was wearing a blue print frock that she'd outgrown, revealing limbs that were too lean, and a scuffed pair of Mrs Harrison's shoes.

'All right, Beth love, you can come in, but only for a few minutes. I'm busy.'

Thinking to steer her towards the kitchen, Laura had calculated without the girl's all encompassing glance. The array of paintings covering the living-room table was spotted beyond the half-open door. There was no persuading Beth away from that.

'Go on then, you can have a look – but only look. No touching, no playing either.' And I hope I'm not wrong in my head letting you anywhere near those designs.

Beth was amazingly careful of them, standing a pace from the table, scrutinising each pattern in turn and then the one scarcely begun.

'Now, that's all there is to see, and you can tell how busy I am,' said Laura, firmly for her. Grasping Beth's hand she led her from the room. As far as the hall everything was fine. Once confronted with the front door the girl stiffened. 'Don't you dare,' Laura breathed through clenched teeth. Just this once, Beth must learn who had the right to say no here.

The yell, predictably, was prolonged, but then Beth's rigidity slackened and she sobbed hysterically.

'I'm sorry but you're going home, young lady.'

Struggling to get the door open and haul Beth through it, Laura caught her spectacles on the edge of the door.

'Now look what you've done!'

The lenses hadn't broken but she saw the bridge had smashed.

'Stand still a minute.' Her grip on Beth implacable, she retrieved them from the carpet, thrust them down beside the telephone.

Beth's weeping was undiminished, wearing down Laura's nerves and embarrassing her because somebody surely would come running.

Wearing garden clothes, Patrick was doing precisely that. He arrived to find Laura, white-faced, shouting over his daughter's cries: 'I just wish I knew what you wanted . . .'

'Paint, paint!' Beth cried, and hiccuped.

'God, by all that's wonderful!' Patrick shot into the house, bundling them with him, then hugging them both to him.

'God, Laura, but you're a marvel!'

Gazing first to his daughter then to Laura, he released them. Laura went to close the door. When she turned, Patrick was down on one knee, a hand on each of Beth's shoulders, his brown eyes earnest.

'What did you say, Beth?'

Three minutes passed terribly slowly, five . . . still Beth remained silent. Each time her father pressed her to speak she stiffened again, clamped her arms firmly around her chest, turned away her head.

'I'll make us a cup of tea,' said Laura.

Beth took her glass of milk, smiled, was prompted by Patrick to say thank you, *commanded* by him . . . but she said nothing.

'Never mind,' Laura whispered, sitting beside him. 'It's a start. We can be patient.'

'*You* haven't waited this long,' he snapped, tension in every angle of his face. He shook his head and gave a rueful grin. 'Listen to me, that's unforgivable. Laura . . .' He grasped her hand. 'This is the most wonderful day yet. I never believed . . .' He paused. 'Look, we'll celebrate, go out for the day.'

'I can't, I'm afraid. I said – I've too much to do.'

'Can't it wait?'

'Not this time, no. I've got to have this right for Monday.'

'Lindley's don't own you, for heaven's sake.'

'And nor do . . .' Too late, she clamped her lips tightly shut.

'As you say.' He rose swiftly, pulled Beth to her feet and with him into the hall. En route for the door he spotted the broken spectacles. 'Did that happen just now?'

'Afraid so.'

'I'll reimburse you, of course, for their replacement.'

'Doesn't matter, I . . .'

'To me, it does.'

'If you'll let me finish, I was saying I was going to get them changed anyway.'

'All the same.'

Suddenly, he looked down at Beth, and then again faced Laura.

'We can't quarrel, not today.' He paused. 'And you can't work either, not without glasses.'

'I'll have to, love, this is my job. Not just something I play around with when I feel so inclined. You don't understand . . .'

'Why must you spoil everything, when this is the day we – *you* have cracked Beth's appalling silence!'

Before Laura could speak, he and the child were gone.

328

Chapter 19

Laura succeeded that weekend in completing the design, if not entirely to her own satisfaction. She was accepting by now that she had become a perfectionist, and rarely was quite content with anything she produced.

What did matter was that on the Monday morning both Roy and, to a lesser degree, Wayland Rogers were delighted with the result. After only a couple of minor adjustments, they were agreed that the pattern could go forward to be set on Jacquards.

By that day's post they received photographs of the hotel for which the carpet was destined, helping Laura to visualise how it would appear, and confirming how appropriate her concept was.

'Is there a chance of my going to London to see it?' she asked Roy again, but he would make no promise.

'Just be glad you're coming along champion,' his father told her, smiling, as he walked in on their discussion. 'It's the first time anybody so fresh to the work has been entrusted with this kind of an opportunity.'

Laura was glad, devoutly thankful that she was being given this chance. She was excited as well. Having someone to share her elation would have stopped it being simply a tight feeling at the top of her stomach and in the back of her throat.

She tried telling Netta over the telephone that Monday evening, but all she got was 'That's nice', and details of the distance Netta had driven alone, plus an account of how the baby was kicking her inside. At Arncliffe, Laura felt wary of seeing Patrick. She knew she'd annoyed him by letting her work take priority, and she in turn was irritated by his refusal to acknowledge the importance of her designing. She wondered about Beth frequently – and was eager to know if the girl had spoken again. But she still left it for a week before enquiring. Evidently there had been no further improvement. So far as everyone in the Arncliffe household was aware, if Beth spoke now it was alone, to herself.

I bet I could get her to talk if she was with me a lot, thought Laura. And sometimes before falling asleep would picture how that might bring herself and Patrick closer again.

In the real world of cycling to the mill on a stifling day or when the rain was tippling down, she acknowledged even that unlikely event would bring no guarantee that any of the other difficulties between them could be solved.

Over the next few weeks, however, Laura felt the awkwardness between herself and Patrick easing. Since completing that important design, she'd resolved to ensure herself at least some time for working on her house and its small garden. The summer would be gone if she didn't watch out, and none of her ideas for the flowerbeds a reality.

Finding her outdoors, Patrick often paused to offer advice, or a cutting or two, or simply to chat. One day he enquired after her important big design whose completion had occupied a whole weekend.

Laura smiled. 'Come on in. Earlier this week I was given the first sample off the loom.'

He smiled back. 'Proof that it works!'

'Aye,' she said over her shoulder as he followed her into the kitchen. She didn't tell him, though, of the crisis she'd had to face when the design was first set up, and didn't come out true. She knew precisely which hour of a certain Sunday morning that section had been completed. And who had prevented absolute concentration. Still, that wouldn't happen again, she wouldn't let it. And she had quickly corrected the flaw, allowing production to commence.

'That's a lovely piece of carpet, Laura. Those colours are superb and you've combined them to perfection.'

'Thanks.' Ridiculous or not, she was glowing with just those few words from him.

'I'd love to see the completed carpet. I'm certainly sure now that I'll be looking forward to the time when you'll begin on the one for our London office.'

'We seem to have such a lot on at present I've not been able to give as much thought to it as I'd like. And you hadn't said all that much about it.' She had begun to wonder if he had been serious.

'No, well – we're having to hold our horses until we see if we are faced with war.'

'Aye, it's still hanging over us, isn't it?' Laura sighed. 'Want a coffee while you're here, or a cup of tea?'

'Coffee would be welcome, thanks.'

They had drained their cups and were sitting, easy with each other again, when the telephone rang.

'That was Roy,' she told Patrick when she returned to him. 'The baby's on its way, our Netta's scriking that she wants me.'

'Shall I drive you over there?'

'It's all right, thanks. There's no rush. If it isn't a false alarm, and knowing my sister it could be, it'll take its time. If I go on my bike I shall know I can get home, or to the mill tomorrow if nothing happens before then.'

Certainly no false alarm, Netta's labour was causing intense pain to her and anxiety to Roy if not to the midwife who was attending. Roy's parents were at the house as well, summoned by their son to sit, like Laura, feeling helpless. When eventually, a little before midnight, cries from overhead declared the arrival of the new Lindley, they all were awakened from intermittent dozing in armchairs.

Roy was heard bounding two at a time down the stairs. He hurtled in to pull his parents to their feet and hug them in turn. 'It's a boy – the grandest little lad ever – and Netta's champion.'

When he turned to Laura tears were spilling out of his eyes, splashing down over the tie hanging unknotted either side of his unbuttoned shirt.

'Congratulations,' she exclaimed, seizing both his hands

and giving his tired face a kiss. 'Is Netta really all right?'

'Go and have a look.'

Nobody had warned her, not ever. The doctor was washing his hands after giving her sister several stitches, the midwife was busy with the infant. When the doctor came back from the bathroom across the landing, Laura was taking root in the doorway of the master bedroom, horrified. How could she have known there'd be *so much blood?*

'Is it – I mean – is she . . .?'

'Perfectly normal? Of course, my dear, and you are . . .?'

'Her sister.'

'Good, good. Well, as you've heard, the young man has a lusty pair of lungs on him. Everything else intact – that's what you all want to know, eh? And Mrs Lindley's a fortunate mother. Her youth has ensured her a flexible body, well able to cope with the actual birth.'

Hardly daring to look, Laura again turned towards the bed. Netta was scarcely recognisable, her hair clinging like tangled ribbons of licorice around her blotched face, her eyes half closed. And lower down, the wrinkled, sweat-stained nightdress was streaked with blood that smeared her lovely legs, and as for the sheet . . .

Laura gulped.

'Why not go back downstairs?' suggested the doctor. 'While we clean her up.'

'In a minute.'

Stiffly, her legs barely under control, Laura crossed to the bed. She took Netta's moist hand.

'It's me, love – Laura. Congratulations, you've been very brave. Just you rest now, you've got your little boy safely here.'

Netta nodded, her half-closed eyes hardly able to focus. After Laura had kissed her clammy forehead, she turned away. The midwife was holding out the baby for inspection. He was tiny and red, and very wrinkly as if his skin was a few sizes too big.

'Mmm – bless him, he's lovely,' said Laura, hoping that was all that was expected of her. Netta appeared to be sleeping already even while they were cleaning her up. Rather hastily, Laura went back downstairs to the others.

'You must be very proud, Roy.' She smiled at him, and at his mother and father who were heading towards the stairs. 'If you don't mind, I'll go home now, have what remains of the night in my own bed.'

Her first impressions of the baby had not made Laura overwhelmingly enthusiastic, but when she saw him again two evenings later she privately admitted he'd improved a lot. The raw look had gone from his skin, leaving him pale-complexioned with a flush to his cheeks. The wrinkles seemed to be disappearing and his head was covered in downy golden hair.

Netta, sitting up in bed, was enjoying reigning over the Lindleys. Inez was staying to care for her daughter-in-law, and Robert Lindley returning with Roy each evening from the mill. He was almost as thrilled as his son, a fact which owed much to the baby being named Kevin Robert. Kevin had been Harry Crabtree's middle name. Laura felt choked when she thought how their father would have loved a grandson.

'When's Mum coming to see you then?' she asked Netta as soon as she had given her a hug.

'Tomorrow, all being well. Our Greta and Sybil won't arrive till the weekend, though, they're working now.'

'Both of them? I didn't know that.'

'There's a new draper's shop opened up, right in the centre of Whitby, and they've both got set on. I think somebody we were at school with is the daughter of the owner.'

'Well, I'm thankful they've found something, after all this time. And I'm glad Mum'll be here soon. Pity she wasn't on Sunday . . .'

'Couldn't be, could she? Not when, as far as she knows, Kevin arrived before time.'

'Eh, I'd almost forgotten. Are you going to keep up the pretence with her?'

Netta shrugged. 'Don't know. Roy says it doesn't matter now. I don't know what to think. Tell you what, though – I'm not going to let that spoil owt.'

Within a month Laura was far more deeply affected by her nephew's birth than she could have anticipated if she had thought of nothing else the entire nine months. He was a splendid baby, promising to have the Lindley physique. With a mother and father as attractive as Netta and Roy, how could he be other than beautiful?

What Laura hadn't reckoned on was being torn through by the sudden craving for a child of her own. Much as she loved her Coach House, its emptiness hit her each time she unlocked the door. And whenever Beth appeared, *not* hugging her to death took self-discipline.

Living so near to Patrick made her feel no better. He gave no hint these days of more than casual friendliness towards her. And although this once had seemed desirable, Laura was beginning to acknowledge that she had grown increasingly fond of him.

Work alone satisfied her, and there was plenty of that. She was involved to a degree in the production of the carpet for the London hotel, and there were other designs to be completed. Lots of folk in the West Riding and beyond liked her patterns, and wanted to make sure of carpeting their homes now before prevented from doing so by war.

War dominated the minds of businessmen, ensuring caution as they made long-term plans. They went from Yorkshire on their trips to London and returned grave-faced, unable to dismiss the sight of trenches being dug in the parks, and sandbags protecting buildings.

Gas masks had been issued. Laura tucked hers away at the back of her wardrobe. Only at her gloomiest did she admit that their distribution might be justified. The mill workers were plagued with notices, urging them to volunteer as Air Raid Precaution wardens, for the Women's Voluntary Services or the Auxiliary Fire Service. She told herself nobody really believed any of these were necessary, especially in Halfield. And then she met Miss Priestley one Saturday shopping in the town.

'I've got a job, Laura, quite an important one, too.' She was beaming, her silver-grey eyes glinting with enthusiasm.

'Eh, I am pleased for you. What're you doing?'

'Learning the switchboard, with the Auxiliary Fire Service.'

'Oh.'

'It's that good to be doing summat useful again!'

Laura was appalled, felt as if Halfield was disintegrating around her. The following Monday first thing she located her brother-in-law in his office. She herself still never had enough time for her work, never mind catching up with what appeared in the newspapers.

'I want you to tell me straight, Roy – are we heading for war?'

He sighed, glanced away, reluctant to confront her with the truth. Despite the way Laura was making a name for herself, he still felt almost as protective of her as he did of Netta.

Noting his reticence, Laura sighed back at him. 'I'm not a little girl, anything but,' she asserted. 'I only *look* like Shirley Temple.'

'Yes, well – it certainly does appear that we're not going to avoid a conflict.'

'How soon?'

'I'm no politician.'

'How will it affect us here then?'

'Lindley's, you mean? As you might have assumed from the way we've been stepping up production for some time now, we can't expect that they'll let us carry on as we are.'

'But – but what'll we do?'

'Whatever the government tells us, unless we're all called up.'

'Blooming heck!'

'Don't get downhearted yet, Laura.'

'But I'm only just establishing myself . . .' She could imagine nothing worse than being prevented from progressing now. 'That big job for London was only the beginning.' She still had more ideas for designs whirling through her head than ever she had time to set them down in draft, never mind on point paper. And there was that lovely gold-coloured carpet with Yorkshire roses for Patrick. She'd been meaning to discuss details with him and then talk it over at work.

'Happen it won't come to anything,' said Roy.

Laura wished she dared believe him. From that day, she made a point of buying at least one morning paper. It was time she kept up with what was happening.

By 16 September she was following in the *Daily Telegraph* the visit of Mr Chamberlain to the Berghof, Herr Hitler's mountain chalet. On the thirtieth of that month it was announced that agreement on a peaceful solution to the Czechoslovakian crisis had been reached. Next morning, 1 October, the *Telegraph* proclaimed:

The Prime Minister was given one of the greatest ovations ever accorded to a British statesman, when he arrived in London last night. He said his mission to Germany had resulted in peace with honour. 'I believe it is peace for our time.'

Kevin's christening was on the Sunday after that, and everybody seemed to be experiencing the same optimism that filled Laura with relief. Neither the Lindleys nor the Crabtrees saw any need to be other than cheerful as they looked forward to the little lad's future.

'What I'd really have liked was a little girl, though,' Netta confided to Greta and Sybil as they squabbled over who had been holding the baby longest. 'So's I could buy her lots of pretty clothes. This time next year, I'll see young Kev's got a sister.'

Even Netta didn't get all she wanted that readily, Laura reflected. But she was not so far off; she had been expecting for six months when that year had passed. For the entire nation as well as the Lindleys, though, prospects were grim.

Ever since war was declared on 3 September apprehension had filled their days and nights. Production at the mill was already winding down. Part of the site was being commandeered

336

for production of munitions, and government departments had intimated that the section permitted to continue weaving would be producing webbing and similar army requirements.

Laura was distraught. 'You'll be sacking us designers,' she said to Roy and his dad.

'Hold your horses,' Roy told her, adding that there might be a use for some of the team in the studio. 'They're looking into the possibility of our camouflaging military tents.'

'Tents? Tents! You mean covering them with splodges of brown and green and so on?'

Robert Lindley nodded. 'Something of the sort, Laura.'

'Well, that'll just be daubed on – nobody can call that designing.'

'Could be the means of ensuring you a safe job here, though.'

Laura didn't want a safe job, especially one that wouldn't utilise one scrap of her skill. She thought of Mavis Priestley in the Auxiliary Fire Service and wondered if she too might make herself useful there. Or women were going into the forces. Enlisting would be doing as much as she possibly could. But it would also mean she would have to leave her lovely home.

Would she be as unhappy as she feared, though, away from Arncliffe? She had recently been made to remember that she had no right whatever to contemplate sharing any sort of life with Patrick.

He had been on the other end of the line one evening when she answered the telephone.

'Do you mind popping over here?' he'd asked. 'I see they've issued your Identity Card along with those for the rest of us here, and I really haven't the time to bring it over.'

'Of course I'll come,' Laura had said readily. Despite all her resolve, she was glad to be seeing him if only for a few minutes.

Patrick seemed preoccupied when she went into his study. Even when she saw the array of Identity Cards on his desk, Laura had no idea why he was so pensive. But then, as he handed over her own card, she noticed the next one to it was in the name of Magda Horsfall.

'I'm hoping this mass registration will at last further my attempts to trace her,' he said. 'I've put in a call, explaining that she is no longer here. Maybe somebody in the network will stand a chance of discovering where she is now.'

His face looked drawn and grey. With renewed yearning, Laura supposed. She could imagine how desperately he must long to see his wife again after all this time. Returning to her own home, she realised how disturbed she was, because she really could not continue to believe anything Patrick had ever said about hoping they might have a future together. And still, no matter how firmly she decided to avoid becoming involved with him, or reminded herself of the gulf between his circumstances and her own, she seemed unable to govern her deepest emotions.

Perhaps getting away until after the duration might be a good idea? she wondered, feeling for once that she'd be glad of almost anything that would remove her from this hopeless situation.

The day a solution was offered, the sheer surprise of the suggestion shook Laura into understanding that she would never escape her feelings by leaving Arncliffe.

It was nine o'clock on a Saturday evening when someone knocked on her door. She tensed, thinking it was so late that if young Beth had arrived she would be obliged to march her straight home again.

Opening the door, Laura was staggered to see who was standing there.

'Michael!' she exclaimed, before inviting him in. 'I've not seen you for ages.'

He smiled. 'Not since I left St Martin's, I know. How are you, Laura?'

'All right, thanks,' she replied, showing him into the living-room and to a chair. 'Not at all happy about what the war is doing to us all at Lindley's, of course. The firm's going over to producing stuff for the war. Which means they don't really need me.'

'But you're still working there?'

She told him how she had stayed on, doing any job she was asked to during the process of winding down production. 'It'll only be a matter of weeks now before there's nowt for me there.'

'And how's your mother, these days?'

Maggie Crabtree was another of Laura's burdens. Both Greta and Sybil were living away, working on munitions. Instead of lessening the weight on their mother's shoulders, this seemed to be making her uneasy about living on her own.

Laura told Michael this. 'I went over to see her last weekend, and rather wished afterwards that I hadn't gone near. She did nothing but moan about being there in the empty house, yet when I suggested she might take in lodgers that didn't suit either. It isn't as if she never sees anybody, you know – Greta and Sybil get home quite a lot, and her and Mrs Tomlinson next door have always been pally.'

'You haven't contemplated work which might take you to live a bit nearer to Whitby then, if only for the duration?'

'What sort of work?'

'Oh, I don't know – on a farm maybe. Haven't you an uncle in farming somewhere out that way?' Michael paused for a second. 'Or you could marry me. I still love you, Laura. I've got a nice little house now within easy reach of Whitby. I'd like to think of you there, safer maybe than amid all the industry here, and waiting for my homecoming.'

'You're not moving on somewhere else already?'

Michael grinned. 'Haven't I said – that is where my home is now. I'm simply going into the forces, least I can do. The Army.'

'Oh, I see.'

'You're still not jumping at the offer of marriage, I notice,' he remarked, but sounding unsurprised.

'Sorry, love – no. I'm too confused about such a lot of things to make up my mind about anything that important.' She wished Michael would forget about her, and free himself for meeting some other young woman instead of continuing on year after year like this.

For days afterwards Laura marvelled at his still considering she might accept his proposal. She could only console herself that he hadn't seemed unduly perturbed by her refusal. And it had proved to her that she felt that this was where she belonged.

With her career threatened, though, Laura was beginning to realise how concentrating on that had prevented her from thinking very seriously about anything else. She felt so lost without the motivation that had existed for nearly as long as she could remember, and wished something would point her in one direction or another.

Laura was cycling up the drive at Arncliffe when she saw a hearse pulling away from the main entrance. Patrick remained standing on the top step, staring after the vehicle. He looked so appalled that she immediately dismounted and, pushing her bicycle, hurried towards him.

'Bad news?' she asked gently.

He seemed to come back from some distance as he noticed her and nodded. 'Mother. She died this morning.'

'Eh, dear. Eh, I am sorry.'

'Thank you. Come in for a minute, will you?'

He led the way into the sitting-room that had so impressed her during her first visit. Today, it felt singularly lifeless and so cold that Laura shivered.

Patrick indicated a chair, but she didn't sit. She simply stood there, looking at him, aching to put her arms round him.

'I can't spare more than a few seconds,' he said. 'The end was quite sudden and rather took us by surprise. There are a thousand things to do, and I must get back to Father.'

'How has he taken it?'

'Not too badly. He'd seen, of course, how seriously she was deteriorating. We both had, even though we hadn't understood it might happen so swiftly. He can feel relieved that she's no longer in all that pain. Afraid I'm not as yet quite so philosophical.'

Patrick continued to be badly hit by his mother's death,

even after the funeral which he pressed Laura to attend. The war didn't help. So many of his contemporaries were either joining the services or taking on war work.

One Sunday morning he arrived at the Coach House just as Laura was making coffee.

'I've decided what I'm going to do,' he began, standing in her kitchen. 'It hasn't been easy, but I can't tolerate contributing nothing to the national effort. But there's Beth to consider. I can't delegate responsibility for her by absenting myself, and it's not the best time to leave Father to cope. That's why I'm offering Arncliffe Hall, or a major part of it, as a military hospital.'

'That's a good idea.'

Patrick seemed surprised that she approved. 'And I'm having most of the estate ploughed up. Ted's advised me on farming it, and I've been given to understand that before I know it Land Army girls will be arriving.'

Laura smiled. 'A bit of company for us, eh? Pity about your lovely grounds though.'

Patrick smiled back ruefully. 'If losing a few acres of garden is the worst we suffer, I'll be very thankful. Must admit I'm rather concerned as to how we'll preserve the interior of the Hall while the military are in occupation. That's if Hitler doesn't demolish it entirely . . .'

'Don't even talk about that,' Laura exclaimed.

'Anyway,' he continued, 'I just wanted to assure you that all these changes should have little effect upon you. Which brings me to what I was going to ask – you do intend staying on here, Laura? You're not thinking of joining up or anything, are you?'

She read in his dark eyes how much having her around mattered to him. After what had happened to his mother, she suddenly knew that she couldn't contemplate leaving for some long while.

Smiling slightly, she shrugged. 'Eh, I don't know what to do for the best. As you'll have gathered, normal production at the mill has stopped, while they make all sorts of stuff needed for the war. None of it's the kind of thing I'll be any use for. If you think of a bit of a job for me, let me know before I'm sent into a munitions factory like our Greta and Sybil.'

The job was anything but small, and was suggested by Patrick within the next few days. He needed somebody immediately to help co-ordinate the alterations being made to the Hall, and also to keep an eye on preparations for farming his land.

'You must say if it's not at all in your line,' he added after his suggestion. 'But all it requires is a modicum of common sense and a systematic manner of working.'

'I'll give it a try,' Laura decided at once. She was aware, though, that being reluctant to leave Arncliffe didn't necessarily guarantee her an easy time here.

Laura was glad to be able to tell the Lindleys that she was taking on different work, and was delighted when both Roy and his father emphasised that she mustn't dream of going anywhere else when the war ended.

Working alongside Patrick was a revelation. Although naturally courteous, he was too demanding a boss for life to be comfortable. Extremely quick-witted himself, he seemed to expect her to adapt swiftly to this totally new work. Having few guidelines for turning Arncliffe Hall into a military hospital, and fewer still for beginning to run the estate as a farm, Laura often felt completely out of her depth.

Patrick's brother-in-law Ted came over when he could to advise on how best to use the land, but his own farm was undergoing changes and he rarely spared enough time to explain details thoroughly to Laura.

Patrick himself relished toiling outdoors alongside the handful of Land Army girls who were allocated to them. He soon found this a healthy antidote to his responsibilities at the building society where staff were being conscripted into the services or munitions, to be replaced by men who came out of retirement to busy counters.

Despite the initial difficulties, Laura realised how happy she was less than a month after she had left the carpet mill. It mattered not at all that the work was unfamiliar and Patrick so demanding. She was seeing him for some part of every day, as well as seeing young Beth more frequently. And since it seemed that the three of them were being drawn more closely together, she had decided at last that she should put Magda Horsfall right to the back of her mind.

Patrick had demonstrated that she herself had a valued contribution to make in their daily lives here. While this remained so, she was going to concentrate on keeping the three of them happy.

Although she assisted in most aspects of running things at Arncliffe, it was as administrator of the farm that Laura was officially employed. She loved welcoming land girls when they arrived and helping them to settle into their quarters in a large outbuilding that had been converted. She calculated their wages and kept the farm books, ordered supplies, and liaised with Mrs Harrison who, with the help of a couple of local girls, had the task of feeding them all.

In some ways, though, it was the hospital side of Arncliffe that most captured Laura's interest. She loved to see and hear evidence of wounded men recovering there, and believed the relative peace of this part of the Yorkshire countryside contributed to their being restored.

The medical and surgical staff were under a lot of pressure which meant that some of the men were rather at a loose end as soon as they became mobile again. Those tending badly wounded men couldn't spare the time for keeping up the morale of others who were no longer in need of so much professional care.

'I wish there was something we could offer by way of an interest,' said Patrick one afternoon when he and Laura were having one of their regular discussions on how things were running.

'What sort of a thing?' she asked.

'Anything on the social side,' he began, and then he smiled, recollecting. 'You dance, don't you? I saw you that first time . . .'

'That's it!' she exclaimed. 'I'll check with the doctors, but I'm sure dancing could be ideal. It'd be a kind of physiotherapy for lots of the chaps, as well as giving them something to do. We could happen rope in the Land Army girls as well – they'd be glad to get to know some of the patients here.'

In this way, dancing at Arncliffe was begun. Delighted to be taking to the floor again, Laura wondered how on earth she had avoided dancing for so long.

Chapter 20

On the first occasion that she organised dancing at Arncliffe Laura relied on her ancient gramophone. Although it was all she had that would provide music, she discovered it was far from ideal. So old it was the kind that needed winding, it obliged her to break off and either attend to it herself or ask someone else to do so. And she had to stop the record every time she interrupted to explain something.

These interruptions were frequent. She had helped Aunt Constance instruct beginners, but that hadn't in any way prepared her for working with the people here. Because of their injuries many of the men were trying to cope while limbs were still heavily bandaged. And some even insisted on attempting to dance virtually immobilised with plaster.

'I'm beginning to wonder if I'm doing the wrong thing,' Laura confided to Mavis Priestley when she came for tea on the following day. 'There's that many of 'em can hardly get about, never name dance, that I might be making it so tantalising it's a sort of torture.'

'Nay, lass – I don't think that. You're not compelling them to attend, are you? And didn't you say you'd had a good crowd turn up?'

'A lot more than I expected. It's just – well, I did catch one or two of 'em just stood there, looking on longingly.'

'Might be no bad thing, that,' said Mavis pensively. 'Give them a sort of target – like becoming a bit more mobile.'

'I just wish I could organise it better, I seem to be forever starting up the gramophone then stopping it again.'

'How did your auntie manage when she was teaching?'

345

'Oh, she had a pianist, that worked very well.'

'There you are then. I'd play for you if you wanted . . .'

'Would you really?'

'Like a shot.'

'I'd be ever so grateful, only I'm afraid I'd not be able to pay you so much. We're not out to make a profit, and we try to lay on a bit of supper for everybody that comes.'

'Don't you worry your head about paying me. I'd love the change of company. I enjoy my AFS work, but there's not so many youngsters among our chaps, and I've always liked to be surrounded by young folk.'

'I'll have to check that Patrick doesn't mind us using his piano, but I daresay he'll not object.'

It was agreed that Mavis should play for the dancing classes whenever her fire service duties allowed, and Laura suggested that she may wish to stay overnight at the Coach House when she came out to them.

Before the next session, Laura had met up with her in the town centre to try and find copies of sheet music. They bought 'Whispering Grass' which everybody seemed to be singing these days, and 'A Nightingale Sang in Berkeley Square', but nothing else seemed suitable.

Having promised to look through the music she had at home, Mavis arrived for the next dancing night laden with copies of 'Over the Rainbow', 'The Folks Who Live on the Hill', and 'I like A Nice Cup of Tea', plus several other pre-war hits.

'That's marvellous,' Laura enthused, helping her off with her coat. 'But where's your overnight things? I did ask you to stay.'

Her friend smiled. 'I know, love, happen I will do one day, but I like to get home really. The AFS know where to contact me then if they want me to do an extra turn on duty.'

'That happens, does it?'

'Quite often, aye. I don't mind admitting it's good to be needed.'

Mavis Priestley soon proved her worth at Arncliffe Hall.

During the first half hour Laura began to appreciate how good it was to have someone there who could play slowly when required, pause while she demonstrated steps, and then continue where they had left off.

Laura's only disappointment that evening was Patrick's repetition of his refusal to join them. Hearing from one of the land girls that he had laboured all day alongside them, planting out the freshly ploughed ground, Laura had made a point of suggesting he had earned a break afterwards.

'I think not, thank you,' he had replied, sounding cool and rather formal. 'I have things to do.'

She had noticed then the folder on his desk. Labelled 'Magda', it seemed crammed with correspondence. She hadn't wanted a reminder that he was still pressing on with the attempts to locate his wife.

I wish he'd find her, as well, thought Laura fiercely. Then we'd all know where we stood. And she herself really would put him out of her mind. How long was it now that she had cared so much – about Patrick, about his daughter? For too long, she decided, and resolved that away from work she would give all her attention to making this dancing scheme succeed. At least that's one thing I understand, she thought, even though she still worried about how best to help men who had been severely wounded.

On this second occasion the whole evening went quite smoothly. More aware of what to expect, many of the land girls chatted freely with the men, and helped them to relax. One or two of these girls already had some experience of dancing and Laura had taken them aside to explain that whilst they wouldn't yet find very skilful partners, they themselves could be of great assistance.

Everyone seemed to be beginning to believe Laura's assurance that it didn't matter what they looked like at this early stage.

'Just get cracking and try to move to the music,' she reminded them cheerfully. 'It's all so's you'll have another way of enjoying yourselves. I don't expect you to be elegant yet.'

After that they laughed more easily, and exchanged rueful glances over their efforts to master the basic steps she was teaching. Very gradually, they were matching their movements to the melody, and with just a few exceptions were dancing quite rhythmically.

This might eventually become the sort of class I intend, thought Laura, feeling exhilarated by the surrounding buzz of pleasure. None of those attending seemed other than glad to be mastering something different. Amid her satisfaction though she still couldn't help regretting Patrick's absence. I just wish I could see why he's keeping away, she thought. What is going on in his mind . . .

Alone after Laura left his study earlier that evening, Patrick had sighed, drawing the folder towards him. There had been no news from the people organising registration – they had been quick to tell him that they had issued Magda's Identity Card with this address for the simple reason that they knew nothing of her living elsewhere.

Glumly, he thumbed through the file, glancing at letters he had written, at replies received. The Salvation Army had come up with nothing, although they alone did profess to continue to hope that time might produce some lead on her whereabouts. He wondered if that was merely their habitual refusal to admit that hope no longer existed.

There were also details of the original enquiries made by the police, which had yielded nothing and reminded him still that adults were considered free to vanish. He shuddered now recalling how they had even investigated the possibility that foul play might have occurred. And how he'd scarcely been consoled when he'd been exonerated, only to be assured that there had been nothing to prevent Magda from wishing to leave him.

He hadn't liked being compelled to consider that his wife might have walked out on him, any more than he had enjoyed police suggestions that she could have had a lover who proved more appealing.

He certainly would never again approach the police for help. But it was what had happened during their initial investigation which was sufficient to keep him away from them for ever.

Grimly, Patrick recalled the hours of being incarcerated in that cell, the questioning and cross-questioning which he'd endured; and all because some keen young detective had heard there was some financial difficulty, and suspected he might have gained from Magda's death. He had never really recovered from the shock of learning that a theory so ludicrous to him could be entertained by anyone.

Admittedly, they might have seen his marriage as suffering from some degree of neglect – he worked long hours, but what man with any ambition didn't? And Magda had known all about that before their engagement, had seemed ever since Beth's birth to have enough to occupy her. The hours he devoted to the building society reaped their reward, enabling him to be generous, providing everything she asked for in the home. She had relished their ability to entertain, and was satisfied that the house was staffed so well that she never needed to lift the proverbial finger.

Wherever she was now, there were days when he envied Magda. Evidently, she was free in a way which he most certainly was not. Since the day he was so nearly accused of her murder, he had spent a large part of his life fighting to overcome the repercussions. Bad though that meeting had been, when he'd only just held on to the confidence of shareholders with the power to oust him, worse had followed. Nothing on this earth could be more harrowing than watching his small daughter withdraw into her own world, from which neither speech nor any show of affection by her had reached out to touch him.

It seemed a long time now since that day when she had spoken so tantalisingly briefly in front of him. Since then Beth had remained so silent that he often believed that momentary improvement had been mere wishful thinking.

It was for Beth's sake now, even more than his own, that he

nurtured this determination to find Magda and free himself. It was through Laura that Beth had begun to improve. She was the one good thing in their lives. And he couldn't begin to court her until he severed all the shackles dragging his past into the present and darkening the future.

'We need Laura,' he murmured aloud. 'And I don't know how the hell to set about being free to approach her.'

He could enlist the aid of a private investigator, he supposed, there seemed no other avenue open to him now. The idea wasn't one that he relished, and must be undertaken with some circumspection. Too many local people had been interested in the furore among his fellow shareholders at the time when police questioning threatened his good name. It seemed he must engage someone from outside the locality, or risk unwelcome rumours being resurrected.

With Mavis at the piano, the dance sessions were going so well that Laura had suggested they might like to increase their practice nights to two per week. The men were enthusiastic although the Land Army girls were less so.

'We'd love it, really we would,' one of them explained. 'But it's getting up so bloomin' early, see? We can manage one late night a week, but we're whacked as it is. More than that and we'd be getting complaints about not being up to working. Leastways that's how it is now. Might alter after a bit when dancing comes easier through not having to concentrate so hard.'

'I wish I could think of a way to get the chaps together more than once a week, though,' Laura remarked, when explaining this to Patrick. He had pleased her by asking after her dancing class, but then had spoiled it all by seeming not to listen while she was replying.

'As far as I'm concerned, feel free to use that reception room whenever you wish,' he said, but rather vaguely, as though much more interested in the farm accounts she had shown him.

'You've no ideas, then – on how we might give them another

interest?' she ventured. It was, after all, his home. And there was her old longing to see him more involved in what was going on here.

Patrick merely shook his head. 'Sorry, too much on my mind as it is.'

Trying to get *her* back, thought Laura yet again. Well, if he wanted it that way, she'd no desire to change his mind for him. These days, there was so much company here at Arncliffe that she was beginning to think less about the Horsfall family. The men who'd been brought here from the war seemed glad of any time that she gave them.

Laura had taken to wandering through the makeshift wards for which most of the upstairs rooms were commandeered. The men she knew called to her or gave a cheery wave, and she paused frequently beside others, newcomers perhaps, fresh from airfields in the south, or from battle fronts overseas.

She wrote letters to the dictation of some for whom writing was difficult, and won the appreciation of nursing staff and doctors whose greatest burden was shortage of time.

The one tiny operating theatre was used to the full, but only for minor surgery; more complex operations required the facilities in one or other of the larger local hospitals. The resident surgeon was a man who had emerged from retirement and, being a widower, seemed glad now to live in at Arncliffe and become truly involved here.

It was often of surgeons elsewhere, though, that many of the men would speak, and mostly – given time and hindsight – in approving terms. Even when limbs had been sacrificed, patients' experience of war had imparted knowledge of the thin line separating life from death. Laura marvelled at the courage of many amputees, and tried not to reveal emotion when, sitting at a table among them, she reflected on how greatly most had suffered.

As time went on, her interest in these men rather overshadowed her earlier concerns and, with the exception of caring about Beth, she felt quite relieved to be less involved with the family at Arncliffe.

Beth remained a regular visitor to her home, and loved to play hopscotch in the courtyard or with her beloved whip and top. And although still not really speaking, she did manage to communicate quite well with Laura.

It was generally only when Beth arrived at the Coach House indicating that she wanted some drawing paper that Laura thought very much about carpet designing. Keeping the books up to date, touring the wards and organising her dances ate up a great deal of time.

Any rare minutes designing were devoted to possible patterns for the building society carpet. She had been determined all along that as soon as Lindley's began producing again when the war ended, she would have ready a design that nobody could fault.

Mavis had been playing the piano at Arncliffe for several weeks when she was obliged one evening to ring and cancel.

'I'm ever so sorry, Laura, I don't like letting folk down. But it's the AFS, you see – the chap that should have been on duty tonight has been took bad, they think it's his heart.'

Although telling her not to worry, Laura was perturbed. They worked so well together that she dreaded going back to depending on her aged gramophone.

She was getting it out of the cupboard in the ballroom when the first of the men came in.

'Where's our pianist tonight then?'

Laura explained. 'Can't say I relish going back to using this thing, but I've nowt else . . .'

'There's other folk can play the piano – what about Maurice?'

'Maurice?'

'Maurice Olivier, don't you know him? You might not, I suppose. Keeps himself to himself quite a bit, though we're working on that. He certainly wouldn't attend your evenings – lost a leg when his Spitfire came down in flames.'

'Do you mean the man who spends so much time reading? He has a foreign accent.'

'That's Maurice. From Jersey, he is. We got him to play the piano the other night when we had a few drinks.'

'Could you – would you mind going to ask him if he would agree to play for us, please?' Several of the other fellows had drifted into the room now, she couldn't really leave them.

Maurice limped straight towards her ten minutes later, smiling as he leaned heavily on one crutch to offer his hand. 'Don't believe we've ever been introduced, Miss Crabtree, but I surely will be happy to be of service.'

'That's great!' she exclaimed. 'I'm absolutely delighted. And everybody calls me Laura.'

She walked with him across to the piano and raised the lid while he was laying aside his crutches.

'We haven't got a lot of tunes, I'm afraid. Sheet music seems to be in short supply round here, but this is what we do have. I've pencilled on for Miss Priestley whether each one's a waltz, quickstep or foxtrot and so on. Oh – and I hope you won't mind that I have to keep stopping you – when I explain a few steps, or if somebody gets in a bit of a mess.'

Maurice grinned, his grey eyes lighting. 'Beats sitting with my nose in yet another book! You just put me right on how you want it.'

Laura warmed to Maurice's manner at once, he seemed so genuinely glad to help. During the course of the evening his self-effacing smile began to convince her that Mavis Priestley's absence had been anything but a disaster.

When they paused for refreshments she offered to bring something across to him and asked if there was any food he hated. Maurice, however, insisted on limping over to the table where everything was set out.

'The lads here rib me enough about not joining in. Maybe I should show them that I'm not stand-offish.'

Later, after the class had ended, Laura thanked him sincerely for all he'd done. 'You're every bit as good as Mavis, and she's been coming here for weeks. I hope I can call on you again when she can't make it?'

'But of course,' Maurice said smoothly. 'Fact is, time hangs heavily, 'specially till I'm fitted with an artificial leg.'

'Any idea when that'll be?'

353

'Not as yet. Afraid I'm not healing too well.'

'Oh, I'm sorry.'

'Yes, well – I'm lucky, I suppose, that I didn't end up entirely a cinder.'

The lines around his thin, sensitive mouth revealed, though, that he hadn't always so unreservedly reckoned this good fortune. Before acquiring those lines he would have been one of those few men who could be accurately described as handsome. His eyes were such a pale grey and their blue-tinged whites were fringed with long bronze lashes. His hair also was a deep shade of bronze, slightly wavy.

Somehow, though, to Laura his accent was the most appealing thing about Maurice, setting him apart from the others, making her believe he was very different from them, even before she began to learn how different he was.

They talked for a while longer, mostly about the war, especially of the Battle of Britain in which his fighter squadron had fought frequent sorties.

'I'm sorry,' he said eventually when a clock somewhere chimed eleven. 'I shouldn't be keeping you when you've worked a full day even before tonight. Do you have far to go home?'

Laura chuckled. 'Only across to the Coach House. Quite handy, you see.'

'Would you object if I walked you to your door? I don't like thinking of you going through the blackout on your own.'

'That's very kind of you, thanks. I've just got to make certain all the lights are off, and then lock up behind me.'

'And I can return by the rear entrance. It's the one we're told to use, I believe.'

'That sounds as if you don't get out much?'

'Fact is, I feel an idiot on crutches.'

'You shouldn't let that bother you here, there's plenty of chaps the same.'

'And worse off. Do you think no one tells me? Makes no difference, Laura. I reckon I'll never stop feeling embarrassed.'

Maurice propelled himself awkwardly around the room,

helping to switch off lights. 'One thing I can manage,' he'd said, making her aware again of how deeply he felt being incapacitated.

This close to the moors, the night was cool for early summer, especially after the heat generated indoors by thirty or so dancers.

'Just look at all those stars,' Laura exclaimed after they had paused briefly to grow accustomed to the darkness. She always thought the one benefit of the blackout was this ability to see all the splendour of night skies.

Maurice, she noticed, was too busy watching where he set his crutches on the paving.

'Thanks for everything,' she said when they reached her door. 'For seeing me home, as well as for your super playing.'

'I've enjoyed it all,' he answered sincerely. 'I hope it isn't too long before your Miss Priestley is otherwise occupied again.'

'I'll look out for you when I'm wandering round the wards. I do that quite a bit, you know.'

'Do you think I haven't noticed you?'

As they said goodnight, Laura felt a tiny shiver of excitement coursing through her. Knowing Maurice had kept an eye on her was very flattering somehow.

From that night onwards she always paused to chat with Maurice whenever he was around as she went about the hospital. He showed her photographs of his home on Jersey, and of his mother, and confided how anxious he'd become since the Germans invaded the Channel Islands in July 1940.

When next she was short of a pianist Laura had enough warning to be able to leave her desk during the day and go to ask Maurice if he could help out.

His ready smile added emphasis to his swift agreement, and Laura immediately began looking forward to having his company once more. The other men were a grand bunch, as were the Land Army girls who partnered them; no one but Maurice, though, had got through to her in quite this way.

Privately, she admitted that his accent added still further to his charm, but more than that, and more even than his handsome features, she was becoming attracted by his gentleness and courtesy.

At the end of this second evening of playing for them, Laura was pleased when Maurice remained behind after all the others had trooped away. Again, they both went about turning off lights, and when they reached the outer door, she smiled into his eyes.

'Thanks again, Maurice, it's lovely having you around. I shall be making a hot drink when I get home, do you want one?'

He admired her cosy living-room where they sat either side of the fire, drinking cocoa.

'I envy you a place of your own,' he said, though without any trace of bitterness. 'I was looking for a flat or something on the island before this lot started. I love my mother dearly, but she was growing too dependent, and with no real need. That wasn't good for either of us.'

'Are there just the two of you?'

Maurice nodded. 'My father was gassed in the last lot. Afraid that finished him – he only lasted until I was ten years old. And I've no brothers or sisters.'

'I can understand your being worried about your mother now.'

'It could be worse, I suppose. We manage to get letters to and fro somehow through friends, which helps. Or at least – makes it rather difficult now, writing to her and not saying too much about . . . the way I am.'

'You mean – you haven't told her?'

'Where's the point? In any case, before this lot ends I'll have the tin leg. She'll be so glad if I survive the war, she'll not be unduly perturbed about the shape I'm in.'

Laura suspected differently, but saying so wouldn't help Maurice. 'You're not married then?' she asked.

He shook his head. 'Just as well, eh? Now. I'd have hated to return like this to a wife who'd feel obliged to stick around.'

'Maurice! You mustn't talk like that, mustn't even think that way. You're a smashing chap, I've never met anybody nicer. That's the sort of thing that counts.'

'Sweet of you, Laura, but you don't have to be kind. I'm no child, you know, I face facts.'

'But they aren't facts at all. Like I said . . .'

Maurice only shook his head. 'I'm just thankful now that things didn't work out a year or two back. There was somebody then. French, she was, we met in Normandy. I thought the world of her, fool that I was. Decided to give her a surprise one weekend, and went over there. I was the one receiving a surprise. I believe they married just before war was declared.'

'Oh, dear.'

Maurice grinned at her. 'I'm over it now, don't look so woeful on my behalf. And as I said, it simplifies a whole lot of things, with this situation.'

As time went on, though, Laura began noticing that Maurice wasn't anything like well-adjusted to having lost a leg. Although she pressed him to come and watch whenever Mavis played for dancing, and he promised to do so, he never put in an appearance when he couldn't be of use there. She discovered also that he was viewing the future as if he was precluded from ever marrying or having a family.

She knew from her own experience how the lack of children could hurt. These days, she was too busy to see a lot of Netta and the baby, but whenever she had been over to visit them she returned acutely conscious of her own yearning.

Perhaps partly to compensate for this, she had obtained Patrick's agreement to her taking Beth for walks around his estate. Whether or not Laura herself was benefiting, the child certainly seemed to enjoy their outings. And one day she became so excited that she at last uttered a few more words.

They had strolled beside the rows of potatoes which had replaced a large expanse of lawn, and were watching one of the land girls who was handling a distant tractor near the brow of the hill.

Suddenly Beth tugged on Laura's hand. 'I want to see, can we?'

Laura was so thrilled that she felt more like rushing the child back to Patrick in order to tell him. But Beth's enthusiasm was too plain to be ignored.

'Yes, of course we'll go nearer,' Laura promised. 'Only you'll have to do as I say and stay close to my side. Tractors can be dangerous, you know. Promise you'll be good?'

Beth nodded, but didn't provide the 'yes' for which Laura was hoping. Once they were within yards of the tractor, the child waved eagerly in response to the land girl's raised hand. In fact, this close the machine proved so noisy that Beth seemed reluctant to approach any nearer. Laura was relieved that there was no reason to restrain her and risk one of the screaming fits with which she still tended to meet opposition.

Standing there while Beth watched every move the girl was making, Laura held on to her hand but allowed her own gaze to travel beyond the nearby boundary of the Arncliffe estate.

On this side it was bordered by woods that spread down into the valley and halfway up the hillside facing them. A sandstone hamlet crowned that next ridge, and beyond that further hilltops drew the eye towards mauve-tinged moors in the far distance.

Somewhere out there was the reservoir that she'd visited with Patrick. Laura longed suddenly to walk that way again, maybe to take Beth with her.

Her wish was confirmed as a possibility when they eventually turned away from the tractor and Beth pointed towards the gate set in her father's boundary wall. Although she couldn't be encouraged to speak again, the urgency with which she attempted to pull Laura in that direction voiced her longing to explore.

'Not today, love, or you'll miss your tea. But we'll go out there one day soon,' Laura promised. And was thankful again when Beth appeared to accept that cheerfully.

As soon as she had handed the child over to Mrs Harrison who had tea waiting, Laura went in search of Patrick.

He was in the office that they shared, but had only just arrived home from the building society and was unloading his briefcase. He looked tired and worn, and Laura realised she hadn't quite dismissed her feelings for him. She wished with all her heart that the situation between them was easier and that she could put her arms round him. As things stood, she rarely knew the best approach to use.

Their relationship now seemed neither one thing nor another. Working alongside Patrick on farming the estate or sorting any problems arising from the use of Arncliffe as a hospital was quite agreeable, but no more than that. The short spell when he had confided in her had faded into the past, almost as though it had never been. And although she found satisfaction in working here, he'd never given her any reason to suppose her presence produced in him anything beyond relief that someone was to hand while he was coping with one of his other responsibilities.

Today, however, she was delighted about this progress of Beth's, which surely would help raise his spirits.

'Hallo,' she began with a smile. 'I was hoping you'd have arrived home. I've something to tell you – Beth has said another few words at last.'

'Really?' He sounded incredulous rather than elated, but listened carefully while Laura gave him all the details.

'That's very good,' he said after hearing her out. 'If only I could get her to begin communicating like any normal person . . .'

'Perhaps if we went and saw her now?' Laura suggested. 'She's only having her tea, it won't matter if we interrupt. And we could catch her before she clams up for ages again.'

But Patrick was shaking his head. 'Leave it with me,' he said swiftly. 'I'll see her as usual before her bedtime.'

Feeling dismissed, Laura made herself smile again. 'Sure, fine. Anything you want to discuss before I go off home?'

'Have you got those cheques ready for signing?'

'On your desk. Together with last month's figures.'

'That's all then, thanks,' he said, and crossed to his desk.

As he turned from her, though, one of the files he'd been carrying slid off the top of the pile. Retrieving it from the floor, Laura took it across to him. Handing it over, she couldn't help noticing that it was the one headed 'Magda'. No wonder he seems preoccupied and worn out, she thought. He's still burning himself up with these efforts to trace his wife.

When the door closed behind Laura, Patrick sighed, sank on to his chair, and stared into space. The day had been hellish. The private investigator he'd employed some time ago had written admitting defeat. None of the means he had used had produced so much as a whisper about Magda Horsfall's present whereabouts. He very much regretted the situation, but without further clues regarding her disappearance he could extend no hope of locating her.

The news that Beth had finally spoken again ought to have offset the gloom induced by yet another failure to find her mother. Somehow, though, the fact that Laura had got his daughter to speak seemed merely to emphasise his own inadequacy. And that was a feeling which was growing increasingly prevalent.

He'd never been like this in the old days. He'd always felt fully in command – of himself, and of those surrounding him. On days like this when his capacity for success seemed drained away, he was reminded all too readily of that dreadful time preceding Magda's departure. He had reacted so badly under all the stress, and now he appeared to be unable to rid himself of the feeling that he could do nothing about this situation in which he was trapped.

He wanted Laura – his longing to make her a part of his life never lessened – but not like this. *He* needed to be the person to encourage Beth to respond, just as he needed to put things right before even contemplating another marriage. Whatever happened in the future, he couldn't even think of coming to depend on anyone, no matter how he might feel about her.

Chapter 21

Patrick reported the following day that Beth had made no attempt to speak to him when he saw her that evening. Laura read in his eyes not only understandable disappointment but also his reluctance to accept that someone else might succeed where he had failed.

Rather at a loss to know how to help, she suggested quickly that he might like to join Beth and herself for a walk, perhaps during the weekend.

'She seemed that eager to go out of the far gate that I could hardly bear to bring her back here. It's such a change, isn't it, from the way she used to cling around her home?'

Although Patrick agreed with that, he didn't jump at the idea of taking a walk with them. Instead, he began speaking of all the tasks awaiting him.

'Do you mind if I take her out then when I have time?' said Laura, yet again convinced that he wished to avoid spending his leisure with her. 'I give you my word I'll keep my eye on her the whole time.'

He didn't doubt that, any more than he doubted Laura's ability to get the best out of his daughter. 'Yes, that's all right with me,' he said coolly, and began discussing the day's business.

Laura was determined that she wouldn't let his attitude affect her determination to help Beth. And nor would it ruin the rest of her life. She had two dancing sessions arranged for this week, the routine practice tonight, and a dance on Saturday, to which some of the land girls were inviting friends.

Going through the hospital wards during her lunch hour,

Laura reminded some of the men of this. 'Just see you all turn up on Saturday, as well. A few of the lasses are bringing partners, but there's more that have invited other girls to come.'

As usual, Maurice greeted her with a smile, and as usual gave her a look when she tried persuading him to attend. 'Not unless you need me to play the piano. You know I can't dance.'

'I'll let you know then, after I've seen Mavis tonight.'

During their break for refreshments that evening, Laura asked her old friend if she was coming on Saturday.

Mavis frowned, surprising her. 'I don't know what to do for the best actually, love. I know I said it'd be all right, but it's with it going on till half-past eleven, you see.'

'You could always stay the night. I've said that all along, but you've never taken me up on it, have you?'

'No – well . . . In one way I'd love to, but in another that'd make it more awkward. It's church, you see – I'd not feel like getting up early enough to make it. And I don't like missing. Especially now we've got the new chap permanent in charge of the music.'

So many men were away in the forces that until quite recently the organists at St Martin's had been temporary, filling the gap left by Michael's departure.

'Don't go worrying about it, we'll manage,' Laura assured her. 'Matter of fact, if this Saturday dance is a success, it'd be a good thing to have Maurice playing regularly for them. It's the only way I can get him to attend.'

'Eh, dear – is he no better at joining in than he was?'

'He's all right when he has something to do. Mind you, he's got a lot on his plate, I can understand if he doesn't feel up to making much of an effort in other directions. They've just fitted him with his artificial leg, and it's taking some getting used to.'

Troubled by the new limb or not, Maurice seemed in fine spirits when Saturday came. There could be no questioning the enthusiasm with which he played the numbers that he and Laura had selected together. And because it wasn't really a practice session, there were few breaks for instruction.

'I think that went ever so well, don't you?' said Laura at the end of the evening, delighted by the number of people who had thanked her as they were leaving. 'I've promised them another Saturday do before so long. I hope you won't mind playing for us?'

'I shall love it, Laura. You ought to know that by now. But what about your friend?'

'Oh, I had a talk with Mavis. She'd rather stick to the weekdays she can manage. Doesn't like to be late on a Saturday.'

'But I thought that was the night everyone wished to go out?'

Laura grinned at him. 'Aye, so did I. Look at you though – you weren't making a set at any of them lasses! Isn't it time you found yourself another girl?' she finished lightly.

Maurice's smile vanished. 'I would not saddle anyone with me, I have told you . . .'

'Oh, come on, love – stop being so serious. It was only a bit of a joke. Tell you what, have a nightcap with me. I want to celebrate how well it went off tonight, and I'd feel proper daft on my own.'

After switching off lights and locking the door behind them, they walked side by side towards the Coach House. The night air felt pleasantly cool after the warmth generated by dancing, making Laura inclined to linger. But Maurice, with his new limb and trying to cope using only one stick, seemed to find strolling awkward.

He still ignored her invitation to sit, however, after going indoors. 'I'll pour the drinks for you first, if you'll allow me.'

Laura opened a door in the sideboard acquired just before the war. 'I haven't got much choice, I'm afraid. I never was a drinker, even before we had shortages forced on us. There's some bottled beer, if that's owt in your line. Or there's sherry. There's a drop of port left an' all. That's what I'll have, I think, with lots of lemonade. It's poor stuff compared to prewar, but the port will disguise it.'

They drank to the future success of similar evenings, then talked of various men on the wards who'd become firm friends, and of others who had now moved on.

'I daresay some of them are on active service again by now,' Laura observed. While others, she knew, had been sent to specialist hospitals for further surgery.

'What will you do when this lot's over?' she asked Maurice eventually. She had never enquired into his civilian occupation. Life here seemed so withdrawn from the normal world that she often found considering that these men had other lives quite difficult.

Maurice smiled. 'My family are market gardeners, mainly growing tomatoes, though I mean to diversify after the war. Fortunately, it's something where I shall still be able to cope.'

'Of course you will. Now you've got the leg you're as good as new. Or will be once you're more used to it. Nobody'll know you're any different.'

Instead of agreeing, Maurice was shaking his head. 'I shall know – always.' Why else would he have been so reticent with this woman who already meant so much to him?

'Eh, love, you mustn't be like that. You're a lovely fellow, nobody's going to let it bother them. If you were my chap I'd just be that thankful you'd survived.'

Even though they talked of other things, Maurice remained subdued. He seemed really down tonight, and Laura couldn't for the life of her think how to help. It wasn't until he was about to leave and had struggled to his feet that he began to reveal that he had further anxieties.

'Where's this lot going to end, Laura, that's what beats me? And even if we do last till the duration, will there be anything to go back for?'

'Maurice? Have you had bad news from home?'

'Nothing concrete. But my mother's far from strong. I gather that food on Jersey is seriously restricted. We always imported most of our meat from Britain. Now people are being forced into being vegetarian.'

'I daresay she'll be faring better than you think, love.'

'I hope so. It's some while since I heard.'

'Couldn't you ring her up? You can use my phone with pleasure, any time.'

'Bless you, Laura, but you don't understand. It was the worst thing of all at the time. With the German occupation, all contact ceased. The Ministry of Information announcement sent a chill right through me. "Telegraphic and telephonic communications have been cut and no further information is at present available," they said.'

'Eh, love, come here.' Laura went to Maurice, thrust her arms around his shoulders and held him to her. 'You've got too much on your mind, haven't you? It's more than one person should have to bear.'

She felt his lips on her ear. 'And it's only with you, Laura, that I even begin to forget.'

Despite the sadness she felt on his behalf, she smiled. 'That's the nicest thing anybody's ever said to me.'

She kissed his lips and his arms drew her closer. Her smile deepened as she realised how right they seemed together. 'Do you want another drink?' she asked, aware now of how empty her home would seem as soon as he left.

'Not just yet. Unless you're telling me it's time I was on my way?' If he was compelled to leave now he would need something strong inside him to ensure any sleep.

'On the contrary,' she admitted. 'I was just thinking it seems too soon for you to go.'

'Good. Splendid.' Maurice hugged her. 'But if you don't mind I would like to use your bathroom.'

'Of course. I'm afraid it's upstairs, though.'

'I can manage stairs – slowly, but I get there. Good practice for me.'

Watching his laborious progress as he hauled himself from step to step, Laura felt her heart aching. How could she fail to love his determination?

Waiting below in the tiny hall she soon heard the bathroom door open again, but then Maurice cursed and seemed to stumble.

'It's okay,' he called hastily.

Laura was already halfway up the stairs.

'I said I'm all right,' he snapped.

'What happened, love?'

Despite his embarrassment, he grinned as she reached him on the tiny landing.

'Nothing much – I just turned more sharply than this damned foot. Now the whole bloody contraption feels to have shifted.'

'Why don't you pop into the spare room and sort yourself out? It's this door here.'

'In a minute.' He was thinking how matter-of-fact she sounded about this abominable leg, almost as if she wasn't as revolted as he himself by its presence. 'You're good for me, Laura,' he said rather huskily. 'Bloody marvellous.'

He reached for her hand and held it to his chest. With his other arm he drew her against him. When their lips met his kisses were very different: searching, lingering, insistent.

He leaned against the wall and hauled her closer still. Laura could feel his need, and her own unmistakable response. When he stirred she couldn't control the echoing movement of her own body.

'God, how I need you,' Maurice gasped.

I know, thought Laura, and understood that this was the reason they had been brought together. If Maurice needed her, she was no less in need – hadn't she yearned for so long to feel she was a bit of use to someone who mattered to her? And hadn't she realised now precisely why she'd been so distressed by his idea that marriage was no longer for him?

He was kissing her again, deeply, urgently.

'You can't be very comfortable with the weight on that leg,' Laura remarked when he paused to draw in breath. 'Shall we find somewhere better?'

Briefly, Maurice hesitated, eyes questioning her. 'You sure? If we move from here, I can't promise I'll hold out . . .'

'I'm sure.'

Taking his arm, she turned towards the spare bedroom.

'It's tidier than mine,' she said ruefully and grinned.

Maurice's answering smile was wry. 'As if I'd notice! I'm far too preoccupied with my own shortcomings.'

'Oh, love – you mustn't be.' Laura turned again and hugged him close. 'You're warm and loving. And I want you so much.'

His mouth again found hers in a flurry of tender kisses which quickly intensified. Against her he felt hard, so demanding that the need was awakened deep within her.

In mutual consent they moved towards the bed. Laura began undressing, but as soon as her skirt was off Maurice checked her with a hand on her wrist. There seemed no hint of awkwardness as he lowered her on to the bed then eased himself on top of her. For moments only he remained pressing close, and then she felt him removing her panties, unfastening his own buttons.

They lay skin to skin, their bodies acknowledging each other.

'You're so beautiful,' he murmured, his voice emotional.

'And you're the most wonderful man ever.'

He entered her slowly at first, then swiftly-grown love overcame caution and every final reservation.

Thrilled and a little startled, Laura savoured each new sensation until the intensity of their loving stilled.

'I hope I didn't hurt you?' Maurice murmured into her ear. Earlier, he had been confronted by too many other worries to consider that she might be so inexperienced.

She smiled against his cheek. 'I'm fine, love. And very happy.'

'So am I, extremely. Except I just wish I didn't have to make my way back to that damned hospital bed.'

'Do you have to? Won't any ward rounds have taken place long before this?'

'Well, yes, but . . .' He couldn't really believe that she would permit him to stay overnight. That would be inviting gossip, criticism. Men like himself could confront any such opprobrium. She, on the other hand, was an innocent young woman.

There was a smile in her voice when Laura spoke again. 'Why don't we undress and be comfortable? Haven't we just shown that we sort of belong here?'

Maurice yearned to spend the night holding her in his arms, and longed as well to love her again. That first time had been for himself; he wanted to demonstrate that he could temper his own needs to match Laura's.

With only the moonlight a thin strip down one side of the blacked-out window, the room was all but totally dark. Suspecting that Maurice preferred it that way, Laura didn't turn on the light. As she discarded her own clothing, though, she was aware of the unstrapping of his leg and a metallic sound as it was set aside. The floor shook as Maurice hopped the few paces to the bed and then he was beneath the covers, but far away on the edge of the mattress.

Laura slid towards him. Her arm went around him and her lips located his mouth.

'I love you, Laura,' he said. 'These past weeks you've given me hope. And now yourself. No man could ask for more.'

'And you've made me so happy.' She kissed him again. 'Really alive, for the first time ever.'

They lay for a while, kissing gently and holding each other, and for a while they slept.

Some time during the early hours Laura awoke and listened to Maurice's even breathing, glad that he was here beside her. Minutes later she became aware that he was no longer sleeping. Smiling, she kissed him, and was drawn close against his powerful body.

'This time, it's to be entirely for you,' he told her. 'Or almost – I have to confess to renewed interest!'

He wooed her tenderly with caressing hands that enticed and awakened, making her reach towards him. Her fingers gentle, she first explored his severed leg, willing herself not to stiffen or reveal her emotion as she traced the taut skin, the scarring low down on the thigh.

'Now I know,' she whispered, and swallowed back tears before kissing him again, 'we'll forget you were ever wounded.

We do seem to have discovered a lovely way of forgetting everything.'

Crushed against his chest, she revelled in the strength of him and the heartbeat that appeared to challenge her to notice his virility. The pressure of his lean body was already alerting all her senses.

Afterwards, Laura realised that no moment in her life had produced such glorious feelings of well-being.

Morning came too soon, awakening her when the alarm clock rang out from her own bedroom.

Returning after hastening through to turn off the din, she was thrusting her arms into a dressing-gown.

'Do you have to?' Maurice teased from the bed. 'It was too dark last night for admiring you.'

Laura gave him a wry look. 'Just be patient with me for a while – don't forget I've done a lot of adjusting in the past few hours.'

He chuckled. 'Fair enough. It's no bad thing, anyway, to hold some treats in reserve. Always assuming that I have acquitted myself well enough to be invited again?'

Laura leaned down to kiss him. 'What do you think? But to come back to earth, shouldn't you be making your way across to that ward now?'

'Unfortunately, yes. I'll just take a quick wash, if I may.'

'I'll go and make some tea. Have you time for breakfast, love?'

'Better not. If I snatch something over the way, it might not be quite so evident that I've been absent all night.'

Laura was humming cheerfully to herself in the kitchen while she filled the kettle and set out cups and saucers. Normally, she turned on the radio first thing. Today, she couldn't bear the rest of the world to intrude on them. She felt quite saddened that Maurice couldn't live here with her completely, but she would exist on his mentioning their being together again until that could be managed.

Insistent knocking on the outer door startled her. She hurried across to see who was there.

'Beth! Eh, love – it's far too early for visiting. Can you come back another time?'

But Beth, who had been taught she was always welcome here, was already over the threshold. Making straight for the kitchen table, the girl drew out a chair, sat, then pulled one cup and saucer towards her. She was beaming up at Laura, her blue eyes so happy and trusting that even the hardest of hearts would have weakened.

'All right then, but you can't stop long,' Laura gabbled, crossing to take out a third cup while she wondered frantically how she would explain Maurice to Beth.

As if to emphasise how inept her own efforts at quick thinking were, she heard the click of the bathroom door and Maurice emerging.

He called to her from the head of the stairs. 'Is the tea poured, my love?'

Laura's answer was drowned in another bout of urgent knocking, this time from her front door. 'Just a minute,' she called back to Maurice. 'It's probably the post.'

The postman it was not. Patrick was standing outside the door. 'Sorry, Laura. Mrs Harrison said Beth went streaking off, is she here?'

'In the kitchen,' she began, then broke off, shaken by his appalled expression. She turned and looked to where he was staring towards the top of the stairs where Maurice was balancing cheerfully on his one leg, a hand on the wall for support, wearing an inadequately draped towel.

'Beth's in the kitchen,' Laura repeated, her voice several octaves higher. 'She can stay for a cup of tea if she wants . . .'

Patrick cut her short. 'I think not, don't you?' he snapped. 'This is no place for my daughter.'

'You'd better take her then,' Laura retorted.

The screams with which Beth protested while her father was removing her from the Coach House gave Laura no satisfaction. No matter how much either she or Beth wished to continue their friendship, it would not be permitted to last. Oh, well, she thought resignedly, they have each other.

Meanwhile, it was up to her to assure Maurice that he need not be perturbed by the altercation that had just taken place.

She ran upstairs immediately and straight into her spare room. Maurice was sitting on the edge of the bed wrestling with the strapping of his leg. The look he gave her emphasised that her presence was the last thing he wanted at that moment.

Briefly, Laura hesitated, about to turn and leave. But then something decided her to remain where she was. Any harm was done already, and this might remove a few more inhibitions about the limb.

'I'll assume you're coping okay,' she said matter-of-factly, 'which is more than I've done downstairs. You saw that was Patrick Horsfall – very much in his Master of Arncliffe mode. If I'd had the sharpness of mind which he seems to possess, I'd have reminded him that this is my house. Where I do what I wish.'

Maurice chuckled. He could have been enjoying the turn events had taken. 'Well, maybe I shan't need to worry about whom we should confide in, eh? Could be our private life will be the talk of the whole place before the day's out . . .'

'Oh, I don't think so,' Laura began.

Maurice remained amused. As soon as he had fixed the leg he rose and came to her. Hugging her to him, he grinned. 'Whatever – it's all right with me, sweetheart. I want the world to know I love you.'

Laura reminded herself repeatedly of what Maurice had said. In no other way would she have survived the day intact. The second shock had followed within the hour. Her late arrival in the office was greeted by Patrick whom she had supposed would long since have left to keep an eye on the farmworkers. She was already wishing that this wretched war didn't enforce a seven-day week. Postponing this encounter for another day might have allowed his fury to cool.

Stony-faced, he glanced up as she entered and spoke without any niceties. 'I am well aware that you are at liberty to conduct your own life as you wish, don't trouble to remind me of that. What I must insist, however, is that your behaviour should not influence my daughter. We both know Beth dotes on you. As a consequence, she is vulnerable. Regrettably, I must refuse to allow any future contact between you.'

He rose without giving Laura the opportunity to speak, turned from her and strode out of the office.

Too shaken to begin work immediately, she sank on to her chair and sighed. If Patrick had tried to hurt her he couldn't have found a more effective weapon. To be fair, though, she could see his point of view. The circumstances of Maurice's presence in her home had been all too evident. She herself had felt embarrassed, but no more than that. She couldn't feel one iota of regret about their lovemaking. It would take more than the upset here to stop her looking forward to this wonderful new relationship developing.

Fortunately for Laura, Sunday was one day of the week when some of the land girls felt sufficiently relaxed to take the odd few minutes away from work and chat to her. She had been sitting preoccupied for only a short while when one of them breezed into the office.

'We're almost out of potato sacks again, said I'd come and let you know. What I really wanted to say, though, was what a smashing time we had last night! That goes for us all. Those of us in our room didn't get off to sleep for ages talking about it.'

Laura smiled. 'Glad you enjoyed the dance as much as I did. The hospital chaps seemed to as well. You can tell the other lasses from me that they're doing champion – getting the men to join in.'

Heartened by this appreciation, Laura began to feel better. She completed the order for potato sacks while she had it in mind, and tackled some of the paperwork which always seemed to accumulate faster than she could clear it.

Although she had never been asked to work Sundays as well as during the week, she had found from the start that it was a good time to handle any backlog. And today she sensed she would be better if her mind was occupied. This relationship with Maurice was so new that she'd been unable to sort out her deepest feelings. Whilst she had no misgivings, time alone would prove whether or not they were both so committed as she now felt herself to be. She needed others to understand their situation. She had been offended by Patrick's insinuation that she would sleep around.

But Maurice loved her, and hadn't been slow to declare his love. Thinking back over their tender moments together, Laura was beginning to understand that only her own growing love for him had made last night possible. I shall ignore anyone who criticises or condemns, she resolved, and concentrate on what's between us. That is the only thing that really matters.

Laura suspected she was going to hate her next visit to the wards. She'd been conscious all along that Maurice's absence during Saturday night must have been noticed, and the mood he was in he would readily reveal where he had passed those hours. She could imagine he would cheerfully brazen it out, and might even consider this enhanced his new image as one of the lads. It was her own nature to keep something so personal between themselves, but she would settle for having others share the joy they had found in each other.

I'll get it over with this morning, she decided all at once. If word has percolated through the hospital wards, I might as well show my face there and prove I'm not perturbed that it's common knowledge.

Initially, Laura avoided Maurice's ward. Judging by her own emotions, he could need a bit of time before they met in public. She was glad when first from one side then another she was greeted by enthusiastic reminiscences about the previous evening. It was heartwarming to have the men reiterate their enthusiasm for the dancing she had introduced at Arncliffe.

She was also beginning to feel relieved – no one, so far, had referred to her relationship with Maurice. Maybe she was being granted some respite in which to get used to what was happening between them.

The second ward she visited produced no untoward comments either, the attitude of the men appeared to be no different from usual. She was still accepted as a pal who'd devised a means of keeping them occupied, someone also who was willing to give a hand on the ward, with reading or writing letters or so on.

Laura was approaching the third ward when one of the doctors on duty hailed her. 'Can you spare a second?' he asked, smiling, as he showed her into the side room used as an office. 'Unofficially, you understand, I just want to congratulate you. About Maurice, yes. I couldn't help but notice he'd gone missing. And I'd have been even less observant than I sometimes appear if I hadn't also noticed his elation this morning.'

'I take it he confided where he'd been?' said Laura rather awkwardly.

'I made him tell me. Not that he needed much persuading. I thought at first – well, maybe one of the Land Army girls . . . When I knew it was you, everything took on a whole new aspect. An affair would have boosted his morale. Knowing it's something more enduring makes it ideal. He's a new man already, Laura – and that's entirely your doing. He'll be okay now, whatever.'

He had paused. Seeing her smile, he squeezed her shoulder. 'I certainly wish the pair of you well. Long may your relationship continue.'

'Thanks,' she said. 'Thank you very much.'

The doctor grinned. 'I dare say you might come in for some ribbing from certain quarters. Wanted to get in first and assure you the news is excellent.'

Encouraged, Laura decided that the next ward she must visit would be Maurice's. And if the lads were in the know by now she felt fully able to stand up to any comments they might toss her way.

Maurice saw her the moment she came through the heavy doors, and rose carefully to limp along between the rows of beds to meet her. A cheer went up from the rest of the men. Laura felt her face colouring, but smiled readily at Maurice before turning to grin at his comrades.

'Glad to make your day!' she heard herself exclaim, and felt Maurice's hand tighten on her arm. 'Sorry we've nowt to celebrate with,' she added. 'I'll have to see what I can rustle up for our next dancing night.'

'You're a marvel, sweetheart,' he whispered. 'Thought this lot might have embarrassed you.'

'It's no good letting folk feel they can't be glad for you, is it?' she remarked. And felt one stab of regret because Patrick had excluded himself from her happiness.

'Are you on the way back to your office now, love?' Maurice asked her. 'I'll walk you part of the way. They're always pestering me to get more exercise.'

Alone in the corridor, his grasp on her arm tightened. 'I do so love you, Laura,' he said huskily. 'I've been thinking this morning – could be you'll have me revising all I said. You know, about no one ever having the chance of taking me on?'

'I'd certainly have no reservations on those grounds,' Laura told him frankly. 'We've got all the time in the world to sort out what we want. I'm just glad that we've started to make a go of it together. I'm going to enjoy getting to know you better, and then we'll see how we both feel after a while, eh?'

'You wouldn't marry in wartime, is that what you're saying? I do understand, my love, if you won't commit yourself to an airman.'

Laura shook her head. 'I don't mean that at all. Happen I don't really want too much to change, not yet awhile. I just want us to be the way we were last night, as close as we were.'

'So you won't stipulate that there must be a ring on your finger? And won't object if I make a habit of finding my way over to your home?'

Laura smiled and kissed him lightly. 'I'll object if you don't. You'd better be there, love, whenever possible.'

Behind them in the corridor a door opened admitting a cool draught of air. A voice all-too-familiar to Laura interrupted.

'I trust, Miss Crabtree, that this isn't an indication of the way in which you intend passing your working hours in the future?'

Furiously, Laura spun round. She drew in a sharp breath. 'I assure you, Mr Horsfall, that I shall remain conscientious.

But I might remind you that today is Sunday. No one pays me for Sunday work so you might consider it wise to refrain from further comment about whatever I might volunteer to do with my time.'

Maurice had turned as well and seemed about to speak, but Laura shook her head at him. 'Let's leave it, shall we?' she murmured. 'You said you were going to walk as far as the office with me.'

Chapter 22

Despite the difficult atmosphere whenever she and Patrick were in the office together, Laura was feeling elated. Almost every night during the past week Maurice had come to the Coach House. He was in good spirits, not only because of their deepening relationship, but on account of the letter he had received from home.

'Mother says she is enduring the occupation quite well,' he had told Laura, hugging her. 'I'm prepared to accept that's true, and take a break from worrying about her.'

'That's good, love. All that anxiety was preventing you getting better as quickly as you should.'

During that week Maurice had surprised her in a way that, as much as anything, convinced her he was indeed greatly improved. She had been feeling pretty pleased with life herself as she greeted Mavis while she was preparing for the dance session. Over the past few days several land girls as well as men from the wards had mentioned yet again how much they had appreciated the Saturday night dance. And seeing her former landlady always provided a link with the old life to remind Laura that when this war finally ended she had an interesting career ahead of her.

It was after the first handful of men had arrived and the girls began filtering in that Laura felt somebody watching her. She turned and her eyes met Maurice's across the room, making her smile broadly. Pausing only long enough to finish explaining the order of dances for the first half, she left Mavis and hurried over to Maurice.

'It's lovely to see you here,' she exclaimed. 'Are you

going to have a go tonight with us?'

Although smiling back, he shook his head. 'I doubt that, sweetheart. You'll have to give me time. But I couldn't stay away.'

Throughout the evening, Laura could feel him watching her, and though they chatted only briefly with interruptions during the refreshment break she remained thrilled that he had joined them.

After the others had left she began tidying the room and switching off lights. For once, Maurice wasn't helping. He seemed pensive and when she neared the place where he was sitting he reached out and caught her hand.

'Seriously, Laura – is dancing something I could manage?'

'Why don't we try? Look, I'll dig out my gramophone, I left it in a cupboard here.'

The record she chose was a foxtrot, slow enough to accommodate his artificial limb.

'Don't even think of trying proper steps,' she advised, going to him and into his arms. 'Just listen to the music at first, and move with me. Keep those steps quite short to begin with.'

He seemed far steadier than she had feared he might be, and they moved quite rhythmically together.

'You must say when you're tired,' she told him part way through.

It wasn't tiredness that ended their dancing. Acutely aware of him as always now, Laura had felt attraction coursing through her to divert attention from their dancing. When Maurice began drawing her closer she recognised that his need of her was growing.

'Coming home now?'

'That's precisely how I think of it,' he confided as she went to turn off the record. 'You've surely made me belong there, sweetheart.'

Crossing the courtyard they paused beneath the stars to kiss, holding each other as if neither could wait to cover that short distance to the Coach House.

As Laura turned after locking the door behind them

Maurice was discarding his stick.

'Oh, my love.' He pulled her sharply against him, kissing her throat, the tender spot below one ear.

He appeared to mount the stairs with more agility. He was waiting on the landing when Laura had quickly checked the downstairs rooms for the night and joined him. He headed towards the spare room which they had always used before but Laura shook her head, smiling.

'I want you in my room, Maurice, from now on.' He was so much a part of her life already, she didn't wish to exclude him from anything here.

She had prepared the bed with freshly washed linen and had smiled in anticipation while making everything ready. Now, though, suddenly they could not delay and sank together on to the bed, snatching away only the garments that would keep them from each other.

'I can never have enough of you, sweetheart,' he gasped, easing himself on top of her.

'I'm just the same about you,' she confessed breathlessly. 'I hope you can tell.'

He smiled against her lips. 'I did get the message.'

Maurice entered her almost at once, reminding her of that first time he had loved her. She relished the intensity of his need. Each time they loved like this she felt that she had waited the whole of her life to know him. While their bodies met and soared the rest of the world and its troubles receded. And now they were free to grow increasingly attuned.

Sated at last, they drowsed, faces close, arms about each other. Awakening, they smiled into each other's eyes before undressing to meet beneath the covers.

The darkness seemed particularly dense, velvet black without the slightest glimmer from the thickly curtained windows.

'We might be the only people alive,' said Laura.

'I almost wish that we were,' Maurice added. 'That way, there'd be nothing to prevent our doing this repeatedly.'

'I haven't noticed much cramping of your style, as it is!' Laura teased.

It was she herself, however, who awakened in the night, longing again to be loved. Rather surprised by her own eagerness, she lay in the darkness, torn between contentment to have Maurice sleeping beside her and awareness that the passion he aroused could hardly be ignored.

Only a short while later, she noticed from the change in his breathing that Maurice also was awake. She said his name and was drawn against him.

'I'm going to spend my whole life with you,' he asserted. 'And I want us to marry. This feels like a honeymoon, I know, but I want to show the world I'm fully committed to you.'

When Laura didn't immediately reply, Maurice persisted. 'Say you'll marry me, sweetheart. I'll live wherever you wish, and I'll make no conditions.'

'I couldn't refuse you anything, love, not now. You mean so much to me.'

Two nights later they talked more practically about marriage. Laura had insisted on cooking Maurice a meal and then they had strolled as far as he could manage before sitting in her tiny patch of garden while the sun dropped towards the distant moors.

'I can see why you love this place,' he said seriously, glancing beyond her home to the hills surrounding them. 'And I meant what I said – if your heart's here, it's where we'll settle.'

'Well, we'll have to see,' Laura began. She had grown up among families whose womenfolk were schooled to accept the man's work was all important and must be accommodated.

'There's your job as well as your home,' Maurice continued. He had heard a little about Laura's carpet designing. 'And as for myself – well, I've seen how readily things are cultivated around here. There's nothing to prevent my establishing a market garden in this area.'

Those words had made Laura more contented than she'd ever expected to be during this period while war separated her from the work she had grown to love. In this part of the West Riding there were few raids to send them running to shelters, a fact that made her feel quite guilty when her own happiness

380

was only disturbed by news of bombing elsewhere. Even the presence of wounded men in the hospital which Arncliffe Hall had become seemed less depressing now that she was getting to know so many of the patients and seeing them improve.

As the newness began to wear off her relationship with Maurice, however, and excitement gradually gave way to serious consideration of the future, Laura was compelled to acknowledge that there would be hardship to face before they finally made a settled life together. Much as his returning fitness delighted her, it did also make her aware that the day would come when Maurice would be fit for rejoining his RAF squadron. He himself seemed to relish that prospect, confident that he had come out the other side of his one confrontation with death, and that active service would provide no further narrow escapes.

Laura was less confident. She seemed unable to forget the danger he would face on returning to the south of England which was taking the brunt of the German air offensive. Their times together became more precious, and somehow more intense. Repeatedly, she reminded herself that she must resolve to think only of their ultimate happiness which would come when peace at last allowed them to make a real home together. She must fix her mind on that, and ensure that so long as Maurice remained at Arncliffe he was unaffected by her private fears.

Her working life was no less busy than before, and even if Patrick's unbending attitude towards her meant that there was no congeniality when he was in the office, Laura's job gave her plenty of contact with other people. When the Land Army girls weren't dashing in with details of supplies that should be requisitioned, hospital folk were referring administrative problems to her.

It had seemed to Laura that ever since their disagreement Patrick had spent fewer hours at Arncliffe, and more at the building society. Most of the time, these days, her desk was the only one occupied. If it hadn't been for this constant stream of people with requests she would have grown to hate having so much of her own company. The only good thing about the situation was supposing that her grasp of the work must be proving satisfactory, otherwise Patrick would soon have given more personal supervision.

Away from the office, Laura lived only for Maurice. It seemed as though instructions had been issued regarding Beth. Certainly, she hadn't appeared at the Coach House during all the weeks since that awkward Sunday morning. On the one occasion when Laura had asked after his daughter Patrick had dismissed her enquiry coolly: 'Fine, thank you.'

The day that Beth fleetingly came back into Laura's life was in early September. Maurice had been having a bad spell with the artificial leg which had chafed his wounded stump. Although able to continue visiting the Coach House, he had been obliged to curtail his walking. Now, at last, both he and Laura were greatly relieved that he was healing once more. After eating Sunday lunch together they took a short stroll through the estate.

As always, people were working the land. Their tasks out here appeared ceaseless. Today, someone was handling a tractor almost out of sight near the boundary wall. Others were harvesting various crops in which Maurice was showing a professional interest.

'It hasn't really occurred to me before, but I reckon I could lend a hand about the estate. Now the leg's bearable again.'

'You'd have to watch you're not on it too long, love, or you might put things back to the way they were a bit since,' Laura warned.

'I know. But I'll have a word with the doctor, see what he thinks.'

Before either of them spoke again, Laura heard running feet on the path behind them and a young voice calling.

'Maddie, Maddie!'

Laura recognised the voice if not her own name. Turning, she was just in time to extend her arms to Beth who was charging full tilt towards her.

Bending down to hug the child, Laura heard Maurice, sounding bewildered.

'What did she call you?'

'Not sure. It sounded like "Maddie" or something. Doesn't matter, anyway, it shows she's still speaking.'

'To you, do you mean?' asked Maurice, still puzzled.

'To anyone,' Laura said hastily. 'Tell you later.'

Releasing Beth from the hug, Laura took her hand. 'We're having a walk – do you want to come?'

Beth nodded enthusiastically, but refused to speak again despite Laura's coaxing. She was trying to get the girl to say which direction she would like to take when they saw the man striding rapidly downhill towards them from the tractor he had evidently been handling.

'Oh, Lord,' she sighed under her breath, and cleared her throat anxiously. 'Hallo, Patrick.'

He didn't return the greeting, and ignored Maurice when Laura would have introduced them. Instead he bent down to face his daughter. 'You know perfectly well this isn't Maddie, it's Miss Crabtree.'

Laura smiled at him. 'It doesn't matter. At least she talks now.'

'It does matter,' he contradicted over his shoulder.

'But she is talking more?' Laura asked. She cared too much to lose the opportunity of finding out if Beth was improving.

'Not with any regularity,' Patrick said wearily. Standing upright, he placed a hand firmly on Beth's shoulder. 'But she fully understands what I have said. You must excuse us now,' he finished grimly, and steered Beth away in the direction of Arncliffe Hall.

'What was all that about?' asked Maurice as soon as the pair were out of earshot.

Laura was almost too disturbed to reply. Eventually she sighed. 'A part of it, you already know. Ages ago Patrick decided I wasn't fit company for Beth.'

'But – that's ridiculous. She obviously idolises you. He can't seriously believe a child her age would be curious about the relationship between the two of us, much less influenced by it.'

Laura shrugged, sighed again. 'It's his privilege, anyway, to have a say over his daughter's companions. I'm just sorry for the pair of them. They're neither of them at all happy.'

'Chap should see sense then,' Maurice asserted. 'You work together, after all. I'd have thought it'd have been in his own interest to be at least civil. And I saw your face – you can't pretend you're not hurt by what he's doing? I've a good mind to have a word . . .'

'No, Maurice, please. It's best just to ignore it.'

Although he had agreed and they'd continued their walk Laura remained disturbed for days afterwards. Knowing in her heart that Maurice was the one person with whom she wished to spend the rest of her life didn't exclude everyone else. Patrick's behaviour that Sunday had reminded her how she had longed from the start to help both him and Beth.

There was Patrick's father as well. She hadn't seen him at all since the day Patrick had encountered Maurice at the Coach House. To Laura, it seemed rather silly. She felt that she still had room in her life for concern about them all. She was becoming convinced that she must try yet again to break down the barriers that Patrick was constructing.

On the Monday morning he was in the office. She seized the opportunity of his rare appearance to ask if Beth really wasn't any more willing to speak.

He gave her a look. 'Certainly not with me,' he replied gravely.

'Oh, I am sorry,' she said.

He must have read the genuine sympathy in her eyes. He didn't snarl or close the conversation.

'And your father?' Laura enquired. 'How is he? I know I haven't asked for ages.'

'He's not too bad actually, thanks. You know the resident surgeon, Alec Simpson? Turns out he and Father attended the same school. They spend a lot of their leisure yarning, and they play chess.'

'That's excellent. You must be very relieved.'

'It's one less worry, yes.'

Since they were at last actually talking again, Laura felt she couldn't let it go without making another attempt to thaw Patrick's resolve regarding herself and his daughter.

'You don't really have to shoulder responsibility for Beth quite alone, do you?' she began. 'You know that she and I get on . . .'

His dark eyes froze as he inhaled sharply. 'Leave it, Laura. There is nothing to discuss.'

'You're busier than ever since the war began. So is Mrs Harrison. I honestly believe Beth's better with plenty of company.'

'I'd have thought you'd enough on with that fellow you've taken up with.'

'I'm trying to tell you that I've still got time for other folk.'

'Nothing's changed, Laura. If you denied that you were sleeping with the man, I'd not believe you. I couldn't.'

'And I wouldn't deny it.'

'You've astounded me, you really have. Never thought you'd take a stranger into your bed.'

'Maurice has never seemed like a stranger, especially since he began coming to our dances. None of the men who attend seem less than very good friends.' And, thought Laura, if you'd put yourself out to attend this situation might have turned out very differently.

She saw by his soaring eyebrows that Patrick even wondered if she'd invited others across to the Coach House.

'No, there's only ever been Maurice,' she told him. 'And if it weren't for the war, we would be married by now. That's how much we love each other.'

'Only you're *not* married,' Patrick reminded her brusquely, stood up and walked out of the office.

Laura listened to his footsteps receding along the corridor. She felt quite miserable. She didn't in the least regret anything about the love between herself and Maurice, but she couldn't help wishing that it had not meant sacrificing her friendship with Patrick and his young daughter.

Autumn around Arncliffe was particularly beautiful. Near at hand the sun was glowing over corn stacked on the estate and trees were turning to red and bronze. Beyond its boundaries, the range of hills beckoned as the woods too changed colour, while moorland heather and bracken increased the variety of shades.

Except for occasional shopping trips into Halfield or rare visits to Netta, Laura hardly ever left the vicinity. Maurice had been advised not to venture too far away from the wards, and nothing would have induced Laura to sacrifice any time which they could manage to spend together.

There was the dancing, as well, taking up her time. Programmes must be planned, a fact which ate into the hours when she was absent from the office.

When, as sometimes happened, she longed for the opportunity to wander through the countryside, Laura would remind herself that in time Maurice would be sufficiently recovered to tackle longer walks. And they had a lot to be grateful for. This part of the West Riding still remained relatively free from air raids. And busy though she was, her work was far more congenial than in any ordnance factory.

The sudden marring of this comparatively happy life arrived out of the blue. Maurice came to the Coach House one evening, his customary smile absent and his eyes shadowed with anxiety. Laura had cooked them a meal after work, but he merely toyed with the food on his plate, even though he divulged nothing when she repeatedly enquired whatever was wrong.

They went to bed early that night. Laura had hoped that the intimacy of her room might encourage him to confide, but still he failed to do so.

His lovemaking seemed quite savage, he might have been protesting against some cruel turn of fate, yet Laura sensed that any ferocity was not directed against herself. Neither of them slept well, but when she asked again while they were getting up he still persisted in his assertion that nothing was wrong.

As he was about to leave he told her. Hugging her to him, he kissed her fiercely time and again.

'It's no good – I can't go without telling you.'

'Go?' Laura echoed, instantly horrified.

'For God's sake don't tell anyone what I'm doing. No one must know. It's Mother, you see. She's seriously ill. Someone – got word through to me. I can't just do nothing. I've got to see her . . .'

Laura was nodding, holding him close. 'I understand, love.' And then she remembered. 'But you can't – Jersey's occupied.'

'It'll be all right. I can't just abandon her there. I've got to get her out, see she has treatment.'

Staring aghast, Laura swallowed. 'But how, with the Germans . . .?'

'There is a way,' Maurice assured her. 'We get mail out, don't we? It will be all right, sweetheart. I don't want you to worry.'

'How can I not? Oh, Maurice.' She knew that he had to do whatever he could, but knew just as surely that she couldn't bear this. 'Take me with you, I'll help somehow.'

'That's nonsense, my love, and you know it. It'd only lead to more risk of being discovered. No, I must tackle this alone, at least until I'm virtually there.'

'And then? Tell me you'll have some assistance, somebody to . . .'

'There'll be help, don't worry. All I ask is that you keep this to yourself. No one must be told. You don't know where I've gone. If you want, you can put it about that I'm trying to rejoin my squadron.'

A moan that wouldn't be suppressed escaped her throat. Maurice kissed her again, tenderly.

'I'll get letters to you, somehow. And I'll be back, Laura, just as soon as I'm able. Because I shall marry you, never forget that. We're going to spend the rest of our lives making up for this.'

Unable to concentrate on work, by ten o'clock that morning Laura took herself off into the hospital section and made straight for Maurice's ward. The tiny area around his bed looked abnormally tidy and he was nowhere in sight. She glanced into the day room, but knew in her heart that she would not find him there.

The day was already feeling abominably long and would be extended. This was the evening for one of her dancing sessions. Laura longed to cancel, but doing so would only draw more attention to her anxiety about Maurice. And nothing would ever induce her to do anything that might worsen the risk for him.

As the men drifted into the lovely old room, she read at once in their faces that they all knew of Maurice's disappearance. 'Why discharge himself?' was the question most of them voiced. 'He was getting on all right. He has you – he's more reason than any of us to put up with things here.'

First to one and then another, Laura said what Maurice had suggested she should, that she imagined he was returning to his squadron. 'I know he's not a hundred per cent fit,' she added. 'But I think he believes he can be of use to them.'

For days she dreaded being questioned by any of the senior medical staff, but an influx of new patients meant they were working overtime to cope with the admissions. It seemed no one could spare time for pursuing a man who had chosen to leave.

Hardly able to sleep, Laura found the nights hardest of all to bear. She caught herself wishing that she and Maurice had kept to the spare room. Alone in her own bed, memories made her acutely aware of the fearful risk that was the reason behind his absence. During the first couple of days she listened to every wireless bulletin she could, ears alert for any mention of action on Jersey. Although she heard no news about the island, she abandoned listening on the third day. Watching the clock for the time to switch on the wireless had only made her still more agitated.

In the office, she was thankful the new admissions to the

wards gave her more paperwork. She was glad also that Patrick seemed to have heard nothing about Maurice's departure and therefore wouldn't be quizzing her about him.

Laura's relief on that score lasted less than a week. He came in one evening straight from the building society and mentioned that he had heard Maurice was no longer at Arncliffe.

'Assuming you're in touch with him, you'd better convey the advice of his doctors here that he should continue treatment. Wherever he is. Alec Simpson was saying last night that he hoped the squadron he's rejoining is based somewhere near the surgeon who performed the initial amputation.'

Laura frowned, her anxiety increasing. 'Is he saying that Maurice's recovery isn't as good as we thought?'

Patrick shrugged. 'No idea. I only know Alec was telling us what he thought of patients who discharged themselves like that.'

Laura sighed. 'There was good reason,' she began, and stopped abruptly before she revealed more than she intended.

The realisation that everybody at Arncliffe appeared to believe the story she had put about concerning Maurice's destination was little consolation. She worried that his condition might prove to be worse than it had seemed, which could increase the difficulties as he tried to reach his mother in occupied Jersey. It wasn't all that long since he'd suffered that renewed chafing. How on earth would he even get around, troubled by that wretched metal limb?

Day after day Laura looked for the postman, and felt depression settling more firmly when he brought no word from Maurice. Weeks passed and the weather grew more wintry, turning the surrounding hills bleak and forbidding. Strong winds surged over Arncliffe, battering its windows and keening in chimneys, and making her Coach House feel isolated from the main building.

In that November of 1940 the German offensive over Britain grew more widespread. Coventry was bombed, along with Birmingham. Sheffield and Manchester suffered as well, bringing the destruction much closer to the area around

Halfield. It seemed to Laura that every bit of news she heard made her yet more conscious of the danger being confronted by everyone outside their own small community.

And still there was no word from Maurice. Plagued by worry, she began feeling quite ill, literally sickened by this fear on his behalf. Somehow, she kept the dances going, though she herself saw how she'd changed from looking far younger than her age to appearing haggard. Mavis often remarked on how drained Laura seemed.

'You're doing too much, aren't you, love?' she said sympathetically one evening. 'Why don't you take a bit of time off, spend it with your Netta?'

Laura hadn't seen her for ages. She had never told her family about Maurice, and had visited her sister only rarely during the entire time that their relationship had continued. The prospect now of seeing her sister wasn't particularly appealing. Netta appeared to be having a war unperturbed by partings and anxiety. Roy had been given the task of directing despatches of the items of equipment now being produced by Lindley's and similar factories. The furthest he travelled seemed to be Leeds or Liverpool. Laura couldn't help envying them the ability to raise their family undisturbed.

Perhaps, though, she ought to go over to Whitby, to learn how their mother was coping. The last she'd heard had been in a telephone call the other week when Maggie Crabtree had been awaiting a group of soldiers who were billeted on her. Surprising Laura, she had seemed to be looking forward to their arrival. Certainly it would be company for her since Greta and Sybil rarely got home now from their long hours doing warwork.

Looking in the mirror that night decided Laura that this wasn't the time for going home to Whitby. Feeling so dreadful that she could hardly eat, the pounds had fallen off her. Combined with the dark staining around her eyes from sleeplessness, it made her look positively ill. Mother would soon start the cross-questioning, she thought. And, no matter what, she mustn't breathe a hint to anybody anywhere about

Maurice and the reason behind his departure from Yorkshire.

Not telling people was putting a strain on all aspects of her life. She had continued her daily visits to the wards. But there, just as during the still popular dancing sessions, she had to guard her tongue with the other men.

I will try to eat more, Laura resolved, I'll force a decent meal down at least once a day. If I don't, I'll not be fit for anything by the time Maurice is able to come back.

The wartime diet didn't help, though. And coming home each evening to the empty house only emphasised that yet another day had passed without news that Maurice was safe. Eventually, Laura decided that eating a hearty breakfast might be the solution. Thinking ahead to the work waiting on her desk would remind her that there was one purpose at least for keeping up her strength.

She fried some black pudding and a couple of slices of bread. She reconstituted dried egg powder which she then scrambled. It was so long since she had cooked breakfast, however, that she had only a minute or two left for eating.

By the time she arrived in the office the food was an uncomfortable lump, barely digested. Rushing down a cooked meal this early in the day was the worst idea she could have had. Sitting at her desk, Laura began feeling hot and then cold, was unable to start thinking about work. After ten minutes or so she realised that she couldn't avoid being sick, and dashed for the nearest cloakroom.

Having rinsed her face afterwards and still dabbing at her eyes with a handkerchief, she emerged to be confronted by Patrick in the corridor.

'You look terrible,' he said. 'Sick?'

Laura tried to smile, but couldn't quite manage it. 'Afraid so,' she admitted. 'But I'm all right now.'

'Take an hour or so off, if you need. Lord knows, you work far and above anything expected of you.'

'No, really. I'll be fine in a few minutes.'

Patrick followed her into the office where he stared at her, his expression inscrutable.

'Are you expecting a child, Laura?'

'No, I'm not,' she responded sharply, and was relieved when he said something about the Land Army girls and hastened out of the office.

As soon as she was alone Laura felt tears welling in her eyes. They had nothing to do with the manner of Patrick's questioning. In that moment she had admitted to herself that she wished with all her heart that she was expecting Maurice's baby. A part of him, on which she might have focused all her love and concern. She would have had something then, some reason for enduring. For with each day that passed she grew increasingly afraid that Maurice himself would not survive to return to Arncliffe.

Chapter 23

Laura seemed to have slept for only a few minutes when the siren startled her awake. Desperately tired, she had decided on an early night, and now it seemed even a decent sleep was denied her. Alerts here were rare, but the spread of bombing to fresh areas of England had ensured they were taken seriously. Reaching for dressing-gown and slippers, and grabbing her eiderdown, she hastened towards the landing.

Yawning, she hurried downstairs and made for the cellar door. In the early days of the war Mrs Harrison had told Laura that she must join the rest of them taking cover from raids in the cellars of Arncliffe Hall. Laura had done so once or twice and had quite enjoyed the companionship among land girls, wounded men and the family. These days, however, she preferred her own company. And the ease with which she could quickly return to bed after the all-clear was a bonus she needed while still exhausted by anxiety concerning Maurice.

She made herself as comfortable as she could, tying her dressing-gown tightly then wrapping the eiderdown around her before settling into the deckchair that she'd installed in the cellar. The lighting here was dim, provided by the low-wattage bulb she had fitted in preference to one that might show a gleam of light around the coal-grate. The coal itself, to one end of the long narrow cellar, was separated from the rest of the storage space by a door so ill-fitting that Laura was afraid forbidden light might escape. And since she always hoped to doze here, if not to sleep, she never brought any reading matter that would require better illumination.

A good keeping cellar which she appreciated during hot

summers, the place felt cold tonight, and if not really damp it often seemed that some moisture hung in the air. Although it was summer now, Laura shivered and thrust both hands into her sleeves while she buried her chin in the eiderdown. Still losing weight, she was prone to sudden attacks of this chill that appeared almost to come from within herself rather than as a result of external temperatures. It certainly wasn't helped, though, by the coolness down here.

Laura herself wasn't helped either by the interruption of her sleep, and this solitude which offered too much time for thinking. There was no word yet from Maurice and her yearning for news of him had been displaced by a growing realisation that she might indeed be compelled to face the fact that he would not be returning. No matter how aware she had been of the difficulties he might experience in getting a message to her, she was beginning to see it was most unlikely that if he were still alive he would have failed to make some contact.

These gloomy thoughts were interrupted by the sounding of the all-clear and Laura thankfully stood up and folded the bulky eiderdown, ready for her journey back upstairs.

Reaching her unlit bedroom, she heard a plane overhead and paused, motionless, listening to its engine whose tone sounded somehow abnormal. The aircraft seemed to be passing low over the house. Perturbed, Laura went to draw back the thickly-lined curtain.

Staring out, she was surprised to find that it wasn't yet dark outdoors. The thoroughness with which she had blacked-out the Coach House had prevented her from knowing that the sky was still a cerulean blue. She could see the horizon with that single dead tree standing erect on the moor. Moving lights and a dark shape outlined against the brightness remaining from the setting sun revealed the lone aircraft, so low in the sky that it seemed to skim the hillside.

The noise of its engine altered again, alarmingly, just as it was travelling eastwards out of sight. And wasn't that smoke issuing from its fuselage – had she imagined the glare of a flame? Dashing along to the window in the adjacent wall,

Laura heard the aero engine falter and cease. The crash followed immediately, shattering her so much that despite being unable to see anything she stood riveted at the window for what felt like over a minute.

Shaking her head as if to rouse herself for action, Laura closed the curtains she had started to open, likewise the ones at the other window. She could be the only person who knew that plane had crashed.

Pausing only to snatch up her keys, she began running towards the Hall. The door nearest to the Coach House was secured for the night. Increasing her speed, she rushed around the back of the building towards the rear entrance. The warren of cellars where residents of Arncliffe always sheltered led off from stairs that descended from the former butler's pantry. If anyone was still up and about, this was where she was likely to find them.

Laura heard voices as soon as she began hammering on the heavy door. Although the sky was darkening fast, there was sufficient light for her to recognise Alec Simpson the resident surgeon, and Patrick's father behind him in the gloom of the passageway.

'Come in, Laura my dear,' Mr Horsfall began. 'We'll just draw this curtain across then we can switch on the lights. Alec was about to do so when we heard you knocking.'

'There was a plane,' said Laura breathlessly. 'I'm afraid it's . . .'

'Crashed,' Alec finished for her. 'We saw it as well. Patrick's telephoning to report it. We thought we noticed German markings.'

'I couldn't make any out from my place, I was dazzled,' said Laura. 'It first appeared just where the sky was brightest.'

They ushered her along and through to the main entrance hall where Patrick was telephoning. Beside him, Beth waited, moving nervously from foot to foot. And then she turned, spotted Laura and raced towards her.

Laura was down on one knee waiting with extended arms to gather the girl to her.

'Hallo, Beth love, are you all right?'

The child smiled up at her and nodded. When Laura stood up a small hand was thrust into her own.

Patrick replaced the telephone receiver and walked briskly towards them. He acknowledged Laura with a nod and addressed them all. 'They knew already. I'm afraid it doesn't look so good. As I feared, the plane was heading for Dale Reservoir. The surrounding plantation is at risk from fire or, worse, the reservoir itself could be damaged. Either way, there could be casualties, apart from the pilot himself and any crew. I said we'd stand by. We're nearer to hand than the main hospitals in Halfield.'

Alec Simpson was already heading for the stairs that led up to the wards where men were heard still moving around after returning from the shelters. 'We'll cope, whatever . . . I'll have the theatre prepared, just in case.'

Patrick's father said he would remain by the telephone. 'That'll free other folk for doing something more useful if we are used as an emergency receiving station.'

Patrick agreed. 'Okay. I'm on my way. Got to see if there's anything I can do. At the very least, I can direct emergency services to this place if we should be needed.' Briefly, he glanced towards his daughter and frowned.

'I'll see Beth's looked after,' Laura said swiftly. 'And I'll stay around in case they need help sorting anything on the hospital side.'

When Patrick had gone out she took Beth towards one of the sofas well away from the front door and any possible draughts. Although summer, it was late at night and the massive hall anything but cosy. 'You sit here, love, by me, and I'll be to hand if your grandpa wants anybody to run messages or anything.'

After they listened to Patrick's car driving away, the big house grew quiet. Above their heads men were settling for the night. Laura pictured the elderly surgeon and his staff preparing the theatre for emergencies. Somewhere in the night outdoors she heard fire engines on the move, ambulances and what she took for police cars. Just waiting here felt useless somehow.

Old Mr Horsfall eventually left the telephone and came to sit near Laura and his grandchild.

'How've you been, Laura?' he enquired. 'We've not seen so much of you lately.'

'Oh – not so bad, you know,' she replied. 'How about yourself?'

'It's done me good meeting up with Alec Simpson again. We've quite a lot in common. And his being so busy with the young chaps here keeps me in touch with a bit of life as well. Which reminds me – I was sorry to hear your young fellow discharged himself. Is he getting on all right?'

'I'm afraid I don't know. Haven't heard a thing since he left.'

Laura felt the old man giving her a curious look. She said nothing. Happen she'd revealed too much already, as it was, letting on that she'd had no word from Maurice. Anybody seriously considering the fact might possibly conclude that he hadn't, after all, rejoined his squadron. It all seemed such a long time ago now, though, that she suspected that nothing anyone here might say or do could jeopardise Maurice's situation on Jersey. Or help him.

Growing restless, Beth wriggled on the seat beside her and then got to her feet. She smiled engagingly at Laura. 'Dance?' she invited.

The effect on her grandfather was startling. Laura had felt him jump when Beth spoke; he immediately gave a short sigh of relief.

'It's true then, she does talk,' he murmured to Laura.

'*You* dance,' she persuaded Beth. 'Show me what you can do on your own, love.'

The child hesitated and then stretched out her arms and, her tongue between her teeth in concentration, began progressing slowly around the hall. Laura was noticing that Beth was nodding to some beat she could hear within her sleek blonde head when Mr Horsfall claimed her attention again.

'It's only to you that she speaks, you know, Laura. Or so far as I'm aware. If Patrick's got more than an isolated word out of her, that's as much. Or so I believe,' he added. 'Not that he confides a great deal.'

To anyone! thought Laura, and swallowed. Suddenly, it all seemed so *daft* – they'd once been such good pals. And here was she, more alone than ever since Maurice had disappeared, while Patrick maintained the aloofness which had seemed so evident when first she met him. Laura thought of Beth as well, and how she might have improved so vastly by now if only Patrick hadn't forbidden them to spend time together. She herself had grown so sure that the girl only needed to learn to relax with somebody who could make her feel at ease.

Laura's thoughts were interrupted by the sound of a car in the drive, and then its door closing and footsteps approaching.

Patrick came in looking haggard and shaken, but before saying one word he gave Beth a curious glance. She, in turn, paused to stare in his direction, and then concentrated on her dancing. Very briefly, the slightest of smiles softened Patrick's mouth. His gaze met Laura's and he gave a tiny nod.

It *isn't* approval, she warned herself silently, don't start feeling elated. There was some hope, however, just a glimmer that he might stop shutting her out of Beth's life.

'What did you see out there?' his father asked him.

Gravely, Patrick shook his head. 'More than I liked, more than enough! It was a Messerschmitt we saw, looked like a stray one that someone took a shot at. By the time I arrived it was embedded in the dam which confines the reservoir. Couldn't have landed in a worse spot. It's breached that dam.'

'Good Lord!' his father exclaimed. 'That means . . .'

'Afraid so,' Patrick continued. 'Millions of gallons pouring towards the valley. The plane was breaking up under the force when I got there, water spilling out around it. I saw Richardson, from a distance.' He paused, added to Laura: 'The civil engineer responsible for its design. He was coming away from the reservoir keeper's place. They'll have done what they can, setting sluice gates and so on. The emergency services are all at the scene now.'

'We heard them,' said Laura. 'Are there any casualties?'

'The German pilot, so far as we know. And – and there was a family swept away, a couple of children and their parents. I don't think there's much hope.'

'And further down the valley?' his father enquired. 'How bad is it really?'

'Well, I managed a word with one of the chaps in charge of the operation. He seemed pretty confident that the water was being checked at source now, just in time to prevent a widespread disaster.'

Even though the following morning they had learned that water had ceased escaping the reservoir and a major catastrophe had been averted, they remained subdued by the crash for several weeks afterwards. The descent of that German plane was discussed endlessly by everybody in and around Halfield, and reported in the local newspapers. Crowds travelled to stare at the scene, which seemed to Laura rather macabre. For her, the only good thing that came out of the incident was the change in Patrick's attitude towards her.

That first day he spent most of his time elsewhere, but returned to Arncliffe long before Laura was packing up for the night. He greeted her with something of the old geniality as soon as he came into the office. And after routine questions about the state of their farm work as well as hospital administration, he seemed eager to talk.

'I made a point of seeing Wolf Richardson today, when I eventually tracked him down. Poor chap wasn't at home this morning. I wouldn't like to be in his shoes.'

'But surely no one can blame him for what happened? It was just unfortunate circumstances . . .'

'Agreed. No, it's what the destruction of the reservoir has done to Richardson personally. He'd had to fight from the beginning to get permission to construct it. Must admit there was a time when I was inclined to oppose the plans, but I soon came round when I saw how well he was treating the local people affected. I was the first to confess that he handled the whole business in an exemplary manner. Then the threat of war meant he'd to ensure his contractors completed before hostilities broke out.'

'And now this,' Laura exclaimed. 'He must be absolutely sickened.'

'I've never seen a man more shattered – wouldn't wish to see another. This bloody war! Life's a struggle enough, normally . . .'

Patrick astonished her then by adding that he considered it high time that they began making the best of the situation at Arncliffe. 'I've been difficult, I know. As of now, you must forget whatever I've said in the past with regard to Beth. Please feel free to spend time with her whenever . . . that's if you still feel so inclined?'

Laura grinned at him. 'Do you need to ask? And I'll give you no cause for anxiety, I'll see someone always knows where we are.'

'Except for occasions when Beth just takes it in her head to go seeking you!'

'Aye, well – I'll admit organising her isn't always easy.'

For a time Laura had believed the softening of Patrick's attitude owed much to witnessing his daughter's continuing enthusiasm for dancing. Some weeks later she began to understand that his changed approach might be due to an altogether different cause.

Again, they were chatting in the office one evening. There were problems to be resolved regarding supplies, both for the wards and to facilitate the smooth operation of the farming side. Following a long discussion of potential solutions they had remained at their desks, neither of them seeming eager to leave.

'Is there still no word from your young man?' Patrick asked suddenly.

'None at all,' Laura told him while wondering what prompted him to enquire.

'I gathered from Father that – well, that was how things stood some weeks ago. You will have been very concerned, naturally?'

Laura nodded, and swallowed. 'I never thought it'd be as bad as this.'

'D'you want to tell me? Whatever you say will go no further. You can't have failed to notice that I can be singularly tight-lipped.'

'I'd given my word that I wouldn't tell a soul where he was really heading for,' Laura began. 'But I don't think anything I say can do much harm after all these months. His mother had become ill, you see – on Jersey.'

'Oh, no,' Patrick groaned. 'He didn't . . .?'

'I couldn't have talked Maurice out of going, and I wouldn't have tried anyway. I saw how worried he was. He was determined to get to her, to get her out so she could receive treatment.'

'But he'd not long been fitted with that tin leg.'

'Quite. He knew as well as anyone that he wasn't fully fit. But he had to try. I thought I'd never be able to bear not knowing . . .'

'No one understands that more than I,' said Patrick. 'I thought I'd go mad if I didn't manage to trace Magda. I was compelled to keep trying.' Suddenly he clammed up. Where was the use in going on about his determination to obtain a divorce? The woman he loved was eating out her heart for that fellow Maurice. 'Have you done anything to try and find out what happened?'

'I couldn't, could I? No one had to know that he even set out for Jersey. If I revealed anything at all, it could endanger him. If it wasn't all too late, any road, after the first week or so.'

'But how in the world did he hope to land there without being discovered and interned?'

'I've no idea. All I do know is that someone was smuggling letters out, getting them to him. That was how he learned his mother was taken ill. I supposed he'd some reason to think that same person, or group of people, could get him ashore.'

'Sounds extremely dangerous,' Patrick observed, then realised that was anything but reassuring. 'Sorry, I mean . . .'

Laura was shaking her head. 'It's all right. I've been fully aware of the potential hazards since the day Maurice left Arncliffe. And I daresay there's plenty of others, not half so likely, that have passed through my mind. Some days, I almost wish I knew the worst. There might be some way then that I could be realistic, and get on with the rest of my life.'

'I know. As I'm sure you've gathered, Magda simply went missing, several years ago now. I came home from the building society as usual one evening and she wasn't in the house. Neither Mrs Harrison nor her husband knew anything. Worse still, Beth had disappeared. We began searching the grounds.' Sighing, he started fidgeting with the ruler on his desk.

'And you found Beth?'

'Eventually. She was in quite a state, dishevelled and utterly exhausted. From the condition of her little shoes, she'd been trudging all over for ages. And she wouldn't speak, not to anyone. No matter how long I myself and everyone else persisted, she would not tell us where she had been, nor when and where she had seen her mother last. As you know, she's hardly said a word since then.'

'But she had talked normally before?'

'She was four years old, extremely bright. The only problem prior to that had been stemming the flow of chatter.' His dark eyes filled.

Laura watched him swallow. 'Thanks for listening, anyway,' she said, and began tidying her desk for the night.

Once this had eased things between them, Laura was glad to start to take Beth for walks, and also for the occasional meal in the Coach House. She wasn't the only woman relieved that this had once again become possible. Mrs Harrison soon revealed her own thankfulness.

'That girl's relied on me too much for far too long, you know. It isn't natural for a young lass like her to cling to an old fogey like me. And besides, I can't give her proper attention, not since we've had so many folk round us.'

Laura had realised all along how true this was. The hospital wards had their own catering arrangements, but with only minimal help Mrs Harrison organised meals for all the land girls.

One Sunday when Laura was planning to take Beth as far as the nearest moors Patrick surprised her by suggesting he should accompany them.

'And we might take a look at the reservoir now that people no longer go there in droves to satisfy maudlin curiosity,' he said. 'I've heard it's been drained for the duration.'

Beth seemed less than enthusiastic about her father's presence, but soon showed how delighted she was to be heading towards Dale Reservoir. Once they were through the estate and she had stopped gazing around her at the young women working the land, she began running along ahead.

The child had grown quite a bit during the past couple of years, but she was still small for a girl of ten, and painfully thin.

'Beth's finally beginning to settle to learning,' Patrick confided. 'You wouldn't believe how thankful I am. Initially, I was trying to tutor her myself, but time is scarce enough. And she doesn't respond well to me. These days, I've got one of the army chaps coaching her.' He mentioned a name, asking if Laura knew him, which she didn't. 'Alec Simpson happened to say the man had taught in civilian life. He's in pretty bad shape, shrapnel lodged near the spine, but that doesn't prevent him being a damned good teacher.'

'I'm pleased to hear it.'

'I could never fathom how to judge if Beth had grasped very much at all, but he's brilliant with her. Has devised all manner of written tests. Fortunately, Beth complies willingly and is proving how much she has learned.'

'That's good.'

'High time! I always dreamed she'd have a decent education. Afraid that went by the board early on. If I'd have sent her to school, she'd have been diagnosed as slow-witted or worse. If only we could get her to communicate, there'd still be time. She might get to a good grammar school, at least; maybe college to follow.'

Laura was saddened by Patrick's obvious disappointment

and anxiety concerning his daughter. Watching her evident enjoyment today, though, it was possible to believe that she could in time improve sufficiently to live a more normal life.

They were nearing Dale Reservoir when they saw on the distant horizon a man who appeared to be gazing through binoculars at the ruined dam.

'Wonder who that is?' said Patrick idly. 'Looks more than curious about the reservoir.'

'It's not the civil engineer then, what's his name – Richardson?'

'I doubt it. I heard Wolf's in the forces now, abroad somewhere. In any case, he's dark-haired.'

Even this far away, they could see this man's hair was quite light.

Beth also had seen the stranger, and seemed excited as she came running back to them. Laura felt embarrassed more than pleased when it was her hand, rather than Patrick's, that the girl seized. With her other hand, Beth was pointing towards the man who now was turning away. Tugging urgently at Laura, she was trying to haul her off across the scrubby ground in the direction the stranger was taking.

'Uncle – Uncle!'

Any satisfaction that Beth had spoken was driven from Patrick's eyes almost immediately. 'Don't be silly, Beth. That's not Uncle Ted, he's not a bit like him. And besides, your uncle and aunt would have come to the house.'

Patrick had intervened to take Beth by the shoulders and was checking her. 'And you're not to pull on Laura like that. You know better than to behave so badly.'

'It is Uncle,' Beth whispered to herself, then jerked away from them to run ahead again.

'Is Ted her only uncle?' Laura enquired, disturbed by Beth's certainty that she knew the man who had now disappeared from view.

'My sister in Canada is married, the one you met at Mother's funeral. But her husband couldn't make it then, could he? In fact, I've only met him the once – over there, before Beth was born.'

'Is there nobody on your wife's side of the family?'

Patrick shook his head. 'Magda is an only one.'

'And there's no one Beth just used to call uncle?'

'Not to my knowledge. She was too small before all this happened to sit up of an evening and chat with anyone I might have invited to Arncliffe. In any case, addressing people as "uncle" or "aunt" when they're not related is a practice I wouldn't encourage.'

The subject lapsed as they drew closer to what remained of the reservoir. Viewed from here none of the damage was noticeable. As they came nearer still, however, and gazed towards the retaining dam at the head of its valley, Laura could see the great gap in the concrete and the cracks radiating from it.

'Lord, but we were fortunate that didn't cause a catastrophe!'

Pausing beside her, Patrick sighed. 'That's what I said to Wolf the following day. I don't think he saw that as much consolation.'

'I don't suppose he would. But it will be repaired, surely?'

'I imagine so, after the war. It's not the sort of project that can be allowed just to disintegrate.'

Skirting Dale Reservoir, they continued along the hillside where the coarse grass gave way to even rougher-textured moor. Far away on the horizon stood the remains of a blackened stone dwelling, long neglected and showing signs of collapse.

'That looks very bleak,' Laura exclaimed.

'Unless I'm much mistaken, it's Top Withens, reputed to be the inspiration for the site of Wuthering Heights.'

Laura smiled. 'I loved that book. If not quite so much as her sister Charlotte's *Jane Eyre*. Certainly, you could well picture Heathcliff or Cathy appearing around here.'

The moorland where they were walking was remote enough, but it seemed to grow even more wild with every fold of the hill.

About them, the wind was keen even on a summer's day like this.

'Want to turn back?' Patrick enquired with a grin.

'I don't mind,' said Laura. 'It's sort of splendid out here – majestic. So long as you aren't on your own. But we mustn't forget about Beth, she could tire more easily.'

Although the girl seemed content enough, chasing up and down among heather and low-growing bilberries and jumping off rocks, they turned and headed back towards home.

Taking a different route, they descended into a steep-sided valley enclosed by woods, eventually emerging from the trees on the opposite hillside to find Arncliffe Hall before them. All its windows glinted in sunlight that enhanced the golden tints of the stone, making Laura aware that it wasn't as soot-darkened as many buildings in the town.

'Are you glad you've put Arncliffe to such good use during the war?' she asked.

'Actually, I am,' Patrick told her. 'It's grand to feel people around you.' Homes the size of his were intended for big families and never ought to be kept up for just one man and his daughter.

Beth too had recognised the house and pointed happily now, taking Laura's hand and smiling up at her.

If only, thought Patrick – if only Laura wasn't now entangled with that fellow from Jersey. And if I were free. The three of us could have the beginning of something so good. More than ever, he needed to know what had become of Magda, to free himself.

Returning to the Coach House, Laura felt refreshed by their outing. She'd been glad Patrick had joined them. She had nevertheless declined his offer of a meal afterwards. These days, she still needed time alone. Time in which to think.

Ever since Maurice's departure she had felt a part of him was dwelling in her home. No room there was without reminders of the glorious time they had spent together, of their love.

* * *

406

Several of the Land Army girls had quite a flair for dancing. Laura was delighted with the way in which they responded to her coaching. And one or two of the men who'd been hospitalised at Arncliffe all the time that she was running her classes also danced quite well. Because of all this, the evenings she organised were relying less for success on the initial premise of simply bringing people together socially.

'You've done ever so well with them,' Mavis told her one night as they were clearing away. 'I'll bet that aunt of yours is looking down on you and feeling that proud!'

Laura laughed, but the compliment pleased her, and the improvement that many members of her class were showing heartened her to continue. Some days it was hard, after long hours at work, to give her mind to organising dancing. And there was, too, the way in which she always missed Maurice so much in the place she'd always thought of as the Arncliffe ballroom. One of the land girls played the piano, these days, whenever Mavis couldn't do so. But the fact that it wasn't another man playing never stopped Laura picturing Maurice at the keyboard.

Finding things to interest Beth was the only good part of Laura's life at present, and the girl did seem to continue to respond to her concern and affection. Although still speaking only rarely, she did communicate quite a lot in her own way, and was eager to accompany Laura on walks that otherwise might have felt very lonely.

After the day when Patrick had gone with them towards Dale Reservoir his daughter seemed to adopt a fixation about the place which made Laura wonder about the child's certainty that, despite his distance from them, she had recognised the man they had seen.

She questioned Beth one day while they were strolling in that direction. 'Did you really think that you knew the man we saw here, Beth, that he was your uncle?'

Beth disappointed her by, as usual, refusing to speak. But she nodded so emphatically that Laura could not doubt the child was convinced.

'But you heard what your father said, it wasn't your Uncle Ted.'

Beth gave her a look which seemed to confirm that Ted wasn't at all the man she'd had in mind. Laura sighed and abandoned the topic. Getting to the bottom of this was virtually impossible until Beth began to talk more regularly. No wonder poor Patrick despairs, she thought. And yet she herself believed quite firmly that the time would come when his daughter would return to normal.

Until then she was doing all she could to fill the child's life with stimulation. Remembering how Beth had loved to sit at the kitchen table and paint, she encouraged her to get out paints again, and provided paper, though it was now of poor wartime quality.

There seemed little hope of an early end to this war despite the fact that January 1942 had opened with an affirmation in Washington by twenty-six countries of the 'Declaration of the United Nations' in opposition to the Axis powers.

Laura realised with a jolt that she herself hadn't touched a paintbrush for ages. So little of her time could be called her own that even when Beth came over to the Coach House, chores had to be finished.

One Saturday she was ironing while Beth was colouring a pleasing landscape. Patrick appeared at the kitchen door and was invited to join them.

'I'll make tea, if you like,' Laura offered, unplugging the iron.

'It's all right, thanks,' he said quickly. 'Jenny and Ted have brought young Patrick over, so I'm here to collect Beth.'

'Sure,' Laura began.

Beth, however, had different ideas. 'No,' she appealed to Laura. 'No, Maddie, no.'

Patrick scowled and dragged the child off her chair. 'Come along,' he insisted sharply. 'And you know that's Laura. She is not your mother!'

At the door he bundled Beth through, and turned back. 'Maddie is the name she always had for my wife.'

As she watched them crossing the courtyard towards the main building Laura wondered which of the pair she pitied the most. Maybe Beth had needed to pretend that she still had a mother around, but Patrick clearly could do without reminders that the woman he loved was missing. How much longer must they all endure this distress?

Chapter 24

Laura was glad afterwards that they hadn't known it would be two or three years before there was any substantial improvement in Beth's condition. When it came, the change was generated by something which neither she nor Patrick could have predicted. Following the D-Day landings in the summer of 1944, the first of what proved to be many Yanks were arriving for treatment in the wards at Arncliffe. And it was these uninhibited men who eventually penetrated Beth's reserve.

Initially, it was one man, nicknamed Mac, who got her talking far more consistently than Laura herself had ever managed.

Mac had interested Laura from his arrival because his injuries were very similar to those affecting Maurice Olivier. While Mac was waiting for the healing necessary before his limb could be fitted, he confided in her a great deal. One of the first things she discovered was that his occupation back home was teaching children with learning difficulties. In confidence, she told him all about Beth who still didn't attend school and was going through a bad time after the death of her previous tutor.

Before long Patrick and Mac had been introduced and lessons for Beth had been arranged. The girl took to Mac at once, but that didn't mean his task became easy. She was now thirteen years old, but still offered only the occasional word and seemed in some ways even to relish revealing the extent of her learning without actually speaking.

'We sure have one difficult girl!' Mac exclaimed to Laura during one of her rounds of the wards. 'I wonder no one's lost patience with her. Lord knows, the kid is bright, and she grasps whatever you tell her. Remembers it as well. But coaxing her to talk all but beats me.'

Beaten, however, was something that Mac was not prepared to be. He had time in plenty and, having no personal involvement, refused to let Beth's reluctance to converse upset him.

Ultimately, though, it was through something altogether different that Patrick's daughter really began to communicate just like everyone else.

For some time Laura had been trying to get Patrick to agree to Beth's attending the first hour of the evening dance classes. He had refused, believing they weren't quite suitable for a girl of her age. But he had consented to her watching from the minstrels' gallery.

'She'll tire of that once the novelty wears off,' he'd said dismissively to Laura.

Rather than Beth's interest waning, it had increased with the weeks, particularly so with the integration of this influx of Americans. Laura hadn't quite known what to do with these Yanks. They didn't appear all that keen on learning ballroom dance routines. They were more in favour of anything that involved hugging the land girls close in smoochy numbers; and although some of the women thought this was great, others remained rather wary. And then one evening the Yanks persuaded Laura to let them demonstrate the jive.

Initially, three Americans took to the floor with three of the more daring land girls. They had got one of their own chaps to take over the piano from Mavis, and soon were moving around the room to the lively beat. Within minutes everyone watching was clapping to the rhythm while big smiles lit jaded faces.

'You'd better teach me,' said Laura to one of the men when the tune finished.

Learning the first few steps of the jive was hilarious, and most of her pupils enjoyed seeing Laura struggling to master something. Her sense of timing helped, though, and by the end of the number she believed she had mastered the basic steps. Coming off the floor, she was thanking the fellow who had taken her in hand when she noticed that Beth had arrived at the foot of the gallery staircase.

Beaming, and her cheeks flushed with excitement, the girl extended a hand towards Laura. 'Teach me,' she begged.

Laura grinned. 'Eh, love – I can't, not yet. I haven't learnt it properly myself.'

'May I try to teach the little lady?' asked the man who was leading Laura off the floor.

'If you like. Go on, Beth. This gentleman will show you . . .'

Their pianist seemed to have a wide repertoire of music suitable for jiving. And now that other people were eager to attempt this new form of dancing Laura hadn't the heart to stop them. Since they were all enjoying themselves so much, she crossed to Mavis and asked if she objected if the Yanks were given their head tonight.

'Nay, lass, of course I don't mind, so long as nobody thinks of getting me to perform any of that lot. It's fair grand to see 'em all letting go like that, isn't it? Including young Beth.'

Beth was, indeed, having a wonderful time. The fellow who was partnering her seemed to have infinite patience, and was encouraging her until she was moving as swiftly and almost as surely as himself.

I wish her father was here to see this, thought Laura, and then realised immediately that he wouldn't necessarily approve. He hadn't authorised Beth's joining in the dancing, and – although it seemed fun – Laura herself wondered if jiving wasn't rather too uninhibited.

The change in Beth was astounding. She came off the floor beaming up at the Yank who had partnered her, and chatting to him.

When Laura crossed to join the girl Beth looked a little uneasy, but as soon as she heard Laura saying: 'Well done, love, you picked that up quickly!' she grinned. And she didn't protest when Laura went on to remind her that joining in had been a special privilege, and now it was time girls of her age were heading for bed. 'You can come again next time we're dancing.'

Instead of the expected objections, Beth reached up and gave her a hug. 'I do love you, Maddie!'

The Americans were jiving again already, with more of them taking the floor, and more of the Land Army girls as well. For a full minute, however, Laura was hardly aware of the activity behind her. She couldn't take her gaze off Beth who was running up the stairs, then dancing light-heartedly along the gallery before pausing to wave before going out of sight.

Laura swallowed, thinking of the frail, listless girl who had met her here when she first visited Arncliffe.

Mavis appeared at her side. 'You can't call her too quiet tonight, any road, Laura love! I hope her father will approve the reason behind this change in her.'

'So do I,' Laura said ruefully. And she had a nasty feeling his enthusiasm might be somewhat diluted.

It was late the following afternoon before Laura had the opportunity to discover what Patrick felt. Even though she herself had been just as busy as usual in the office, her mind had wandered frequently to what his reaction might be. In the event, she soon learned that he knew of no change in his daughter's behaviour.

'Has Beth said anything to you about last night?' Laura enquired.

He was standing unfastening his briefcase after checking that the day here at Arncliffe had produced no difficulties requiring his attention.

'No. She didn't say one word at breakfast, why?'

'Well – actually, last night she became really animated.'

His dark eyes adopted the cautious look with which he often greeted Laura's reports on his daughter. 'Oh? And what brought that about?'

'I hope you won't be annoyed, but – well, we were trying a dance that was new to us. And Beth was so intrigued I hadn't the heart to stop her having a go. I did limit her to just the one attempt, because I know you think she's a bit young yet.

Anyway, she picked up the steps ever so quickly. Far quicker than I did, in fact,' she added. She realised at once that he might be curious about the reason why she herself wasn't teaching. 'Best of all, though, when the music stopped I noticed Beth chatting to the man who'd been demonstrating.'

'Good, good,' he said, but again Laura recognised Patrick's reservations, and could only sympathise with his wish to be the one person who did most to release his daughter from her silence.

An hour or so later, sitting over her evening meal, Laura was still thinking about Patrick and Beth. Was it just cussedness that always stopped the girl speaking with her father while she seemed now to be beginning to talk to other people? Or was there some specific reason for her reticence with him?

Laura was washing the dishes when the possible answer occurred to her. She had been considering situations in which people clammed up, if only about one particular matter, when she recalled how she herself had become almost as reticent. After Maurice's disappearance she had gone out of her way to avoid speaking of his departure, *because of his instructions*.

Was it too outrageous to suppose that someone, Beth's mother perhaps, had told her never to talk to her daddy about something that had occurred? Could a child, only four years old at the time, even have interpreted that as never speaking to him again? Or was it all just a part of the evident trauma of her mother's disappearance? Patrick had said what a state Beth had been in when she was found.

Laura's concern lessened on the following day when Patrick came into the office first thing and smilingly announced that he had coaxed Beth into a proper conversation with him the previous evening.

'I think we're winning, at last, Laura. And it was thanks to your tip about the dancing that I got her to confide. She wasn't exactly garrulous, I admit, but it's a good start. Can't help but think it must have something to do with the free-and-easy style those Yanks have. At least, Beth said they "talked funny" so I gathered they were the ones responsible.'

'Er – yes. They were jiving, all very energetic. I suppose that would appeal more to a youngster.'

'Perhaps, but you have had her dancing from the start. I shan't forget.'

Warmed by his words, Laura felt more contented than for some long while. She might be compelled to resign herself to accepting that Maurice's disappearance could be permanent, but there was a lot for her here. Especially now that both Beth and Patrick appeared to be happier. Somehow, they might all manage to make the best of things.

The privations of war had grown more evident still during the past year or two, making the need to cheer themselves up more imperative. As well as all the limitations enforced by food rationing, even bathing had seemed like a luxury since February 1942 when people were asked to use no more than five inches of water. And there was no possibility of buying a new outfit except when really necessary. Not only were coupons required for clothing but the items available were regulated by government restrictions. Laura remembered when, about the time that bath water was curtailed, Patrick had been complaining that no man in his building society would be smartly clothed now that suits must not cost more than £4.18s.8d.

'By the end of this war, even those of us who're fortunate enough to have homes still standing will look like wrecks ourselves!'

Laura recalled how she had been forced to smile to herself. She could believe that the suits which men of his standing possessed would keep them well-presented for many a year yet. The need to adhere to the 'Make do and Mend' campaign wasn't really hitting him hard.

Despite such reminders of the differences in their circumstances, however, she was conscious of the return of the affinity which had at first seemed to be developing after her arrival at Arncliffe. These days, though, they were often only alone together in the office, and never for more than the odd short period.

Patrick still put in several hours weekly working on the land, as well as keeping an eye on the farming operation. Together with running the building society and coping with administrative problems in the Arncliffe hospital, this gave him a full life. For so long they had met only through work that Laura was surprised when he suggested one Saturday that they should take Beth for another long walk.

'And then you're to come and have a meal with us,' he added. 'I won't take no for an answer.'

Laura had intended arranging to see Netta and Roy that day. She couldn't even remember when she'd seen them last, though she had managed a weekend at home in Whitby. She wanted to assure Netta that their mother had looked very well. Rejuvenated by the work she was doing for the WVS and for the men billeted on her, Maggie Crabtree was livelier than ever Laura remembered her.

As soon as Patrick made his suggestion, however, she knew what she wished to do. She immediately began looking forward to spending time with them, especially now that Beth had grown more forthcoming.

For once, the war seemed distanced from them for, leaving behind the rows of vegetables in Arncliffe's grounds, there was little evidence of any change from normality on the hills about them.

'Selfish or not, I can't help being thankful that this part of Yorkshire hasn't been ruined by bombing,' Patrick admitted, as they headed towards the moors. 'At least the alterations in and around Arncliffe are such that it will in time be restored to something like its old self.'

Within Arncliffe Hall, despite inevitable wear and tear, most of the fabric of the building remained in prewar condition; and many of the furnishings had been put away carefully for the duration. Out of doors was, of course, a different matter.

'I expect it will take quite a while to re-lay all your gardens as they once were, though,' said Laura.

'I shan't try,' Patrick replied. 'I shall have a long think, once we are at peace, then get in a good landscape gardener when I have the new ideas clear in my mind.'

'Can I help, Daddy?' asked Beth. 'It is my home as well.'

Patrick was pleased that she finally seemed happy to contribute something. 'Why not? After all, you're the one who will have to live for years with the result.'

Beth smiled at that, but said nothing further. She still spoke less than most girls of her age. Today she seemed content to walk with them and absorb the late-summer air and sunshine.

'Will they reconstruct that after the war?' asked Laura suddenly, pointing to the distant shell of Dale Reservoir.

'I can't think of any reason why they wouldn't,' said Patrick. 'If it was essential before, it should come in for government consent once reconstruction does begin countrywide. It served industry, don't forget, as well as homes.'

'That'll be good,' said Laura. She hated to see any place that had been destroyed.

Beth appeared pensive while the reservoir was in sight, making Laura recall her old interest in the area, and in the man whom they had glimpsed there years ago.

Later that day when they had returned to Arncliffe and the two of them were waiting for Patrick to finish a telephone call, Laura asked Beth if she remembered that previous visit.

'Of course. When I saw Uncle.'

Laura nodded. 'But Uncle *who*, Beth? What was his name?'

'I don't know. Just Uncle.'

'How did you know him, love?' Laura persisted, anxious to learn more at last about the existence of this man who had made such an impression upon the girl.

Laura hadn't noticed that Patrick was standing in the open doorway now. Only when he spoke did she swing round and catch sight of his frown. 'Laura, I don't think . . .'

She had to wait to learn what that was. Mrs Harrison appeared at that moment to announce their meal was ready. But as they headed towards the dining-room Patrick fell into step beside Laura.

'You're not doing any good with your cross-questioning of

418

Beth, can't you see you're distressing her?' he hissed.

Laura didn't believe Beth looked at all distressed, but she wouldn't spoil the rest of the day by saying so. She remained certain that getting to the bottom of this whole business could only help to unearth what had happened all those years ago, and thus enable Beth to begin adjusting.

Patrick's father joined them that evening, and after they had eaten put on a selection of classical records. Although Beth grew restless and went off to her room to read, Laura enjoyed the music which induced a feeling of calm, lacking in her for much too long.

When she eventually rose to return to the Coach House, Patrick offered to walk her there. As they made their way through the corridors, sounds reached them of patients and hospital staff getting ready for the night.

Crossing the ballroom Patrick smiled. 'I'm glad you've put this to good use, Laura. Your dances have done a lot to make our Land Army girls happier, as well as the men. For me, it's been great to hear voices in here and music, keeping the place alive.'

'And yet you never join us. Why don't you?'

He shrugged. 'Maybe I haven't felt it was quite me.'

'Why ever not? You ought to think about it.'

Returning the way they had come, Patrick was thinking. There were reasons enough why he had never joined the dancing that Laura organised. In the beginning, he'd felt he didn't wish to share her with anyone. He would have been disturbed to watch her dancing with other men, as he knew that she must. During the time of her affair with Maurice Olivier he'd have done anything to avoid seeing them together. And since then? He had been all too aware of her yearning for Maurice, without placing himself in a situation where he might risk reminders that she was still committed to the man.

For years now he had sensed that only by keeping their relationship as it was could he hold on to what little they had. Any change might end these brief moments when they seemed to share some affinity.

During the next weekend Laura finally made time to see Netta and Roy, and wondered while she was there why she didn't visit them far more often. Netta had matured a great deal during these war years, working with Roy at the factory as they produced whatever the government required of them. Ages ago, Roy had offered to show Laura what they were manufacturing by way of tents, webbing and so on. She had declined with a smile. She needed to remember Lindley's as it was – the place to which she would return to design all the carpets that remained lodged somewhere in her imagination.

Today, however, Roy was optimistic that it wouldn't be all that long before the war ended and they were free to take up normal production again.

'D-Day was the beginning of the end of this lot, I'm sure,' he asserted. 'The Allies have a job to finish, I know. But there's no talk now of the war lasting for ever.'

'Roy's promised he'll still find me work in the office,' Netta announced. 'That's unless I've started another baby by then.'

Her husband was smiling when he turned to Laura. 'That should convince you we're sure the worst's over. I wouldn't countenance adding another child to the two we have while we were at war.'

'It hasn't all been bad, though,' said Netta. 'There's Mum, for instance. It's been the making of her, hasn't it?' She began asking Laura for details of her visit to their old home in Whitby. What the men were like who were billeted there at present.

Travelling had been difficult during these past few years, as well as unnecessary journeys being frowned on as unpatriotic. Neither of them had gone as often as they felt they ought to the east coast, and in fact Netta had visited Greta and Sybil more frequently. She had seen them the previous month and was happy to enlarge on what she'd already told Laura while keeping in touch by telephone.

In many ways, though, it was her nephew Kevin who delighted Laura most during that visit. Now five years old, he was an engaging child who had inherited Roy's golden hair and handsome features.

'I could hug him to death!' Laura admitted to the boy's parents after he had given her a kiss before going obediently to bed.

'Eh, you should have given him a good hugging then,' Netta exclaimed. 'He hasn't quite grown out of being affectionate yet. Roy's always having to remind me that I haven't to make him soft.'

'He's beautifully behaved, though,' Laura remarked.

Roy laughed. 'Sometimes!'

But Kevin was well mannered, nobody could have faulted him at the table. And he had none of the moodiness displayed by lots of children, including his younger sister Petra. Laura had played Snakes and Ladders with him, and he had chortled just as cheerfully when she won a game as when he himself won. She could believe he would accept most of life's ups and downs with similar equanimity.

Sitting in the blacked-out bus on the way back to Arncliffe, Laura remembered that Beth must have been rather younger than Kevin was now at the time of the trauma which reduced her to silence. And this year she was thirteen. No matter what Patrick said, it was high time somebody really got to the root of the trouble, and freed her once and for all from any remaining inhibitions that it had induced.

Laura tackled the problem as soon as it was feasible to invite Beth to the Coach House for a meal. These days, thankfully, the girl didn't hesitate to converse, which made entertaining her infinitely easier. They chatted about this and that whilst eating, then washed up together in the kitchen that still pleased Laura because of being well-fitted, but most of all her own.

Afterwards, sitting before the living-room fire, Laura brought up the subject which had bothered her for so long.

'We've always been friends, haven't we, Beth? That's why I want to help you, if I can, by showing you how things that happened a long time since don't have to make your life today unhappy.'

'You mean about Maddie, don't you – the real Maddie?'

'Your mother, yes.' Laura didn't quite know how to proceed. Beth had shaken her by coming straight to the point.

Now, however, the girl seemed unable to continue being so direct. For quite some time she paused, and then she sighed and began speaking again. 'I don't know what happened, I don't think I've ever known. But it couldn't have been Uncle's fault. It couldn't, could it?' she added desperately.

'I'm afraid I can't say, love. I didn't know your uncle . . .'

'And you didn't know Mad . . . my mother.'

'What was she like?'

'I can hardly picture her now. But her hair was the colour of mine, only wavy and short, a bit like yours. She was very pretty, and laughed a lot. Or she did when we were with Uncle. When we were out, that is – I was made to go away and play when he came to the house.'

'He came to the house then?' Laura was surprised. Patrick had seemed unaware of any man whom Beth might have called Uncle.

'Oh, yes. He came a lot, I'm sure he did. He brought me sweets and things, presents.'

'So – he was a friend of your father's, after all?'

'No, I don't think so. He was Maddie's friend. It was always her that he came to talk to.'

Laura digested this information which Beth appeared to be too innocent to find significant. Poor Patrick, she thought, if his wife was carrying on behind his back. And she could sympathise with him if this fellow, whoever he was, had also charmed his daughter with gifts. But then, Patrick might not have known that any of this was going on: his busy life could have kept him from noticing that something was occurring in his absence.

'When you went out, Beth – with your mother and this man – did you go far from Arncliffe?'

'It seemed a long way always, to me. They teased me a lot for dawdling, and sometimes Uncle carried me on his shoulder.'

'And where was it you went?' Laura persisted, eager for some clue to how this man had fitted into their lives.

'Can't remember, sorry. Except – sometimes it was to the reservoir. You know, the one we've seen with Daddy. Only it didn't have water in it, I think. It was nearly like when we've seen it since the plane crashed there.'

So, thought Laura, that must have been while Dale Reservoir was under construction. Although she had learned quite a bit from Beth, the childlike account of events gave only a sketchy picture of what the situation might have been at that time. Enquiring further just now, however, might only cloud the picture forming in her own mind. She needed to be alone to think, to make some kind of sense of what she had learned. And to examine her reactions to hearing that it seemed Patrick's wife had been unfaithful.

After Beth had left, Laura sat up to the fire re-examining everything that she had been told. Before very long her own motivation for questioning the girl began troubling her. Because now, alongside all her concern for everyone who had been affected by this trauma, new emotions were arising. And strongest of all was this massive relief – if Magda were proved unfaithful, wouldn't Patrick then be more likely finally to turn from her? To Laura herself . . .? With something of a shock she realised that she had become resigned to losing Maurice. How otherwise had she again grown so concerned for Patrick? Had she always intended not so much to help Beth overcome the past as to find a means of freeing her father?

Disturbed like this, Laura rather dreaded meeting him again. When he was waiting for her in the office next morning she realised with alarm that he looked extremely angry.

'Beth tells me you've been questioning her,' he began without any preamble. 'I've asked you before to desist. I am telling you now that I will not permit this to continue. Damn it, Laura, we've fought long enough to get her to emerge from that uncanny silence. Are you determined to make her retreat into it again?'

'Anything but,' she said earnestly. 'I believe Beth will only be helped by learning what really happened and then being guided to accept it.'

'Guided by you, I suppose?' he snapped, then quelled his long-standing resentment that she so often got through to his daughter. 'I'm sorry, but I must insist that this is handled in the way that I consider fit. I won't have her cross-questioned. Can't you see the girl would do anything to avoid facing the truth?'

'Or is it you who would?' Laura asked, then checked, appalled that she had spoken her thoughts aloud.

His dark eyes chilling further, Patrick gave her a prolonged stare. 'You know my views now. The matter will not be discussed again.'

Before Laura could say anything he had swung away and left her.

Throughout that day and for some long while afterwards Laura remained disturbed. She had only so recently come to realise how much it mattered to her that Patrick should relegate all thoughts of his wife to the past. And now, because of her own intervention with Beth, she had antagonised him yet again.

Only Beth made the ensuing months bearable. The affection she and Laura shared seemed undiminished by Patrick's annoyance, and Laura was glad that at least he hadn't forbidden her contact with the girl.

The two of them roamed the countryside, sometimes taking bus journeys which Beth declared great fun. They spent a day exploring Haworth and afterwards Laura loaned her a copy of *Jane Eyre*, then later *Wuthering Heights*. Beth adored reading, and became obsessed with the Brontës. Laura suspected the girl felt some affinity with these sisters whose lives had been as strange as her own seemed.

On several occasions when they walked in the vicinity of Dale Reservoir Beth referred to the past, but she never revealed anything fresh connecting her mother with the place. And Laura knew better than to ask further questions. Her relationship with Patrick now hung on the slender thread of contact concerned with running Arncliffe. Another slip from her could result in that fragile link being severed.

Signs that the war would eventually end were increasing. Laura was determined that she would keep things as they were for the duration. With the liberation of Paris in August hopes of peace had become more substantial. Despite the flying bombs assailing London and the south east, Britain could take heart. And in that same month the Germans occupying the Channel Islands withdrew. Following the Allied advance on Brittany the strategic usefulness of the islands had evaporated.

The news gave Laura mixed emotions. Hearing that the first priority was to provide the Channel Islanders with food, and especially meat, she felt glad that people like Maurice's mother might eventually be helped. But this did bring home to her that if by some chance Maurice was safe over there she could possibly receive word from him. Her feelings about him were terribly confused. Their love, glorious though it had been, was all a long time ago. They had known each other for only a matter of weeks. And if it should turn out that he had survived but had neglected to let her know he was alive, she would find it hard to forgive the anxiety he had caused her.

As weeks passed and no news of Maurice reached her, Laura couldn't help feeling quite relieved. One day, she would try and discover what had happened. For the present, she had enough here at Arncliffe to exhaust her capacity for concern.

The set-back of the battle of Arnhem brought massive admissions to their hospital, stretching facilities to the limits. Laura was kept busy trying to obtain additional medical and surgical supplies, and ringing round to get hold of more beds to erect in corridors and any odd corner that might accommodate a wounded man. Or woman, for one of their wards was now given over to servicewomen.

Laura had asked if the time had come for her dancing sessions to cease. They seemed almost irrelevant amid so much earnest effort to care for still more people battered by war. A massive protest ensured that dancing continued and, although at her wits' end to know how to fit in those evenings, she was glad to know they were still valued.

Attendances became far higher than ever she had intended, filling that exquisite room with men and women, many of whom were working off in exuberance all the tensions of open battle. Again, it was the Yanks who appeared liveliest, many overcoming quite severe injuries to jitterbug around the room until the entire floor vibrated.

Although she herself retained some reservations about this form of dancing, Laura was compelled to acknowledge that it did seem to have them throwing off cares along with any inhibitions. She was saved some of the time which she would have given to preparing to coach in traditional ballroom dances, and Beth had somehow obtained her father's consent to join wholeheartedly in the fun.

She's going to miss this once the war's over, thought Laura, watching Beth's glowing face and noticing how she never hesitated to chat with her partners.

Whatever will happen to her when this lot's ended? Laura worried. With no real education behind her, the girl stood little chance of finding work commensurate with her undeniable brightness. Beth had missed so much through the years, lost within that awful silence. Somebody, some time, would have to bring her out into the real world. Even now that she was so much better she remained more naive than even a child of ten would be. Without proper handling of her future, these circumstances could be dangerous.

I suppose the truth is that what she needs most is her mother, Laura reflected. And found herself wishing sincerely that Magda Horsfall might at last be located.

Chapter 25

Peace came to Europe in the May of 1945 amid troubling reports of the continuing Far Eastern conflict, and horrific pictures from German concentration camps. But peace it was, however overshadowed by the truth now emerging of the havoc war had created.

To the folk in and around Halfield this promise of better days ahead brought a determination to celebrate with the rest of Britain, and to implement plans already made for getting back to normal.

Eager for news that Lindley's would soon return to manufacturing carpets, Laura grew impatient when told by her brother-in-law that the changeover might take some time. She had been longing for months to escape the office at Arncliffe. Although well aware that the troops in its hospital would require treatment for some long while, she had warned Patrick already that he must not count on her staying any longer than it took for Lindley's to begin carpet weaving again.

His expression had remained about as enigmatic as it had ever since their last disagreement, convincing Laura that she'd be happy to revert to only having him as a neighbour. There would be stresses enough in readjusting to her old job. Although she couldn't help feeling that the past few years had equipped her for making light of any problems the carpet mill might produce! And she would still reserve some of her leisure for Beth. *If* the girl continued to spend all her time at Arncliffe. Laura had heard that Patrick was looking into the possibility of sending his daughter to a special school.

Laura felt that she ought to endorse anything which might

help Beth to tackle life as it really was, yet she herself was uneasy about the possible effect of tearing the girl from her roots.

'I guess Daddy will think now's the time to pack me off,' Beth was saying on the evening of VE-Day as she and Laura walked up the hill to watch beacons being lit at intervals over the surrounding countryside.

'Well, we'll wait and see what happens,' said Laura, trying to sound reassuring. 'Your father's got a lot of other things to attend to as well.' The land on the estate was undergoing less intensive cultivation as, gradually, the Land Army girls were dispersing. He had spoken of his plans for the ground and that, together with the question of the future of the hospital, occupied him.

'At least he's unlikely to find me a place until the new term in the autumn,' Beth continued, though a sigh revealed her dread of any change.

Suddenly, their discussion of the future was halted as Dale Reservoir came into view, signs of great activity near its containing dam. From the quantity of plant and machinery visible, they gathered that preliminary work towards its reconstruction had begun. What puzzled Laura, and Beth as well, was the sight of police officers along with the workmen on the site.

'I wonder what they've found?' said Laura. 'Happen it's bits of that Messerschmitt that were embedded in the concrete.'

For a few minutes they paused to stare. This far away, however, they could discern very little, and Beth was losing interest. When, with the increasing darkness, the first of the local beacons was lit, they turned their attention to spotting others flaring from the highest point of each surrounding hill.

'I wish we lived in a street,' murmured Beth wistfully. 'Then we'd have a party. That's what everybody else is doing, isn't it?'

'Well, we're having one at Arncliffe too, don't forget.'

'You mean when Auntie Jenny and Uncle Ted bring little Patrick over? Not exactly exciting, is it?'

'No, I didn't mean that.' Laura hadn't even thought that the Horsfall family would have a gathering. 'We're getting all the hospital patients and staff together. There'll be some dancing, but other things as well – for those who can't get about yet.'

'I don't expect I'll be allowed to be there,' said Beth, sounding so dejected that Laura was forced to smile.

'Nay, love – you're supposed to be celebrating peace in Europe, not going round with a long face.'

'Sorry, I know I'm being a mope. It's just that I'm always the wrong age. I'm years older than Cousin Patrick, being with him is no fun. Yet Daddy always thinks I'm too young really for joining in the things you're organising.'

When they turned and headed back towards home Laura was thinking that maybe school wouldn't be all that bad a thing for Beth. As they approached the house, however, everything else was driven from her mind by the police car she spotted near the main entrance.

Beth appeared to be taking very little notice of the car, and Laura was wondering how to get the girl past and into the house without alarming her when she saw Mrs Harrison waiting on the doorstep.

'I was just looking out for you. Come along in, Beth love,' the housekeeper began. She sounded quite brisk and cheerful, but her eyes revealed her anxiety. 'I'll have a word with you just as soon as I can,' she whispered to Laura after Beth had said goodnight and hurried in through the front door of Arncliffe Hall.

No matter how hard she tried to rationalise that it might prove otherwise, Laura couldn't help feeling there was some connection between the police car here and the officers out at the reservoir.

Arriving at the door of her own home she wondered if she ought to have gone inside with Beth, and waited until there was an opportunity for Mrs Harrison to confide in her. Really, though, this was none of her business and such an action might have been construed as being over-curious. Especially these days, while Patrick seemed to have so little to say to her.

Attempting to dismiss the subject, Laura switched on the wireless to listen to reports of the celebrations taking place up and down the country. But even though she could feel thankful for this first ceasefire, she remained perturbed about events nearer to home.

It was almost ten o'clock when somebody knocked on the Coach House door. Going to answer it, Laura felt relieved that Mrs Harrison was finally coming to put her in the picture.

Patrick was standing on the path, his face even in the darkness looking haggard.

'Eh, love – come on in,' she exclaimed. 'Whatever's happened?'

'In a minute . . .'

He waited until she had shown him through to the living-room and he had sunk into the chair she offered.

'I believe you saw the police car when you returned with Beth,' he began at last.

'Aye, I did an' all! What is it, love? Some sort of accident?'

He shook his head. 'Stupid of me, really, to be so shaken – it was what I'd half expected for many a year. She couldn't really have disappeared so completely if – if she hadn't been dead.' He was staring down at his hands, perhaps intending to conceal from Laura the shock so evident in his eyes.

'You mean, they've found your wife?' Her legs suddenly weak, she sat in the other armchair.

'They've found a body, yes. Positive identification may take some long while. It looks like a suspicious death, they say. She – she was at the reservoir.'

'She'd drowned then? But how was it she hasn't been discovered till now? It's been drained for ages.'

'This person hadn't drowned. They think she had been buried at the time the reservoir was being completed, underneath an area later set with concrete. That certainly makes the period coincide with her disappearance.'

Laura immediately wondered how enough of the woman had remained for anyone to link her with Magda Horsfall's

430

disappearance, but that wasn't something she would ask. Patrick was disturbed already.

He told her anyway, in staccato sentences. 'There's little more than a skeleton. A few shreds of clothing. There are rings to identify. When they permit their removal. And a gold locket.'

Patrick paused after that, as if he had no energy left. Laura rose and poured him a brandy. He sipped in silence for a while before continuing.

'It's her locket, all right. Knew it at once. So did they, for that matter. It's quite large, a family thing. I'd had it engraved with both our names. My gift on our wedding day.'

'Oh, Patrick – I am sorry.'

He sighed. 'Don't know what I feel, not really. Numb, disbelieving. For so long I've needed the truth, now . . .' He shook his head.

Patrick sat in silence while he finished the brandy, then rose abruptly. 'Thought I'd tell you myself, before you heard Thanks for this,' he added, handing her the glass. 'And for listening.'

'I'm only glad I was here. If there's anything I can do, anything at all . . .'

'I'll let you know.' He thanked her again, began walking towards the hall, every step an effort.

He would have to identify the body, what there was of it. 'If you want somebody with you at any time,' Laura offered.

He shook his head. 'Ted's volunteered. I rang them, of course. And most of the conclusive identification will be from dental records.'

'Have you told Beth?'

'Not yet. No point in upsetting her until we are absolutely sure. Don't know whatever I'll tell her. I know I can rely on you not to let it out first. Be good to her, Laura – while I'm distracted.'

In every sense of the word! she thought as she watched him stomping sombrely across the courtyard towards his home.

* * *

431

She found the next few days trying, and could imagine how much worse they must be for Patrick. Despite holidays declared to celebrate VE-Day, they had been obliged to have the office open just to keep the hospital running. Laura wasn't sorry to have somewhere to go. Ever since hearing the news, she had felt too agitated to think about anything but Magda's having been found. Even the Coach House was too far away from Patrick.

Two or three times a day, he wandered into the office and said a few words, but never about the matter concerning them so greatly. The only thing Laura did learn was from the local newspaper which confirmed what she had supposed – that the body had been found when damage created by that enemy plane was being assessed prior to reconstruction. It wasn't until the rest of the world went back to normal and the building society opened up that Patrick appeared to be recovering from the shock.

He caught Laura that evening just as she was about to head across to her home.

'It's definitely Magda,' he said, sounding relieved. 'Her dentist has proved that, not that I had any real doubts. There'll be an inquest, of course, various other formalities. Either Ted or Jenny will accompany me, wherever . . .' he added, making Laura wonder if he was glad to have a reason for not relying on her.

'Does Beth know now?'

'I'm telling her in the morning. This isn't the best time of day for unloading that news on her. I shall take tomorrow off, be around for her. Whether that helps nor not.'

'Of course it'll help her.'

He gave her a look. 'Don't just say what might be expected of you, Laura. We've been friends for too long for that. You know and I know that Beth doesn't confide in me very much.'

'Maybe she will now. This is something you're in together.'

Patrick shrugged as he went out.

Laura hardly slept that night. Not for the first time since the body had been discovered, she lay there wondering what

Patrick must really be feeling now. She was thankful that she had kept to herself all that Beth had told her. If, as it seemed, Magda Horsfall had been having an affair, that fact had died with her. She was glad Patrick needn't suffer that additional hurt.

The dread that was to plague Laura endlessly came to her the following night when, again, she found sleeping virtually impossible. Working her mind to and fro over all that she'd ever learned about Patrick and his relationship with his wife, she remembered something she had heard years ago.

Patrick had been closely questioned by the police around the time of Magda's disappearance. There had been problems concerning their finances. He'd had to overcome difficulties with his own board at the building society. And hadn't there been some insinuation that he might have stood to gain from his wife's death? Right from the start, Michael had cautioned her against him, even dear old Clem Hargreaves had warned her as well. Surely – surely to God no one now could even think that he was the person responsible for her death?

I'll go to that inquest, Laura decided. I shall have to be there now in case Patrick has to face some accusation. I've got to show I stand by him.

Beth had taken the news of her mother's death quite calmly, and by the time Laura saw her afterwards appeared to have accepted all that she had been told.

'Daddy explained as much as he knows,' she said as she sat in Laura's kitchen, looking quite relaxed for a girl who had been given such terrible news. 'We don't know why she died, and we might never know, but it was a very long time ago now.'

Laura swallowed, unable to think what to say, or how to utter it. And Beth continued anyway.

'We shall remember her as she was, but we already have this very different way of life. She would never have wished us to be miserable for ever.'

After Beth had left Laura wondered if the girl really did have nothing to remember about what had occurred at Dale Reservoir. Had she, mercifully, perhaps done no more than

433

wander about the estate looking for her mother? Laura fervently hoped that Beth would have nothing worse than that stored anywhere in her memory.

As soon as identification of the remains had been confirmed, everyone in and around Halfield seemed to be full of the story. Laura went over to see Netta and was greeted with her exclamations.

'Isn't it an awful thing to happen – Patrick's wife being found dead after all this time! Has he said anything to you?'

'Well, naturally. It's not a thing you ignore.' But Laura felt uncomfortable now, was afraid she might let slip something Patrick had said. And she considered their conversations on the subject confidential. 'I'm just very sorry for him, and for Beth. But I didn't come here to talk about that, love.'

'Oh, don't be so stuffy, Laura. You must know more than's in the papers. You're as bad as Roy, he got quite ratty and told me to shut up about it.'

'I dare say he's got a lot on his mind, trying to get the mill organised for going back to producing carpets. I wanted to ask him when they'd be starting up again. Is that where he is now?'

'On a Sunday night? I don't think so, he just said he was going out for a bit. It's starting to come dark as well, I hope he's not so long. I'm a bit worried about him. Happen he is concerned about Lindley's. He's been sort of quiet lately, and snappy with me.'

'We all have our off days.'

'I bet you're right, Laura, and it is to do with wanting to get cracking with carpets again, I hadn't thought of that. But he was on about it on VE-Day. Mother rang me up that day, did I let you know? Just to say she was all right, like. She was having a party for the chaps that were billeted on her.'

'That's good. I wonder what she'll be like when they've all left to be demobbed?'

'Miserable, I expect,' said Netta, and laughed. 'Any road, she'll have our Greta back home afore so long. Not so sure about Sybil – last I heard she'd got a fellow. Serious, we think.'

Laura grinned. 'Don't sound so surprised. You're not the only one that likes the idea of being married, you know.'

'Ah, but they aren't all like Roy, are they? Chaps. There's nobody like him.'

Laura grew quiet, reflecting on how well the unlikely pairing of her sister and Roy Lindley had turned out. She hoped they would now have the third child for which Netta longed.

'Do you hear much from Roy's brother?' she asked; she rarely remembered to enquire.

'Alan? He's with a convoy somewhere, off Russia, I think.'

As soon as he qualified Alan had signed on as a naval doctor. During most of the war his family had had only a vague notion of where he was serving.

'It's going to mean big changes for a lot of folk when this lot's really over, the Japanese war as well,' Laura observed.

'Changes for the better, though, surely?' said Netta.

'Oh, of course, that's what I meant.' But would it be for the better in Patrick's case? thought Laura. He had battled for so long to learn what had happened to his wife, to get her back. And all he'd ended up with was a bundle of bones. 'Just a bundle of bones,' she murmured, without realising she had spoken aloud.

'Is that all she was when they found her – Magda Horsfall?' asked Netta, intrigued.

'Eh, I don't know, not really. There'll be an inquest, any road. You'll be able to read all about it then.'

There seemed something distasteful about anybody being this eager to read about the death which had so surely shattered all Patrick's hopes of a reconciliation with his wife. Suddenly needing to get away, Laura began making excuses that she must be heading for home.

As she was leaving, however, she suggested to Netta that they might go over to Whitby together before long to see their mother.

Their old home looked very different these days, with evidence in all the downstairs rooms of their long-standing use as a billet. The men for whom Maggie Crabtree had made a home evidently settled so well that they spread forage caps, army belts and boots around just as they might in a place of their own.

'Heavens, it's worse than when we were growing up here!' Netta said with a grin, looking round the living-room.

'Well, it comes a close second!' Laura exclaimed.

But it was in their mother herself that the war had wrought the most dramatic change. Laura had thought previously that Maggie had become far more capable through coping with the influx of army and airforce personnel. Today, she also appeared excited.

'It was one of my young chaps put the idea into my head,' she confided to her daughters who were sitting at the kitchen table while she rolled out pastry for a pie. 'As soon as they have to leave I'm going to start taking folk in. For their holidays, you know.'

She went on to assert that there would be plenty of people coming to the east coast again. And even while food remained rationed, she could at least provide rooms for them.

'We shall have to see how things go – it might be best if they buy their own stuff in and I cook it for them. I've been talking to some that were landladies afore the war, and they reckon that's going to be the best way of organising things afterwards.'

'But aren't you going to find that a lot of hard work?' asked Netta.

Laura could have shaken her sister for putting a spoke in just when their mother seemed to be looking forward contentedly. But Maggie Crabtree had thought this all through, anyway, and wouldn't be deterred.

'I'll prefer that to sitting twiddling my thumbs in this great empty house. You don't have to worry, neither of you. If I could manage through the war with one batch of lads after another, I'll cope with owt.'

Maggie was so full of her plans that it was only when Laura and Netta were saying goodbye that she remembered she had news for them.

'Eh, I nearly forgot – I had a visitor last Sunday. Michael Dawson. He looked ever so well, and he had a young lady with him. Very nice, she was, talks posh – from down south somewhere. A nurse, she is. They met while he was serving abroad. Can't remember where.'

Laura instantly felt thankful that Michael had found someone. The relief was enormous. There would be no risk now that he would turn up again with hopes that she might take up with him.

During the train journey back to Halfield Netta revealed that she had her own reasons for thankfulness.

'It's early days yet, but I wanted you to know, Laura. I'm expecting again. I've missed twice now.'

Laura congratulated her and smiled as she listened while Netta went on about how lovely it would be to have another kiddie. When she reached her home, though, Laura couldn't help wishing that there was some prospect of ever having a family of her own.

The Coach House seemed full of Maurice tonight. Even after all the intervening years, she pictured him vividly about the place, fancied that she recalled the exact timbre of his voice with that lovely Jersey accent.

I thought I'd put all that behind me, she reflected as she yawned and went up to bed. It's high time I did. And yet somehow she needed something, word of what became of him perhaps, to enable her to relegate Maurice to the past.

Despite their tiring day she lay awake for hours, wrestling with her memories of Maurice and willing herself to let him rest. She could be more use here if she surrendered the past completely. And in their present situation Patrick and Beth couldn't be more in need of practical sympathy.

The moment she saw Patrick the following morning he certainly took Laura's mind away from everyone else.

'The inquest's tomorrow,' he said grimly. 'And from what they've gathered from the post mortem, it's likely to be quite a shaker. It seems they're sure that Magda was strangled. They think a dog lead was what was used. It was still around what remained of her neck. Anyway that will all come out in the coroner's court.'

'Would you like me to be there?'

Patrick shook his head but smiled slightly. 'No, thanks. Ted is coming over. What I would like you to do, please, is keep an eye on Beth. You don't have to be in the office all day, but in any case I'd like you to have her with you.'

'Of course I will. Anything . . .'

Before he set out for the building society Laura asked Patrick how much Beth knew about the supposed cause of her mother's death.

'Only that it is being investigated, and should be discovered by the coroner. I'm not telling her more until their suppositions are confirmed.'

'And presumably there's no clue as to who might have been responsible?'

'Well – there are clues. That dog lead, for instance, is heavily fingerprinted. But without anything to go on, there's little hope of matching them up.'

'But how had the lead survived like that, if her clothes and so on were disintegrating?'

He shook his head. 'Search me. Maybe leather takes longer to break down. No doubt that will emerge. I'm just very thankful it was so. The fingerprints meant they were quick to eliminate me.'

To Laura's relief, Beth wasn't unduly disturbed on the day that the inquest was taking place.

'We have to get to the bottom of what happened,' she told Laura, in words which clearly echoed her father's. 'It can't last for ever, Daddy says,' she added, confirming that Patrick had offered her a matter-of-fact means of dealing with the trauma.

Fortunately, there was little requiring Laura's attention in the office, and she and Beth spent most of the day out of doors watching the few remaining Land Army girls who were servicing the tractor and other machinery. The war with Japan had finally ceased, bringing nearer the return to peacetime occupations.

'I wonder what they'll all do now the war's over? Where will they go?' said Beth.

'Back to their homes, I expect. To their old jobs.'

'Like you, Laura. Will you be glad to design carpets again?'

'You bet. Can hardly wait for the day Lindley's get back to normal.'

'Daddy was telling me that you used to say you'd design a carpet for him, for their main London offices. Only he thought you'd have forgotten after all this time.'

'I haven't forgotten at all.' And she was delighted that Patrick still had it in mind. She must mention this to Roy when she next saw him. It couldn't hurt to have new projects in hand for when the looms were operational again. And, whatever the ups and downs of relations between Patrick and herself these past few years, she was glad to know something had survived.

Laura had been hoping to be able to ask how the inquest had gone but after hearing the car in the drive as Patrick and his brother-in-law returned, she only saw Mrs Harrison who came to bear Beth away. And she wasn't going to go out of her way to ask questions and encourage Patrick to think her unduly inquisitive.

Throughout the next day, until the local evening paper arrived, Laura was obliged to contain her anxiety about the verdict. The report confirmed what she'd already been told – that it appeared Magda Horsfall had been killed by strangulation, the instrument being a dog lead. Due to the advanced decomposition of the body, the time of death could not be established, and no success whatsoever had been achieved in attempting to locate her killer. The account continued that, so far as Mr Patrick Horsfall was aware, his wife had known no one who might have cause to harm her.

So he certainly didn't suspect Magda had been engaged in a potentially explosive relationship, thought Laura. And he apparently had never thought anything further about the 'uncle' whom Beth claimed to have known. A man who seemed, in the girl's mind, to have been connected with the area around Dale Reservoir. But Patrick isn't stupid, Laura reflected, she couldn't really believe that he had dismissed that man entirely.

Only a couple of days later she learned that he was anything but content to let the matter rest. He arrived back early from the building society and came into the office where she was balancing hospital accounts.

'Can you leave that please, Laura?' he began. 'I have an appointment this evening, and I need somebody with me to witness anything that might be said. I'll explain in the car.'

Laura readily agreed. She was glad that, at last, Patrick seemed to want her with him.

As soon as she was beside him in the car he began speaking. 'I rang Wolf Richardson today – the man who designed the reservoir. I'm hoping that he might come up with something, however slight, which could point us in the direction of Magda's murderer. It's obvious she was involved with somebody . . .'

'Er – yes,' said Laura awkwardly, and knew that she must continue. 'And there was the chap Beth seemed to recall – the one she thought of as "Uncle".'

'Don't think I've failed to dwell on that,' he said quite sharply. 'But for my resolve to spare Beth further traumas, I'd have aired that earlier. I won't have her interrogated, though, however determined I am to get at the truth. We've suffered for something like ten years over this. I'll see that there's a reckoning!'

'Has Beth never said anything to you about – about the time just before her mother disappeared?' asked Laura hesitantly.

She watched the line of his jaw tightening.

'Evidently she has to you,' he said tersely. 'You'd better tell me. I don't honestly think it can be much worse than all the possibilities I've raked back and forth over the years.'

'Well, you appear to be right. There was somebody that – that Magda was seeing.'

'Ah.'

440

'I am sorry to have to be telling you this . . .'

'Oh, Laura, grow up,' he said, though not unkindly. 'These things happen. We might not understand the reason, but there's usually one there. And I really am not about to throw a fit after hearing what seems to be a fact. I just hope this meeting now will throw some light on the matter.' And then, he thought, please God, I can inter everything concerning Magda, and concentrate on this woman beside me now.

Wolf Richardson's home was large and imposing, though cold and with a neglected feel to it which suggested to Laura that he had only recently returned from the war. And yet she was sure she'd heard that Richardson had been invalided out of the army after D-Day. The man himself was tall and gaunt, and had the air of a solitary male who wasn't given to looking after himself.

She was surprised again after they were introduced. Wolf ushered them through to a once elegant room and a woman rose to greet them.

'I'm Rhona Brightstone,' she announced, as Patrick began introducing Laura to her. 'Wolf and I are old friends. I just happened to call in on my way to visit someone who's a mutual acquaintance of ours. I've told Wolf that it's fine with me if you wish to talk in private.'

Patrick shook his head. 'Do feel free to stay. I'm just hoping there might be some sort of a lead, however slight, to link somebody with my wife's death. The fact that she is dead is plastered all over the papers now, so it's a bit late for me to seek privacy.'

Wolf Richardson offered them drinks but Patrick declined. 'Not for the moment, thanks. I'd rather get down to business. You've read the account of the coroner's court proceedings?'

Wolf nodded. 'Not very satisfactory, I imagine, for you.'

'Quite. That's why I've asked you to search your mind for anything you might have seen in or around the reservoir at the time it was being built.'

'I've thought about it a great deal. And I have to say you might have done better going straight to the construction company who worked to my plans. I can put you in touch, if you wish. Meanwhile, I can only tell you what bit I can recall.'

'Go on,' prompted Patrick, wishing people wouldn't be quite so circumspect about the possible effect of their words on his emotions. He wanted this over and done with, once and for all. It was that simple now.

'You asked if there had been anybody employed at the site who might have become involved with Mrs Horsfall? Frankly, I think that extremely unlikely. From what you tell me, and indeed from what I know of my own former wife, I don't believe the workmen there would have been in the running.'

'I was afraid not. Magda's tastes were somewhat sophisticated.'

'And expensive?' Wolf enquired, with a touch of sharpness that made Laura wonder what his ex-wife had done to wrong him.

'There's only one possible candidate that I can recall,' he continued after a moment's pause. 'And I'm afraid I don't know who he was. I only remember him because he trespassed at the site more than once, and didn't desist without a blazing row.'

'Do you remember at all when this happened?'

'Not exactly, though we were working on the containing wall of the dam.'

'So it could fit in. Is there anything you can tell me about him? What he was up to, wandering about there on his own?'

'Oh, he wasn't alone. Sorry – did I convey that impression? He always had a woman with him, sometimes a child . . .'

'Boy or girl?' Patrick enquired while Laura watched his expression stiffen.

'Not certain. Sorry. I only know I was concerned that the child must be kept well away from the plant and machinery.'

'How old was this child?'

'Afraid I'm no judge.' He turned to Rhona Brightstone. 'How old's Chrissie now?'

'Five.'

'About that age then, maybe rather younger.'

Patrick glanced towards Laura. 'It fits.' His attention returned to their host. 'And the woman, can you describe her?'

Wolf shook his head. 'Difficult after all this time.'

'Well, was she fair or dark?'

'Couldn't say, I'm afraid. She always wore a hat.'

Patrick sighed. This felt as slow as extracting teeth, and the pain was far worse than any sustained in a dentist's chair.

Wolf noticed his dismay and smiled sympathetically. 'It was the man with whom I had the altercation.'

'Tell me about him then.'

'He was about my own height, I suppose, quite well-built. I do recall his hair – it was fairish, though not absolutely blonde.'

Patrick shrugged. 'Means nothing to me. Not that I thought it would. I've never supposed it might be someone of my acquaintance.'

Wolf Richardson apologised for being unable to help very much, and insisted that they should have something to drink. When tea was chosen Rhona Brightstone rose to go and make it. Thinking the men might talk more readily alone, Laura offered to help.

The large kitchen seemed rather stark, underlining the absence of homeliness elsewhere. And yet Laura noticed that her companion went unhesitatingly to various drawers and cupboards. More for something to say than anything, she asked Rhona if she and her husband were old friends of Wolf Richardson.

Rhona turned from the cups she was setting out on saucers. Smiling, she shook her head. 'Tim never knew Wolf. Ours was a wartime marriage, in Kent where he was stationed. He was in the RAF – he was shot down . . .'

The words brought back Maurice's story so forcibly that Laura ceased listening. But suddenly Rhona had sensed this and was coming to take her by the arm.

'What's wrong?' she asked gently. 'Did that happen to somebody you were fond of as well?'

'Yes. Only Maurice survived. Or survived the plane crash.'

'So did Tim, actually,' Rhona told her, going to attend to the kettle. 'He died in a prison camp; ironically, of some gastric complaint.'

'I've never heard what happened to Maurice,' Laura began, and all at once the whole wretched business was spilling out. When she reached the present and how she couldn't accept not knowing the truth, she saw Rhona had remained motionless throughout, still holding the teapot.

'How awful for you, Laura. I suppose not having had the chance to marry Maurice was the reason no one's ever kept you informed. You haven't ever contacted the Air Ministry then?'

'Do you know, I've never even thought of that. Happen because of being so conscious that we weren't actually married.'

'I'm sure you weren't by any means the only ones. If you explained I think they'd tell you anything they might know. It's worth a try.'

It certainly is, thought Laura. And if only she could at last discover what had become of Maurice, this evening would not have been such a waste of time as it had seemed.

Chapter 26

For days after their visit to Wolf Richardson Patrick was restless and subdued. He also felt so angry because Beth had somehow been involved in the liaison that he almost wished he'd never attempted to learn the truth. The little that he had unearthed was of no real practical help, and if it seemed to confirm the supposition that his wife had taken to going around with someone else, the man's identity remained tantalisingly out of reach.

It could be anybody on this earth, he thought wearily. There wasn't a thing to link a specific person with Magda's death. And he himself was unlikely to dredge up any clue from memory. He had been so immersed in his business affairs during that period that he'd been away from home even more than normal, and thus had provided the pair with ample opportunity for pursuing their clandestine relationship.

If only I could forget, he thought for the thousandth time, put it all behind me. And begin again with Laura. Except that even yet he couldn't be sure that she would look at him. He'd been shaken to learn that she was writing to the Air Ministry. It seemed she still cherished some hope that Maurice Olivier was alive.

Viewed together or independently, both their lives certainly appeared to be in a mess. And he felt to have lost the energy which might have helped him to discover how they might provide a bit of support for each other.

Privately, he was also troubled by the prospect of Lindley's reopening for carpet manufacturing and Laura's inevitable withdrawal from the office here at Arncliffe. He'd asked Beth if she knew when that was on the cards, and hadn't enjoyed being told that Laura was looking forward to designing again in the near future.

It wasn't until a month or so had passed and Laura had indeed returned to the mill, that it occurred to Patrick that he had every reason to increase his contact with her. Once recalled, the idea of the carpet that Laura had called Yorkshire Gold was something to which he clung. He must at least enquire what kind of production would be taking priority, and remind her of the promise to design for his building society.

The day that he went across to the Coach House with this query was a Saturday in late November. Earlier that week they had had snow, which although a pleasant aspect out on the surrounding hills was reduced to grimy patches of ice nearer to home.

Laura smiled when she admitted him, and he followed cheerfully as she led the way into her living-room. He'd always liked the intimate atmosphere of this place which still resurrected memories of chatting with Jenny in the old days while Ted was busy at the farm. He missed his sister now, particularly since the end of the war had reduced his responsibilities so dramatically. Even the hospital wards were winding down, with the transfer of most of the patients to regular hospitals. Every last Land Army girl had long since departed, leaving only a small quantity of paperwork to be finalised.

'What's it like to be back on designing?' he asked as Laura took the armchair across from his own.

'Chaotic, as yet,' she exclaimed ruefully. 'But Roy's gradually getting some sort of production plan together.'

'Is he in sole charge now, what about his father?'

'Oh, he's still very much involved, but more on the financial side. And I gather there are some loose ends still, regarding the stuff they produced during the war. In fact, there's a lot of government stock in the warehouse over yonder. Folk keep grumbling that there'll be no room for our carpets when they come off the looms.'

'And what's the order situation – plenty of work?'

'From the way Roy talks, as much as we can handle. There was a backlog, of course, from when production ceased for the war. And from what I gather there's plenty of orders coming in from folk who were unable to get anything made these past few years.'

'Any chance of our London office carpet being produced?'

Laura smiled. 'You really want us to go ahead then? That's great! Of course, it's not for me to say, but I don't suppose they'll be turning down work. I'll have a word with Roy, he's the one who's responsible for all decisions on design now. We lost the head of our studio to one of our competitors. Not that I'm sorry, I never took to the man.'

There were masses of other people in the mill, however, whom Laura was delighted to be seeing again. Some were just once-familiar faces with whom she was glad to pass the time of day, others were old friends. Amos Kitchen had worked there throughout the war, glad to be given the opportunity to try his hand at more than the scouring process. And his wife was the first person Laura saw in the canteen, a very different woman now that her marriage to Amos had provided security and a cheerful home.

'My lad's coming back as soon as he's demobbed,' she was quick to tell Laura. 'Mr Roy's promised he'll be given a good chance to continue trying to better himself.'

And now with the news that Patrick was seriously considering making the order for a carpet a firm one, Laura felt delighted that she would have this link between her working life and him.

'If you like, I'll ask Roy to come over here so you can talk about your ideas with him,' she suggested.

'Is that necessary?' Patrick asked. 'From our earlier discussions I was confident that you were entirely in tune with my requirements.'

'I still think you'd better speak to Roy,' said Laura. Maybe because he was her brother-in-law, she didn't want him imagining she was taking too much upon herself.

'Okay then, fine,' Patrick agreed readily. And in the meantime he had something else in which he wished Laura to take an interest. He reminded her how he had kept the tapestries covered throughout the war years, protecting them from accidental damage while so many people were free to move about Arncliffe Hall. They had also needed preserving against any potential blast in the event of bombing.

'I'm going to unveil them any day now, and wondered if you would care to inspect them with me?'

Laura was happy to agree, and looked forward to going across to the main house on the evening they had chosen.

'You must have a meal with us as well. Father's always complaining he never sees you now that you're not working with me. And Beth is becoming really quite animated . . .'

The difference in her these days was the one thing which could lift Patrick out of the weariness induced by the unsatisfactory conclusion of investigations into Magda's death. As schools were reopening in their original buildings since the end of the war, he had begun enquiring about a possible solution to the difficulties that had resulted from Beth's long years of silence.

After some time he'd been rewarded with the name of a suitable school, and the head had been persuaded to accept Beth as a pupil. The staff seemed particularly adept at assessing their charges' abilities and shortcomings, with the result that Beth was already progressing in subjects like English and Mathematics, and was beginning to catch up in some of the others.

'She might never become an academic, as such,' he had told Laura. 'But she will be equipped to cope with normal life.'

'Has she any idea what she wants to do?'

For a moment, Patrick appeared embarrassed. 'Actually – well, she says she wants to be like you, and design carpets. Of course, it's early days yet.'

'Naturally, I'd do all I could to help. And she always has loved colour, and having a brush in her fingers.'

Beth seemed altogether happier these days, so much so that Laura privately hoped for her sake that nothing more would ever emerge concerning her mother's death. For her own sake, she was less certain what she hoped. Patrick clearly hadn't relegated that part of his life to the past. And yet, even though she hardly admitted it to herself, she couldn't help wishing that there was some way in which they might finally find happiness together.

Their common interests seemed very much to the fore when Laura went across to Patrick's home to examine the tapestries with him. Although cool and wintry, the day was bright and the afternoon sun gleamed into the long gallery.

'As you see, I've uncovered the first of the tapestries,' he began. 'I couldn't even wait till you arrived. From the quick look which is all I've had time for so far, it seems unharmed by remaining covered for so long. I'm glad now that I took expert advice on ensuring they were preserved.'

After examining the work close to and then standing back to admire the overall effect, Laura nodded her approval. 'That certainly looks fine to me.'

Together they moved on to unveil the next tapestry, and then the one after it, all the way along the wall. With each they experienced a rush of excitement as they found it as beautiful as they remembered.

'I often consider they're more satisfying than paintings, you know,' Patrick remarked as they finally gazed along the whole length of the gallery. 'There must be more skill required, surely, to create something of such colour and expression by incorporating yarns?'

His words made Laura think – not only of the obvious connection between her own work and tapestry, but about Patrick himself and how very much she wished to discover more of this side of him which so often appeared submerged and shut away.

The thought of perhaps establishing a more satisfactory relationship with Patrick returned more forcibly to Laura on the day just before Christmas when she at last received a reply from the Ministry concerning Maurice.

She recognised the letter at once by its formal envelope and paused for several seconds before picking it up from the doormat. There was other correspondence as well on that Saturday morning and she opened those letters first and read them before even slitting the envelope of the one about Maurice.

As soon as she read that they regretted the need to convey the result of their investigation, Laura had to steel herself to read through to the end. The news was much as she had feared since those first early days following Maurice's departure. They had succeeded in discovering that he had set out, as intended, for his home in Jersey. But they had only discovered this because the tiny boat in which friends had tried to bring Maurice ashore there had been intercepted by a German patrol vessel. Together with his companions, Maurice had been shot. It was from the disc he was wearing and documents he carried that his identity was established and the War Department informed.

They added that they were pleased to tell her that his mother had survived the war and was now living near St Helier. If Miss Crabtree wished to communicate with her, they would be happy to forward any correspondence.

Laura would need to think about that one. She was more shaken than she'd expected by having Maurice's death confirmed. She couldn't at present see that any purpose would be served by contacting Mrs Olivier. The old lady should have learned by now to come to terms with his loss, and could quite easily be distressed by having another reminder that, for her, this peace must be tinged with regrets. And for herself Laura could only think that she would do better to leave matters as they stood. She had loved Maurice, deeply and sincerely, but could not continue to mourn him for the rest of her life.

Now that I know for sure, she decided, I'm going to put Maurice out of my mind for a while. This first peacetime Christmas was upon them, and mustn't be marred by too many backward glances. Her mother and Greta and Sybil were coming to Halfield for the holiday period. The triplets were to be all together in Roy and Netta's home, while Maggie Crabtree was to stay in the Coach House.

Netta's third child, Margaret, had been born in early December and Netta herself had recovered swiftly with the prospect of family celebrations in store.

Preparing the spare room for her mother, Laura couldn't help being rather amused by her own delighted anticipation. It wasn't that long ago that she'd have done anything rather than encourage Maggie to stay here. She was glad of the changes which had ensured that they got along so much better these days, just as she was thankful that her mother was viewing the future with such active enthusiasm.

One of the nicest things that occurred, however, concerned Beth rather than Laura's own family. Having all spent the whole of Christmas Day at Roy and Netta's and had lunch on Boxing Day at Lindley Lodge, Laura was preparing tea for everyone in her home when Beth arrived.

'I know you're busy, Laura, and Daddy says I mustn't stay long, but I must thank you for the set of paintbrushes – they're super! And I couldn't wait to show you this.'

Beth stood quite still, holding out for inspection the heavy gold locket suspended from her neck on a thick chain. 'Daddy gave me this,' she exclaimed, her blue eyes shining. 'It was Mother's, you see. I'm to wear it a lot, he says, but while remembering her I've got to stop feeling sad about her. He and I have started planning to be happy in the future.'

Thank goodness those two are really communicating at last, thought Laura, and what a good time to make such a resolution. Admiring the locket, she saw how beautifully engraved it was.

'And has it got photos of your parents inside?' she asked, expecting to be shown.

Beth shook her head. 'Don't know, I'm afraid. It has a tiny little lock, you see – here, in the engraving. We can't find the key.'

'She's a nice girl,' Maggie Crabtree remarked after Beth had left. 'And you say she's the one who lost her mother so tragically?'

'That's right. Any road, it sounds now as if both she and her father are picking up again. I'm ever so relieved. They're lovely people, and have had such a lot of trouble, they deserve happier times at last.'

When her sisters arrived shortly afterwards with baby Margaret, Petra and Kevin, Laura was surprised that Roy wasn't with them.

'What's wrong?' she asked Netta at once. 'Where is he?'

Netta smiled back unconcernedly. 'Don't look so worried. It's only that Roy's over-eaten already. He said to tell you he was sorry but he couldn't face another meal.'

'But he could have come, anyway. I wouldn't have minded if he didn't eat owt. He hardly ever comes here, as it is,' Laura added. And thought then that she couldn't, in fact, recall one occasion when Roy had accepted an invitation to the Coach House. And he hadn't taken up the suggestion that he should come over to discuss the carpet that Patrick had had in mind since before the war.

During the course of the meal and afterwards, however, there was so much chatter between the triplets and so much fussing over the baby and Petra and Kevin, that Laura began to feel the occasion was quite animated enough, no matter who was absent.

She watched her mother, watching the other three and the kids, and realised that Maggie had acquired the ability to enjoy her family. It was unfortunate that in the past she had allowed her life to be dominated by so much stress, but she was compensating now in good measure.

The first few days back at work helped Laura to overcome the regret that she'd experienced when the time came for Greta, Sybil and their mother to return to the east coast. The Coach House had felt very empty in the stillness after they had left, but Laura had immediately busied herself tidying the place. She had then felt justified in looking out the design which she had begun for Patrick's carpet.

'Yorkshire Gold,' she murmured to herself, examining the

details, then leaning back in her chair to test the colour combination and overall effect. Tomorrow at the mill she would show this to Roy, try again to persuade him to meet Patrick so that a firm order might be given them.

To Laura's astonishment, he felt no such meeting was necessary. 'Look, love, you can do all that's needed yourself,' he told her. 'Find out exact specifications – the area of carpeting he has in mind. He must have a record somewhere of the dimensions of their floor space. For their London head office, did you say?'

'That's right. I think he believes they should have something better there than linoleum or wooden flooring or whatever . . .'

'Well, this design of yours looks just the thing to me. Get him to approve the shades, and your interpretation of their cypher, exactly. Once the size is confirmed we can begin planning production. With a one-off like this, at least we have only the one client to satisfy. Should be far easier than having to consider what would please a wide range of folk if a carpet's to be offered in the shops.'

Laura made a point of seeing Patrick that evening, taking with her the latest version of her design.

'I'll have someone calculate the exact area of the floor to be covered,' he told her quickly, smiling as though he was almost as delighted as Laura herself that the carpet could go ahead.

'Do I take it that your people will then work out the quantity of carpet required?' he asked eventually, walking with her to the door.

'That's right. We have someone who's a genius at such calculations, and providing advice to the fitters later as to the best way of laying the finished carpet.'

'All very interesting. If not before, I must ensure when it's finally in place that you have a trip to London with me to inspect.'

With that prospect to look forward to, Laura worked harder than ever, transferring the building society design on to point paper at home so that the job wouldn't be neglected whilst she worked in the studio on patterns already in hand.

The confidence which both Patrick and Roy had in her ability made her feel that she would work day and night if need be to prove she could tackle everything they expected. She was finding life at the mill more enjoyable than ever in the past, and realised that the war years hadn't entirely been wasted. Coping with such a lot of very different work had made her mature enough to speak up for herself. And maybe, she reflected, had produced a self-confidence that meant she could prove she was adequate without saying one word.

Once again, Laura was spending so much time on designing that she rarely saw anyone unconnected with work. She was glad now that having Roy for a brother-in-law enabled her to check regularly that Netta and the children were all right.

Although her sister seemed quite capable, these days, Laura still had her old feelings of responsibility for Netta.

Beyond her own family and those in the immediate neighbourhood of Arncliffe Hall, the only person who gave her much concern was Mavis Priestley. Now that the AFS was being disbanded Laura was very much afraid that her old friend would miss her work and the company there quite terribly.

Towards the end of January Laura set aside a Saturday afternoon for calling on Mavis. With each week that passed the mill was getting busier, and she knew that when a production date was set for the Yorkshire Gold carpet her work would be even more time-consuming.

'Bien-être' looked just as neat as ever from the outside as Laura approached, although her long absence seemed to have made the whole terrace of houses appear much smaller. The smell from the toffee works was overwhelming, and the clattering of machinery that emerged indicated that, despite the continuation of sweet rationing, they were in full production.

Feeling glad that she had found a home away from here in the hills surrounding the town, Laura nevertheless knocked on her friend's door with a rush of anticipation.

Mavis came bustling downstairs and admitted her with a grin that seemed to say that Laura's anticipation was justified.

'Eh, love – come on in. I've got such a lot to tell you. Go on through, you know where my sitting-room is.'

Even before Laura had taken the proffered chair, Mavis was hurrying on again excitedly. 'I were busy upstairs clearing out drawers and cupboards.'

Laura smiled. 'Yes, well – there's always plenty of tidying up to do, isn't there?'

'Oh, this is a bit more than that. I'll be leaving here afore long.'

'Will you? I hope you're not going too far, I'd miss you.'

'Eh, bless you, love, no. I'll nobbut be a few streets away. What do you think – I'm getting wed! Just fancy, me, at my age . . .!'

'Do tell me all about it. Come along, sit yourself down.'

'Well, I was going to put the kettle on first, but happen I'll just put you in the picture beforehand. Gerald was in charge of our station in the AFS. A right grand chap, he is. Been a widower for years. We'd been quite good pals all through the war, then t'other week when everything was being wound down we got talking. We both said how we were going to miss the company, like. Him and his brother run a little business – a tannery. I gather Gerald doesn't see that many folk through his work.'

Mavis went on to recount how she and Gerald had begun going to the theatre in Halfield together, and had decided before long that they were so well suited that keeping two homes going was pointless.

'I'm not saying it's a big romance,' she added. 'But some of them don't turn out as good as folk think. We're simply planning to fit in around each other, as you might say.'

On the way home that evening Laura decided that the kind of relationship Mavis and her fiancé planned sounded very good. Happen that was the kind of thing she herself would settle for in another few years. I must be getting old, she reflected ruefully. Resigning herself to accepting a relationship based on less than being in love wasn't something she would have contemplated years ago.

By the time Laura's designs for the Yorkshire Gold carpet had been approved and transferred on to the Jacquard system she was even busier than she had anticipated, and scarcely able to find time to plan meals for herself, much less think about anybody else.

She was particularly pleased that her old friend Dennis Jagger, recently returned from a German prisoner-of-war camp, was to be in charge of its weaving.

'I'll never forget how much you taught me all those years ago,' she told him. 'I couldn't have chosen anybody better if Roy'd asked me who I wanted to tackle this.'

Dennis laughed. 'Nay, Laura, you want to hang on a bit afore you go making rash statements like that. You'll have to wait and see if I'm any good now at weaving!'

The initial sample, though, was beautiful. Laura felt her breath catch in her throat when she was shown the first few feet of the carpet. The shade of gold she had selected for the background was so rich and further enhanced by the depth of pile which made it look like velvet. Each large white Yorkshire rose had petals outlined in the slightly deeper gold that also embellished the building society cypher.

'Gosh, I am pleased with that!' she exclaimed to the weaver. 'Thanks ever so much, love.'

Both Roy and his father were equally delighted. Robert Lindley made a point of congratulating Laura on her work, and on securing the contract for them.

'If you weren't such a damned fine designer, I'd be encouraging you to join our sales force! Seriously, we are aware of how outstanding your work is. We'll always make sure you're given something interesting to tackle.'

For the present, though, all Laura wanted was to be able to show this sample to Patrick. As soon as enough had been woven, she was given a piece to take home to Arncliffe.

She rang Patrick that evening at around seven-thirty, by which time she believed he would have finished dinner. She herself had been unable to eat. Thrilled though she was by the carpet, she had developed a sudden dread that Patrick might not approve it.

'Let's have a look then,' he prompted her as soon as she arrived at his door with the sample roll beneath her arm.

'Don't you want to go into one of the other rooms?' she asked, looking about her in the ballroom where beyond the windows the spring sky was darkening.

'I didn't think you'd wait that long!' he exclaimed with a smile, and went to switch on a nearby wall-light.

'Just a minute,' said Laura, noticing the red lampshades. 'We really shan't get the true colours in here.'

They went through to the adjacent room where Patrick turned on every light while Laura knelt down to unroll the Yorkshire Gold sample.

'That is superb, Laura!' His exclamation was too instantaneous to be anything but heart-felt.

Laura smiled up at him and her eyes filled in undiluted happiness. 'Thank goodness you like it.'

'Like it? That *is* an understatement.'

Patrick came to kneel beside her, inspecting the pile at close quarters, running his fingers into its luxurious depth. And then he rose slowly and assisted her to her feet, all the while gazing down at the carpet she had designed for him.

Laura felt his arm go about her shoulders, squeezing them. 'A grand job, my dear. I couldn't have imagined anything half as lovely. I just can't wait now to see it completed.'

She grinned sideways at him. 'You'll have quite a wait for that, I'm afraid. It's one of the biggest orders of a special design that Lindley's have ever done. Oh – that reminds me, both Roy and his father Robert said I was to tell you they are delighted you entrusted the order to our firm.'

'And I must speak to them. Right away. I'm going to phone and assure them of my complete satisfaction. Shan't be long. Why don't you go and chat to Beth, she's around some-where . . .'

Beth had heard and, as her father hurried away to the

telephone, opened a door further along the corridor and called to Laura.

'Hallo, I'm glad you're here. Got something I'm dying to show you.'

'Hallo, love,' said Laura, going into the room. 'What've you got there then?'

Rushing back to the table, Beth sat down and motioned Laura to take the chair next to hers.

'Daddy's just given me this, it's Mother's jewellery. Not the best bits that she had, most of those were sold or something. But there's lots here. These are the things I've tried on already.' Several necklaces and a brooch plus several pairs of earrings were placed to one side of the open box.

Beth was rummaging through the rest of its contents. 'There are some sparkly buttons that I want to stitch on a frock, but I need six and I can only find five. And there's a ring with a blue stone that'll exactly match my best blouse . . .'

Smiling, Laura watched while Beth prodded around in the box, moving aside the items that she hadn't yet examined. It would have been far quicker to tip everything out on to the table, but this way seemed more fun.

'Gosh!' Beth exclaimed suddenly. 'Here's a key. I wonder if . . .' She struggled to unfasten the gold locket that she was wearing, then gingerly tried the key in the minute lock. 'Got to be careful. If it's the wrong one it could damage it.'

The key, however, was turning. All at once, though, Beth was overawed by what was happening. She hesitated before opening the locket. 'There should be a picture of Mother,' she said breathlessly.

'Or perhaps a lock of hair,' added Laura, almost as excited as the girl herself.

Very slowly, Beth released the locket catch and gazed inside. 'That's not her hair,' she gasped, disappointed. 'It was always as fair as mine, and look . . .'

She drew strands of her own long hair across the lock inserted beneath the tiny oval of glass. The hair framed there was several shades darker, more golden than blonde.

'Never mind,' said Laura. 'Let's see the photograph – is that her, or your father?'

'No,' said Beth dismally. 'It isn't either of them. I don't know who he is. If I've ever seen him it's such a long time ago I can't remember.'

'Perhaps your father will know. Let's have a look though I don't suppose I'll be any use, I haven't lived round here long enough.'

Laura glanced at the photograph, then examined it more carefully. Shaken, she only just managed to contain her gasp of astonishment. She swallowed, trying to regain composure, and heard someone enter the room behind her.

'I spoke to Robert Lindley. He's glad I'm so pleased with the sample of carpet,' Patrick said evenly. 'What have you got there?'

'It's the locket, Daddy – we found its key. But we don't know whose picture this is.'

'Nor do I,' he said grimly after a brief inspection. All his good humour had drained away.

Laura felt sympathy for him surging through her. He must have realised the man depicted was likely to be the person who had supplanted him in his wife's affection. The way that he turned from it seemed to suggest that the photograph was of no one he recognised.

I wish to goodness I could say the same, thought Laura, and heard herself making excuses about having to get back home. She needed to recover, and most of all needed to think. Disturbed and terribly confused, she certainly couldn't remain here while all she could wonder was why on earth her brother-in-law's photograph should be in Magda Horsfall's locket.

Chapter 27

The telephone was ringing, rousing her from the sleep into which she had fallen only an hour or so ago. Sighing, Laura dragged herself out of bed and, almost staggering with weariness, hurried downstairs.

'It's only me, Laura – Mavis. I forgot to say when you were here, the banns are being called on Sunday. I thought you might like to be there. Then you could have a spot of dinner with us, meet Gerald . . .'

'I'd love to,' said Laura. 'But I'm not sure if I can manage Sunday. I'll let you know.'

'Okay then, love. I say, Laura – are you all right?'

She tried to reassure her friend. 'Fine, thanks, don't worry. It's just that I had a bit of a bad night.'

That was quite some understatement, she thought, heading for the kitchen. It had felt like the worst night of her life. She'd been distressed often enough in the past. When her dad was lost at sea. After Maurice had left for Jersey. Around the time Magda's body was found. Nothing that had happened previously, though, had placed her in such an appalling dilemma.

If she told Patrick that she knew the identity of the man whose picture had been placed in his wife's locket, that would invite the inevitable conclusion that Roy had been Magda's lover. The likelihood was that Patrick would realise, as she herself had, that Roy could have been involved in Magda's death. Patrick would go to the police. Roy would, at the very least, have to face an interrogation.

And Roy was Netta's dearly loved husband, the father of

their new baby and of another daughter and of Kevin who had brought so much joy to their marriage. They were her own nieces and nephew, her mother's first grandchildren. How could she do this to her sister, how do it to them all? There were the Lindleys to consider as well – Robert, who had demonstrated his faith in her ability from the start and who with his wife had always been kindness itself to her.

All night long Laura had weighed each possible action, and now with daylight increasing beyond the surrounding hills she seemed further than ever from reaching any conclusion. Revealing what she knew would destroy the lives of so many people. People whom she loved, people who relied on her. Even if Roy were questioned and proved innocent, the damage would still be great. And she knew in her heart it was possible he could have been involved with Magda.

If she confided the truth to no one, who would be harmed? Patrick and Beth both appeared to have accepted that Magda had died at the hand of someone unknown. It might even prove better for Patrick if nothing further occurred now to resurrect the hatred he naturally had felt towards that person. He and Beth would live with the mystery unsolved, live this life that they were already reconstructing. He was beginning to enjoy having a daughter. Beth was growing increasingly well-adjusted. Following this discovery, however, Laura couldn't picture herself taking much part in their lives ever again; she would be too preoccupied with the necessity of guarding her tongue. Only so long as she kept silent would Netta and the rest of them continue oblivious of Roy's connection with the Horsfall family.

How though, Laura thought bleakly, could she exist quietly alongside Netta's in-laws while acutely aware of this association? How assume any sort of normal behaviour while all the time harbouring such grave suppositions about Roy? How might she go daily to the mill, to work with him, and display no hint of the dreadful assumption that she had reached?

Unable to face anyone that day, Laura telephoned the mill. When Roy answered at the other end, she felt agitation increasing her heart-rate and pounding in her ears.

'I'm sorry, I'm not very well. I shan't be in today, though I'll be all right tomorrow,' she said in a rush.

'Nothing serious, I hope?' Roy asked genially. He didn't seem to expect a reply which made Laura thankful. 'I daresay you've been overdoing things,' he added. 'Don't worry about taking time off, I can't remember your ever doing so before.'

He had sounded so sympathetic, so nice, that she now felt even worse than earlier. How could she even contemplate revealing what she knew?

Laura spent a wretched day. Despite feeling empty – yesterday, excited about the carpet, she had hardly eaten – she found now that she couldn't face a proper meal. Somewhere around mid-morning it started to rain and a strong wind arose to moan about the Coach House and lash the downpour against its windows. Feeling she was trapped here with this terrible quandary, she stared out through the rivulets coursing down the glass.

The distant moors, together with some of the nearer hilltops, were virtually obliterated, increasing Laura's feeling of isolation. On one side she could see little more than that solitary dead tree as it bent before the wind. Watching it being battered, Laura felt she was equally fiercely beset. And she was just as alone as she struggled to think clearly.

The wind had blown itself out and the rain had settled to a steady drizzle by early evening when she finally acknowledged to herself that all along there really had been only one decision that she could make.

Her ears were straining for the sound of a car. By the time that Patrick had placed it in the garage and walked the short distance to the main entrance of Arncliffe Hall, Laura was waiting there.

'Laura, what's wrong?' he enquired, pausing before inserting his key in the lock.

'Can I talk to you? It's very important.'

'Come on in.' He stood aside to let her precede him then extended a hand indicating the door to their left even before he'd closed the front door after them.

'Take a seat,' he said, offering her a chair and then putting aside the briefcase and newspaper that he was carrying. 'Now, what is it?'

'You know yesterday, when we were looking at that locket with Beth?'

Patrick nodded. Already his expression had set grimly.

Laura sighed. 'Happen I ought to have said something then, but I was so upset. Confused. You see, I know who it is. The man in that photograph. God, this is so awful . . .'

'Take your time, Laura,' he said in concern.

She shook her head. 'No, I've got to get this over with. It's – it's Roy Lindley.'

'Belonging the carpet mill, you mean? Your boss?'

Laura swallowed. 'One of them, yes, the son. But that isn't the worst. Have you forgotten? It's Roy who's married to our Netta.'

'Oh, Lord . . .'

'Terrible, isn't it?' Laura exclaimed, although now that her mind was made up and she had begun revealing the truth she felt slightly better. 'I couldn't not tell you,' she added.

'I certainly appreciate how difficult the decision must have been. You must have seen already that I shall be compelled to mention this to the police.'

'I've thought of nothing else since yesterday. And Roy will need a damned good story if they're to dissociate him from Magda's death.'

'I'm afraid so. It's a connection we've both assumed immediately. I believe the police always suspect those in closest contact with a murder victim.'

'Quite. And even if it should turn out nothing can be proved against Roy, his being accused will do a lot of damage.'

For several minutes neither of them said anything. Eventually, Patrick sighed as he began speaking again.

'Lord knows, I've wanted nothing more than getting to the truth about Magda's killer, but suddenly I can't helping feeling that I'd do anything to avoid shattering even more lives by speaking up. How will your sister cope, Laura? She's only a slip of girl . . .'

'Netta's grown up a bit since the time she was living here with me, but I can't pretend she'll accept a blow like that without going to pieces. Still – I only told you because I'm sure it's right that Roy should at least be questioned.'

'And you are one hundred per cent certain of the man's identity?'

Laura nodded. 'It isn't only the photo, there's that lock of hair as well.'

'You don't wish me to get the locket now so you may take another look?'

'I will if you like. But I really have no doubts at all.'

Patrick fetched the locket nevertheless, and the tiny key which had revealed this shattering fact to them.

'Yes, it's Roy. That's exactly how he looked when I first met him.' After a moment she glanced towards Patrick, her anxiety increasing. 'Will you phone the police, please? I can't bring myself to do it.'

'Of course,' he said gently. 'You've done all you should by telling me. They will want to question you, though.'

'I'm prepared for that. I don't suppose there's many possible consequences that I haven't considered.'

'Do you want to remain here and see them with me? Or I could bring them round to the Coach House when they arrive . . .'

'Would you mind?'

'Just wherever you'll feel more comfortable. It might be best, anyway, to have any discussion there. Keep Beth out of it as long as we can.'

Laura had barely settled at her kitchen table with a cup of tea when Patrick knocked on the front door.

'This is Chief Inspector Muggeridge and Detective Sergeant Wilson,' he said, introducing them to Laura before she led the way through to the living-room.

The chief inspector began by thanking her for passing on the information. 'Mr Horsfall has explained the relationship between your sister and the person you identify as appearing in this photograph. In consideration of the delicate nature of your situation in this, we shall try to spare you a confrontation with the man.'

Laura nodded. 'Thanks,' she said, but was unable to smile.

'As you will appreciate, however,' he continued swiftly, 'some proof of identification will become necessary should the gentleman in question refuse to admit to any involvement with the late Mrs Horsfall.'

'I know nothing about this is going to be easy,' said Laura. 'I'll do whatever has to be done, just to have everything settled as quickly as possible.'

'Much the best for all concerned,' said Chief Inspector Muggeridge.

The sergeant opened his notebook as the questioning began. First of all they wanted to know how long she had known Roy Lindley, and how well acquainted they were.

'I began working for Roy and his father in 1937. Except for the interval during the war years when carpet production ceased, I've worked there ever since.'

'And did you meet the Lindleys through your sister perhaps?'

'No – quite the reverse. Netta came to stay with me for a while and was given a temporary job at Lindley's. She and Roy got married before the war.'

'So we can assume then that nothing in his behaviour since you've known him could have any bearing on his having had a relationship with Mrs Horsfall,' the chief inspector murmured. 'We're pretty sure she'd been dead for a year or two before your arrival on the scene.'

'Yes,' Laura agreed, thankful that at least she couldn't be called upon to witness to anything that might have occurred during those crucial years.

The officers had begun speaking in more general terms of their impending approach to Roy, and the probability of his being required to appear initially before the magistrates court. Laura had started to feel relieved that the worst of her part in all this seemed to be ending when Muggeridge spoke again.

'Before we reach that stage, I'd like you to tell me in confidence, Miss Crabtree, what your own impression of Roy Lindley has been.'

'He's good at his job. He's made my sister happy since the day he met her.'

'And his attitude to other women, have you always found that – well, proper?'

When Laura hesitated to reply the two officers exchanged a glance. Quelling a sigh, she swallowed. At least she hadn't said anything about the way Roy had behaved towards herself in those early days. And if she wished the question unasked and the conclusions reached from her silence less obvious, there was nothing she could do to erase the officers' opinions.

To her relief, Chief Inspector Muggeridge nodded as if satisfied that nothing further could be gained from questioning her at this stage. He and his sergeant departed in the direction of the main building where they had indicated Patrick would be asked to confirm details of the statements he'd already given.

Sickened by the part she'd been obliged to play, Laura was still sitting near the fire in her darkening room when Patrick returned.

'I had to come over,' he said, 'see you were okay. Quite an ordeal for you, wasn't it?'

'And for you, surely?'

He nodded. 'I'm used to it by now.'

'But it's raking it up again, and will do even more so if . . .'

Patrick interrupted her. 'Whoever was proved responsible, that would be the case. Or to some degree maybe even if no one were charged it could prove less easy finally to let the matter rest. I just can't help wishing now that Lindley might be able to prove there was no involvement – for your sake and your family's.'

'Thanks. Trouble is – well, I wouldn't have told them, but Roy used to be a terrible ladies' man. He tried it on with me till I made it plain that it cut no ice. You won't let on about that, will you, Patrick?' she added, already regretting her impulse to tell him the truth. 'I've done enough already to make things bad for him.'

'I shan't give a hint. After all, something like that's merely hearsay now. No use in obtaining a conviction. And there are plenty of men who could be said to have an eye for the ladies.'

'I only wish Roy wasn't one of them.'

'There's one thing, Laura – if that's the way he's always been, there'll be lots of people besides you around Halfield who are aware of the fact.'

True though that might be, it made Laura feel no better. Even if other folk went so far as to prove what Roy had been like with women, that would only spare her conscience at the expense of worsening things for Netta.

They talked for a while longer, speculating about how likely it was that the police might feel they had enough on Roy to arrest him, and eventually both Laura herself and Patrick concluded that they would not have enough to make a case.

By the time Patrick went back again to the Hall, Laura felt she was nearly asleep on her feet. But for the second consecutive night as soon as she got into bed she began struggling with her overactive mind which refused to let her rest.

Dismally, she watched daylight increasing within her room the following morning. Today, she would have to force herself to go over to the mill. She must then try, somehow, to behave normally with her brother-in-law. How on earth she might manage that while feeling so utterly drained, she could not imagine.

Laura was drinking a cup of coffee in the hope that it might revive her more than tea when the telephone rang. I bet that's Patrick, she thought. He had seemed very concerned about her last night.

'Netta?' she gasped as soon as she recognised her sister's voice. Her heart began thudding within her chest. It couldn't have started already, could it?

'It's Roy – something awful's happened,' Netta gabbled breathlessly.

Laura realised that her sister seemed to be weeping. And

what the cause of her distress would be.

Netta was shrieking into her ear: 'Oh, Laura – the police have taken him away. They've been here half the night. Summat to do with that body they found ages ago.'

'Eh, love, I am sorry. But what did the police say?'

'Not so much in front of me, especially when they checked that I hadn't even been living here at the time the reservoir was built and wouldn't know anything. They took him off into another room. All I discovered was what Roy told me. When they allowed him five minutes to get his things together. He – he just said it was all a dreadful mistake. That he hardly knew the woman. But they've arrested him, Laura. I don't understand. And I'm that scared!'

'All right, love, all right. I'll get there as fast as I can. The buses should be running by now.'

Laura threw on some clothes and found her handbag then went rushing down the drive to the bus stop. All the way into Halfield and out again to her sister's, she sat wrestling with her thoughts. How could she tell what she ought to do when she got there?

Her lovely dark hair awry and her blue eyes wide with shock, Netta greeted her at the door.

'Thank God you've come – oh, thank God! I don't know whatever to do, you see . . .'

'Nor do I, love, really. But we'll have a good think. What time did you say they took Roy away?'

'Just before I rang you.'

'Has he arranged for his solicitor to be with him?'

'I don't know. They just took him. It must be a mistake, Laura, mustn't it? It can't really be to do with that body they found, can it? Not my Roy?'

Laura would never bring herself to tell Netta that she knew full well that there had been a connection between Roy and Magda Horsfall. But she needed to discover how much the police had learned since leaving Arncliffe. 'Now tell me again, love – what exactly did Roy say to you?'

'That he did know this person whoever she was, but he'd

never known her well. And that I wasn't to worry, he'd soon sort it out. Only . . .'

'Yes?' Laura prompted. Her sister's anxious face revealed that she was far from convinced that Roy would be able to sort things.

Netta gulped, sank on to the settee and scrubbed at her eyes with a saturated ball of handkerchief. 'He was that upset, Laura. I've never seen anybody look so shaken. As if the bottom had dropped out of his world. Yet if he has nowt to worry about with the police he shouldn't be so perturbed, should he? He'd just clear it up, like he said, then come home. And it'd be all right again. Nothing's altered here, we're still here waiting for him, me and the children . . .'

Out in the hall a clock chimed, reminding Laura that she would have to tell somebody she wouldn't be at the mill again today. And then she remembered the appalling fact that it was not only Roy but his father who ran the carpet factory. What would having his son arrested do to Robert Lindley and his wife?

'Did anybody let Roy's mum and dad know what was happening?' she asked gently.

'I don't think so – unless they rang them from the other room.'

Or from the station, thought Laura, but decided it was best not to keep talking about where Roy was.

'I'll speak to his father, if you like,' she volunteered. She felt she owed so much now to Netta, to all the Lindleys, that she'd never be able to do enough to compensate.

It was Inez who answered, her voice so strained that Laura knew immediately that she had been informed of Roy's arrest. 'Oh, it's you, Laura. Has Netta told you?'

'About Roy? Yes. I can't tell you how sorry I am . . .'

'It's been such a shock. Dreadful. I was just thinking about Netta and the children, whether to bring them over here . . .'

'I'm with her now. Do you want me to get her?'

'How is she?'

'Shattered, naturally.'

'Tell you what – don't bother her just now. Can you stay there for a while?'

'I was going to. I'm afraid I didn't feel up to going to work, anyway.'

'No – well, I don't suppose Robert will make it, either, certainly not this morning. If Roy's taken before the magistrates, he will be there to stand by him.'

'Oh, they can't have got as far as that, surely?'

Inez sighed. 'Something's convinced the police that Roy had some connection with that poor woman. None of it makes any sense to me, though. It's all so totally out of the blue. I mean – whatever could there be to link him with – with her death?'

Laura gulped, willed herself to contain the words that would reveal her own involvement in Roy's arrest. If the Lindleys started to blame her for any of this, that might also turn them against Netta. And the poor lass was going to need all the support she could get from everybody.

'They questioned us, you know, late last night,' Inez went on. 'I couldn't see the point of it, all about Prince – a dog we had long before the war. Asking all sorts of daft questions, like what became of him.'

'And what did happen to him?' Laura enquired, wondering for a moment why that should be significant.

'We had to have him put down. He'd gone missing, slipped the leash or some such and ran off. You know the way they do. When he eventually turned up again here he was in a bad way, emaciated, and he'd been hit by a car.'

Laura felt that Inez was rambling on about the dog to avoid facing Roy's arrest. She let her talk, was glad to be relieved of the need to say very much herself.

The conversation ended with Inez promising to let them know as soon as she had any news. 'I'll probably be round there later on, but I wanted to hang on here in case Robert tries to get hold of me.'

When Laura replaced the receiver she could hear both the baby and Petra crying somewhere upstairs. It would only be a matter of time before Kevin came down to ask what was wrong. Netta was still on the settee, looking so dazed that Laura could believe she was oblivious to their cries.

Laura crossed to her and gave her shoulder a gentle shake. 'Come on, love, the kids have to be seen to,' she said, and was thankful that they were there to give her sister something to do.

When Inez arrived it was late afternoon and she had her husband with her. The pair of them looked to have aged by at least ten years.

'Try not to worry, love,' Robert told Netta at once. 'Roy will have the best lawyer I can find.'

He went on to tell them that Roy was still being questioned by the police who expected that he would appear before the magistrates next day. He himself had no idea how or why they believed his son could have been implicated in Magda Horsfall's death. He added that he could only hope that someone would soon come to the conclusion that this had all been a terrible mistake.

That night he and his wife insisted on taking Netta and the children home to Lindley Lodge. Although glad that her sister was being cared for, Laura felt very keenly this removal of the opportunity to do anything for her.

Arriving back at the Coach House, she glanced all around her, shivering, feeling isolated again with this turmoil into which she had been plunged.

After waiting until she felt certain Patrick would have eaten his evening meal, she rang him.

He told her at once that he had some news. 'Can you come over here? We'll be free to talk. Beth's out until nine o'clock. She's finally making friends at that school of hers.'

Patrick greeted her with concern as soon as he opened the door. 'Laura? You look rough – because of your sister?'

'I suppose so, mainly. I've been with her most of today. You do know Roy's been arrested?'

He nodded as they went through to the sitting-room where

he offered her a chair. 'And that the police are convinced they have a case against him. A lot of it's circumstantial, but they think there are signs that he will crack.'

When Laura swallowed, Patrick sighed. 'I know this is dreadful for you, but the good news is that there's more than that locket to link Lindley with the murder. The chief inspector made no secret of it when we spoke earlier today. You may not recall, but there was a dog lead buried with Magda. It was quite well preserved – certainly that was the way it looked originally when they asked me if I could identify it. I told them we'd never kept a dog. Anyway, it transpires that the lead was covered in fingerprints, most of them identifiable as Lindley's.'

'But they can't convict on that alone, surely? Anybody could have got hold of that lead, have used it to . . .'

'Then there's the photo and Beth's account of the "uncle" whom her mother used to see – a man of similar colouring to him.'

'Is Beth being called to give evidence?'

'If it can't be avoided. To date, Muggeridge has talked to her. Very gently, I'm glad to say.' Seeing Laura's expression, Patrick nodded again. 'I was horrified, too. But, so far, she's standing up to it very well. I explained to her, of course, that we must do all we can, not only to find her mother's killer but to prevent anyone else being harmed.'

'Beth – Beth didn't witness it all, did she?' Laura asked, suddenly realising the whole business might be even more dreadful than they had supposed.

Patrick shook his head. 'Not according to what she's said. Her version is that they were setting out to walk, but then her mother and – and this man she refers to as "Uncle" began arguing. They hadn't even reached the boundary of the estate, and Beth was told to wait there and play.' He paused. 'That seems to tie in with the way that she was found wandering the grounds.'

'But if she'd seen nothing, why was she so distraught? In such a state that she didn't even speak again for years?'

Patrick seemed about to say something, but then his lips

stiffened into a grim line and his eyes became veiled.

Laura sighed. 'Oh, it's all such a mess! Hateful. There's nothing I can do, either, for anybody. Robert and Inez Lindley have taken Netta and the kids to stay with them.'

'Best for all concerned, surely? Inez'll be there to keep an eye on them, whereas you will be at work during the day.'

'I shall have to be from tomorrow. I didn't make it today, again. I meant to ask Roy's father what was happening at the mill, but it was the last thing on my mind.'

'I'm sure. Still, it'll do you good to have something else to think about.'

'If I can concentrate at all. I haven't slept for two nights. As soon as I'm on my own I begin mulling everything over.'

'Then don't go off to the Coach House. Or only to fetch the things you'll need. Mrs Harrison always has at least one spare room ready. I was going to fix myself a stiff drink. It wouldn't do you any harm to try one.'

Laura was tempted to agree. She and Patrick seemed to have become closer through the events of the past couple of days. Her old original feeling of being drawn to him had certainly returned.

When she didn't reply at once he persisted. 'You look all in, my dear. You might allow me to do a little to show my concern. After all, it's entirely through involvement with us that you've been dragged into this trouble.'

Beth came in while they were talking and went straight to Laura to kiss her. 'Lovely to see you, Laura. You don't spend enough time over here since you went back to working at the mill.'

Her father smiled. 'Matter of fact, I was just trying to persuade Laura to spend the night here. Don't like to think of her on her own with being in the thick of all this.'

'Oh, you must stay,' Beth enthused. 'You can have the room next to mine. Shall I go and tell Mrs Harrison?'

Still smiling, Patrick glanced towards Laura with one eyebrow raised. 'Well?'

She smiled at them both. 'Oh, why not! I'll certainly be glad to break the routine of going to my own bed only to toss and turn all night long.'

When she had dashed as far as the Coach House to collect her overnight things, Laura returned to the Hall feeling greatly relieved. This is only for the one night, she told herself, it mustn't develop into a habit. But it was very good to know that both Patrick and Beth wanted her here.

'Mrs Harrison is just laying out clean towels and things,' Beth told her as soon as she reappeared.

'I hope I'm not putting everybody to a lot of trouble?'

Patrick smiled again. 'Not in the least. And don't forget you're not the only one needing to break the routine.'

The three of them relaxed as Beth chatted about the evening spent with her friend. Evidently, she was a girl who loved classical music and had a large collection of records.

'I wish I had,' Beth remarked, but cheerfully without any sign of envy. 'I'm getting to like music a lot.'

'You must speak to your grandfather, he's got a splendid collection of the classics,' Patrick reminded her.

'I will as soon as he comes home.'

'Is he away then?' asked Laura. 'Thought I hadn't seen him for a while.'

'Daddy persuaded him to go out to Canada, to stay with my Auntie Elaine. I wanted to go as well, but I wasn't allowed.'

Patrick gave her a look. 'You know perfectly well that your trip's only delayed. We might both go out there during the long school holidays, let you meet her husband and family.'

'I know. And you're a love to promise me. But you know what I'm like – can't wait . . .'

That's not surprising, thought Laura, after all the years you wasted waiting to join in anything.

'Did you finish tonight's homework?' Patrick asked.

'Almost. I've just got a few lines of an essay to do. It won't take me a minute in the morning.'

'Do it now,' he told her. 'You know how rushed mornings tend to be.'

'Oh, must I? Not now that Laura's here.'

'I'll call in and say goodnight when I come upstairs,' Laura promised.

Pausing only to hug each of them in turn, Beth went obediently from the room.

'Thanks,' Patrick said. 'You do wonders with her, you always have.' He rose and looked down at her. 'How about that drink? What would you like? Gin, whisky? Whisky's usually the one I resort to.'

'Can't say it's something I go for, but I'll give it a try.'

'Just one thing about tomorrow, then we'll put the whole wretched business to the back of our minds,' said Patrick, handing her a glass before returning to his chair. 'Make sure I have your phone number at Lindley's. Then if I hear anything from the police, I'll let you know.'

For half an hour or more they talked of other things. After saying goodnight to Patrick, Laura went wearily upstairs and knocked on his daughter's door.

Beth, her homework finished, was sitting at the dressing table, a hairbrush in her hand. Her long blonde hair had been released from the ribbon in which she tied it back.

'Want me to brush it for you?' Laura volunteered.

'I'd love it, come on.'

Her hair was still as soft and fine as a little girl's, cool beneath Laura's fingers. It smelled clean, faintly scented from recent shampooing. For a short while they both remained silent while Beth luxuriated in the action of the brushing.

'I wish you lived here all the time,' she suddenly said.

God, but I do love you, thought Laura.

When Beth spoke again, though, it was to bring into the room the one shadow that no one could forget. 'This sounds silly, I know, but I don't want them to prove that man killed Mummy. It's going to be so upsetting.'

And you don't know one half of it, thought Laura.

Chapter 28

Robert Lindley called Laura into his office first thing the following morning.

'How are things?' she enquired before he could speak. He looked so terrible that she could only believe the worst.

'Roy will appear before the magistrates today,' he said grimly. 'I understand from our solicitor that the police are certain they have a case. This is going to be tough, Laura.'

'I know. How's Netta today?'

'Haven't seen her this morning, Inez decided to let her sleep. We had a long talk last night, tried to reassure her that she and the children would always have a home with us, if need be. Whatever . . . Of course, there's no way of being certain she would wish to remain with us.'

'But she's always been very fond of you both. As I have.'

'Well, we'll just have to see. Anyway, I'm counting on you here, I'm glad you're in this morning, Laura. I appreciate that. This whole business must be difficult for you, my dear.'

'I can't argue with that. Although I never knew her, Magda was Patrick's wife. And he must have thought a great deal of her. Even during the war he was still trying to trace her.'

'Really?'

Robert sounded surprised. Laura couldn't think why. Unless he knew more about his son's friendship with Magda Horsfall. But they ought to be trying to shelve all this and get on with some work.

'Were you coming through to the studio?' she asked him. 'After two days away and this lot on my mind, I can't be sure what the situation is there.'

'Yes, I'll take a look at what's going on. Got to start somewhere.'

Most of the other designers were in already, though not at their desks. Laura could believe that they, and everyone else at Lindley's, were preoccupied with the accusations that had been made against Roy.

She had nothing but admiration for his father as he went from one desk to the next, inviting the men to explain their current work. He reached Laura last of all and inspected the roughs of the design she had begun after the Yorkshire Gold carpet had been set up for production.

As the door of the design studio closed behind Robert Lindley, a dreadful thought surfaced in Laura's mind. Patrick had been too disturbed to say one word about the carpet for his building society, but was it even possible that he would allow them to continue with production now? How could he want it to be manufactured by the family firm of the man accused of his wife's murder?

Dully, she willed herself to forget that aspect and get on with her present design. The others were working steadily, speaking hardly at all. She was reminded by the silence of her initial uneasy months in here all those years ago. And yet the studio, basically, had seemed a much pleasanter place since the war. Not all of the original team had returned, and those who had appeared simply to be glad to be back in the work for which they had trained.

When the telephone call came through for her Laura expected it to be Patrick. It was Mavis Priestley.

'I tried to get you at the Coach House last night only there was no answer.'

'Sorry, I was out. What is it, Mavis?'

'I only wanted to ask how you were. I read in the paper that somebody was being questioned about Magda Horsfall's body. Then I went into town and I heard folk saying as it were Roy Lindley they've arrested.'

Laura groaned. If it was all round Halfield already, she could just imagine how news would spread once the magistrates' decision was learned.

'I'm afraid I can't talk about that, especially here. But I am all right, thank you for ringing . . .'

'You sound far from all right,' her friend interrupted. 'And I just wanted to say that if it gets on top of you, with you being out at Arncliffe, like, you must come to me for a bit. Now think on – I know everything's topsy-turvy with me packing up, but there's allus a bed for you.'

Laura thanked her again and put down the receiver. She had been too concerned about the effect on the people she was fond of even to consider how interested local folk would naturally become. From now on, assuming that Roy was sent for trial, there would be nowhere that she could escape the pressure of gossip.

Throughout the rest of the day Laura made herself concentrate on work. Nothing she might do could alter Roy's situation. But her job was of use to the Lindleys, she still had a living to earn, and she needed some occupation to help preserve her sanity.

That evening when Laura got off the bus and began walking up the drive at Arncliffe she felt as though she had lived through one of the longest days of her existence. Patrick hadn't telephoned her at the mill, and she didn't know what to think of that. She would like to believe that Roy had been released, and therefore Patrick had no desire to share the news, but still she felt in her heart that Roy's innocence wouldn't easily be proved.

Deep in thought, she scarcely noticed the sound of a car turning in off the main road. When it drew up alongside her and Patrick opened the passenger door, she was startled.

'Hop in, Laura. We've got to talk.'

'You've heard something then?' she asked, settling into the seat beside him.

'Yes. There was a delay on the previous case. Lindley didn't go before them until much later than the police hoped. He pleaded not guilty, naturally, and he's elected to be tried by jury.'

'I see. Does that mean – well, will he have to stay in prison until the case comes up?'

'It's unlikely he'd be granted bail when it's such a serious offence.'

They had reached the main entrance of the Hall and Patrick noticed the distraught expression in Laura's blue eyes.

'Oh, come on in,' he insisted, 'can't talk out here.'

He was closing the door behind them when someone spoke from the doorway of the room nearest to them.

'That's right, Laura – you and him stick together.'

'Netta! What are you doing here?'

Before her sister could reply the person who'd been with her in the room stepped forward. It was their mother. And she seemed well aware of Laura's part in Roy's being arrested. 'Nay, Laura – I'm surprised at you,' she exclaimed. 'You can't have thought, not for a minute, what this will do to your sister. To all on us.'

'I have thought, Mother, very deeply,' Laura said quietly. 'But why all this . . .?'

Maggie straightened her back. 'You didn't think I'd stop at home, did you, while one of my own was going through agony? The minute I heard, I got my coat on. Our Netta's heart's broken, can't you see?'

'I know how upsetting this must be,' Laura began.

Netta immediately contradicted her. 'Oh, no, you don't. You're the last person who'd ever understand. It's you that's done this to me. I hope you're satisfied now. Roy's been locked up, he could even be hanged. And it was *you* identified him.'

'Now, just a minute,' Patrick began, but Netta wouldn't let him speak either.

'She was your wife, wasn't she, and you're determined to get somebody for it, aren't you? That's why you got Laura to speak up. Go on – admit it.'

'There is nothing to admit,' Patrick put in calmly. 'There has been absolutely no collusion between Laura and myself. There was no need for any. The arrest was made, as you must know, on evidence found at the site.'

480

'Not only that,' Netta sobbed. 'They'd never have known about the photo in that damned locket if she hadn't spoken up.'

'Nay, Laura,' Maggie exclaimed. 'Couldn't you have kept your trap shut?'

Appalled, Laura simply stood there, tears spilling down her face while she watched her sister and mother rage against Patrick.

'If you had to fight this, you should have done it yourself. You didn't have to set my daughter against her own sister.'

Netta was nodding fiercely. 'You got her on to your side, and you made her turn against my husband.'

'It wasn't like that at all,' Laura insisted. 'Patrick never tried to interfere in what I felt obliged to bring to everyone's attention. I couldn't lie about the photo in that locket. I wished I was able to, but I just couldn't.'

'Happen not,' snapped Netta. 'You didn't have to lie but if only you'd held your tongue nobody would ever have known of its existence.'

Patrick inhaled slowly. When he spoke it was with infinite control. 'Believe me, I am deeply sorry that it is your husband who has been charged with Magda's death. I would far rather never have known who was responsible than have this come between yourselves and Laura. But since it has, I can only suggest that we all take time to allow the situation to cool. I will drive you to wherever you are staying now.'

'No, thank you,' said Maggie firmly. 'I'd not get into a car with you, not if I were dropping in my tracks.'

'Then I will order you a taxi, it will be here within minutes. If you would please return to the room where you were waiting? I won't have either of you distressing Laura any further.'

She couldn't let her mother and sister leave while they felt so much animosity towards her. 'No, Patrick, let's get this sorted out now. I'll be all right.'

He remained adamant. 'This is my home, and I won't permit you to suffer in it. They are to leave, and I suggest you go along to my study or somewhere in order that we may restore some kind of quiet.'

Patrick sought her out ten minutes later, coming into his study and crossing immediately to put his arms round her.

'They've gone now, my dear. And it truly is for the best. In such heat, unforgivable things are said, and I don't want that for you. After a while you can approach them again, try and put across the truth. I'll go with you, if you wish, anything . . .'

'Oh, Patrick, this is all so hideous. How did they get in here, anyway?'

'Mrs Harrison found me to explain. She saw them standing around outside your house, felt she shouldn't leave them to wait out there.'

'No, I don't suppose she could. What are we to do now, though?'

'Get through first one day and then the next, it's the only way. We can't suspend life until the time when that court case comes up.'

'But whatever will I do? Netta might even make her father-in-law give me the sack.'

'I doubt that. Robert Lindley will use his own judgement. And besides, you've more than one job to see through there, haven't you? Things like my Yorkshire Gold carpet.'

'You still want that to go ahead then? I thought, I was afraid – well, that you'd not want to give Lindley's any business.'

He drew her even closer to him. 'You're responsible for that carpet, aren't you?' he said simply, as though nothing else could be important.

'Will it be a long time before Roy's trial?' she asked eventually when she was calmer.

'I'm afraid so. Always remember, though, Laura – we're together now, we'll see this through.'

The months did indeed seem long, and very uneasy, while all the evidence was gathered and investigated. The police came and went repeatedly at Arncliffe, sometimes simply for discussions with Patrick, frequently with Beth as well.

It was to Laura that the girl confided her disturbance as she gradually recalled more and more of what had occurred on that day when she was only a child of four.

'I'm not supposed to talk about it, they say, but I know you won't let any of this go any further. And I don't want to bother Daddy. She was his wife, after all, this is bad enough for him as it is.'

She then repeated to Laura everything that she had told the police. About setting out for a walk, and the quarrel between her mother and the man whom she was now convinced was Roy.

'It was something he wanted her to give him, and she kept saying she couldn't. And then they noticed I was listening. Mummy got hold of me by both arms, I can still remember her long fingernails digging in, hurting. "You're not to tell anybody, think on. Not one word about any of this."

'And then he bent down until his face was in front of mine. "Just keep your mouth shut, or you'll be sorry." I was frightened. I'd never seen him cross before, he'd always been so kind. Then Mummy said something else. That I mustn't talk, most of all not to Daddy.'

Eh, love, Laura had thought when hearing this, and had that been enough to make you stop talking altogether?

On another occasion Beth had told her about the dog. 'He came with Uncle, every time, and he was like my friend. I used to call him and he'd come, and we ran about together. But then he'd gone away, and so had Mummy. And I didn't see Uncle any more.'

And your father was distressed, thought Laura, too preoccupied with his own bewilderment and loss to realise that you were only little and should be helped to understand.

Disturbed though she was by wondering what effect these recent developments must be having on Beth, Laura remained even more upset about the attitude of her own family.

On the Saturday after the quarrel she had telephoned Inez Lindley to check if her mother and Netta were still there. It was mid-afternoon when she arrived at Lindley Lodge. Netta was just coming downstairs with the baby in her arms; Petra and Kevin rushed into the hall to see who was visiting.

The lad flung himself at Laura and she had gone down on one knee to hug him when Netta descended the last few steps. At the same moment Maggie Crabtree emerged from the sitting-room. Both women were stony-faced, staring her out.

Laura swallowed. 'I've come to see if we can patch things up, we can't fall out forever over this.'

'That's what you think,' snapped Netta, ignoring a warning frown from Inez.

'Talk's easy,' said Maggie. 'It's not your husband that's been locked up.'

'Oh, please –' Inez interceded. 'Things are quite bad enough. Let's wait, shall we, at least until something is proved? If Roy is declared innocent the whole of this will have been unnecessary.'

Netta gave her mother-in-law a look, then continued to Laura: 'I don't know how you've the cheek to set foot in this house after what you've done to us. I shan't forgive you, whatever you might say.'

Laura turned in her tracks and walked resignedly back to the door.

Inez reached her side: 'I'm sorry, Laura, this is most unfortunate. But it does look as though you ought to keep away for a little while.'

'Don't worry, I shan't come again. I really did hope to put things right. I can see now that's beyond me.'

Being defeated in her intention had made Laura even more distressed but she hadn't allowed that to deflect her from attending the trial. She had checked with Robert Lindley that he didn't object to her taking time off work and, given the situation, he had been remarkably understanding. 'I can appreciate your being concerned,' he'd added. 'And once this is behind us, we'll all have to make up lost time.'

When the first day of the trial finally came Laura felt a strange mixture of emotions. She was dreading the whole experience, yet at the same time felt deeply thankful that none of them need wait much longer to learn the outcome.

On Patrick's insistence, she was sitting alone in the public gallery. They had travelled to Leeds together with Beth and outside the courtroom had met up with Patrick's sister and her husband. Jenny had arranged to look after Beth who would be waiting in an anteroom ready to give evidence if she was called. Beth was bearing up well, seeming as upset that the locket had been taken from her until after the trial as over anything else. And Wolf Richardson had identified photographs of Roy Lindley and Magda as the couple seen at the reservoir site, making Patrick hope Beth wouldn't have to appear. Just as he was anxious to spare his daughter, he was determined Laura should not further antagonise her family by sitting with him.

She spotted Netta almost at once, pale but composed in a new dark green coat and hat, and flanked by her mother and mother-in-law, with Alan and Robert Lindley in the row behind them. Laura was glad, in a way, that her own mother was present. Robert Lindley had mentioned that Maggie's previous visit to Halfield had been brief; her returning was proof that she shirked nothing these days.

Mum has turned out to be a strong woman after all, Laura reflected, and hoped that her support would help the whole Lindley family as well as Netta. From what Patrick had confided, the police were confident of a conviction. For herself, Laura could only hope that the trial would not be protracted. She had felt she was being torn apart during all these months while her concern for Patrick and Beth struggled against family loyalties and the additional pull of her allegiance to Lindley's factory. Only when the trial ended would she be able to marshall her feelings into any kind of coherence and make decisions regarding her future.

Or have them made for her, she thought grimly, realising yet again that Robert Lindley was quite likely to cease employing her. She had been involved in his son's identification and arrest; and for years she had made no secret of her friendship with Patrick Horsfall.

The jury were entering one by one, then being sworn in.

Around her in the courtroom, Laura felt the tension building. Both defending and prosecuting lawyers looked gravely confident to her, equally intimidating. She tried not to stare towards the dock where Roy stood between escorting prison officers.

She turned her attention to the clerk of the court as he began reading the charge aloud for the benefit of the jury. Nothing in Laura's life before had prepared her for hearing someone she knew so well accused of unlawful killing. She had to contain a gasp in the momentary silence at the end of the indictment.

Some distance away, Patrick glanced towards Roy, then seemed to turn his gaze thankfully towards the judge. Laura could well understand if he could not bear to look at the man charged with the death of the wife whose loss had ruined life for him.

Roy's 'Not guilty' sounded very firm, yet Laura sensed that too much that she had learned over the years pointed to his being responsible for Magda's killing. I don't want to be here, she thought in panic, yet knew in her heart that she could not have kept away.

The prosecuting lawyer rose, and so began the lengthy procedure to which listening became less easy even than Laura had expected. Despite the agony of waiting to begin learning the truth, snatches only of what seemed the relevant facts were reaching through the turmoil of her own emotions.

The first surprise was that there was no longer any dispute regarding the identity of the man frequently seen accompanying Magda on walks through the countryside. Roy had ceased to claim that he had hardly known Magda and was now admitting they had enjoyed a loving relationship. These words drew Laura's glance again to Patrick. He seemed to flinch, and she missed the following few sentences while she yearned to comfort him. But a picture was emerging of Magda Horsfall, a lively and attractive woman who, perhaps through her husband's preoccupation with business matters, had been driven to turn elsewhere for affection.

It sounded reasonable to Laura that Roy would have responded to her interest. She could imagine that his defence would make much of the way that he had grown so attached to the beautiful woman that he would be the last person to wish her any harm.

The story of their association widened to include Beth, the lovable child who had accompanied them on their walks. Laura watched Patrick again, saw him sigh, and felt with him the agony of reliving the way in which his daughter as well appeared to have been drawn to Roy Lindley.

Patrick must be being made to feel terribly inadequate, she thought, and ached to reassure him. She knew he had experienced financial difficulties around that time, could picture how hard he would have worked to resolve them. If only his wife had been more understanding of this, there might have been no liaison, no unwarranted killing . . .

Thinking about Patrick, Laura had failed to hear a whole chunk of the tale. She was jolted to attend by the admission that Roy and Magda had been lovers. To her, this fact seemed to emphasise Magda's need of Roy, and thus to increase Patrick's shortcomings.

The judge's expression was inscrutable though intent. Laura gazed towards the jury. Were they already – even before his lawyer had spoken on his behalf – sympathising with the man who had brought love and interest into the life of a neglected woman? Or were they capable of believing the man accused had, for some reason not yet uncovered, killed her?

For days the trial continued. Laura travelled back and forth with Patrick and his daughter each day while, because of Beth, they talked around the trial without discussing the harrowing details. Too drained for conversation every night, Laura retreated thankfully to the solitude of her home. Whatever the effects of this case upon these two dear people, she could endure no more than the taxing hours spent in that courtroom. She longed for a conclusion to be reached, when they would at least have the trail behind them. And the freedom at last to consider the future.

Laura was already very much afraid that if the judgement went against Roy she would not bring herself to remain in Halfield. As well as the awkwardness that was bound to exist between herself and the Lindleys, if her connection with them continued that would be a constant reminder to Patrick of what their son had done. Somehow, she would have to try and make things right between herself and Netta, and was toying now with the possibility of their making a home together somewhere where she might help with the children. By going right away, she would free Patrick and Beth to adjust to the present without the fetters of the past.

The fourth day in court began with a tightening of the atmosphere. Laura could feel tension between the opposing lawyers, in the sharp attention of jury members. The truth was coming, and nothing would be the same when it emerged.

Roy himself seemed restless, she noticed, whereas earlier he had shown remarkable calm. She had even admired the way he'd conveyed the impression of a man bravely reliving the circumstances leading up to the loss of a woman greatly loved.

The moment everything really changed was as he was questioned on their setting out on that fateful day. The defending lawyer seemed to be leading up to calling Beth as a witness to the discussion allegedly begun between Magda and her lover. But Roy shook his head. He would not have the girl endure cross-questioning.

'I'll admit we argued,' he began. 'It was a private matter, Beth was not involved. We left her inside the Arncliffe estate, told her to return to the house.'

No one could dispute that this concurred with evidence already received. But the prosecution seized on this admission of an argument. While the courtroom hushed as though in anticipation of crucial details, Roy suffered an onslaught of cross-questioning.

'This quarrel with Mrs Horsfall – did you become heated?'

'Not really. And I said argument, not quarrel.'

'Argument then – was it the first between yourself and Mrs Horsfall?'

'So far as I recall. Normally, we got along so well that no differences arose between us.'

'None at all? Not even lovers' squabbles?'

'None that I remember.'

'So what had occurred on this particular day, Mr Lindley, to produce an argument?'

'Nothing very much. Just – something that seemed rather disappointing.'

'In what way disappointing? Did it relate to your possible future together?'

'No. I never believed that Magda would leave her husband.'

'What then? Surely only by telling us more, Mr Lindley, will you reassure the court as to your loving attitude towards the deceased?'

When Roy did not reply, the lawyer tried another tack. 'Well, then – if this did not concern your future relationship, did it perhaps have something to do with more material matters, with money?'

Laura noticed that Roy flushed and then turned deathly pale. Still he said nothing.

'Magda Horsfall was the wife of a wealthy man,' the prosecution persisted. 'One cannot automatically assume that her financial situation had no bearing on her relationship with those about her. It was common knowledge around the time in question that Mr Horsfall was suffering certain financial pressures.'

Hearing this, Roy seemed to sway in the dock. He clutched at its wooden panelling for support. Briefly, he closed his eyes.

'Were you aware of this, Mr Lindley?'

'Yes,' he murmured, his voice rasping. He cleared his throat. 'Yes, to some degree.'

'Really? "To some degree", is that all? I am going to suggest to you, Mr Lindley, that you know far more than anyone here present today about the full extent of Mr Horsfall's financial embarrassment. Because you were responsible for the gradual draining of his personal funds.'

'That's ridiculous! Lindleys are mill owners, have been since way back last century.'

'Agreed, but at the time we are discussing you were decidedly junior to your father. What young man, finding himself in your situation, wouldn't have striven to invest in his own future, to seize an opportunity to start up his own business, perhaps?'

'Is ambition so very wrong – criminal?'

'No, Mr Lindley, but the means one employs to further that ambition might well conflict with the law.'

Visibly perturbed, Roy stood shaking his head. Laura was reminded that he had looked exactly like this after the dyehouse accident.

The prosecuting lawyer nodded sympathetically. 'Take your time now, think carefully. It is a perfectly ordinary reaction to meet refusal with annoyance. We can all understand if you had built up your hopes, only to have them founder when no more funds were forthcoming.'

'It was to be a loan, that was all,' Roy murmured huskily.

'Would you repeat that, Mr Lindley?'

'A loan, that's all it was. I couldn't bear it when I thought she was lying to me – saying there was no more money left . . .'

'Really?' The reaction to this admission was quite cool. 'So, what happened next? Was that when your quarrel sharpened?'

Dismally, Roy shook his head. 'We were going to walk it off. I needed to think. I was too fond of Magda to let the money come between us.'

'So what happened?' the lawyer repeated.

'I only wanted to make things right between us. I wouldn't have dreamed of hurting her . . .'

'Then why did you?'

When he spoke, Roy seemed to answer from a long way away. 'It started again over that damned locket. She would persist in wearing the thing, though she'd sworn it meant nothing to her.'

'You are speaking, I presume, of the gold locket which we see before us here. Exhibit – er, exhibit C?'

'That looks like the one from here. A family thing,' she said. Magda began teasing me, said it had a secret . . .'

'The secret, perhaps, which we all now know to be the fact that the locket contains your photograph?'

'I knew of no photograph then. It has a lock, you see. I thought – well, first . . .' Roy faltered, stopped speaking.

'First there was the money which would no longer continue coming your way, is that what you are saying, Mr Lindley?'

'No, nothing to do with money. We'd discussed that, decided to forget it. We'd made up our differences, were all right again.'

'Really? We'll leave that, shall we, for the present. So, next you were provoked by Mrs Horsfall's refusal to take off this locket. Did you snatch it from her neck, was that how its chain snapped?'

'I don't think so, can't be sure. It's a long time ago . . .'

'But you were angry, disappointed.' The lawyer paused, adjusted his wig. 'Where exactly was your dog throughout all this, Mr Lindley?'

'Dog? What's that got to do with any . . .?'

'Your dog – Prince. He was with you, I take it, on that day?'

'Running loose somewhere. You know what they're like out on the moors. Chasing all over . . .'

'Not on a lead then?'

'No, I always released him once we left the estate.'

'And the lead was still in your hand?'

'I suppose so. Or my pocket. How would I remember that all these years afterwards?'

'I put it to you, Mr Lindley, that you would remember very well. Unless, that is, you have chosen to put such unpleasant memories from you. That dog lead was what you used, wasn't it, to strangle Magda Horsfall? Wasn't it?'

Biting his lip, Roy stared distractedly about the courtroom, as though seeking some release from this trap. Finding none, he sighed.

'I wouldn't have hurt her for worlds. Only it was all

crumbling – our love, my plans – because she was still tied to *him*. When the chain of that locket broke, I thought – it seemed for a minute that that was it, that her being tied to Horsfall was ending. And then all at once I knew. Or I thought I knew. Why did it have to be only when it was too late, years too late, that I learned it contained my photograph?'

Roy gulped, took several seconds to recover sufficiently before he continued. 'She was looking down at the thing, nearly moaning over it. "Don't you realise how much this matters to me?" she asked. And there were tears in her eyes – not for me, or so I believed, not for *him*, for a lump of gold. I wanted to make her care, really to care, about somebody. About me . . .'

'And?'

'She moved away from me, only a few paces, but she'd turned her face towards the reservoir . . .'

'That is where you were then – near the reservoir?'

'Oh, yes. We'd started going there for Beth, she liked to watch the men working.'

'But Beth wasn't with you that day?'

Roy shook his head, the lovely golden waves gleamed. 'I said, didn't I? We left her inside the estate.'

'While you attacked her mother?'

'It wasn't an attack. It wasn't like that. I wanted her to look at me, that was all, to face the truth about us. She refused. I walked towards her, but she kept her face averted. I must have had the loop of the lead in one hand, then I grasped the catch that fastened on the collar. I was just going to pull her towards me . . .'

'Only . . .?' the lawyer prompted softly.

'The lead settled higher than I intended, on her shoulders. When Magda moved slightly, as if to walk away, it lay across her throat. "Go on," she goaded. "Finish me off now there's no more money." I tried to make her understand. I was shouting that it was her I wanted, reminding her how we'd only just agreed to forget all that. But she laughed. She sounded hysterical. She wouldn't even look at me. I shook her a bit. She

492

seemed to stumble, and she slithered against me, to the ground.'

'Didn't you think to get help from somewhere? The workmen at the site?'

'They'd all finished for the day. And she had no pulse. I checked and checked and checked, there wasn't even a flutter.'

Grimly, with frequent pauses now for Roy was growing increasingly distraught, the tale unfolded of his search for somewhere to conceal Magda. And how the setting sun had reflected on the still wet concrete of the retaining dam.

'I couldn't just leave her. There was a lot of plastic material lying around the site. I manoeuvred her on to the largest sheet I could find. I sort of rolled her towards the edge where they'd been working. The plastic was all tattered by then, I just tipped it all in with her.'

The prosecuting counsel was nodding, well-satisfied. The defence lawyer, however, was calling a witness. Surprise rippled through the courtroom.

Laura recognised Wolf Richardson and listened while he took the oath and was invited to relate what he recalled of the day on which Magda Horsfall died. He glanced towards Roy and then began speaking.

'It was only when asked about circumstances surrounding this case that I checked the date in my diary for that year. I had an appointment that evening, attending the board of governors of a local school. I had driven over by way of the reservoir – to inspect the concreting they'd completed – and was continuing on when it happened.'

'Yes?' Roy's lawyer prompted.

'A dog bolted across the road. I was in no danger of hitting him, but the car coming towards me had to swerve. I thought he might have caught him a glancing blow. We both braked, naturally, but the dog had run off. The other driver and I exchanged a rueful look.'

'And then?'

'I thought the dog appeared familiar. Then I saw the

defendant and the woman I'd encountered in the past. I was furious. They were mucking about, laughing and hugging, not taking a blind bit of notice of their dog. It could have caused an accident.' The rest of Wolf's evidence confirmed that at some stage Roy and Magda were reconciled. At least Roy's testimony was being backed up to some extent.

As Wolf stood down the judge looked at his watch. Moments later he had adjourned the case until the following day.

Laura went to find Patrick among the crowd and told him she would make her own way back to Arncliffe. Whatever was proved concerning the state of his relationship with her on that day, Roy had as good as admitted to killing Magda. Laura's place now was with their Netta.

Chapter 29

Netta was sobbing as they emerged from the public gallery. Laura was afraid that she would again find herself dismissed. But Robert Lindley, one arm around Netta and the other through his wife's, greeted her, albeit wearily.

'Looks like, with Richardson's evidence, we might just get a verdict of manslaughter,' he said. 'I keep telling Netta that, but . . .' He broke off and sighed.

'I know. But whatever happens, Netta's bound to feel this dreadfully.' Laura turned and spoke intently to her sister. 'You're going to need folk to see you through this, love. Won't you let me help?'

'Nobody can,' she wailed inconsolably. 'How can they?'

'But you'll let me try?' Laura persisted. 'Happen in a day or two when we've all calmed down a bit?'

'I don't know,' her sister sighed. 'I don't know owt any more, except that I want Roy.'

'You've done your best, Laura,' said their mother, wiping her eyes as she came round from behind the group. 'I'll talk to her later on. I daresay we were a bit hasty afore, blaming you. You know what I can be like, all spit and wind. It means nowt.'

Laura moved towards the Lindleys again and grasped Inez by the hand. 'I hope it doesn't turn out too badly for Roy when the jury reach a decision. Seems this waiting will soon be over, any road.'

Although she had tried to sound thankful about that fact, at least, Laura discovered on the way home that her own spirits couldn't have sunk much lower. Exhausted, she found the bus journey back to Arncliffe and the long walk up the drive quite debilitating. Glad though she was that the few minutes with her sister and mother appeared to have generated a better understanding, she almost wished she had ridden back here with Patrick and his family.

Having seen at such close quarters the distress of Netta and her in-laws, Laura was sure she wouldn't get them out of her mind at all during the solitary evening and the night that followed.

She was looking in her handbag for her key when someone called to her across the courtyard.

'Laura – have you got a minute, please? Can I come over?'

It was Beth. Laura managed a smile. 'Of course, love. Come on.'

Beth followed her into the living-room and stood by the empty fireplace. She looked almost as pale as she used to in the old days, and her blue eyes were shadowed.

'How did today go for you?' Laura asked. 'At least you weren't called to appear in court. Don't suppose you will be now.'

'I guess not. It was all right, I think, just too much waiting around, and everybody all on edge and that. Auntie Jenny was as good company as anybody could be there. Only – well, I couldn't stop wondering what Daddy must be feeling. Whenever they adjourned, Uncle Ted would come to tell us what had been going on, but Dad's said hardly anything since.'

Beth had paused. When she spoke again it was rather awkwardly. 'It's about Daddy that I wanted to see you. He seems different today – angry.'

'That's understandable, love. After having all this raked up about how your mother was taken from him.'

'Is it?' said Beth, inexplicably.

Laura was confounded, unable to respond to the remark which seemed to imply that Patrick hadn't reacted angrily to that. When she didn't say anything, Beth pressed on about her reason for coming over.

'This is going to sound an awful cheek but I'm going back with Auntie Jenny. She wants me to babysit while she goes to the WI. Uncle Ted's got his books to do. I don't want Dad to be on his own tonight, and I wondered if you'd mind terribly asking him across to have a meal with you?'

Laura considered for a moment. 'I haven't got very much in. Shopping's been the last thing on my mind this week.'

Beth grinned. 'Well, I just heard him telling Mrs Harrison he couldn't eat anything.'

'Omelettes then? Does your father like them?'

'He certainly likes eggs.'

'Well now – let me see . . . Happen it'll be best if I give him a ring. You dash back over there.'

'You won't hang on about our little chat?'

'If you don't want me to.'

Patrick arrived while Laura was cracking eggs into a basin.

'Glad you could make it,' she said, opening the front door to him. 'I wanted to tell you – I had a word with our Netta, my mother as well. I think they might forgive me, in time, for being involved in Roy's arrest.'

'That's good,' said Patrick tersely, but he appeared anything but thankful.

Laura showed him into the living-room and began setting the table. She could see he was still under a lot of strain which wouldn't just evaporate if she left him and disappeared towards the kitchen.

Although she told him to take a seat he only remained in the chair for a matter of seconds before beginning to prowl about the room. When Laura eventually headed towards the kitchen, he followed and began stalking there, up and down, up and down, until she caught herself counting his steps.

'I've a bottle of wine somewhere here,' she said, looking in one of the cupboards. 'Open it, will you? I think we need something.'

When she had told him where to find glasses, he poured wine for them and set hers beside the cooker where she was busy. But he still did not sit, and Laura had to summon concentration to be able to prepare their simple meal.

'We'll have to make do with salad to accompany this,' she

497

told him. 'I've only got a couple of potatoes in the house.'

'Fine with me.'

Even during their meal Patrick appeared no less edgy. Laura was very glad that at least the wine had relaxed her sufficiently to make her feel she might cope with him. She reflected ruefully that dreading being on her own tonight hadn't necessarily meant she'd cheerfully settle for having this strain inflicted on her.

Almost as soon as the thought passed through her mind, though, she remembered again that Patrick had spent the past several days (to say nothing of the preceding months) dwelling on his wife's death. How could she expect him to be other than tense?

When they had moved to armchairs only to sit in almost total silence, Laura decided that the time had come to try and show how concerned she was for him.

'I hope, with luck, they'll get this wretched trial over with tomorrow. If only for your sake, Patrick. You've had too long thinking about Magda, all that happened . . .'

He merely shrugged.

Laura watched his drawn face for a minute and then began again: 'Maybe you ought to take a few days off afterwards? I can see how gruelling it's been for you. You must hate Roy Lindley . . .'

'I hate him for all but ruining me!' Patrick sprang to his feet, startling her. 'For conning her into dipping into my money. I knew damned well Magda had no cause to be milking our joint account. I provided every mortal thing she could have wanted. That's what I said on that last day when I confronted her with the statement showing what was missing.'

'But I don't understand,' Laura began.

Patrick gave her a look. 'Have I never said? I shouted at her that day. In front of Beth as well. Accused her of withdrawing cash because she mismanaged the allowance I gave her. And ever since I've been left feeling *I* was the one who mishandled the situation. Drove her away. That I always react badly under stress.'

Very briefly, Laura smiled. Patrick didn't miss the glimmer of amusement.

'Okay,' he snapped. 'So that *is* how I react – it's what I'm doing now. But only because of him, because of being done! In my work I'm responsible for many thousands of other people's money. How could a chap like him manipulate her so that she fleeced me?'

When Laura said nothing he paused in one circuit of the room and swung round to face her.

'My anger's justifiable, surely? I've every right to be vexed.'

Laura swallowed uncomfortably. 'I'm just – well, frankly, a bit surprised that you seem more annoyed about Roy doing you out of your brass than about – about what he did to your wife.'

'And don't you understand the reason? Don't you?'

Laura could only shake her head, bewildered. Had she never understood him? She couldn't believe she could even have liked this man who seemed to value money more highly than his wife.

Patrick broke into her thoughts. 'Leave it for now, eh? Thanks for the meal. I'll pick you up as usual in the morning,' he added, heading smartly towards the door.

Even in the courtroom the following day Laura still felt perturbed by Patrick's attitude. He no longer seemed at all like the man she believed she had known all these years. How could anybody in his situation only be annoyed about the money he had lost? It was people who mattered most. The folk you grew attached to. Her own one bright moment this morning had been when both Netta and their mother had nodded in her direction as they all filed back into court.

She felt so shaken by how seriously she had failed to assess Patrick correctly that even these vital closing stages of the trial scarcely penetrated.

When the judge reached his summing up, she tried to match her concentration to that of the jury members, and she d hold her attention there long enough to learn that, in absence of tangible proof of malice aforethought, the judge was directing them to consider the charge of manslaughter. She felt a wave of relief wash over her. At least Roy seems as if he'll escape sentencing for murder, she thought, and reiterated her own silent thanks on Netta's behalf.

After the jury returned following their deliberations and their foreman declared Roy guilty of manslaughter, Laura watched Netta for signs of breakdown. Her sister, however, was sitting upright in her seat, staring straight ahead. Nobody could have anything but admiration for her today. Few women would have displayed such composure.

I'll make it up to her, Laura thought. To her and the kiddies. We all will. We'll all rally round, see that she's never left on her own to brood. She herself would begin today, as soon as the judge had pronounced sentence. All the Lindleys had seemed glad to see her again. And Robert, entering the courtroom at Laura's side, had reminded her that he was relying on her to keep good designs going for their looms. Becoming involved again there would be far simpler than she had expected.

Laura sensed someone moving behind her. A hand grasped her shoulder.

'We can catch up on details of the sentence later,' Patrick whispered against her ear. 'I've got to talk to you. Coming?'

Laura couldn't credit that he could believe anything more important than learning the extent of Roy's sentence. But as soon as they were outside, Patrick hustled her towards his car. 'I've borne with the need for you to show your own family that you were not siding against the Lindleys. Now it's my turn, at last.'

He opened the passenger door for her and closed it gently once she was seated.

'You said last night I needed a break,' he began, getting in behind the wheel and reaching towards the ignition. 'If I do ng to get away, that's not to be on my own.'

As they picked up speed and he eased out on to the road, miled. 'This is where we begin tackling the future, Laura.'

'We?' she asked. 'Now, just a minute . . . You'd better hear what I have to say. Because all I foresee is devoting my time to our Netta. Somebody will have to keep an eye on her and the kids for years.'

'The Lindleys will do that, and there's also your mother.'

'That's not good enough. I can't abandon Netta.' And, she realised, it looks as if I'm going to have to make a choice now. Patrick was hardly going to encourage her to invite to his estate the wife and children of the man who'd killed Magda.

'All right,' he was saying as he headed away through the outskirts of Leeds. 'I accept that you'll need to give them some time. But not the whole of your life. And besides, making Netta unduly dependent upon you again wouldn't necessarily be the best thing for her.'

'There's my work an' all, don't forget. Robert said he's going to be relying on me a lot.'

'Not surprised. You're a dependable woman.'

'Thanks. But I don't really see . . .'

'No, but you will – very soon.'

He was driving swiftly now, not dangerously but very quickly. Laura felt quite uneasy. She decided not to distract him again until they reached wherever it was that he seemed determined on going.

When Patrick eventually parked the car there was an expanse of moorland about them, and a valley falling sharply away in the middle distance with further hills beyond.

'Let's walk,' he said, and got out of the car.

He locked both doors the minute she joined him on the rough path, and then he took her hand.

'Time, at last, to talk about us.'

Laura shook her head. 'I don't think there's much to say.'

'Why ever not? We've known each other for years . . .'

Laura dragged her hand free of his. 'That's just it, Patrick. We haven't. Or I haven't known you. Not what you're really like. I'm sorry. I must have been blind or something – stupid. And now I can't let you say any more.'

He stared straight ahead, avoiding her eyes. 'That's w

has made me determined to have this out with you. Since yesterday especially, you don't even – *like* me, do you?' he said, sounding shaken.

'I don't like some of the things you believe. You shook me badly last night. I'm sorry but I cannot understand someone who cares more for money than for the wife he lost.'

'Only because you don't realise the havoc it caused at the time. The rest of the building society board learned my personal finances were in a critical state. They expressed their lack of confidence. And they'd already heard I was being questioned by the police. They didn't know that was concerning Magda's disappearance.'

'Look, I can see it was all very unfortunate. And I do sympathise because you had to put up with so much trouble at once. But I still can't understand why you haven't been more upset about Magda since the day her body was found.'

'I should have thought that was obvious.'

'Not to me, I'm afraid.'

When Patrick stopped walking and gazed down at her Laura felt bewildered. The expression in his dark eyes revealed a wry amusement along with his concern. 'Lord, have I failed that abysmally to put you in the picture? Haven't you seen all along how little I cared about her?'

'How can you say that? You've spent hours and hours writing letters, telephoning folk all over the place, because you were that determined to trace her.'

'A search which intensified after I met you. Falling in love with you, Laura, soon showed me how shallow marriage to Magda had been.'

'But you never said,' she murmured.

'There seemed hundreds of reasons why I shouldn't. You appeared too young to be taxed with my problems. I needed to locate Magda first and divorce her, if only to minimise the ﬁfficulties, before beginning anything with you.'

Patrick sighed, grasped her hand again, and when she ﬁ't resist urged her to walk on once more towards the skyline. Presently, he shook his head and spoke.

'The thing that deterred me most, though, was the way I'd lost my temper with Magda on that fatal day. As I've said, I thought I'd frightened her away. I was equally convinced that witnessing our quarrel was what had driven Beth into that infernal silence. I was in no state for trusting myself in another relationship.'

Laura didn't know quite what to say. She was beginning to find his attitude more explicable but, wearied by the trial and all that had preceded it, she had grown accustomed to doubting her own judgement.

'And there was something else,' Patrick continued reluctantly. 'Just when I was feeling utterly thankful that you and I were working together, there was your affair with that RAF officer.'

'That wasn't just an affair,' Laura told him sharply. 'Maurice and I were deeply in love, intended to marry.'

'And now? Are you still eating your heart out over him?'

Laura shook her head. 'I don't suppose so. Maurice was an important part of my life, but even before I knew for sure that he was dead I felt certain that I'd have to adjust to not seeing him again. I'm only thankful that my memories of him are good ones.'

'But that's it, don't you see? For me, it's totally different. It isn't because Magda's no longer alive that I feel free of her, it's because I've seen her as she was. Every last illusion went with the realisation that she was incapable of loyalty. To me, or to that poor sod charged with her death. Whatever she and I had been to each other had gone just as surely as she'd drained our account.'

Silently, Laura walked on at his side, absorbing Patrick's words, letting them remove some of the misgivings aroused by her fears that he was completely materialistic.

Around them the hills offered vistas that changed with their progress towards the summit but remained substantially similar, with their wide expanse of wooded valleys and moors, all darkening now beneath the evening sky.

'Beth seems to have survived all the traumas of the past months quite well,' said Laura.

Patrick smiled. 'Ah – Beth.' His tone of voice implied that he'd been waiting for her to enter Laura's thoughts. 'You've given my girl a good life, you know, Laura. Made her what she is today. I've been trying to resist the impulse to remind you how happy she would be if you and I could make a go of it . . .'

Laura gave him a look. 'But supposing we didn't? There've been so many ups and downs between us over the years.'

'But I love you, Laura, I have all along. The difference now, though, is that I'm not afraid to say so. Would you consider taking me on?'

He had stopped walking to draw her against him. Holding her close, he pressed his lips into her hair.

Laura closed her eyes, sighed. 'I don't know, not any longer. I'm sorry, but I really do not know. I wish I did, that something would show me.'

Opening her eyes, she looked up at him, willing him to comprehend this weight of uncertainty, and to find some means of taking it away.

She stirred in his arms and something glinted on the far horizon, catching her attention. Gazing towards it, she recognised water, gleaming, gilded by the last rays of the sun.

'Is that Dale Reservoir, Patrick?'

'That's right. The day Wolf Richardson attended court he told me reconstruction was completed.'

'We must go there soon,' she said, and smiled. Restoration of the reservoir seemed reassuring, reminding her that devastation need not be everlasting.

And nearby was Arncliffe. 'Let's go,' she said suddenly, and squeezed his hand. 'Take me home, love.'